*Larks' Eggs*
New and Selected Stories

*To the students who befriended me at the*
*University of California, San Diego.*

# Larks' Eggs
## New and Selected Stories

Desmond Hogan

THE LILLIPUT PRESS
DUBLIN

First published 2005 by
THE LILLIPUT PRESS
62–63 Sitric Road, Arbour Hill,
Dublin 7, Ireland
www.lilliputpress.ie

ISBN   1 84351 071 5


1 2 3 4 5 6 7 8 9 10

Set in 11.5pt on 13.5pt Centaur
Printed by MPG Books, Bodmin, Cornwall

# Contents

Captive everywhere
the street that I walk
the vehicles I avoid
put away the things I have bought
all visionary excursions into your realms—
my foot trips—hurts
a detour into your dwellings—

Deborah was stabbed by stars
and yet sang triumphant hymns
when the mountains dissolved
and on white—gleaming donkeys like prophets
the troop of horsemen moved on

But silence is where the victims dwell—

NELLY SACHS
(trans. MICHAEL HAMBURGER)

*Larks' Eggs*
*New and Selected Stories*

# Blow-Ball

What was it for, why was it they came? Perhaps because it was just there, the house. Perhaps because she might have been there, the lady, and she was in a way their object of pursuit.

The house was Georgian and summer languished around it. The fields beyond had a greenish feel, laid with hay cut just as it was turning colour. Men, separate, unobtrusive, were working in the fields and here and there were sprays of poppies. On the pond in front of the house was an accumulative growth of water lilies; still, strange to the children.

They were drawn to it in a group. Bubbles, whose hair was as bog cotton with the sun in it. A ragged ribbon fell on her forehead. Hanging over them, keeping her apart from the others at times was her class background. But she was vital because summers were blanks; something had to be made out of them. This required imagination, a special talent almost. Bubbles above all had it. Pee-Wee was gentle then; he drooped at the shoulders, an unawareness about him. There was a department in his mind where the word was fantasmagoria. He was undertaking a study of ghosts. Dony reached him through his oddities, because of them he was Pee-Wee's best friend. Dony was thirteen, the oldest.

There were others, their younger brothers and sisters whom they brought with them. Other children who trailed along but never really committed themselves. Also Bubble's English cousin who had buck teeth and told Bubble's mother sometimes that she had been with the boys. But none of them mattered. Bubbles, Pee-Wee and Dony were the instigators.

They had it to themselves, the house. It looked so contained. In a way it was just like going to the pictures. Pictures which showed sleek skies and coral swimming pools which made phosphorus trails of smoke when someone dived into them, the sort of pictures they went to see. At the pictures love was something important. The house made love important too. It had a mythology of sex, of violence, of the supernatural evolved from the generations of landowners who once lived in it. There was a book written about it, written by a young lady of the house, Lady Loughbown. That was the name of the house, Loughbown. The children knew how the lady looked. There was a photograph of her in the book, a photograph of a ghost-like figure in a tapering Edwardian dress. They liked to think that she was buried in the grave in the garden. But most people said it was her dachshunds that were buried there. Pee-Wee wished to see her ghost. Bubbles and Dony wanted to get through to her too.

The book itself had black covers and they usually brought it with them. They took a delight in the suggestiveness of some of the phrases, phrases like 'We were very attached to one another.'

To one side of the house the framework of a greenhouse had broken down into a bed of nettles, among the trees nearby were sleeping crab apples. The visits to the house were always somehow ineffectual, there wasn't much to do. They'd stand by the pond, they'd stroll about, looking at things. Sometimes they brought food and had picnics. Bubbles could never bring anything more than milk and brown bread and butter. She always frowned when she produced them, did nothing more. On one of these occasions it began raining. They sheltered under a rug in the garden, eating bananas, the rain beating down ceaselessly. It meant laughter and pulling. The smell of girls' knickers. Total madness.

Often as the others searched about Bubbles and Dony would sit by the pond and talk. They'd talk about the future. Dony intended to be a priest, and go to Africa. Bubbles had an extravagant wish. She was going to be an actress.

Bubbles was a peculiar girl. Unconsciously she imitated adults in her way of talking, in her way of walking, in her smile. After seeing a film she managed a hint of the star in her demeanour.

Sitting by the pond like that she'd brush Dony's hair in the way she liked to have it. She always carried a brush and a comb in a funny, worn bag. There was no explanation for it.

When Dony changed to long pants that summer it was Bubbles he wanted to see him in them. She seemed to understand. It was just she who mattered. Her family wasn't important. It didn't matter that her uncle had been in court for interfering with young children. It wasn't even important when everybody knew that her older sister had shamefully had twins. Her sister went to England afterwards. Dony was at the station when she was leaving. There were two trains, one going to the sea and the other to Dublin. Dony was going to the sea with his mother, to a day of candyfloss, of grey ebbtide, of cold. The girl was going to Dublin. She was a bulky girl, in a pink cotton dress, lying against the wall. She looked mute, a little hurt. Bubbles was there to say goodbye to her and she eyed Dony. Dony sensed disdain and rejection on his mother's brow when she glanced their way.

But she couldn't have suspected his friendship with Bubbles. She couldn't have suspected that he'd be with the girl the following morning, that he was with her almost every day of the summer. They were fugitive hearts, all of them.

But nothing happened to them and they were impatient. Their refrain became: 'I wish something would happen.'

They were baffled when suddenly, unexpectedly, summer was almost over. Their sensibilities changed, the pang of schooldays so near again. More children joined their group, others followed them to the house, spying on what they were doing.

One morning at Loughbown Bubbles decided to do something climactic. She fell on the terrace with a little yelp. She let the others help her up. Her eyes were round and deceiving.

'I've seen a lady,' she said. 'She was all white.'

'It was her,' Pee-Wee started.

They wanted to know more about the lady but Bubbles was vague. All she could remember for them was that the lady had seemed to have beckoned to her.

They believed because they wanted to believe. It would have been a breach of trust if they hadn't. But Dony said bluntly to her: 'You're lying.' Bubbles looked at him, her eyes begging. It was as if he'd said something irrevocable. 'I'm not,' she cried.

She turned, letting out a little sob, and ran down the steps to the stone seat beside the pond. She was apparently transfixed there, her hands hiding her face. Pee-Wee went and put an arm around her, the others standing back ineffectually. One of the younger ones was crying now too; she said she'd seen the devil at a window.

The group was split. They drifted home separately, no need to hurry. It was already long past their lunchtimes. They'd be scolded at home, interrogated for the truth. But their parents wouldn't understand the truth anyway.

It was warm as Dony ambled home, bits of fluff blowing across the lane as it they'd been released from somewhere. He turned as he heard a cry from behind. It was Bubbles who couldn't get over the gate. He went back and helped her across. Her hand felt so tiny as he tugged it; it was white and complete. They walked home together, a little quiet with one another. Bubbles was wearing a pinafore, her head inclined from him, something on her mind.

'I didn't see a lady,' she admitted. 'I'm a liar.' Her voice was just a suggestion, soft. 'I wanted to make you notice me,' she added. Dony wasn't sure what she meant, what she was hinting at.

She spoke about the colour of his eyes, the colour of her eyes, other things, her words slurred. She lowered her eyes and smiled shyly when she said: 'You're the nicest boy in town.'

Coming near her house she pressed his hand suddenly and left him.

The next week they were back at school and they had few opportunities of seeing one another. They depended on a chance to meet. Often they encountered each other in the library, the two boys and Bubbles. They were usually bundled in mackintoshes and they'd speak behind a bookshelf. The librarian's eyes would glance at them sporadically. These moments were memorable, mellifluous; the light strained from the rain outside, winter evenings mostly wet.

Once Dony found himself sitting in front of Bubbles at the pictures. It was a picture in which Ingrid Bergman was having a love affair with Humphrey Bogart in Paris. Ingrid Bergman's pale, clear, Nordic face was touched by a Paris lightness. Bogart brought her for a drive to Normandy, a chiffon scarf about her neck, tied out in two wings, fluttering in ecstasy.

Sometimes Dony caught Bubbles' eyes and it might have been that they were sitting together. They really enjoyed the film for that. But already things separated Dony from the previous summer. Awful nightmares, a new recourse in sex; carnal dreams. Pee-Wee was smoking. He'd merged with a group of boys and hadn't much time for Dony.

Somehow he failed to meet with Bubbles for a long time after that and in the spring her family emigrated to England. She called him into a yard one evening beforehand to tell him. She'd changed, she wore earrings, very tiny, very minute ones; her hair was in a bun. It was during Holy Week. There was an array of old tractors in the yard, a broken-down threshing machine. The fields about were rimmed by flood water; something inexorable about it. It made Holy Week more real. One strange remark Dony remembered from that conversation: 'Wasn't Jesus very good to die for us?' Bubbles had said.

She suggested they go to the house, to Loughbown, before she went. But this would have been ambiguous now and it was never achieved.

If it had been at any other time that Bubbles went they might have made it dramatic. But summer was almost forgotten and her departure was of little significance. She just slipped away.

# Foils

The lane slanted from the Protestant church that stood amid trees above the town. The elderly Protestant lady who lived at the top of the lane could often be seen in the prayerful September evenings as she swept the dust outside her home, a view of a sedate interior distinguishable from the reflections on the window behind her. There was a frailty about her movements, plait encircling her head of frayed white, a precariousness about her figure in a long frock and woollen stockings, She looked unreal. Like a rag doll. She was a reminder of the Protestant stratum who once dominated the town, a remnant of it.

Geraniums peeped at her from the opposite window, the base window of Miss Duffy's house. Miss Duffy had lived alone since her sister had died, the front of her house shabby, a sobriety about it, the paint black, the curtains drawn.

She'd sit on one of the benches under the Protestant church in the progression of September evenings. Dressed entirely in black she was as familiar to the scene as the old dogs that strayed about. A tiny figure stretched at the edge of a bench, hand on her chin, she always looked dishevelled. Strands of hair struggled from under a beret, her coat parted on an unwieldy bosom, her bosom almost voluptuous in the shining black material of her frock. She looked abandoned as she sat there, something plaintive about the way she'd greet every passer-by, calling out to them.

The only other person who regularly sat on one of the benches was a boy who lived at the end of the lane. He came to read every evening, sitting near Miss Duffy, totally engrossed in what he was reading, his dark head bowed over the book. They spoke only briefly until one bright October Sunday. There was a funfair in operation on the fair green below them that day, dizzy shrieks rising above the blare of music and the noise of the machinery. An orange sweater made the boy conspicuous in the sun. They both seemed equally lonely, excluded from the enjoyment of people thronging among the amusements on the fair green. Miss Duffy called the boy over and asked him an unnecessary question, something about a relative of his who happened to be ill at the time. But it was only an excuse for conversation.

She made a series of useless remarks about his family, telling him how holy his mother seemed, how quiet his father was. She showed curiosity as she queried him about school, about his career. Her reaction was unexpected when he told her that he hoped to be a writer. She waved her hand sceptically, a hen-like noise escaping her, her face squeezing up in scorn. 'Don't be silly. Don't be silly,' she scoffed at him.

But as he tried to explain that it wasn't so impossible the idea became more acceptable to her. She agreed that he might succeed if he persevered. Perseverance was the most important thing, she said sagely.

They continued speaking about writing. But the world of the young writer, a world of aspirations, was far removed from that of Miss Duffy. It turned out, however, that she had some knowledge of books and outdated authors. She had been fond of reading once, she told him, but she no longer had time for it with all the housework she had to tackle. There was a note of complaint and at the same time something self-assertive in the way she said this. It was as if she wanted to believe that she was a busy, overstrained housekeeper.

There was an inkling of truth as she added in a low voice, 'It's been hard to manage since poor Cissy passed away.' Cissy had been her sister. At the mention of her name, Miss Duffy's eyes automatically sought the distance where a row of old houses stood in sunshine and seasonal tranquillity, at the base of a wooded hill. There was a sense of pain on her brow as she lapsed into silence for a few moments.

Everybody had known how she'd missed her sister. Once they'd seemed inseparable, her sister a tall, melancholy figure in a long fawn coat, a beret sidewise on her head, a pronouncement of despondency on her face. She'd been a foil for her small fat sister.

They'd been so contented together that they hadn't taken a precaution against death. Death had come treacherously. The little sister had been found in bed one morning clinging to the other's corpse.

Recovery from the shock of death and loss had been difficult. In trying to come to terms with living in a vacuity Miss Duffy had become something of a curiosity among the townspeople. She did her best to muster a sort of independence, refusing all offers of help from her neighbours though her house had fallen into a state of utter disorder. Dirt was everywhere, her cats freely soiling the carpets and furniture.

Something about the October Sunday, something about the tingling clarity of the faraway countryside made her drift into recollection of her sister. She spoke of the life they'd shared, lingering on the irrevocable things. Things that had been part of their yearly routine. The holiday they used to take in a resort on the south coast each September. The apple jelly they used to make at this time every year.

The harrowing loneliness in her voice, in her eyes, was unmistakable. It was as if she realized the hopelessness of her position. Only religious belief sustained her, belief that she was living in an interim, to be reconciled with her sister after death.

The boy listened to everything she said, nodding his head responsively, probably the first person to have listened to her for a long time. When at last he got up to go she complimented him gratuitously: 'Lucky is the girl that wins ye.' As he made off she called after him. Her hand was at her neck as she tried to explain something. 'I hope you wear the collar—you know—the Roman collar,' she faltered.

On the following evenings they often sat on a bench together, a sort of relationship being established between the two segregated people. Miss Duffy would tease the boy about girls, not realizing that there were none in his life.

She'd had a boyfriend when she was young and it gave her

immense pleasure to talk about it over and over again. Her parents had known nothing of it and she made it seem as though there'd been something fugitive about the liaison, something illicit, something perilous about every kiss.

But her mind seemed to wander as she described walks with him to the mansion where the local landlord had lived, a profusion of animal life on either side of the woodland lane leading to it, a profusion of flowers spreading in conflagration around it. The mansion and its surroundings had been another realm to her then. But the landowning classes were on a brink at the time, threatened by national events, their end imminent. Now, after the span of a lifetime, the mansion represented an idea of beauty and change to Miss Duffy, an idea embedded in her youth.

The boy listened with interest. It was as if he were picking up fragments of her life and mentally piecing them together.

Soon it was too cold to sit on the benches any longer. Miss Duffy was confined to her home. She caused some horror among her neighbours in mid-November when the pipes broke. It didn't occur to her to call a plumber and she could be seen carrying her dirt out in buckets to empty it on the hilltop.

She rarely saw the boy now. But sometimes he passed as she languished outside her home. She never failed to compliment him, remarking on some aspect of his appearance or some item of his clothes. 'Your hair is lovely today,' she'd pipe, or, 'You've got a beautiful jumper.' There was no way of acknowledging her compliments and the boy could only smile inanely.

One day he passed her wearing caramel trousers, a bright, modish shirt randomly open at the neck. Under his arm he bore a record, the spectral faces of a pop group peering from the red netherworld on the cover. The record drew an inevitable question from her. 'Do you like music?' she called. The boy said he did. Then for some reason she added, 'I think you have great times,' a look of endearment, a look of envy, in her eyes. She equated youth and good looks with happiness and activity. The boy didn't say anything, just looked at her with his non-committal smile.

They didn't meet in the following weeks, no sign of Miss Duffy in those weeks except at mass which she never missed. Kneeling at the very back of the church she always seemed rather bewildered, her expression similar to that of a child attending its first church service.

On Christmas Eve the boy passed her on the street. It was late, the street crowded. Her coat open, her body was thrown forward as she walked stolidly in front of the lighted windows. She seemed to be engulfed by the bustle and the crowd, a threatened look on her face. The boy greeted her brightly, trying to catch her eye. But she didn't hear him. She was probably unaware of where she was, the time of year. It was the last time he was to see her. Some weeks afterwards Miss Duffy heard he'd cut his wrists and was undergoing treatment in a psychiatric hospital. It was totally unexpected. It caused shock, a wave of speculation. There was something remote about suicide cases and suicide attempts, they were among the few extraordinary things in the undercurrent of small town life and people relished them for that.

Miss Duffy felt left out of all the talk. However, one neighbour told her that the boy had been living under severe mental strain in the past months. He'd been suffering from acute loneliness. The neighbour also informed her that the boy's doctors were discouraging people from visiting him as too much attention now would make his recovery impossible when he returned to normal life.

Though Miss Duffy had come to know him quite well she felt no immediate sympathy for him now. The incident was unreal, part of the growing unreality of life around her, an unreality which was hedging her in.

While he was away she herself disappeared. A nephew sent her to a hospital in some faraway town. She wasn't really able to look after herself anymore.

In the course of the year some of her neighbours heard that she'd died. But she'd been away too long and her death was like an unnoticed exit. Most of those who knew her remained unaware of it.

Her house fell into a state of perpetual neglect, the paint wearing off. It looked reproachful among the cleanness, the order of the other houses.

# Teddyboys

With a curious sultry look they waited, diamonds in their eyes, and handkerchiefs, thick and scarlet, in their pockets. They stood around, lying against the bank corner, shouldering some extraordinary responsibility, keeping imagination, growth, hope alive in a small Irish town some time around the beginning of the sixties.

Then mysteriously they disappeared; all but one, Jamesy Clarke, gone to Birmingham, London, leaving one solitary Teddyboy to hoist his red carnation. It was a lovely spring when they left. I was sorry they'd gone. But there was Jamesy.

He bit his lip with a kind of sullen spite. His eyes glinted, topaz. His hair gleamed. His shirts were scarlet and his tie blue with white polka dots.

As spring came early young men dived into the weir.

I wanted, against this background of river teeming with salmon, to congratulate Jamesy Clarke for staying to keep the spirit of dashing dress and sultry eyes alive. Instead I followed him, ever curious, watching each step he took, knowing him to be unusually beautiful and somewhat beloved by the gods. Though nine years of age, going on ten, I knew about these gods. An old fisherman by the Suck had once said, 'The gods always protect those who are doomed.' I harboured this information. I told no one.

Jamesy had stayed to look after his widowed mother. He lived in the 'Terrace' with her, behind a huge sign for Guinness, bottles abandoned, usually broken, children running about, a cry and a whine rising from them that aggravated the nerves and haunted like other signs of poverty haunted, dolls broken and destroyed, old men leaning against the men's lavatory, drunken and abused. His mother was allegedly dying from an unspoken disease, sitting among statues of Mary that surrounded her like meringues, and cough-bottle-smelling irises.

I'd never actually seen his mother. But I knew she dominated the tone of Jamesy's life, the prayers, the supplications, the calling on Our Lady of Fatima. Our Lady of Fatima was very popular in our town. She adorned most houses, in some more agonized than others, and a remarkable statement under her in my aunt's house: 'Eventually my pure heart will prevail.'

The fields about the river were radiant with buttercups, fluff amassed and fled over the Green and odd youngsters swam. I noticed Jamesy swimming a few times, always by himself, always when evening came, taking off his clothes, laying them in the stillness, jumping into the water in scarlet trunks. He never saw me. He wasn't supposed to. Like a little emissary of the gods I wandered about, taking note, keeping check, always acute and waiting for any circumstance that could do him harm. He was much too precious to me. His shirts, scarlet and blue, impressed me more than Walt Disney movies. But it was his eyes that awed me more than anything, eyes faraway as the Connemara mountains and yet near, near in sympathy and in sensation, eyes that saw and kept their distance.

Scandal broke like mouldy Guinness when apparently Jamesy was caught in the launderette making love to a girl. The girl was whizzed off to England. Clouds of June gathered; the Elizabethan fortress by the river stood out, one of the last outposts of the Queen in Connaught. Jamesy kept his distance. He didn't seem troubled or disturbed by scandal. He went his way. It was as though this girl was like washing on the line. She hadn't altered his life, hadn't changed him.

He smoked cigarettes by the bank corner, alone there now. Their scents accumulated in my nostrils. I took to naming cigarettes like one would flowers. A mantra rose in my mind that ordered and preoccupied a summer: Gypsy Annie, Sailor Tim. I called cigarette brands new names. I exploited all the knowledge I had of the perverse and applied it to Jamesy's cigarettes.

Ancient women sold pike in the Square. Sometimes they looked to the sky. They'd never seen a summer like this, broken cloud, imminent heat.

Old men wiped their foreheads and engrossed people in conversation about the Black and Tans. Everything harkened back; to the Rising, to the War of Independence, to the Civil War. Forgotten heroes and cowards were discussed and debated. The mental hospital looked particularly threatening; as though at any moment it was going to lurch out and grab. Jamesy swam. He had no part in conversation about the Rising, in talk of new jobs or new factories. Where he was financed from I don't know but he led a beautiful life and if it hadn't been for him the summer would not have been exciting and I would not have eagerly waited for the holidays when I could follow him along the railway tracks, always at a distance, until he came to a different part of the river from the one he swam in, sitting there, thinking.

When he started going out with a tailor's daughter I was horrified. I knew by the way she dressed she did not have his sense of colour. She walked with an absence of dignity. His arm always hung on her shoulder in a half-hearted way and she led him away from the familiar spots, the bank corner, the river.

I saw them go to a film. I observed him desert the summer twilights. I felt like writing to his friends in England, asking them to come back and send him out or feeding his mother with poison to make her complaint worse. Even the hold his mother's disease had on him seemed negligible in comparison to this girl's.

I noticed the actresses who starred in the films they went to see, Audrey Hepburn, Lana Turner, and privately held them responsible. I looked up at Lana Turner one night when they'd entered the cinema and told her I would put a curse on her.

I learnt about curses from a mad stocky aunt who lived in the country, was once regarded with affection by all our family until an uncle had a mongoloid child. Then attention diverted from her and she started cursing everyone, making dolls of them and putting them in fields of corn. I knew it worked. About the time she did one of my mother, my mother went to hospital. I knew it was an awful thing to do. But there was too much at stake.

The more I cursed her though, the more defiant Lana Turner looked, her breasts seemed almost barer. I stopped cursing her and started swearing at her, swearing at her out loud. The local curate passed. He looked at me. I said, 'Hello Father.'

He wondered at a child staring at a poster of Lana Turner, calling her by all the foul names my father called my mother.

Come July young men basked by the river. The sun had broken through and an element of ecstasy had come to town, towels, bottles of orange thrown about. Ivy grew thick and dirty about the Elizabethan fortress, gnats made their home there and a royal humming commenced then, a humming and a distillation of the voices of gnats and flies.

The evenings were wild and crimson; clouds raged like different brands of lipstick. That's one thing I'll say for Jamesy Clarke, he still took the odd swim by himself. In the silence after twilight he took off his clothes and dived into the water. Threads were whispered over the grass by the spiders. Wet descended. The splash of water reverberated. There were moments of silence when he just urged through the water. I waited across the field, my head in my lap. If I could I would have built him a golden bridge out of here. I knew all that was piled against him, class, the time that was in it, his mother. It no longer mattered to me that this town should have him. What I wanted for him was a future in which he could puff on smart cigarettes in idyllic circumstances. But much as I racked my brain I could think of nowhere to place him. London and Birmingham sounded too dour, Fatima was already peopled by statues of the Blessed Virgin and other places I knew of I was uncertain of, Paris, Rome. There just might have been a place for him in Hollywood but I knew him to be too elegant for it, there were more than likely simpler and more beautiful places in the United States into which he could have fitted. I wanted him more than anything to be safe, though safe from what I didn't know.

He held his girlfriend's hand about town. He sat on the fair green with her. He hugged her to him. He'd discarded jackets and wore orange T-shirts. A bracelet banded his arm, narrowly scathing hairs on his skin, which was the colour of hot honey. I looked to the sky above them, clouds like rockets in it. Perhaps his girlfriend did have something after all, a hunch of his existence. Nobody could have seduced him for so much time away from bank corner or river without responding to something in him. I forgave her. I gave up ownership. I played with the notion of being present at their marriage. I had it already arranged in my mind. He'd be dressed in white. She in blue. There'd be marigolds as there were outside the courthouse and his mother, virtually dead, would be in a movable bed in the church.

Then one day things changed. The weather broke. Clouds that had been threatening, sending shadows coursing over wheat and water, now plunged into rain. The heat evaporated and a sudden cold absorbed all that was beautiful, warmth in old stone, the preening of daisies in sidewalk crevices. I shook inside. I had to stay in. I played with dinkies. I looked through books. I found no information relevant to life. I burnt a total of three books one evening, two about horses and one an adventure story set in Surrey. I became like a little censor, impatient and ravaging anything that didn't immediately allow one in on the mystery of being. Dickens was merely sent back to the library. He was lucky.

I wrote a letter to Jamesy; he stood stranded by rain.

*Dear Jamesy,*
*I hate the rain. I wish I lived in a country where it didn't rain. How are you? I'm not too well.*

*I've decided I don't like books anymore. I prefer things like clothes. My mother keeps giving out. She was giving out when the sun was shining and she gives out when it's raining. How's your mother? I said a prayer to Our Lady of Fatima for her yesterday.*

*It's raining outside now. I'm going to draw a picture of Mecca. I was just reading about Mecca where all the Moslems go. I'm going to draw a picture of it and colour it in. See you soon I hope.*

*Desmond*

I didn't send the letter of course. I coloured it in too, drawing pictures of Teddyboys along the sides. I also drew a scarlet heart, pierced by an arrow, the number three, emphasizing it in blue, and a tree trunk.

I bore it with me for a while until one day it fell out of my pocket, the colours washing into the rain.

Jamesy had had a row with his girlfriend. That was obvious when the sun shone again. He looked disgruntled. An old woman, member of a myriad confraternities, reported that he spat on the pavement in front of her. 'Disgusting,' the lady said. 'Disgusting,' my mother agreed. 'A cur,' the lady said. 'A cur,' my mother said. And the lady added, 'What do you expect from the likes of him. His eyes,' she screeched with outrage, 'his beady eyes.'

It was true. Jamesy's eyes had changed, become pained, narrow, fallen from grace. He wore a white jacket, always clean though in his despair, and his features knotted in disgruntlement as cold winds blew and a flotsam of old ladies wandered the town, gossiping, discussing all shapes of misdemeanour with one another in highly pitched, off-centre voices.

Jamesy edged into the voice of autumn, his dislocation, his pain, and his eyes spitting, a venom in them now.

He began seeing his girlfriend again. This time he tugged her about town. She was a vehicle he pushed and swayed. Though a tailor's daughter she had her good points, grace I had to admit, and an almond colour in her hair, always combed and arranged to a kind of exactitude.

Lana Turner never graced our cinema again. There were posters that showed motorcycles or men in leather jackets, their faces screwed up as they unleashed a punch on someone. I lost Jamesy on his trail more than often.

Women whispered about Our Lady of Fatima now as though she was threatening them. Voices spoke of death, a faint shell-shocked murmuring each time a member of the community passed away. Death was wed into our town like a sister, a nucleus about which to whisper, a kind of alleyway to the Divine.

Almost as suddenly as it went, the fine weather returned, revealing a curious harvest, tractors in the fields, farmers brown as river slime on bicycles. Then young men of town returned to the river. They were quieter now, something was pulling out of their lives, summer, imperceptibly, like a tide.

Northern Protestants had come and gone, daubing a poster on the mill overlooking the weir, 'What shall it profit a man, if he shall gain the whole world, and lose his own soul?'

I couldn't find Jamesy. There was no sign of him in the evenings, swimming. I started an odyssey, seeking him through field and wood. Birds called. I thought I heard Indians once or twice. Horses lazed about, the last flowers of summer sung with bees, standing above the grass, lime and gold. The bold lettering of the poster above the weir was in my mind, its message was absent. I did not understand it.

My travels led me to wood and to a Georgian house lying outside the town. I hadn't forgotten Jamesy but I kept looking, pretending to myself I'd see him in far-flung places.

I sat on a hill one day and looked at the river beyond. My T-shirt was red. My mind was tranquil. I used the moment to think of Jamesy, his eyes, his anguish. I had seen that anguish cutting into his face in the course of the summer, into his eyes, his cheekbones, his mouth. I had seen a sculpture gradually realizing itself and the sculpture, like beautiful stamps, like stained glass in the church, spoke of an element of human nature I did not understand but knew was there, grief. It was manifest in Jamesy. I wondered about his mother, her journey towards death, his attitude to it, his solitary trails about town, the manifold cigarettes, the grimaces.

I imagined his mother's bedroom as I had visualized it many times, one statue standing out among the statues of Mary, that of Our Lady of Fatima, notable for her beauty and the snake writhing at her feet. That snake I identified now as a curse, the one that blighted Jamesy's face, the one that blighted Ireland, trodden on by the benign feet of one whose purity might, as she claimed, ultimately prevail.

My searching for Jamesy was becoming more spurious, a kind of game now, an unspoken fantasy; gone was the grandeur of odyssey. I observed thicket, nettle and flower.

Then one evening late in August unexpectedly I came on Jamesy. It was virtually dark, by the river, letters standing out on the poster, and as I wandered by the Elizabethan fortress noise became apparent to me. I looked over a hedge. There in the grass by a tributary of the river Jamesy was making love to the tailor's daughter.

The skirmish of a bird with a bush could not have been more noiseless than me, the running of an otter in the grass. I made my way home, shaken by what I had seen.

I hated him, yet I hated him with a hatred that transcended Jamesy. I hated him for what he was doing, for the image he had given me, for this new distortion on stained glass.

I wanted to share his simplicity, an empathy with his face. But there was more to him than a face and in the silence of my room, a wind rushing on the river outside as swans flew over, in the tradition of my rural aunt, in the tradition of Gypsies and the country Irish people rummaging with broken dolls, I cursed Jamesy.

He should not have told me what I didn't want to know, that the human spirit is tarnished.

Jamesy's girlfriend left town, a silent pageant by the station, she was going to a job in Dublin. He was there to say goodbye to her, a Teddyboy on a summer day, platform shorn of all but marigolds. I watched him now, assisting him towards his doom.

He swam again in summer evenings alone, silently racing across dew-moistened grass to dive into the water, and one evening when I wasn't looking he was drowned.

I wanted to tell everyone it was me who did it, I wanted to announce my guilt and be penalized for it. But in my T-shirt red as a balloon in the late-summer radiance no one listened; I was denied any sense of retribution. I was ignored.

His funeral occurred two days before I returned to school. Young girls with the look of girls from the 'Terrace', faces pinched and yet knowledgeable, marched behind a hearse piled with masses of red carnations. He had many cousins, young females, and thereby many wreaths were donated.

The town came out in throngs, people loving funerals, and he being young, they accepted his death, excusing him all, his background, his spitting on the cement as he passed old ladies.

'Sure he stayed to look after his mother,' women slurred, and his mother, risen from her deathbed, looking fine and healthy, was there, a woman in black with a scarf of emerald and white on her head.

The prayers were read; a woman of the community, respectable, stood out from the crowd, a single tear in her eye.

Glass was reflected around the cemetery, domes bearing images of the sky and other wreaths, and when they were all gone I stayed.

I knew he had departed forever, his death seemed inevitable like so many things, autumn, and the poster on the weir.

I told him I was sorry. I apologized. I knew, however, the grief of his death would fill my life and whether I was responsible or not I'd always see him wherever I went, his eyes, his tie with the colonnade of polka dots.

His mother assumed perfect health in the next few months, whether assisted by Our Lady of Fatima or not I'll never know, but one thing I understood, over school books, in the anguish of the classroom I knew by looking out the window that somehow she had triumphed as she said she would. The lady with iron eyes, blue drapes on her robe, her hands joined in prayer and her feet squelching a snake, had prevailed.

Our Lady of Fatima, touchstone of the miraculous, had claimed unto herself a soul before it knew the damp of winter or the drought that issued from the human heart.

# The Last Time

The last time I saw him was in Ballinasloe station, 1953, his long figure hugged into a coat too big for him. Autumn was imminent; the sky grey, baleful. A few trees had become grey too; God, my heart ached. The tennis court beyond, silent now, the river close, half-shrouded in fog. And there he was, Jamesy, tired, knotted, the doctor's son who took me out to the pictures once, courted me in the narrow timber seats as horns played in a melodramatic forties film.

Jamesy had half the look of a mongol, half the look of an autistic child, blond hair parted like waves of water reeds, face salmon-colour, long, the shade and colour of autumnal drought. His father had a big white house on the perimeter of town—doors and windows painted as fresh as crocuses and lawns gloomy and yet blanched with perpetually new-mown grass.

In my girlhood I observed Jamesy as I walked with nuns and other orphans by his garden. I was an orphan in the local convent, our play-fields stretching by the river at the back of elegant houses where we watched the nice children of town, bankers' children, doctors' children, playing. Maria Mulcahy was my name. My mother, I was told in later years, was a Jean Harlow-type prostitute from the local terraces. I, however, had hair of red which I admired in the mirror in the empty, virginal-smelling bathroom of the convent hall where we sat with children of doctors and bankers who had to pay three pence into the convent film show to watch people like Joan Crawford marry in bliss.

Jamesy was my first love, a distant love.

In his garden he'd be cutting hedges or reading books, a face on him like an interested hedgehog. The books were big and solemn-looking—like himself. Books like *War and Peace*, I later discovered.

Jamesy was the bright boy though his father wanted him to do dentistry.

He was a problem child, it was well known. When I was seventeen I was sent to a draper's house to be a maid, and there I gathered information about Jamesy. The day he began singing 'Bye Bye Blackbird' in the church, saying afterwards he was singing it about his grandmother who'd taken a boat one day, sailed down the river until the boat crashed over a weir and the woman drowned. Another day he was found having run away, sleeping on a red bench by the river where later we wrote our names, sleeping with a pet fox, for foxes were abundant that year.

Jamesy and I met first in the fair green. I was wheeling a child and in a check shirt he was holding a rabbit. The green was spacious, like a desert. *Duel in the Sun* was showing in town and the feeling between us was one of summer and space, the grass rich and twisted like an old nun's hair.

He smiled crookedly.

I addressed him.

'I know you!' I was blatant, tough. He laughed.

'You're from the convent.'

'I'm working now!'

'Have a sweet!'

'I don't eat them. I'm watching my figure!'

'Hold the child!'

I lifted the baby out, rested her in his arms, took out a rug and sat down. Together we watched the day slip, the sun steadying. I talked about the convent and he spoke about *War and Peace* and an uncle who'd died in the Civil War, torn apart by horses, his arms tied to their hooves.

'He was buried with the poppies,' Jamesy said. And as though to remind us, there were sprays of poppies on the fair green, distant, distrustful.

'What age are you?'

'Seventeen! Do you see my rabbit?'

He gave it to me to hold. Dumb-bells, he called it. There was a fall of hair over his forehead and by bold impulse I took it and shook it fast.

There was a smile on his face like a pleased sheep. 'I'll meet you again,' I said as I left, pushing off the pram as though it held billy-cans rather than a baby.

There he was that summer, standing on the bridge by the prom, sitting on a park bench or pawing a jaded copy of Turgenev's *Fathers and Sons*.

He began lending me books and under the pillow I'd read Zola's *Nana* or a novel by Marie Corelli, or maybe poetry by Tennyson. There was always a moon that summer—or a very red sunset. Yet I rarely met him, just saw him. Our relationship was blindly educational, little else. There at the bridge, a central point, beside which both of us paused, at different times, peripherally. There was me, the pram, and he in a shirt that hung like a king's cloak, or on cold days—as such there often were—in a jumper which made him look like a polar bear.

'I hear you've got a good voice,' he told me one day.

'Who told you?'

'I heard.'

'Well, I'll sing you a song.' I sang 'Somewhere over the Rainbow', which I'd learnt at the convent.

Again we were in the green. In the middle of singing the song I realized my brashness and also my years of loneliness, destitution, at the hands of nuns who barked and crowded about the statue of the Infant Jesus of Prague in the convent courtyard like seals on a rock. They hadn't been bad, the nuns. Neither had the other children been so bad. But God, what loneliness there'd been. There'd been one particular tree there, open like a complaint, where I spent a lot of time surveying the river and the reeds, waiting for pirates or for some beautiful lady straight out of a Veronica Lake movie to come sailing up the river. I began weeping in the green that day, weeping loudly.

There was his face which I'll never forget. Jamesy's face changed from blank idiocy, local precociousness, to a sort of wild understanding.

He took my hand.

I leaned against his jumper; it was a fawn colour.

I clumsily clung to the fawn and he took me and I was aware of strands of hair, bleached by sun.

The Protestant church chimed five and I reckoned I should move, pushing the child ahead of me. The face of Jamesy Murphy became more intense that summer, his pink colour changing to brown. He looked like a pirate in one of the convent film shows, tanned, ravaged.

Yet our meetings were just as few and as autumn denuded the last of the cherry-coloured leaves from a particular house-front on the other side of town, Jamesy and I would meet by the river, in the park—briefly, each day, touching a new part of one another. An ankle, a finger, an ear lobe, something as ridiculous as that. I always had a child with me so it made things difficult.

Always too I had to hurry, often racing past closing shops.

There were Christmas trees outside a shop one day I noticed, so I decided Christmas was coming. Christmas was so unreal now, an event remembered from convent school, huge Christmas pudding and nuns crying. Always on Christmas Day nuns broke down crying, recalling perhaps a lost love or some broken-hearted mother in an Irish kitchen.

Jamesy was spending a year between finishing at school and his father goading him to do dentistry, reading books by Joyce now and Chekhov, and quoting to me one day—overlooking a garden of withered dahlias—Nijinsky's diaries. I took books from him about writers in exile from their countries, holding under my pillow novels by obscure Americans.

There were high clouds against a low sky that winter and the grotesque shapes of the Virgin in the alcove of the church, but against that monstrosity the romance was complete I reckon, an occasional mad moon, Lili Marlene on radio—memories of a war that had only grazed childhood—a peacock feather on an Ascendancy-type lady's hat.

'Do you see the way that woman's looking at us?' Jamesy said one day. Yes, she was looking at him as though he were a monster. His reputation was complete: a boy who was spoilt, daft, and an embarrassment to his parents. And there was I, a servant girl, talking to him. When she'd passed we embraced—lightly—and I went home, arranging to see him at the pictures the following night.

Always our meetings had occurred when I brushed past Jamesy with the pram. This was our first night out, seeing that Christmas was coming and that bells were tinkling on radio; we'd decided we'd be bold. I'd sneak out at eight o'clock, having pretended to go to bed. What really enticed me to ask Jamesy to bring me to the pictures was the fact that he was wearing a new Aran sweater and that I heard the film was partly set in Marrakesh, a place that had haunted me ever since I had read a book about where a heroine and two heroes met their fatal end in that city.

So things went as planned until the moment when Jamesy and I were in one another's arms when the woman for whom I worked came in, hauled me off. Next day I was brought before Sister Ignatius. She sat like a robot in the Spanish Inquisition. I was removed from the house in town and told I had to stay in the convent.

In time a job washing floors was found for me in Athlone, a neighbouring town to which I got a train every morning. The town was a drab one, replete with spires.

I scrubbed floors, my head wedged under heavy tables: sometimes I wept. There were Sacred Heart pictures to throw light on my predicament but even they were of no avail to me; religion was gone in a convent hush. Jamesy now was lost, looking out of a window I'd think of him but like the music of Glenn Miller he was past. His hair, his face, his madness I'd hardly touched, merely fondled like a floating ballerina.

It had been a mute performance—like a circus clown. There'd been something I wanted of Jamesy which I'd never reached; I couldn't put words or emotions to it but now from a desk in London, staring into a Battersea dawn, I see it was a womanly feeling. I wanted love.

'Maria, you haven't cleaned the lavatory.' So with a martyred air I cleaned the lavatory and my mind dwelt on Jamesy's pimples, ones he had for a week in September.

The mornings were drab and grey. I'd been working a year in Athlone, mind disconnected from body, when I learned Jamesy was studying dentistry in Dublin. There was a world of difference between us, a partition as deep as war and peace. Then one morning I saw him. I had a scarf on and a slight breeze was blowing and it was the aftermath of a sullen summer and he was returning to Dublin. He didn't look behind. He stared—almost at the tracks— like a fisherman at the sea.

I wanted to say something but my clothes were too drab; not the nice dresses of two years before, dresses I'd resurrected from nowhere with patterns of sea lions or some such thing on them.

'Jamesy Murphy, you're dead,' I said—my head reeled.

'Jamesy Murphy, you're dead.'

I travelled on the same train with him as far as Athlone. He went on to Dublin. We were in different carriages.

I suppose I decided that morning to take my things and move, so in a boat full of fat women bent on paradise I left Ireland.

I was nineteen and in love. In London through the auspices of the Sisters of Mercy in Camden Town I found work in a hotel where my red hair looked ravishing, sported over a blue uniform.

In time I met my mate, a handsome handy building contractor from Tipperary, whom I married—in the pleased absence of rela- tives—and with whom I lived in Clapham, raising children, he get- ting a hundred pounds a week, working seven days a week. My hair I carefully tended and wore heavy check shirts. We never went back to Ireland. In fact, we've never gone back to Ireland since I left, but occasionally, wheeling a child into the Battersea funfair, I was reminded of Jamesy, a particular strand of hair blowing across his face. Where was he? Where was the hurt and that face and the sen- sitivity? London was flooding with dark people and there at the beginning of the sixties I'd cross Chelsea bridge, walk my children up by Cheyne Walk, sometimes waiting to watch a candle lighting. Gradually it became more real to me that I loved him, that we were active within a certain sacrifice. Both of us had been bare and desti- tute when we met. The two of us had warded off total calamity, total loss. 'Jamesy!' His picture swooned; he was like a ravaged corpse in my head and the area between us opened; in Chelsea library I began reading books by Russian authors. I began loving him again. A snatch of Glenn Miller fell across the faded memory of colours in the rain, lights of the October fair week in Ballinasloe, Ireland.

The world was exploding with young people—protests against nuclear bombs were daily reported—but in me the nuclear area of the town where I'd worked returned to me.

Jamesy and I had been the marchers, Jamesy and I had been the protest! 'I like your face,' Jamesy once said to me. 'It looks like you could blow it away with a puff.'

In Chelsea library I smoked cigarettes though I wasn't supposed to. I read Chekhov's biography and Turgenev's biography—my husband minding the children—and tried to decipher an area of loss, a morning by the station, summer gone.

I never reached him; I just entertained him like as a child in an orphanage in the West of Ireland I had held a picture of Claudette Colbert under my pillow to remind me of glamour. The gulf between me and Jamesy narrows daily. I address him in a page of a novel, in a chip shop alone at night or here now, writing to you, I say something I never said before, something I've never written before.

I touch upon truth.

# Afternoon

She lay in the hospital which she hated with nuns running about and nurses slipping with trays of soup.

The soup was awful, simply awful. 'Package soup,' she complained to Mary. Not the strong emerald and potato soup of the bog-roads. 'I'll die if I stay here much longer.' Mary looked at her. Her mother was ninety-one and the doctors had stated there was little hope for her. The tribe of the Wards was expecting death as their children would watch for the awakening of stars at night on beaches in Connemara.

Two Madges came and two more Marys came to see her later that night. They stood like bereaved angels gazing at the old woman who had mothered fifteen children, ten living, one a doctor in London, one a building contractor in California. The one who was a doctor had been taken by English tourists before the Civil War. He'd been a blond two-year-old, her youngest at the time. They'd driven up in a Ford coupé to the camp, admired the child, asked if he could spend the summer with them. They never gave him back. Jimmy Joe was a building contractor in California. He'd gone to the golden state in 1925, seeking gold. He now owned a big house in San Francisco and Tim, her great-grandson, had only that summer gone to him and installed himself in the house, 'jumping into a swimming pool' it was whispered.

Eileen lay dying. As the news spread Wards and even McDonaghs came to see her. They came with cloaks and blankets and children. They came with caps and with fine hats from London. They
smoked pipes. They looked on with glazed eyes telling themselves
about history of which she had seen so much.

Mary recalled the wake for her husband twenty years before in
the fair green in Ballinasloe, loud mourning and the smell of extin-
guished fires. In the fair green of Ballinasloe now bumpers bashed
and lights flashed to the sound of music and the rising whine of
voices and machines.

Tinkers from all over Ireland had come to Ballinasloe fair green
as they had for hundreds of years, bringing horses, donkeys, mules.
Romanies even came from England and Gypsies from the South of
France.

Eileen in her hospital bed often thought she heard the voice of
the carnival. She'd first gone to the fair at the age of ten in 1895 when
Parnell was still being mourned as this area was the place of his infa-
mous adultery, adultery among the wet roses and the big houses of
Loughrea. You could smell his sin then and the wetness of his sex.
Her parents made love in their small caravan. In Ballinasloe there'd
been the smell of horse manure rising balefully and the rough scent
of limestone. A young man had asked her age and said she'd make a
fine widow some day.

She'd married at fifteen and her husband went to sea. He sailed
to South America and to South Africa and the last that was heard
of him was that he'd married a black woman on an island.

Eileen had had one child by him. The child died in the winter of
1902 on a bog-road outside Ballinasloe. It had been buried in a field
under the mocking voices of jackdaws and she swore she'd become
a nun like the Sisters of Mercy in their shaded gardens in Ballinasloe.

But Joe Ward took her fancy—he'd become a Tinker king in a
fight in Aughrim—beating the previous king of the Tinkers, who
was twenty-five years older than him, in a fist-fight. He'd been handsome and swarthy and had a moustache like British Army officers,
well designed and falling like a fountain.

They'd wedded in St Michael's Church on St Stephen's Day,
1906. Her father had told the bishop in Loughrea her previous hus-

band had been eaten by sharks and the marriage had taken place without bother. She'd worn a Victorian dress, long and white, which the lady of the local manor had given her, a woman who'd performed on the London stage once with bouquets of paper roses about her breasts.

The priest had proclaimed them man and wife as celebrations followed on the Aughrim road, whiskey and poteen downed where a month before two children had died from the winter chill.

There had been dancing through the night and more than one young girl lay down with an older heftier man, and Eileen slept with a warm-legged man, forgetting about the odd clinging piece of snow and the geese fretting in the fields.

She became pregnant that cold, cold winter, holding her tummy as March winds howled and their caravans went west, trundling along Connemara roads to the gaps where the sea waited like a table. They camped near Leenane Head. Fires blazed on June nights as wails rose, dancing ensuing and wood blazing and crackling with a fury of bacon. They were good days. They'd sold a troop of white horses to the Gypsies of France and many men went to bed with their women, stout in their mouths and on their whiskers.

They saw ships sail up the fjord at dawn and they bought crabs and lobster from local fishing men. When her belly had pushed out like a pram she found Joe on the lithe body of a young cousin.

Her child perished at birth. She had thirteen children by Joe. They grew up as guns sounded and Tinker caravans were caught in ambushes in East Galway. Joe was in Dublin for 1916. He saw the city blaze and he was bitterly disappointed as he'd come to Dublin to sell a mare and eat a peach melba in an illustrious ice-cream house in Sackville Street. He returned to Galway without having eaten his ice cream.

Michael Pat, her oldest, found a dead parish priest lying in the bushes like a crow in 1921; the Tans had smitten him on the head. The Tinkers had covered his body and fallen on their knees in prayer. The police came and a long stalwart ambulance.

The body was borne away and Eileen and her children attended his funeral, bringing bouquets of daffodils stolen from the garden of a solicitor and banners of furze which were breaking to gold.

He was the last victim Eileen knew of, for Britain gave the men with their long moustaches and grey lichen-like hair their demands and as they arrived in Ballinasloe for the fair there was more anger, more shots, and buildings in flame in Dublin.

Irishmen were fighting Irishmen. A young man was led blind-folded to a hill above the Suck and shot at dawn and the fair ceased for a day because of him and then went on with a girl who had a fruity Cork accent bellowing 'I'm forever blowing bubbles' across the fair green where lank and dark-haired Gypsies from France smoked long pipes like Indians.

Eileen opened her eyes.

Her daughter Mary, sixty-two, looked like Our Lady of the Sorrows.

'O Mother dear you're leaving me alone with a pack of un-grateful children and their unfortunate and ill-behaved children.'

Mary was referring to her drunken sons and daughters who hugged large bottles of Jameson in Dublin with money supplied by social security or American tourists.

'Sure they have picnics of whiskey outside the Shelbourne,' Mary had once told her mother.

As for their children they were Teddyboys and thieves and drunkards and swindlers or successful merchants of material stolen from bomb sites in Belfast. There was a group who went North in vans and waited like Apaches swooping upon bomb-sites after the IRA had blown a store or a factory.

It was whispered that the IRA and the Irish Tinkers were in league, blowing the Unionist kingdom to pieces for the betterment of the Travelling people and for the ultimate ruinous joy of a dishevelled and broken province. Middle-aged men sat in parlours in Belfast thanking God for each exquisite joy of destruction, a bomb, a bullet, while they drank to the day there'd be a picture of Patrick Pearse in Stormont and a shoal of shamrocks on the head of Queen Victoria's statue. 'It's a bad picture of the Travelling people folk have,' Mary had told her. And yet more and more were becoming peaceable and settling in council houses in Swinford or Castlerea. These were the ones you didn't hear of. These children who attended school and were educated and those parents who worked and who tidied a new house of slate grey. 'They say Tommy Joe is in the IRA,' Mary had said. Tommy Joe was Eileen's fifth great-grandson. Apparently he wore roses in his lapel and turned up in distant places, meeting agents or big-breasted young women, negotiating deals of arms. He ran off to Libya at the age of seventeen with an Irish melodion player who was a secret agent for a Belfast regiment.

That started him. 'It's been gin and tonic and sub-machine-guns since,' Mary had complained to Eileen before illness had confined her to Portiuncula Hospital, Ballinasloe.

As Eileen lay in bed surrounded by bustling seagull-like sisters from South America news filtered through of violence in the fair green.

It was the first year there'd been trouble at the fair other than brawls and fights and lusts. Men had been beaten with bottles. A caravan had been set alight and an old man in the country had been tied in his bed and robbed by two seventeen-year-old Tinkers.

Eileen grabbed her beads.

It was the North, the North of Ireland was finally sending its seeds of ill-content among the Travelling people. Young men who'd been to Belfast had caught a disease. This disease had shaped greed, had shaped violence like a way of grabbing, a way of distrusting, a way of relinquishing all Eileen had borne with her through her life.

Talking to Mary now, she said, 'England brought me great luck.'

She and Joe had travelled the length and breadth of Ireland as mares grew thin and men looked like mummers. They'd settled outside Belfast, dwelling on a site beside a graveyard while Joe, being a man of intelligence and strength, found work in the shipping yard. She'd had eleven grandchildren then and they hung their clothes like decorations on the bushes as her sons sauntered about Antrim on white horses repairing tin objects. One of her granddaughters fell in love with a minister's son. Eileen like her grandmother. She followed him about and when he ignored her she tore off her blouse, laying her breasts naked and her nipples like wounds, and threatened to throw herself into the Lagan.

Peader her grandson led her away. The girl cracked up, became babbling and mad and ever after that went off with an old Tinker called Finnerty, telling fortunes from palms, staring into people's eyes in Ballinasloe or Loughrea, foretelling people of death or scaldings or bankruptcy.

In the winter of 1935 Joe was beaten up and a young child seized by an Antrim lady who wouldn't let him go for two days, saying he was a heathen.

The sky dropped snow like penance and the Wards moved off, wandering through Donegal, past the mass rocks and the hungry bays and the small cottages closed to them and the hills teeming with the shadow of snow. There was no work for them and Brigid her youngest died of tuberculosis and four grandchildren died and Peader and Liam took boats to America and were not heard of till they got to Boston and were not heard of again until 1955 when both were dead.

'It's like the Famine again,' said Eileen, recalling days close to her birth when the banshee howled and young men and old men crawled to the poorhouse in Ballinasloe like cripples, seeking goat's milk.

Wirelesses blared jazz music as doors closed on them and Eileen cursed the living and the dead as she passed bishops' residences and crucified Christs hanging like bunting outside towns.

Her mother and father had survived the Famine but they lived to report the dead bodies lying over the length and breadth of Ireland like rotten turnips. They'd reported how men had hanged their children in order to save them and how at the Giant's Causeway Furies had eaten a McDonagh as though he was a chicken. 'We'll leave this land,' she said to Joe. They tried to sell their mangy mares, succeeded in Athenry in selling them to an Englishman as thin as the mares and they took off.

'Our people have been Travelling people since the time of St Patrick,' said Joe. 'We should have been treated better than this.'

Sister woke her.

'Wake up, Mrs McDonagh. It's time for breakfast.' She was not Mrs McDonagh but the nun presumed all Tinkers were McDonaghs.

Breakfast was porridge thin and chill as the statue of Mary standing somewhere near.

Eileen ate as a young nurse came and assisted her as though shovelling earth into a grave.

'The tea is putrid,' complained Eileen.

'Whist,' said the nurse. 'You're only imagining it.'

Outside mists clung like a momentary hush. Winter was stealing in but first there was this October imminence, standing above sweetshops and council houses.

She took one more sup of the tea.

'This is not good enough.' She called the nurse. A country girl made off to get her stronger tea as Eileen bemoaned the passing of tea thick and black as bog-water.

They'd set up camp in Croydon in 1937, and from that spot moved across England, repairing tin, selling horses, rambling north along ill-chosen seaside paths, paths too narrow for jaunty caravans. They surmounted this island, rearing right to its northmost edge, the Kyle of Lochalsh, John o' Groat's.

They camped in winter in mild spots where men shook herring from their nets as Eileen's daughters shook daughters and sons from their bodies, as the Wards germinated and begot and filled England with Tinkers.

During the War they craved their little spot in Croydon, venturing north but once, shoeing horses in Northumberland, taking coast roads, watched by ancient island monasteries. They settled in Edinburgh winter of '42 but Eileen got lonesome for talk of Hitler and the air-raid shelters squeezing with people and she left a city of black fronts and blue doors and went south with Joe and her daughter Mary, widowed by a man who jumped into the sea to save a bullock from drowning.

They camped in Croydon. Mary married a cockney tramp and they broke Guinness into an old bath and feasted on it. Mary had three children and more people of their clan joined them.

At Christmas they had the previous year's trees fished from rubbish dumps and they sang of the roads of Ireland and ancient days, bombs falling as they caroused without milk or honey.

He didn't come back one day and she searched London three days and three nights, passing rubble and mothers bemoaning their dead children until his body was found in a mortuary. She didn't curse Hitler or his land. She fell on her knees and splayed prayers and lamentation over his dead body as further sirens warned of bombs, and, as her body shaking with grief became young and hallucinatory, imagining itself to be that of a girl in Connaught without problems.

They buried him in London. The McDonaghs and the Wards and the McLoughlins came and as it was winter there were only weeds to leave on his grave but the women shook with crying and the men pounded their breasts.

Above Eileen saw geese fly north.

She woke with tears in her eyes and she wiped them with hospital linen. Joe, Joe. My darling lover. Joe, Joe, where did you go, times when bombs were falling like bricks and little girls were lying in the rubble like china dolls.

She was leading woman of her tribe then. Her family gathering, hanging their washings like decorations.

At Christmas 1944 a duchess drove up with presents for the children. She had on a big hat of ermine grey and Eileen refused her gifts, knowing her kinsmen to have fought this aristocracy for nine hundred years and realizing she was being made a charity of. Once in Ballinasloe she'd known a lady who'd been a music hall artiste in London and who married the local lord. That lady had addressed her as her equal.

Eileen had had hair of purple and red then and she'd had no wish of charity. The lady of the house had found companionship in a girl living in a tent on the edge of her estate.

'We'll go back to Ireland,' her son Seamus said at the end of the War.

Eileen hesitated. She was not sure. The last memories had been mangy. She and her family were English-dwelling now and they received sustenance for work done and they abided with the contrasts of this country.

She led her family north before deciding. Up by Northumberland and seeing a fleet of British planes flying over she decided on embarking.

The customs man glared at her as though she was an Indian.

'Are you Irish, ma'am?' he said.

'Irish like yourself,' she said.

He looked at her retinue.

'Where were ye?' he said. 'In a concentration camp?'

They travelled straight to Galway. Its meadows still were sweet but on the way men had looked crossly at them and women suspiciously. This was the land her parents had travelled. It had not even a hint of the country beset by famine. Cars were roaming like hefty bullocks and in Athenry as they moved off from Ballinasloe little Josephine Shields was killed.

A guard came to look at the crash.

'I'm sorry,' he told Eileen. 'But you can't be hogging these roads. Something like this has been bound to happen.'

They buried the little girl in Galway. There was a field of daisies nearby and Eileen's eyes rose from the ceremony to the sea spray and a hill where small men with banana bellies were playing golf.

I'm leaving this land, she told herself.

They journeyed back to Liverpool, erupting again on the face of England, germinating children like gulls. They moved north, they moved south and in Croydon, standing still, Eileen met Joseph Finnerty, half-Irish Tinker, half-French Gypsy by his mother's origin. They married within two months. He was thirty-nine. She was sixty-two. She was a good-looking woman still and welcomed his loins. Their marriage was celebrated by a priest from Swaziland and performed in Croydon. Tinkers came from Ireland, more to 'gawp', said Eileen, and Gypsies, wild and lovely from France.

'My family has broken from me like a bough,' said Eileen. 'Now it's my turn for the crack.'

Men of ninety found themselves drunk as hogs in hedges about Croydon. A black priest ran among the crowd like a hunted hare and a young girl from Galway sang songs in Irish about deaths and snakes and nuns who fell in love with sailors.

Eileen looked at the London suburb as though at the sea.

'I can return to Ireland now,' she said.

She brought him back and they travelled widely, just the two of them for a while.

She brought him back to old spots, Galway and the Georgian house where the gentry lived and the girl from the London music hall of the last century. They went to the sea and marvelled at the wayside contrasts of furze and rhododendrons in May.

Joseph played a tin whistle and there was dancing along the way and singing and nights by high flames when a girl stepped out of Eileen like a ballerina.

'The years have slipped off your face,' people told her. They went to a dance one night in Athenry where there was jazz music and they danced like the couples with the big bellies and the bouncing hair.

'I'll take you to my mother's country now,' said Joseph, so off they went in a van that wheezed like a dying octogenarian through France.

They passed houses where they heard music the like Eileen could not understand, thrilling music, music of youth, music of a cosmos that had changed.

They passed war ruins and posters showing brazen women. They weaved through towns where summer lingered in February and rode hills where spring came like an onlooker, gazing at them with eyes of cherry blossom. They lingered on a mound of earth as they caught sight of a blue, blue sea.

They got out.

'This is my real home,' Joseph said. 'The Camargue. My mother's people came from here. This is the heart of the Tinkers' world. I was born here, of a father from Kerry and a mother from Saintes Maries de la Mer. I was gifted with second sight and feet that moved so I spent my first days in Ireland and saw the fighting and the flags and the falling houses and then I came back here and danced the wild dances and loved the strong women. From Marseilles I went south.' He pointed. 'Over there is Egypt. I arrived there when I was twenty-six and from there my life flows. I recall the palm trees and the camels as though it was yesterday. I went there and understood, understood our people the world over, the Travelling people, men who moved before gods were spoken of, men who—who understood.'

'We are of an ancient stock, my father used to say,' said Eileen. 'We were here before St Patrick and will be when he's forgotten.'

'Our secrets are the secrets of the universe,' said Joseph, 'a child, a woman with child, a casual donkey. We are the sort that Joseph was when he fled with Mary.'

Sand blew into Eileen's eyes as she drank wine for the first time. In March she watched young men with long legs from Hungary ride into the sea with red flags. It was the feast of St Sarah, patron saint of Gypsies.

They carried her statue like a bride betrothed to the sea and praised her with lecherous and lusty tongues.

The sea was already taking the shape of summer, a blue, blue sea.

'In October they come again to celebrate,' Joseph explained. 'They are faithful to their saints.'

She sat on sands where she drank bottles of wine and bottles of Coca-Cola and walked by the sea, which asked of her, 'Is this folly?'

She wanted to go home. She wished like a child fatigued of fun to see Ireland again.

'I'd like to take off soon,' she said to Joseph but she saw coming across his face a villainous look. He was drunk with red wine and wandering by the sea like an old man in Leenane. 'I want to go,' she told herself, 'I want to go.'

Summer edged in. She plucked wild flowers and wondered about her children and her children's children and asked herself if this her cup had not brimmed too high. 'Was it all folly?' she demanded of herself. Was it a madness that drove people littler than herself into Ballinasloe mental hospital to enquire daily if they were saints or sinners? She began to wonder at her own sanity and placed wine bottles full of wild roses on the sands of Carmargue before crying out, 'Am I going mad? Am I going mad?' They brought her first to a priest, then to a doctor in Marseilles. They left her alone in a white room for two days.

'Joseph Finnerty I curse you,' she said. Then he came and took her and placed her on a horse and rode towards their caravans in Camargue. 'We're going back to Ireland,' he said.

They arrived on a June morning and they set tracks to Connaught. The day was fine and on the way they heard that O'Rourke, king of the Tinkers, was dead. 'You'll be the next king of the Tinkers,' Eileen said.

She arranged he fight Crowley his opponent in Mountshannon. Women stood by with Guinness and cider and children paddled among the fresh roses and geraniums. She saw her lover strip to the waist and combat a man his senior and she recalled her father's words, 'Lucky is the man who wins ye.'

This man over the others had won her.

She wrapped a shawl about her as they fought and fell to the ground. In the middle of combat her gaze veered from fight to lake where birds dropped like shadows. 'I have travelled at last,' she said. 'There's a hunger and a lightness returned to my body. A grandmother and mother I'm not no more but a woman.'

After Joseph fought and won they drove off to a pub pushing out from a clump of rhododendrons and celebrated.

'Jesus, Mother,' said Mary. 'Have you no sense?'

'Sense I haven't but I have a true man and a true friend,' she said.

She was held in high esteem now and where she went she was welcomed. Age was creeping up on her but there were ways of sidling away from it.

She'd jump on a horse and race with Joseph. He was a proud man and faithful to her.

Also he was a learned man and conversed with school teachers.

In Cairo he'd had tuition from French Jesuits. He spoke in French and English and Romany and could recite French poets or Latin poets.

When it came to his turn at a feast he'd not play the whistle but sing a song in the French language.

Finally he grew younger before her eyes as she grew older. In France she'd fled because it was a bad match. Here there was nowhere to go.

It was lovely, yes, but her eyes were becoming criss-crossed like potato patches.

'I have reached an age that leads towards the grave,' she wept to herself one evening, 'I am an old banshee.' Joseph comforted her, not hearing, but maybe knowing.

She watched him bathe in the Shannon and knew he should be with a woman younger than her but that yet she loved him and would cut her throat for him. She saw in his eyes as he looked from the water the stranger that he was and the stranger that he was going to be.

In 1957 he fell from a horse in the fair green in Ballinasloe and was killed.

She remembered the curse on him in the South of France and knew it to have come true.

She watched the flames burning and coaxing at the wake and recalled his words in France. 'Our secrets are the secrets of the universe, a child, a woman with child, a casual donkey. We are the sort that Joseph was when he fled with Mary.' He was educated by French Jesuits and held comers in his tongue and twists in his utterances. He was a poet and a Tinker and a child of the earth.

She recalled the lady in the manor long ago who'd befriended her, to whom she'd go with bushels of heather on summer evenings.

Why was it that woman had been haunting and troubling her mind recently?

It had been so long since she'd known her yet she bothered her. Had it been warning of Joseph's death? All her life despite the fact she was just a Tinker she'd met strange people.

From the woman in the manor who'd asked her to tea one day, to the French Gypsy who'd become her lover as old age dawned upon her. He'd been the strangest of all, brown face, eyes that twinkled like chestnuts in open pods. Yes, he'd been a poet as well as a lover. He'd been of the earth, he'd gone back to it now. He'd possessed the qualities of the unique like the cockney music-hall girl who'd attracted the attention of an Irish peer and came to live in a manor, finding a friend in a Tinker from a hovel of tents and caravans.

She watched the flames dance and saw again the white horses of Camargue, flurrying in uncertain unison, and would have walked into the fire ablaze had someone not held her and comforted her and satiated her as her moans grew to the sound and shape of seals in bays west of Ballinasloe.

'Eileen wake up. Do you know what's happened? They've killed an old man.'

Eileen looked at her daughter. 'Who?'

'Tinker lads.'

Eileen stared. So death had come at last. They'd killed an old man. 'May they be cursed,' she said, 'for bringing bad tidings on our people. May they be forsaken for leaving an old way of life, for doing what no Travelling people have ever done before.'

As it happened the old man was not dead. Just badly beaten up.

Some Tinkers had gone to rob him, took all and hit him with a delft hot-water jar.

'The Travellers have already gone from the green.'

'Ballinasloe fair week without the Tinkers,' Eileen said. 'What a terrible sight the green must be.'

She saw more Tinkers than she'd ever seen before.

They came like apostles as a priest rummaged with broken words.

'Is it dying you think I am? Well, it's not dying I am,' said Eileen.

She saw five children like the seven dwarfs. 'These too will grow to drink cider outside the Gresham in Dublin,' she thought, as candles lit and the priest talked about the devil.

Her great-grandson Owen was living with a rich American woman in an empty hotel in Oughterard. 'What next?'

Her head sunk back.

She saw Joseph again and the flames and wanted again to enter but knew she couldn't. She woke.

'If it's dying I am I want to die in peace. Bring me to the cross-road in Aughrim.' A Pakistani doctor nearly had concussion but the solemn occasion speeded up as a nun intervened.

Young nurses watched Eileen being carted off.

They laid her on the ground and a Galway woman keened her. The voice was like sharp pincers in her ears.

Now that they were saying she was on the verge of death ancient memories were budging and a woman, the lady of the manor, was moving again, a woman in white, standing by French windows, gazing into summer.

She'd had fuzzy blonde hair and maybe that was why she'd looked at Joseph more closely the first time she saw him. She had the same eyes, twinkling brazen eyes.

She heard again the lady's voice. 'No, I won't go in,' answering her husband. 'It's not evening. It's just the afternoon.'

Eileen woke.

The stars shone above like silver dishes. The bushes were tipped with first frost.

She stirred a bit. 'Is it better I'm getting?' she wondered. She moved again and laughed.

Her bones felt more free. She lifted her head. 'They might be killing old men but they won't kill me.'

She stirred. A girl heard her.

Women shook free from tents and gazed as though at Count Dracula.

In the morning she was hobbling on a stick.

She hobbled down the lane and gazed on the Galway road. 'I'll have duck for dinner,' she said. 'Ye can well afford it with all the shillings you're getting from the government.'

At Christmas she was able to hobble, albeit with the help of a stick, into the church, crossing herself first with holy water.

# The Man from Korea

Afterwards it had the awkward grace of a legend; a silence when his name was mentioned, an implied understanding of what had happened. Few know what actually happened though, so to make it easier for you to understand I will make my own version.

I was five when he came to town, a child at street corners. I was an intensely curious child, a seer, one who poked into everyone's houses and recalled scandal, chagrin and disgrace. I know all about the Hennessys and if I don't let me pretend to.

He came in 1956. He was a young man of twenty-nine but already there was something old about him. He recalled the fires of the Korean War. He'd been an American pilot there. I'm not sure what he saw but it left his face with a curious neglect of reality; he stared ahead. Sometimes a donkey, a flying piece of hay, a budding tree at the end of the street would enthral him but otherwise silence. He kept quiet. He kept his distance. He shared very few things but he talked much to me. By a fire in the Hennessys', flames spitting and crying out, he talked of the sacred places of Asia, shrines to draconian goddesses, seated statues of Buddha.

I always nodded with understanding.

I suppose that's why he trusted me. Because, although a child of five, I was used to lengthy conversations with fire-brigade men, painters, road-sweepers. So he and I discussed Buddha, Korea and sunsets that made you forget war, long raving sunsets, sunsets of ruby and a red brushed but not destroyed by orange. The air became red for odd moments in Korea; the redness stood in the air, so much so you could almost ensnare a colour.

He had blond hair, sharpened by glints of silver and gold, a face tainted by a purple colour. It was as though someone had painted him, brush strokes running through his appearance, a glow, a healthiness about it, yet always a malign image before his eyes that kept him quiet, that compelled an austerity into eyes that would otherwise have been lit by handsomeness in the middle of a strange, arresting and, for an Irish small town, very distinctive face.

He came in April, time when the hedgerows were blossoming, time when Tinkers moved on and anglers serenely stood above the river. Light rains penetrated his arrival; talk of fat trout and drone of drovers in the pub next door to the Hennessys in the evening.

The Hennessys were the most auspicious young ladies in town. Margaret and Mona. They'd been left a small fortune by a father who won the Irish Sweep Stakes once and the pools another time. Their father had spent his whole life gambling. His wife had left him in the middle of it all. But before he died he won large stakes of money and these passed to his daughters. So his life wasn't in vain. They made sure of that, gambling and feasting themselves, an accordion moving through the night, taking all into its rhythms, sound of a train, flash of a bicycle light. The Hennessy girls sported and sang, inflaming passions of spinsters, rousing priests like devils, but retaining this in their sitting room, a knowledge of joy, a disposition for good music and songs that weren't loud and sluttish but graced by magic. Such were the songs I heard from bed up the road, songs about the Irish heart forever misplaced and wandering on Broadway or in Sydney, Australia, miles from home, but sure of this, its heritage of bog, lake and Irish motherhood.

The Hennessys had no mother; she'd gone early but their house was opened as a guesthouse before their father won his fortunes and so it continued, despite money and all, less a guesthouse, more a hospice for British anglers and Irish circus artistes. One travelling painter with a circus painted the Rock of Cashel on the wall. A fire blazed continually in the back room and the sweetness of hawthorn reigned.

You don't bring hawthorn into the house, it's bad luck; but the Hennessys had no mind for superstition and their house smelt of hedgerow, was smitten by sound of distant train, and warmed by a turf fire. Karl came to this house in 1956.

He meant to stay for a few weeks. His stay lasted the summer and if he did go early in autumn it was only because there was hurt in his stay.

The girls at first kept their distance, served him hot tea, brown bread, Chivers marmalade. He spent a lot of time by the fire, not just staring into it but regulating his thoughts to the outbursts of flame. He had seen war and one was aware of that; he was making a composition from war, images of children mowed down and buildings in flame. He came from a far country and had been in another far country. He was a stranger, an ex-soldier, but he was capable of recognizing the images of the world he hailed from in the flames of a fire in a small town in Ireland. I suppose that's why people liked him. He had the touch, just the touch of a poet.

Margaret and Mona nursed him like a patient; making gestures towards his solitude, never venturing too far but the tone of their house altering; the parties easing out and a meditativeness coming, two girls staring into a fire, recalling their lives.

Their father had brought them up, a man in a coffee-coloured suit, white shirt always open. They'd been pretty girls with ribbons like banners on their heads. Their father would bring them to the bog, bring them to picnics by the river, bring them on outings to Galway. Not a very rich man, he was a rent collector, but eventually won all around him and left them wealthy.

Karl when he came sat alone a lot, walked the limestone street, strolled by the river. His shirt, like their father's, was white and open-necked, his suit, when he wore it, granite grey but more than often he wore jeans and shirts, dragon-red with squares of black on them.

Even his eyebrows were blond, coming to a sudden quizzical halt.

He often smoked a cigarette as though it was a burden. Sometimes a bird seemed to shock him or a fish leaping with a little quiver of jubilation. The mayfly came, the continual trespass of another life on the water.

I followed Karl, the stranger, watched him sit by the river, close to the sign advertising God. 'What shall it profit a man, if he shall gain the whole world, and lose his own soul?'

An elm tree sprayed with life in a field. A young man sat on the grass by the river. The Elizabethan fortress shouldered ivy.

Karl spoke little and when he did it was in the evening, in the pub, to the drovers. He was 'The Yank', but people tolerated this in him. He had no big car, no fast money, an urgency in his quietness, a distinction in his brows.

Margaret and Mona accustomed themselves to him and brought him to the bog with them. On an old ass and cart. Two young ladies with pitchforks in the bog, bottles of orange juice readily available, plastic bags of ice, and the summer sun at its height above them, grazing their work with its heat, its passing shadows, its sweltering fog towards evening. He helped them, becoming tanned; the complexion of sand on him, in his face, above his eyes, in his hair. He worked hard and silently. The ass wandered by the river and the girls frequently assessed the situation, sitting, drinking orange.

Margaret was the youngest but looked older; tall, pinched, cheekbones like forks on her and eyes that shot out, often venomously, often of an accord of their own, chestnut eyes that flashed and darted about and told an uncertain tale.

Mona was softer, younger-looking, mouse hair on her, a bush of it, and eyes that were at once angelic and reasonable. Her eyes told no tales though.

The river running through the bog was a savage one, foraging and digging, a merciless river that took sharp corners. Donkeys lazed by it; cows explored it; reeds shot up in it; in summer a silver glow on it that seduced.

Margaret and Mona were tolerant of me, using me to do messages, paying me with Goldgrain biscuits or pennies. I talked to them though they didn't listen. They made a lot of cakes now and I sat licking bowls. Karl received their attention with moderate ease. He was slightly afraid of it yet glad of their kindness.

I felt him to be gentle though I wouldn't go so far as to say he hadn't done terrible things; however, what was more than likely was that he was haunted by the deeds of others.

In mid-July an American aunt came and visited Margaret and Mona, a lady from Chicago. She was from Karl's city and Karl visibly recoiled, going out more, seeking bog and river. This lady danced around, trimmed her eyebrows a lot, polished her nails.

She kept the girls in abeyance, talked to them as though talking to pet dogs. She had a blue hat that leapt up with a start, a slight veil hanging from the hat. She challenged everyone, me included, as to who they were, where they were from, who their parents were and what their ambition in life was. Karl was unforthcoming. I told her I was going to be a fire-brigade man in China, but Karl said nothing, pulled on a cigarette, his eyes lifting a little.

She wanted to know where in Chicago he hailed from. He muttered something and she chattered on again, encompassing many subjects in her discursiveness, talking about the weather, the bog, her relatives in Armagh, Chicago, the Great Lakes, golf, swimming, croquet, timber forests, Indian reservations, the Queen, Prince Philip and lastly her dog, who'd jumped under a car one day when he'd been feeling—understandably—despairing.

Karl looked as though he was about to go when she left. The girls moved closer then, tried to ruffle him a bit, demanded more of him. He sang songs for them, recited poetry about American Indians. They listened. Mona had a song or two, songs about death and the banshee's call to death. Margaret was jealous of Mona's voice and showed her jealousy by pursing her scarlet lips.

They had parties again, entertaining the roguish young clerks. They had dances and sing-songs, the gramophone searing the nights with Ginger Rogers.

Karl went to church with them sometimes. He looked at the ceremonies as though at something difficult to understand, the hurried Latin, the sermons by the priest always muttered so low no one could hear them.

Mona went to Dublin early in September and bought new clothes. Margaret followed her example in doing this.

I went into the sitting room one evening and Margaret had her arm on Karl's shoulder. He talked about the War now for the first time, the planes, the screams, trees and houses fighting for their lives, the children moaning and the women grabbing their children. He recalled the fighter planes, the village targets; he spoke of the mercilessness of war. People asked for alms. They got war. Margaret recounted her father's tales about the Black and Tans, the butcheries, the maiming, and Mona philosophically added, 'Thank God we didn't have Churchill or Hitler here. Those men were just interested in the money.'

Margaret chirped in: 'About time someone got interested in money. They're starving beyond in England and Germany for want of money. We're lucky here.'

Ireland was the land of full and plenty to them, legends about other countries somehow awry.

Margaret boldly got up, put on the gramophone while I was there one evening and asked Karl to dance. Whereupon he threw off his shoes and danced with her, a waltz, the kernel of the music binding them together.

Mona watched, quiet, but not too jealous. They'd always been strange together and now the strangeness emerged. They saw in Karl a common ideal. They wanted to get him come hell or high water. High water came with the floods in early October. Mona outshone herself, russet in her hair, a dress of lilac and her arms brown from summer. Margaret became pertinent to the fact that Mona was more attractive than she, so she did many things, wore necklaces of pearl, daubed her lips in many colours, wore even higher high heels. She stood above Mona and was nearly as tall as Karl.

Their house had a bad reputation and now Margaret began appearing like an expensive courtesan; she wore her grandmother's fur to the pictures while all the time Mona shone with the grace of a Michaelmas daisy.

Geese clanked over; bare trees were reflected in water. The sun was still warm, the vibrancy and health of honey in it. The leaves had fallen prematurely and the floods had arrived before their time but still the days were warm and Mona wore sandals while Karl sported light jackets.

The ladies of town noted the combat between the two girls, or rather Margaret's unusual assertiveness. They were overjoyed and sensed a coming downfall on a house that had distressed them so much with its joyful sounds.

Karl had taken to talking to me, talking about Korea, Chicago, war, the race problem. He found a unique audience in me and I listened to everything and I watched his silences, his playing cards by himself. I started accompanying him on his walks; he sometimes sitting to read Chinese poems out loud while cows mooed appreciatively.

He took my hand once or twice and distilled in me the sense of a father. I suppose with Karl holding my hand then I decided I would have a child of my own some day, a male child.

Karl spoke, spoke of the weather in Chicago, winter storms over the Great Lakes, ice skating, swimming in the huge oblong winter pools. There was something Chicago didn't yield him, though, despite multi-layered ice creams or skyscrapers always disappearing into the clouds, and that was the sky of Ireland, clouds over the mustard-coloured marshes, Atlantic clouds heaving and blowing and provoking rancour in the bog-water. He'd come to our town looking for the ease of an Eastern shrine, found it. Now two young women were vying for him.

He spoke about his mother, his father, Americans, scoffed at the American belief in war. I told my parents that Karl didn't believe in war and they didn't hear me. I told my grandfather. Eventually I told our dog.

To the women of town Margaret and Mona were as courtesans, they'd stopped going to mass. God knows what they were doing with that American.

They made cakes, desserts, cups of tea for him. Eventually he tired of their intricacies and reached for them. One evening I came in the front door, pulled back the curtain to see Karl with Mona in his arms, her dress at her waist, her breasts heaving in her bra. I sped off.

I returned some evenings later, peeping through the curtains to find Margaret in a similar position.

Then one evening I came and the lights were off except for one red bulb that Karl had inserted. He and Mona were dancing to music from the radio in semi-darkness, the fire splurting and a rose light overlooking them, holding them.

This time I waited. I watched through the curtains as they danced, Karl reaching to kiss Mona. Their kiss was tantalizing. He removed her ribbon. Hair shot out like a hedgehog's prickles.

I knew Margaret to be in Dublin. I watched them leave the room. He followed her. I looked at Our Lady on an altar and she looked back at me quizzically. Outside a cat protested.

I don't know what happened that evening. I always imagine Margaret returned prematurely from Dublin and found them sleeping. But Karl left without saying goodbye and of all hurts I've had in my life that remains the most instant, the first hurt of life. My father, brother, friend, didn't acknowledge that a farewell was necessary.

It doesn't seem like a major incident looking back, but it took the rainbow from the girls' eyes, the flush from their cheeks, the splendour from their dress. Jealousy created a barrier. It created an iron curtain. Jealousy came and sat where Karl had once sat. Jealousy came, another tenuous stranger.

He was a celibate and didn't wish to make love to either but took Mona as an off-chance and showed to Margaret all that was missing in her: real physical beauty, a good singing voice.

Mona under the weight of Margaret's acrimony became plump, looked like an orphan in the convent.

No more parties, no more songs; many guests, much work.

And then in spring Mona left on the evening train. I went to the station with Margaret to say goodbye to her. Margaret looked like a lizard, fretful. Mona was wrapped like a Hungarian refugee. The sisters didn't kiss but I can still see the look in Mona's eyes. She'd been betrayed by Margaret's loss of faith in her. She undid her own beauty, the beauty of her soul as well as the beauty of her body to satisfy an impatient sister.

Years later when Mona was dying of cancer in a Birmingham hospital Margaret visited her. There was still no forgiveness, but both of them had forgotten what it was exactly that had come between them; a burgeoning of possibilities in the form of a young ex-soldier, an eye to another world. I doubt if either of them ever for a moment reached that other world but they were left with an intuition of it long after their father's money had run out.

Mona died a few years ago.

Margaret still runs the guesthouse. And me?—I put these elements together to indicate their existence, that of Margaret and Mona, their enchantment with a young man who came and unnerved us all and left a strange aftermath, way back there in childhood, a shadow on the water, the cry of a wild goose in pain, an image of tranquillity in far-off Asia where candles burned before perennial gods, gods untouched by war, by the search of a young man, by the iniquitous failure of two young women who reached and whose fingers failed to grasp.

# The Hedgehog

The valley was situated somewhere in the Cevennes. It was mid-August when Dony stayed there, red berries fired in the blue air, the ground covered with fir cones. To one side the valley was encompassed by blue conical mountains. On the other side the Alps sometimes reigned in the faraway sky, their crests rose-coloured, tenuous.

Dony was brought to the valley by the Jouvets, the sallow-skinned, drably dressed Parisian family with whom he was staying on an educational holiday, during this, the seventeenth summer of his life, only a few days left before he was to return to Ireland.

Paris where he'd spent his first three weeks had been vastly disappointing. There'd been a tiredness after the students' revolution of the previous May and the weather had been autumnal—cold, rainy—a delirium of cloud over the tourist-infested city. He'd been mainly confined to the Jouvet apartment—a Van Eyck reproduction transfixing the marriage of Giovanni Arnolfini on the otherwise unadorned wall—his time occupied by reading back issues of glossy French magazines and by listening to Wagner and Beethoven on record, the music crashing his brain. Altogether his stay in Paris had been a very lonely experience.

He hadn't expected much of an improvement in the final stage of his vacation. But he had hoped for some change.

They were staying in a holiday colony, forest darkness encroaching on the bungalows that were grouped on the side of the valley. There was a tennis court nearby, boys and girls running, jumping about, reaching out, white shirts and shorts contrasting with the dark of their bodies. Everywhere were signs of activity. Children being banded off on picnics by chaperones. Groups of young people wobbling off on bicycle tours. Tours in a countryside of clear air, antique farms, leisurely peasantry.

Dony ventured to the community centre on his first evening in the colony. It was there he met Claire. She was sitting by the fire as though in contemplation when he was introduced to her, a radiance about her cheeks, a sense of poise about her. Her creamy blonde hair fell loosely, grooves of dark green shadow in it. Her pink blouse was pale where her breasts were defined.

He sat beside her as they spoke, his head largish over an orange T-shirt, charcoal brows converging on his eyes, an acne faded on his face. In his fragmentary French he told her about himself, Ireland, his hometown—the business town anchored in the rainy Midlands—the reds, blues, yellows of the fire filling his mind. The conversation touched on many subjects and finally led to politics, which provided ground for common discussion. Dony gave his views on the patchwork wars in Vietnam, Biafra, the Middle East, and expressed a lively hatred for the regimes in South Africa and Greece, targets of youthful concern.

Dony's politics overlapped with the remonstrance of Joan Baez and Donovan, delicate downtending faces on the covers of his record collection.

When he'd finished speaking Claire told him that he was an idealist.

Just then a youth approached. Claire introduced him as Remy. He wore a scarlet shirt, his hair bronze—indented with curls—masculinity concentrated in the expression on his face. He sat down, stretching his legs, remaining silent as the conversation was resumed.

Suddenly Claire pointed to the window. Sunset had accumulated outside. She went to see it, Dony following, looking over her shoulder. Between distant, extinct volcanoes the sky was glowering pink and purple. The pink was strange. It reminded Dony of the undersides of mushrooms.

But he was conscious of Remy slouching behind them, a sort of resentment about him, an expression of boredom on his face. Feeling that he ought to go Dony said goodnight to Claire, shaking her hand which entered neatly into his grasp.

As he made for the door he heard her say of him, 'Il est gentil.'

'Trop,' Remy replied caustically.

Despite that final uncomplimentary remark, Dony harboured hope after that night. He'd felt an awakening of romantic emotion as he'd spoken with Claire, an awakening of romantic trust.

At home he didn't involve himself with girls, overburdened with shyness.

He'd found an opportunity at last to make a relationship with a girl. However, something in him cringed at the prospect, he wanted to retreat into himself.

Next morning he started on a lone walk along the road that led from the holiday colony. On either side fields of corn rose in celebration of blue sky, children scrambling upwards, tiny figures lost in the clean glisten.

He passed a few people sitting in sun dapple on a tree-shaded bench as they imbibed the morning beauty together. The women wore straw hats, spotted dresses. An old man who looked like one of Cézanne's peasants leaned forward on a walking stick. The group watched Dony with mask-like expressions.

As he walked on he noticed many things and he fitted them into a nook in his mind as though he wanted to retain them.

Suddenly his attention was caught by a dead hedgehog that lay on the open road, blood dried on its bristles, the tender little creature utterly mutilated. He stood over it for a few moments, considering it. But it was just an object of curiosity, a detail of the morning.

Further on he encountered Claire and Remy who were returning from a nearby village together, a shopping bag in Claire's hand, ripples of colour in it. Her midriff was bare under a white blouse, her body slim, tapering in slacks.

'Tu es tout seul,' she exclaimed. It seemed to surprise her, shock her even that he should have been alone. But it was as if she extended affection to him by using the second person singular.

He accompanied them back to the colony, feeling a little awkward as he straggled to one side of Claire, something unreachable about her blondeness, her self-contained body. She told him about a woodland picnic that had been arranged for the following evening, the evening before he was to return home. She made him promise that he'd come.

The remaining part of his holiday was mainly taken up with touring in the surrounding regions with the Jouvets, new impressions converging on him, colours interchanging, the hard exhilarating greens of the upper valleys with the gradations of blue in the plains.

But he was back on time to join the picnic on his final evening. The young people gathered outside the colony, bags in their hands, an air of expedition about the picnic. They trekked in a group to the forest, Dony walking alongside Claire, exchanging views on films they'd both seen. Remy was somewhere ahead in the crowd, absorbed in conversation with two girls, their buttocks clenched tightly by blue jeans.

They found a suitable spot by the stream. It was twilight as they piled wood on a fire, sunset trailed in the sky, bells tinkling in nearby fields where goats moved in the growing dim.

The picnic began as potatoes, sausages, scraps of meat were roasted over the fire. There were half-hearted attempts to start a sing-song. A man wearing a traditional costume of the Auvergne played folk tunes on a pipe, the music filling the air.

The heat became intense, sparks crackling upwards towards the stars that were beginning to illumine the sky.

Dony's face and forehead were burning. He got up and sought the quiet of the stream, standing over it. He could no longer stand the heat, the crowd, the din. There was still a faint reflection of twilight on the stream and the sounds of water were soothing, the tinkling of bells still coming from the fields.

Suddenly a little boy touched his arm and thrust some cheese at him. 'Voulez vous du fromage?' he piped.

Dony accepted it, thanking him. Glancing about he saw Claire's eyes fixed on him, her cheeks heated as she sat by the fire, a glimpse of colour in her cravat. She'd obviously spotted him by the stream and had sent the little boy with cheese for him. But there was a questioning expression on her face now, the points of her eyes indicated by the flames, knees hugged to her.

He stood transfixed there, uncertain of himself, hoping that she'd come to him. But when he looked in the direction of the fire again she wasn't to be seen.

The group was diminishing as he crouched by the flames once more, couples withdrawing, their writhing bodies distinguishable among the trees. With utter disappointment Dony realized that Claire was among them. She'd probably taken Remy as her partner or perhaps she'd secured someone else, participating with him in the grove among the other couples.

He started back to bed, hoping that no one had noticed his ignominious departure. But it didn't matter. He'd never see these people again, never see Claire again.

They were representative of an interim in his life, a few suspended days away from home, their images embedded in those days. But they had confirmed the apparent failure of his life, his failure to merge with other people of his own age, to enter their world, to endure the hops at home, the smoky atmosphere, the shrieking music.

The past day had been like a piece of paper curling in intense heat, the edges becoming brown, the paper gradually diminishing, falling into ashes.

Sleep intersected his misery, a night in the bungalow, his case packed beside him. He was woken at about seven o'clock the following morning, the prospect of the long journey before him. M. Jouvet was to drive him to Lyons where he would get a train to Paris. From Paris he was to catch an evening flight to Dublin.

The morning was bright outside, trees innocently chequered by sunshine, but the light offered no consolation. There was a spectral quality about it as the previous evening was remembered.

As he dragged his case into the kitchen M. Jouvet was bent over a transistor set, listening to it intently as though to some important news. It had just been announced that the Russian army had invaded Czechoslovakia during the night, taking it over in one shattering move.

The news overhung the car trip to Lyons, M. Jouvet talking about it, valleys awakening in evanescent sun, mist drifting idly about orange and green tents, the first signs of activity in low-lying villages.

But the event was lost in the heat of the train journey, place names hailing him—Dijon, Fontainbleau—each stage of his journey bringing him nearer home, nearer to the lies he'd have to tell. He'd have to pretend that he'd enjoyed his holiday.

It wasn't until he was in a plane bound for Dublin that evening, a fantasia of moving cloud outside, that he recovered his earlier sense of dismay. The evening papers ranged before him, proclaiming the news of the invasion, displaying the first dazed photographs. The photographs showed ominous tanks, showed the bewildered faces of a people who didn't realize as yet that they were caught up in history.

The images were swathed in a new emotion. They'd never be forgotten—the tanks, the faces, the flags—they were seized upon by a moment of youth, the fires in Prague inerasible in the mind.

# Embassy

She ran a pub where old men slouched over
Guinness and where the light was always dark. Two or three regular
customers were always there and the conversations revolved around
sick dogs or bottled ships as these were an important property in the
community, symbolizing social status and a good clean home.

The calendar in the pub literally looked as though it was about
to fester and give. A doll-like model was represented on it. She was
leaning over a log and her lips were red.

She had blue eyes, delicately outlined by black. She wore a brown
coat and despite the snow on distant pines she did not look at all
cold.

Sheila would stand by the counter talking to all who came in,
occasionally cleaning a glass, rubbing it with a cloth.

Her husband had left her five months now and her children
were gone, married, working on the bogs in the Midlands and she
was alone.

But she was glad she was alone. The house was falling down. A
brown faded photograph of a distant Edwardian relative stood askew
on the stairway. Nettles brandished themselves in the garden, the
odd Guinness bottle thrown among them, but she was happy. She
went to bed at night with Saucepan, the big brown cat, on the eider-
down and she slept peacefully, dreaming of girlhood dances when

she waltzed at the crossroads, framed in a black dress with a topaz necklace on her white bosom.

She'd been a famous beauty then and even in the big house with raging Virginia creeper beyond the canal there weren't girls to come near her in beauty.

She had a quality ministers' daughters or doctors' daughters, lawyers' daughters or senators' daughters couldn't rival. She had black hair wild and as crossed as blackberries and her skin was rich and olive. She had six sisters, none to come near her in beauty, and as such she was marked out and her sins counted.

She'd dance at the crossroads with the doctors' sons and the lawyers' sons and often there'd be coloured lights nearby or a caravan with the lakes of Killarney painted on it as an excuse for a carnival.

Girls at the village molested her with stares but she didn't care and went to Mullingar with doctors' sons who had rich woollen jerseys and bright broad bones in a country where other men stood silently on streets, holes in their trousers and handkerchiefs trailing out of their pockets.

They were good old days to talk to her customers about and she didn't really care if they had not attended the dances. She didn't really care if no one else remembered the day Dr Dehilly's son pinched her cheeks and said they were the colour of scarlet. He had been the boy she mostly had her eye on. He had red check handkerchiefs spilling out of his pocket and he always looked at though he was about to swing a golf club, alert, agile. He took her five times to a dance in Mullingar and once to dinner in Dublin.

When she came back he stopped seeing her and she had the ire and jealousy of local girls to deal with. But she didn't care. Her own sisters were cruel and cutting, and to make things worse she'd been jilted by him, but she raised her head and kept it high and if they breathed bad words about her hadn't she had his good looks and his smile for five weeks and the pleasure of his company in Dolphin's Hotel in Dublin?

Her clothes were cheap and often second hand which caused scandal to her family but it had to be admitted at a dance she looked better than the most refined of the young, a 'French painter's model' someone said. She had good taste and if she had the looks sure she might as well make use of them.

It was going too far, however, when she started roaming the fields in summer with farmers' sons. The streets of the village were bare and deserted, the canal usually low on water and if there weren't poppies in the fields there'd be no colours other than green of grass or gold of hay.

What she did in the fields with those young men no one knew but one rather mad young man gave her a mother-of-pearl bead owned by his grandmother and another said afterwards she was as fine to be with as a whore in Dublin. She didn't care. She raised her head higher and walked the one main carnivorous street of the village, waiting to be chastised, knowing she never would be openly, defiant if you like, brave.

There was a priest at the time with a rhubarb neck whom people said the African sun had made somewhat crazy and he hollered each Sunday as money rattled.

He collected money at funerals and weddings and it would almost make you cry to see the bereaved at a funeral give their silver to a little lizard of a man who with the priest was like the local mafiosi.

This priest hollered one Sunday about Jezebels and daughters of Satan, and Sheila felt like standing, ordering her stance and making a speech in favour of sin. She'd discovered sin to be warm and vibrant and thoroughly to be recommended.

That was in the bad old days. Now Ireland had changed and her nieces courted men on the pavement outside and priests talked about sex and the papers wrote about it. Behind her counter Sheila felt glad that somewhere she'd inaugurated it and laughed at the dreary dirty jokes of her customers.

Five months before her husband had left her. Her husband used to run the pub with her and read Joyce's *Portrait of the Artist as a Young Man* over the counter but then he tired of her fits and got the mail boat from Holyhead and went away.

Sheila's fits were known to all her family. She'd threaten to burn the house down or kill herself, or she'd stand on the stairway at night shouting abuse at her son. No one knew why she did it.

She was the black sheep of the family, always isolated, always blamed and as such into middle age she felt she ought to drag an element of nuisance.

She tried to choke her husband one night, not seriously, but in a fit of anger with herself alighted on him. He stared back. Once he'd loved her. But as she'd grown older she'd made such a nuisance of herself that he tired of her.

He backed a lot of horses. He drank a lot of Guinness.

She'd call him names if he spilt porter on the floor; make him clean it up. As her daughter grew up she grew jealous of her and gave her a difficult time. As her son grew up she was more relaxed but often lost her temper with him and boxed him in the ears. Then she was sorry. But it was too late.

They tried to put her in a mental hospital many times but she refused to go. She knew her rights and laid them on the table. People stared at her exasperated, but that didn't bother her. There was something more she wanted to know about.

She'd go into the garden and recognize the supreme quality of untidiness there and ask herself why she hadn't tended a garden like the local lawyer's or the Protestant minister's with its orange undercurrent blaze of nasturtiums in autumn or its bed of baby raspberries in summer.

What was wrong with her inheritance?

She took a broom one night and set it alight; after that her husband left her. He got a job in Shepherd's Bush in London and lived with two young labourers.

'Driven from house and home,' people said. He returned two months later for his daughter's wedding when there were pound notes stuck about the house and when people danced at the crossroads again. The pub wasn't doing too well so she borrowed clothes from her sister in Ballinasloe and she danced at the wedding, regardless.

I know what they're saying, she thought. They're saying I'm odd and queer. I have a hat the wrong way round and my shoes are too big for me. That doesn't stop me from dancing, does it?

Her son went to work in Bord na Móna, the Irish peat company, and one evening in the pub she read that they'd found an ancient Irish crozier in the bog where he worked. 'Wonders never cease,' she told an old man dormant on her counter. He didn't reply.

She poured herself a bottle of Guinness and toasted her children, her daughter married to a rich garage owner, her son living in a flat in a town in the Western Midlands with a jukebox in the restaurant below him.

'He'll be listening to Elvis tonight,' she thought, recalling Elvis's latest song 'In the Ghetto'.

Things went from bad to worse. People stopped going to her pub altogether and she hardly had sixpence.

No wonder she tried to burn the house down one day. That was it. She was carted off to the hospital in Mullingar. She wondered what she'd done wrong or why it was she was always doing things people didn't favour, like driving her husband away or boxing her daughter's ears or burning her house down. There must be something wrong with me, she thought, yet she resented being the troublesome one of the family. That made her worse. It made her more war-like.

Yet how could she have told anyone how happy she'd been in that house that was falling apart. She'd seen a total of nine mice in it, thought she heard a rat, but alone, left in her ways, she cut an edge on happiness.

Then one night she had a nightmare in which her dead mother chased her downstairs and Sheila rose and systematically tried to burn the house to the ground.

'Why did you do it?' her sister from Ballinasloe asked and she could only answer, 'I got bored.'

Sheila had a retinue of faithful relatives, she provided a focus for their misgivings on life and also a centre point about which they could talk of their endless problems.

Sheila was the biggest problem of all. Yet no one had noticed she'd been happy in her second-hand clothes at her daughter's wedding.

The mental hospital didn't suit her. 'All of them queer people,' she told her sister. 'Can't I get out of here?'

By a stroke of luck a job was secured for her in an embassy in Dublin. They packed her off with good clean clothes and she took up the post of charlady in a big mansion off Ailesbury Road. She had a little room to herself and was fascinated to see a row of red-brick houses when she woke in the morning instead of trees and grass wasted by bad earth.

She rose at early hours and did her chores, bringing tea to the ambassador and his workers.

She cleaned carpets scrupulously and sometimes stopped to look at portraits of Scandinavian dignitaries or oil paintings of Irish scenes by leading Irish artists.

In her village there'd been an artist among their flock of maidens, but the girl had been so cantankerous that it might have put you off art for life. Looking at these pictures now Sheila felt a blue day dawning in her. Gone were her memories of her children's adolescence and her husband's exasperation with her. She felt a lightness in her womb, like a birth.

Here they had honey on their toast in the mornings and they served wine with lunch.

She loved it. If she'd had a close female friend she'd have written to her all about it but as she'd had none she kept silent. Her husband now seemed like a stranger and her children, always angry with her, would never understand.

But there was a unique growth which she herself understood and wanted to describe but there was no one to tell about it so she became devout, praying, because at least God could hear and know that one was grateful.

Croissants were brown and crispy in the mornings and serving them she hummed the only song she knew of, 'Non, je ne regrette rien'. The ambassador liked her cheerful face and seeing herself in the mirror she wondered why she hadn't smiled more often.

It was proper to have a happy face and then she remembered her lineage, her birth into a dour family and wondered at what chance she could have had. But replacing that understanding was a clean new emotion, there was a beginning which was eroding the past and its lack of peace. She was beginning again.

As her wages were high she found herself buying new clothes and picking up lace and delicate things. She bought herself a ring with Connemara marble at the centre of it and often admired it on her finger as she dusted a carpet. It symbolized all growth in her. She went to a window and looked out and instead of one magpie as she'd seen on her wedding day there were two. 'One for sorrow, two for joy.' She remembered chanting that on her way from the church with her husband. He was in England now. He'd been working as a foreman in his peat factory. She'd driven him away, yet why worry, she told herself. She remembered his skinny body in his pyjamas in bed and she rejoiced she was here in Dublin, away from home and family. She arrested an insect in his march across the wainscot and shook him into the air.

A delegation of dignitaries passed her. She rose. They smiled at her. She continued work.

A man who worked as secretary in the embassy smiled at her more than anybody else and one morning when she was having coffee he approached her and offered her a cigarette. He had thick blond hair, though he was about fifty, and he had a large handsome smile. He enquired her name of her and she told him. He seemed pleased. He introduced himself as Dag. They smoked cigarettes and gently he eased information from her about her environment. He'd worked in the United Nations. He liked Dublin, he said, liked the Irish. He was interested in this country.

She acted like a child under surveillance. He left her but later in the afternoon, when she was cleaning the waiting room, he came behind her and indicated a painting. 'Carl Larsson,' he said. 'A Swedish painter.'

The painting showed children feasting in a summer scene with a bottle thrown amid the grass. 'That is how it was,' he said, 'when I was a child.'

Sheila looked at him. He seemed odd and beautiful. Maybe he was lonesome for home.

He talked to her often after that. She didn't know why. He talked of the city whence he came, rivers running through it, water reeds growing, church towers dark and threatening and rain, rain always falling. A biscuit snapped in Sheila's teeth.

'You like it here better?' she asked.

'It's fun,' he said simply.

She wondered why he approached her so much. Would she become coquettish, she wondered.

She stared at a box of marigolds outside a window one day.

What was it that led her here, she wondered, was it the force of salvation itself? Her thoughts came easier. A stranger was making conversation with her and she was glad, glad of words, talk, coffee to accompany them.

He told her about trees in his city that they tried to cut down but which the people did not allow. He told her about a poet who stayed in the trees in a hammock. He described how they still stood, green and bold in summer and how the young ate strawberries under them. Sheila thought of her own young and a wisp of guilt flew through her.

He was a kindly person. He liked books. He talked of the Town Hall in his city where great men had been honoured by the Nobel Prize. Sheila looked at him and said, 'Isn't it a funny thing how men reach their goals?' He smiled at that remark and said it was beautiful.

'Would you like to join me for dinner tomorrow?' he asked.

Sheila was delighted. 'Where?' she asked. He suggested the Shelbourne.

She met him there and he fondled her warm hands as though they were gloves and they ate veal. She didn't want wine. It was too much of a luxury. He talked again of his home country, mentioning the far lands up north where snow fell and the sun never set in summer, where the Laps wandered, a people clothed in deerskin with caps, and eyes staring from caps—like moles.

It was the country of his youth, he said, everyone has a country of their youth.

Sheila considered her own hometown and regretted so much those moments that there had been no such place in her youth but was comforted when he talked of children dying in Asia. Other people had their problems too.

She said goodbye to him at the top of Grafton Street and felt ridiculous and left, going back to work. Staring at the Larsson picture she noticed odd things about the figures and would have asked the artist to correct them if he'd been about.

She met him again the following morning as he smiled but he didn't stop to talk to her.

He was busy. She saw him having coffee with some diplomats and was glad he didn't talk to her because she understood his work to be more important than her. She dusted oak and pinewood and was glad of its sweet smell, near her nose as she bent to dust it.

There was one room in the embassy where there was a chink of stained glass and Sheila went there, in awe of it. She loved its particularity and one day she was standing there when he put his arm on her shoulder. She laughed.

He laughed. He sat and asked her what it was about Irish women and she said she didn't know and he spoke about his dead wife, Elizabeth, and he cried.

She gave him her new clean handkerchief and he said more than anything he wanted children but his wife had had no children.

'There were alderberries around our summer home,' he said. 'I always wanted to share their taste with children.'

She put her arm about him and he held her, quite platonically, and then he let go of her and apologized. His wife was beautiful, he said. They didn't get on.

And he intimated darker things about her death.

Sheila was living in a world miles from the one she used to inhabit. She rose in the mornings, serene, calm and dressed herself neatly. She understood herself to be miles beyond pain and thought they would never reach her here, they being relatives and the mangy dogs of her village.

She went about her chores and each day took time off to talk to her new friend, not about the problems of the Third World which he knew so much about but the areas of pain, loss that the human being encounters.

He whispered things about his home country, about wheaten-coloured grass and boats on the Archipelgo and she in turn thought of golf-playing doctors in the hungry fields about her home.

He took her one day in the pantry and kissed her. She walked about for two days, understanding this kiss, knowing it was not from passion it was given but from appreciation.

Her sister wrote to her and asked her how she was getting on. She didn't reply.

Her friend asked her to dinner and she turned up in a new turtle-brown suit. They had white wine and now she laughed more freely and her eyes were becoming wider.

They were in Wynn's Hotel, which caters for priests and nuns. Suddenly over a table she saw her sister. Her sister looked at her, half from embarrassment. Sheila jumped up and introduced her friend. Her sister smiled a sad knowledgeable smile and left.

They left her alone for three weeks and then began writing suddenly, asking her how she was.

They hadn't written before, her husband, son, daughter, sister but suddenly a barrage of letters came.

She didn't reply to any of them. She had a picture by Carl Larsson in her room and the plant on the window she watered carefully.

In August her friend told her he had to go back to his country on urgent business. She said goodbye to him as if he was only going for a few days and walked about the town where French students were thronging. It was there she met her sister again. Her sister recognized her happiness and her ability to cope and smiled.

They went to a café and had tea.

Her sister asked her questions about work but Sheila could not reply the way she would have done once, she knew other things now and the things she knew about did not make her despair.

Her friend did not come back and she went to the zoo and looked at the polar bears and thought of him. She shopped for herself and at Christmas bought perfumes for her daughter and sister. But still there was no word about him.

She went to mass on Christmas morning in the Carmelite church off Grafton Street and shared Christmas with the char-woman.

Her husband wrote from London. She never finished his letter. Her daughter and son sent customary greetings. Her sister wrote a short note.

In the new year when he didn't come and when it snowed she felt an august closeness to him, crossing the Green, partial to light and golden shadow. She knew that in his country the earth would be covered like this. She wanted to write to him but didn't have his address, all she desired to do was to register this complicity again.

The mornings were clean and blue and she looked at the sky when she rose and realized now she was happier than ever.

Her sister sent her some clothes and her husband asked her about separation. Her daughter wrote an abusive letter to her, just suddenly out of the blue, accusing her of cruelly ruining her adolescence. Sheila put the letter from her but she realized somewhere she was crying inside. Yes, she had been bad.

She crossed streets now by herself and sometimes found herself crying in a café. She drank tea, looking about suspiciously, fearful of someone alien to her entering.

At night she began having nightmares. These nightmares disturbed her suddenly. They were like someone with a red-hot poker. She'd rise, almost as though there was a substance present. She'd reach out but there'd be no one there and she'd go back to sleep, dreaming of the canal at home and the houses staring like spinsters.

Sometimes over work she'd break down crying.

These times were noted with compassion and a doctor was brought. The doctor gave her pills but then one day her daughter arrived, hatred in her eyes, telling her maybe she should have a 'rest'. She knew what they meant.

She allowed them to lead her as though in a trance, wishing punishment for all her sins.

After three weeks it was understood there was nothing wrong with her so she left the mental hospital but her job had been filled and she had to go back to her house. She reopened her pub. The old faces returned like dreary dogs. She sat in the pub and sometimes didn't move but waited, waited as though for fate to punish her.

It didn't come and she spent three months like this.

Her relatives checked her but found she was not creating fits. Her husband obtained a legal separation from her. Her children never wrote.

She knew the wrong she was doing herself and often thought to leave but something kept her here, the weight of the past, the time she boxed her daughter's ears, the time she hit her son with a brush.

Flame burned in front of the Sacred Heart. There was no piety for such a figure in her heart.

She went about her work. She fed her cats.

One day, however, she did go to Dublin. She got a train from Mullingar.

She had a handbag under her arm. She had a brown hat with a velvet ribbon on. She wore a grey suit.

It was like going back to a dream, a dream not tested before, an interim in her life when all made sense.

She walked up Grafton Street and nearing the top she had a heart attack.

It was outside a bookshop and a priest tended to her and her people were both glad and shocked. They were glad she was dead but shocked at the suddenness of her finish. But none of them knew the secret she shared with a diplomat miles from this place.

Approaching the Green she saw that the trees were in bloom and she observed that the leaves were pushing through the railings. She thought of a city faraway where trees were saved from being destroyed by the response of the people and she knew that because they stood, those trees, something was alive that neither her death, nor the death of others, her sadness, nor the sadness of others, could destroy. They buried her without much ceremony.

Her daughter wept. Her son stood as though paralysed.

The figures walked away. One figure stood alone, that of her daughter, her ears still ringing with the memory of a punch from her mother long ago.

But the occasion moved her to wait.

She walked away minutes later. They sold her house, the cats were sent to a cats' home and people ultimately were relieved.

It was as though by closing her off they were putting a seal forever on all of life's misfortunes.

# Jimmy

Her office overlooked the college grounds; early in the spring they were bedecked with crocuses and snowdrops. Looking down upon them was to excel oneself. She was a fat lady, known as 'Windy' by the students, her body heaved into sedate clothes and her eyes somehow always searching despite the student jibes that she was profoundly stupid and profoundly academic.

She lectured in ancient Irish history, yearly bringing students to view Celtic crosses and round towers marooned in spring floods. The college authorities often joined her on these trips, one administrator who insisted on speaking in Irish all the time. This was a college situated near Connemara, the Gaelic-speaking part of Ireland. Irish was a big part of the curriculum; bespectacled, pioneer-pin-bearing administrators insisted on speaking Irish as though it was the tongue of foolish crows. There was an element of mindlessness about it. One spoke Irish because a state that had been both severe and regimental on its citizens had encouraged it.

Emily delayed by the window this morning. It was spring and foolishly she remembered the words of the blind poet Raftery: 'Now that it's spring the days will be getting longer. And after the feast of Brigid I'll set foot to the roads.' There was that atmosphere of instinct abroad in Galway today. Galway as long as she recalled was a city of Travelling people, red-petticoated Tinkers, clay-pipe-smoking sailors, wandering beggars.

In Eyre Square sat an austere statue of Pádraic Ó Conaire, an Irish scribe who'd once walked to Moscow to visit Chekhov and found him gone for the weekend.

In five minutes she would lecture on Brigid's crosses, the straw symbols of renewal in Ireland.

There was now evidence that Brigid was a lecher, a Celtic whore who was ascribed to sainthood by those who had slept with her but that altered nothing. She was one of the cardinal Irish holy figures, the Isis of the spring-enchanted island.

Emily put words together in her mind.

In five minutes they'd confront her, pleased faces pushing forward. These young people had been to New York or Boston for their summer holidays. They knew everything that was to be known. They sneered a lot, they smiled little. They were possessed of good looks, spent most of the day lounging in the Cellar bar, watching strangers, for even students had the wayward Galway habit of eyeing a stranger closely, for it was a city tucked away in a corner of Ireland, peaceable, prosperous, seaward-looking.

After class that day she returned to the college canteen where she considered the subject of white sleeveless jerseys. Jimmy used to have one of those. They'd gone to college in the 1930s, Earlsfort Terrace in Dublin, and Jimmy used to wear one of those jerseys. They'd sit in the dark corridor, a boy and a girl from Galway, pleased that the trees were again in bloom, quick to these things by virtue of coming from Galway where nature dazzled.

Their home was outside Galway city, six miles from it, a big house, an elm tree on either side of it and in spring two pools of snowdrops like hankies in front of it.

Jimmy had gone to Dublin to study English literature. She had followed him in a year to study history. They were respectable children of a much-lauded solicitor and they approached their lives gently. She got a job in the university in Galway. He got a job teaching in Galway city.

Mrs Carmichael, lecturer in English, approached.

Mrs Carmichael wore her grandmother's Edwardian clothes because though sixty, she considered it in keeping with what folk were wearing in Carnaby Street in London.

'Emily, I had trouble today,' she confessed. 'A youngster bit a girl in class.'

Emily smiled, half from chagrin, half from genuine amusement.

Mrs Carmichael was a bit on the Anglo–Irish side, taut, upper-class, looking on these Catholic students as one might upon a rare and rather charming breed of radishes.

'Well, tell them to behave themselves,' Emily said. 'That's what I always say.'

She knew from long experience that they did not obey, that they laughed at her and that her obesity was hallmarked by a number of nicknames. She could not help it, she ate a lot, she enjoyed cakes in Lydons and more particularly when she went to Dublin she enjoyed Bewleys and Country Shop cakes.

In fact the Country Shop afforded her not just a good pot of tea and nice ruffled cream cakes but a view of the green, a sense again of student days, here in Dublin, civilized, parochial. She recalled the woman with the oval face who became famous for writing stories and the drunkard who wrote strange books that now young people read.

'I'll see you tomorrow,' Mrs Carmichael said, leaving.

Emily watched her. She'd sail in her Anglia to her house in the country, fleeing this uncivilized mess.

Emily put her handkerchief into her handbag and strolled home.

What was it about this spring? Since early in the year strange notions had been entering her head. She'd been half-thinking of leaving for Paris for a few days or spending a weekend in West Cork.

There was both desire and remembrance in the spring.

In her parents' home her sister, Sheila, now lived. She was married. Her husband was a vet.

Her younger brother, George, was working with the European Economic Community in Brussels.

Jimmy alone was unheard of, unlisted in conversation.

He'd gone many years ago, disappearing on a mail train when the War was raging in the outside world. He'd never come back; some said he was an alcoholic on the streets of London. If that were so he'd be an eloquent drunkard. He had so much, Jimmy had, so much of his race, astuteness, learning, eyes that danced like Galway

Bay on mornings when the islands were clear and when gulls sparkled like flecks of foam.

She considered her looks, her apartment, sat down, drank tea. It was already afternoon and the Dublin train hooted, shunting off to arrive in Dublin in the late afternoon.

Tom, her brother-in-law, always said Jimmy was a moral retrograde, to be banished from mind. Sheila always said Jimmy was better off gone. He was too confused in himself. George, the youngest of the family, recalled only that he'd read him Oscar Wilde's *The Happy Prince* once and that tears had broken down his cheeks.

The almond blossom had not yet come and the War trembled in England and in a month Jimmy was gone and his parents were glad. Jimmy had been both a nuisance and a scandal. Jimmy had let the family down.

Emily postured over books on Celtic mythology, taking notes.

It had been an old custom in Ireland to drive at least one of your family out, to England, to the mental hospital, to sea or to a bad marriage. Jimmy had not fallen easily into his category. He'd been a learned person, a very literate young man. He'd taught in a big school, befriended a young man, the 1930s prototype with blond hair, went to Dublin one weekend with him, stayed in Buswells Hotel with him, was since branded by names they'd put on Oscar Wilde. Jimmy had insisted on his innocence but the boy lied before going to Dublin, telling his parents that he was going to play a hurling match.

Jimmy had to resign his job; he took to drink, he was banished from home, slipping in in the afternoons to read to George. Eventually he'd gone. The train had registered nothing of his departure as it whinnied in the afternoon. He just slipped away.

The boy, Johnny Fogarthy, whom Jimmy had abducted to Dublin, himself left Ireland.

He went to the States, ended up in the antique trade and in 1949, not yet twenty-seven, was killed in Pacifica. Local minds construed all elements of this affair to be tragic.

Jimmy was safely gone.

The dances at the crossroads near their home ceased and that was the final memory of Jimmy, dancing with a middle-aged woman and she wearing earrings and an accordion bleating 'The Valley of Slievenamon'.

Emily heard a knock on the door early next morning. Unrushed she went to the door. She was wearing a pink gown. Her hair was in a net. She had been expecting no caller but then again the postman knocked when he had a parcel.

For years afterwards she would tell people of the thoughts that had been haunting her mind in the days previously.

She opened the door.

A man aged but not bowed by age, derelict but not disarrayed, stood outside.

There was a speed in her eyes which detected the form of a man older than Jimmy her brother but yet holding his features and hiding nothing of the graciousness of which he was possessed.

She held him. He held her. There was anguish in her eyes. Her fat hands touched an old man.

'Jimmy,' she said simply.

Jimmy the tramp had won £100 at the horses and chosen from a variety of possibilities a home visit. Jimmy the tramp lived on Charing Cross Road.

Jimmy the tramp was a wino, yes, but like many of his counterparts near St Martin-in-the-Fields in London was an eloquent one. Simply Jimmy was home.

News brushed swiftly to the country. His brother-in-law reared. His sister, Sheila, silenced. Emily, in her simple way, was overjoyed.

News was relayed to Brussels. George, the younger brother, was expected home in two weeks.

That morning Emily led Jimmy to a table, laid it as her own mother would have done ceremoniously with breakfast things and near a pitcher, blue and white, they prayed.

Emily's prayer was one of thanksgiving.

Jimmy's too was one of thanksgiving.

Emily poured milk over porridge and doled the porridge with honey from Russia, invoking for Jimmy the time Pádraic Ó Conaire walked to Moscow.

In the afternoon he dressed in clothes Emily bought for him and they walked the streets of Galway. Jimmy by the Claddagh, filled as it was with swans, wept the tears of a frail human being.

'Emily,' he said. 'This should be years ago.'

For record he said there'd been no interest other than platonic in the young boy, that he'd been wronged and this wrong had driven him to drink. 'I hope you don't think I'm apologizing,' he said, 'I'm stating facts.'

Sheila met him and Tom, his brother-in-law, who looked at him as though at an animal in the zoo.

Emily had prepared a meal the first evening of his return. They ate veal, drank rosé d'Anjou, toasted by a triad of candles. 'One for love, one for luck, one for happiness,' indicated Emily.

Tom said the EEC made things good for farmers, bad for businessmen. Sheila said she was going to Dublin for a hairdo.

Emily said she'd like to bring Jimmy to the old house next day.

Sure enough the snowdrops were there when they arrived and the frail trees.

Jimmy said as though in speed he'd lived as a tramp for years, drinking wine, beating his breast in pity.

'It was all an illusion,' he said. 'This house still stands.'

He entered it, a child, and Tom, his brother-in-law, looked scared.

Jimmy went to the library and sure enough the works of Oscar Wilde were there.

'Many a time *The Happy Prince* kept me alive,' he said.

Emily dressed newly, her dignity cut a hole in her pupils. They silenced and listened to talk about Romanesque doorways.

She lit her days with thoughts of the past, rooms not desecrated, appointments under the elms.

Her figure cut through Galway. Spring came in a rush. There was no dalliance. The air shattered with freshness.

As she lectured Jimmy walked. He walked by the Claddagh, by Shop Street, by Quay Street. He looked, he pondered, his gaze drifted to Clare.

Once Johnny Fogarthy had told him he was leaving for California on the completion of his studies. He left all right.

He was killed.

'For love,' Jimmy told Emily. He sacrificed himself for the speed of a car on the Pacific coast.

They dined together and listened to Bach. Tom and Sheila kept away.

Emily informed Jimmy about her problems. Jimmy was wakeful to them. In new clothes, washed, he was the aged poet, distinguished, alert to the unusual, the charming, the indirect.

'I lived in a world of craftsmen,' he told Emily, 'most alcoholics living on the streets are poets driven from poetry, lovers driven from their beloved, craftsmen exiled from their craft.'

They assuaged those words with drink.

Emily held Jimmy's hand. 'I hope you are glad to be here,' she said.

'I am, I am,' he said.

The weekend in Dublin with Johnny Fogarthy he'd partaken of spring lamb with him on a white lain table in Buswells, he told Emily.

'We drank wine then too, rosé, age made no difference between us. We were elucidated by friendship, its acts, its meaning. Pity love was mistaken for sin.'

Jimmy had gone during the War and he told Emily about the bombs, the emergencies, the crowded air-raid shelters.

'London was on fire. But I'd have chosen anything, anything to the gap in people's understanding in Ireland.'

They drank to that.

Emily at college was noted now for a new beauty.

Jimmy in his days walked the streets. Mrs Kenny in Kennys Bookshop recognized him and welcomed him. Around were writers' photographs on the wall. 'It's good to see you,' she said.

He had represented order once, white sleeveless jumpers, fairish hair evenly parted, slender volumes of English poetry.

'Remember,' Mrs Kenny said, 'the day O'Duffy sailed to Spain with the Blueshirts and you, a boy, said they should be beaten with their own rosary beads.'

They laughed.

Jimmy had come home not as an aged tramp but as a poet. It could not have been more simple if he'd come from Cambridge, a retired don. Those who respected the order in him did not seek undue information. Those puzzled by him demanded all the reasons.

Those like Tom, his brother-in-law, who hated him, resented

his presence. 'I sat here once with Johnny,' Jimmy told Emily one day on the Connemara coast. 'He said he needed something from life, something Ireland could not give him. So he went to the States.'

'Wise man.'

'But he was killed.'

'We were the generation expecting early and lucid deaths,' he told Emily.

Yes. But Jimmy's death had been his parents' mortification with him, his friends' disavowal of him, Emily's silence in her eyes. He'd gone, dispirited, rejected. He'd gone, someone who'd deserted his own agony.

'You're back,' Emily said to him cheerily. 'That's the most important thing.'

His brother, George, came back from Brussels, a burly man in his forties.

He was cheerful and gangly at encountering Jimmy. He recognized integrity, recalled Jimmy reading him *The Happy Prince*, embraced the old man.

Over gin in Emily's he said, 'The EEC is like everything else, boring. You'll be bored in Tokyo, bored in Brussels, bored in Dublin.' Emily saw that Jimmy was not bored.

In the days he walked through town, wondering at change, unable to account for it, the new buildings, the supermarkets. His hands were held behind his back. Emily often watched him, knowing that like de Valera he represented something of Ireland. But an element other than pain, fear, loneliness. He was the artist. He was the one foregone and left out in a rush to be acceptable.

They attended mass in the pro-cathedral. Jimmy knelt, prayed; Emily wondered, were his prayers sincere? She looked at Christ, situated quite near the mosaic of President Kennedy, asked him to leave Jimmy, for him not to return. She enjoyed his company as though that of an erstwhile lover.

Sheila threw a party one night.

The reasoning that led to this event was circumspect. George was home. He did not come home often. And when he did he stayed only a few days.

It was spring. The house had been spring-cleaned. A new carpet now graced the floor. Blossom threatened; lace divided the carpet with its shadows.

All good reasons to entertain the local populace.

But deep in Sheila, that aggravated woman's mind, must have been the knowledge that Jimmy, being home, despite his exclusion from all ceremony, despite his rather nebulous circumstances, his homecoming had by some decree to be both established and celebrated.

So neighbours were asked, those who'd borne rumour of him once, those who rejected him and yet were only too willing to accept his legend, young teacher in love with blond boy, affair discovered, young teacher flees to the gutters of London, blond boy ends up in a head-on collision in Pacifica, a town at the toe of San Francisco, California.

The first thing Jimmy noticed was a woman singing 'I Have Seen the Lark Soar High at Morn' next to a sombre ancient piano.

Emily had driven him from Galway, she beside him in a once-in-a-lifetime cape saw his eyes and the shadow that crossed them. He was back in a place which had rejected him. He had returned, bearing no triumph but his own humility. Emily chatted to Mrs Conaire and Mrs Delaney. To them, though a spinster, she was a highly erudite member of the community and as such acknowledged by her peers.

Emily looked about. Jimmy was gone. She thrust herself through the crowd and discovered Jimmy after making her way up a stairway hung with paintings of cattle-marts and islands, in a room by himself, the room in which he had once slept.

'Jimmy.' He turned.

'Yes.'

'Come down.'

Like a lamb he conceded.

They walked again into the room where a girl aged seventeen sang 'The Leaving of Liverpool'.

It was a party in the old style with pots of tea and whiskey and slender elegant cups.

George said, 'It's great to see the country changing, isn't it? It's great to see people happy.'

Emily thought of the miles of suburban horror outside Galway and thought otherwise.

Tom slapped Jimmy's back. Tom, it must be stated, did not desire this party, not at least until Jimmy was gone. His wife's intentions he suspected but he let it go ahead.

'It's great having you,' he said to Jimmy, bitter and sneering from drink. 'Isn't it you that was the queer fellow throwing up a good job for a young lad?'

Emily saw the pain, sharp, smitten, like an arrow.

She would have reached for him as she would have for a child smitten by a bomb in the North of Ireland but the crowd churned and he was lost from sight.

Tom sang 'If I Had a Hammer'. Sheila, plagued by the social success of her party, wearing earrings like toadstools, sang 'I Left My Heart in San Francisco'.

A priest who'd eyed Jimmy but had not approached him sang 'Lullaby of Broadway'.

George, Jimmy's young brother working in the EEC, got steadily drunker. Tom was slapping the precocious backsides of young women. Sheila was dancing attendance with cucumber sandwiches.

Jimmy was talking to a blond boy who, if you stretched memory greatly, resembled Johnny Fogarthy.

The fire blazed.

Their parents might have turned in their grave, hating Jimmy their child because he was the best of their brood and sank the lowest.

Emily sipped sherry and talked to neighbours about cows and sheep and daughters with degrees in medicine and foreign countries visited.

She saw her brother and mentally adjusted his portrait, he was again a young man very handsome, if you like, in love in an idle way with one of his pupils.

In love in a way one person gives to another a secret, a share in their happiness.

She would have stopped all that was going to happen to him but knew that she couldn't.

Tom, her brother-in-law, was getting drunker and viler.

He said out loud, 'What is it that attracts men to young fellows?' surprising Jimmy in a simple conversation with a blond boy.

The party ceased, music ceased. All looked towards Jimmy,

looked away. The boy was Mrs McDonagh's son, going from one pottery to another in Ireland to learn his trade, never satisfied, always moving, recently taken up with the Divine Light, some religious crowd in Galway.

People stared. The image was authentic. There was not much sin in it but a lot of beauty. They did not share Tom's prejudice but left the man and the boy. It was getting late. The country was changing and if there had been wounds why couldn't they be forgotten?

Tom was slobbering. His wife attended him. He was slobbering about Jimmy, always afraid of that element of his wife's family, always afraid strange children would be born to him but none came anyway. His wife brought him to the toilet where presumably he got sick.

George, drunk on gin, talked about the backsides of secretaries in Brussels and Jimmy, alone among the crowd, still eloquent with drink, spoke to the blond teenager about circuses long ago.

'Why did you leave Ireland?' the boy asked him.

'Searching,' he said, 'searching for something. Why did you leave your last job?'

'Because I wasn't satisfied,' the boy said. 'You've got to go on, haven't you? There's always that sense that there's more than this.'

The night was rounded by a middle-aged woman who'd once met Count John McCormack singing 'Believe me if all those endearing young charms'.

On the way back into Galway Emily felt revered and touched by time, recalled Jimmy, his laughter once, that laughter more subdued now.

She was glad he was back, glad of his company and despite everything clear in her mind that the past was a fantasy. People had needed culprits then, people had needed fallen angels.

She said goodnight to Jimmy, touched him on the cheek with a kiss.

'See you in the morning,' she said.

She didn't.

She left him asleep, made tea for herself, contemplated the spring sky outside.

She went to college, lectured on Celtic crosses, lunched with Mrs Carmichael, drove home in the evening, passing the sea, the

Dublin train sounding distantly in her head. The party last night had left a strange colour inside her, like light in wine or a reflection on a saxophone.

What was it that haunted her about it, she asked herself?

Then she knew.

She remembered Jimmy on a rain-drenched night during the War coming to the house and his parents turning him away.

Why was it Sheila had thrown the party? Because she had to requite the spirit of the house.

Why was it Jimmy had come back to the house? Because he needed to reassert himself to the old spirits there.

Why was it she was glad? Because her brother was home and at last she had company to glide into old age.

She opened the door. Light fell, guiltily.

Inside was a note.

'Took the Dublin train. Thanks for everything. Love Jimmy.'

The note closed in her hand like a building falling beneath a bomb and the scream inside her would have dragged her into immobility had not she noticed the sky outside, golden, futuristic, the colour of the sky over their home when Easter was near and she a girl in white, not fat, beautiful even, walked with her brother, a boy in a sleeveless white jersey, by a garden drilled in daffodils, expecting nothing less than the best life could offer.

# The Sojourner

He lived in a little room in Shepherd's Bush. There was a bed for himself and above a little compartment for visitors. One climbed by ladder to this area. A curtain separated it from the rest of the room. It was this area he'd reserved for Moira.

Around the walls were accumulated Italian masterpieces, pieces of Titian, pieces of Tintoretto, arms by Caravaggio, golden and brusque. Dominating all was a Medici face by Botticelli. Above the fireplace a young man, stern, glassy eyes, his lips satisfied, his stare resigned to the darkness of the room, a darkness penetrated by the light of one window.

Jackie worked on a building site. He'd worked on one since he'd come over in February. Previously he'd been a chef in a café in Killarney, riding to and from work on a motorbike. But something made him go, family problems, spring, lust.

The room had been conveniently vacated by two Provisional Sinn Féin members from Kerry. He'd scraped Patrick Pearse from the wall. They were gone to another flat.

He'd risen early on mornings when Shepherd's Bush had been suffocated in cold white fog, a boy from Ireland hugging himself into a donkey jacket. He'd been picked up in a lorry, driven to diverse sites. Now the mornings were warm. Blue crept along the corners of high-rise flats, lingering bits of dawn. Jackie was enclosed in a routine, last night's litter outside country and western pubs. Guinness bottles, condoms, the refuse of Ireland in exile. The work was hard but then there was Moira to think of. At odd moments when life was harsh or reality pressing her image veered towards him; as he sat in the lorry, tightening his fists in the pockets of his donkey jacket, as he sat over a mug of tea in the site office. Moira Finnerty was his sister, at present in a mental hospital in Limerick but shortly to be released. She was coming to London to stay with him.

Jackie and Moira had grown up on a lowly farm in the Kerry mountains. Their parents had been quiet, gruff, physically in love with one another until their sixties. A grandfather lived with them, always telling indecent stories. There'd been many geese, cows, a mare always looking in the direction of the ocean, a blizzard of gulls always blowing over the fields. Life had been hard. Jackie had gone to school in Killarney. Moira had attended a convent in Cahirciveen.

Jackie had peddled dope at fifteen in the jukebox cafés of Killarney. His first affair had been at sixteen with the daughter of a rich American businessman, sent to the convent in Killarney by way of a quirk. After all Killarney was prettier than Lucerne or Locarno and it was possessed of its own international community. Sarah was from Michigan, randy, blonde, fulsome. She'd always had money, a plethora of nuns chasing her. However, she'd avoided the nuns, sat in jeans, which always looked as though they were about to explode, in cafés, smoking French cigarettes, smattering the air with French fumes.

Sex for Jackie until now was associated with the sea; recalling Sarah he thought more of an intimacy with the sea, with beaches near Ballinskelligs, inlets with the spire of Skellig Michael in the distance, an odd mound in the sea where monks once sang 'Deus Meus', the chants of Gaelic Ireland before Elizabethan soldiers sailed westwards on currachs.

Sarah had gone. There'd been many girls, Killarney was full of girls. He did his Leaving Certificate twice which led to nights lounging in cafés in Killarney, Valentine cards circulating from year to year, and one ice-cream parlour in Killarney where a picture of a Spanish poet stood alongside pictures of Powerscourt House, County Wicklow, and Ladies' View, Killarney, one tear dropping out of his eye, rolling up in a little quizzical ball and a bullet wound in his head. It was an odd cartoon to show in a café but then the owners were Portuguese so one accepted the odd divergence more easily.

Jackie had gone to Dublin, worked on building sites, peddled dope; lived like a prince in Rathmines. However, the arm of the law fell upon him. He was imprisoned for six months, returned to Kerry. A good cook, he got a job in a café in a world of provincial Irish cafés, always the jukebox pounding out the bleeding heart of provincial Ireland, songs about long-distance lorry drivers and tragic deaths in Kentucky.

His sister emerged from convent school about this time, got a job in a hospital in Limerick. It was supposed to be temporary but she stayed there. Moira, when she hadn't been at school, had spent her adolescence wandering the hills about their home. There'd been few trees so one could always pick her out. She'd rarely gone to dances and when she had she'd always left early before the other girls, thumbing home.

They rarely spoke, but there was always something there, a mirror-like silence. Jackie saw himself in Moira, saw the inarticulate disparate things, a moment of high on an acid trip in Rathmines, a moment of love in a café in Killarney, a moment of reverie by the sea in Ballinskelligs. The West of Ireland for all its confusion was full of these things and it was these people Jackie veered towards, people who spoke a secret language like the Tinkers' Shelta.

You discerned sensitivity in people or you didn't. Jackie was an emotional snob. He was a snob in clothes, in cigarettes, in brands of dope even. But one thing he never minded was working and wending his way among the semi-literate.

Moira had spent two years in Limerick when she had an affair with an older married man. The usual. He made love to her, took every advantage of her shy, chubby body. Then returned to the suburbs. It was more than that which made Moira crack up. Her parents seemed content to leave her, not to expect anything remarkable of her. By solicitude they condemned her to a life of non-achievement.

Jackie had gone by the time Moira was put in the mental hospital in Limerick. Her face pressed on him. At first he thought to go back and rescue her. But he relied on time and patience. Moira was to be let out in June. He wrote and asked her to come and stay with him. For a while.

Early June in Shepherd's Bush, the young of London walked along the street. Bottles flew. Bruce Lee continually played in the cinema. Irish country and western singers roared out with increasing desperation and one sensed behind the songs about Kerry and Cavan, mothers and luxuriant shamrock, the foetus of an unborn child urging its way from the womb of a girl over for a quick abortion.

Sometimes Jackie allowed himself to be picked up. He'd long lost interest sexually in women. The last girl he'd actually wanted to make love to had been in Dublin, a blonde who ran away to a group in California, mystical and foreign to the Irish experience. Walking in Shepherd's Bush was like walking among the refuse of other people's lives, many bins in the vicinity. He read many paperbacks. On colder days he lit fires in his room and sat over them like a Tinker. Above the door was a St Brigid's cross, which traditionally kept away evil. He'd bought it at the Irish tourist office in Bond Street. There was a desk in his room on which he wrote letters home. He thought of his mother with her giant chamber pot that had emerald patterns of foliage on it. She'd bought it in an antique shop in Listowel. He thought of his father, a randy look always in his eye. As children they'd hear their parents making love like people in far-off cities in a far-off time were supposed to. He could still distinguish his mother's orgasms, a cry in the air, a siren which was sublimated into the sound of a gull, the sound of a train veering towards Tralee.

They'd only had one another, he and Moira. They'd made the most of it.

Now he wrote to her.

*Dear Moira,*
*Expecting you soon. The weather is changeable here. The job's hard. I think I may go to Copenhagen in autumn. See you soon.*
*Love,*
*Jackie*

She arrived unexpectedly one morning. The doorbell exploded. He jumped up. Oddly enough he was on the upper tier. He'd gone up there for a change. He climbed down the ladder, went to the door.

He'd overslept. She was there, with two cases, scarf on her head, something more moderate about her face, less of the mysticism.

They kissed. Her breath smelt of Irish mints.

As there was no coffee he made her tea which they had on the floor. He was late for work but he decided to go anyway as he was on a nearby site. She'd sleep. He'd be back later. He bid her goodbye. She lay asleep in the upper bed. Before closing the door he looked around this den of loneliness. Moira's slip lay over a chair.

She had the room tidy when he returned and she herself looked refreshed, having bathed in the grotty bath with its reverential gas flame bursting into life. Her scent had changed. There were perfumes of two kinds of soap in it.

This time she made tea and they sat down. He didn't want to ask her about the mental hospital so instead he queried her about home. Moira didn't want to talk about home so instead she imparted gossip about DJs on Irish radio.

Jackie made a meal, one he'd been preparing in his mind for a long time, lamb curry. Afterwards they had banana crumble and custard, eating on the floor. Moira said it would be necessary for her to get a job. Jackie didn't disagree. Moira read the little pieces of print stuck about. A line from Yeats. An admonition from Socrates. Soon a point came whereby there seemed nothing else to talk about so both were silent.

They went for a drink before going to bed. Jackie apologized for the grottiness of the pub. Moira said she didn't mind, her eyes drifting about to young Irish men holding their sacred pints of Guinness.

Afterwards they returned through the dustbins and slept in their individual beds.

It being summer Moira got a job in a nearby ice-cream parlour, dressing in white, doling out runny ice cream to West Indian children. In a generally bad summer the weather suddenly brightened and Jackie was conscious of himself, a young Adonis on a building site. His body had hardened, muscle upon muscle defining themselves. His hair was short. His face more than anything was defined, those bright eyes that shot out, often angry without a reason as though some subconscious hurt was disturbing him.

What he resented was the young Irish students who were arriving on the building site. They brought with them a gossipy close-ness to Ireland and a lack of seriousness in their separation from that country. However, he and Moira were getting on exceedingly well. There was less talk of trauma than he'd anticipated. They had drinks, meals, outings together. On Sundays there was Holland Park and Kensington Gardens. They had picnics there. Sometimes they swam in the Serpentine. Moira's head dipped a lot, into magazines, into flowers, into the grass. The vestiges of wardship were leaving. Jackie often felt like knocking back a lock of Moira's hair. Something about her invited these gestures, her total preoccupation with a Sunday newspaper cartoon, her gaze that sometimes went from you and turned inwards, to that area they both held in common.

Moira cooked sometimes. She was a plain cook but a good one. She made brown bread much like his mother's. Jackie's cooking was more prodigious, curries that always scared Moira, lest there be drugs in them, chicken paprika, beef goulash, moussaka, and then the plates of Ireland, Limerick ham glazed in honey, Dublin coddle, Irish stew.

The divisions in the room were neatly made, borders between her area and his. Both were exceptionally neat.

For the first time she mentioned the mental hospital. It slipped out. There had been a woman there who'd had nine children, whose husband had left her, who scrubbed floors in a café and who'd even-tually cracked up. In a final gesture of humiliation she'd wept while mopping the floor one day so that the proprietor reckoned she should see a psychiatrist. 'Jesus, I'm crying. I'm just crying,' she'd shouted. 'I'm just crying because they told me life would be better, men helpful. I'm just crying and I'm not ashamed. I can manage. I can manage myself.' They'd told her she couldn't and quietly stole her children, placing them in homes. It was then she'd cracked up, looking like all the other mad visionary women of Ireland, women who claimed to have seen Maria Goretti in far-flung cottages.

'They force you to crack up,' Moira said, 'so that they can be sat-isfied with their own lot. After all the idea of pain, real pain, is too big to cope with. Pain can be so beautiful. The pain of recognizing how hopeless things are yet accepting and somehow building from it.'

His sister had grown. More than that she'd become beautiful, her Peruvian eyes calm and often a scarlet ribbon in her hair. Playing a game they'd played as children both of them dressed up at nights and went to showband concerts. Whatever her other sophistications Moira had not relinquished the showband world so they traipsed off to pubs, Moira in a summer dress, Jackie in a suit, a green silk Chinese tie on him, girls from Offaly moaning into microphones. You were scrutinized at the doors lest you were not Irish. Often there was some doubt about Jackie until he opened his mouth. Inside people jostled, a majority of women edged for a man. Lights changed from scarlet to blue and somehow Moira in her dreamy, virginal way seemed at home here, lost in a reverie of rural Ireland.

Shyness had gone, a kind of frankness prevailed. Often Jackie sat around his room in just trousers. Moira washed in her slip, sometimes it falling over her hips.

'You know we made a pact, didn't we, when we were growing up?' Jackie said one evening. 'Mammy and Daddy never seemed to notice us.'

It was true. Against their parents' carnality they'd chosen a kind of virginal complacency.

Once in Kerry, looking at the moon, Moira had stated that this country had always been a country of nuns. In ancient times nuns had built cottages by nearby beaches.

It was less that they were a nun and a monk, more that they had to resist. Resist their parents' self-absorption, resist the geese, the skies, the dun of the mountains, the purple changing to green of the rocks.

Jackie had had his affairs. In fact Moira had hers. But it was as though they'd made a vow of celibacy when Jackie was thirteen and Moira eleven; they didn't want to fall into the trap of closing themselves off. They wanted to be open, romantic, available. Looking into Moira's eyes before going to bed Jackie saw that in fact they were closing themselves off in a different way.

They were outsiders, resigned to be outsiders, and were making a fetish of this role. Moira had picked up a little teddybear in Shepherd's Bush market. In her bed she held it. She was sitting up in her slip. 'Goodnight Jackie,' she said.

The teddybear slept with her.

That night Jackie walked the environs of Shepherd's Bush, sat in a café, spoke to a man from Ghana. He waited some hours. The first light came. He returned home, picked up his things for work, waited for a lorry on Shepherd's Bush Green.

She wanted to dance now so she danced with him. They travelled to Kilburn and Camden. Saturday nights in ballrooms, the London Irish swung to visiting showbands. Despite this venture in a foreign city Moira had a lonesomeness for the decay of rural Ireland, for its fetishes. Jackie dancing with her, cheek to cheek, wondered if he could cure it.

It was a miserable summer weather-wise. Early in August there was a much-advertised march against troops in Northern Ireland. Jackie and Moira saw it by accident, young English people shouting about women in Northern Ireland jails.

Later that month the Queen's cousin was blown up in County Sligo. Moira and Jackie didn't listen to the radio much but they heard a jumbled commentary on the events. Jackie wondered about the provisional Sinn Féin people who'd lived in this room once, that was their domain, instant and shocking deaths in the cause of Ireland. He smiled. No one in the whole of London reprimanded Jackie or Moira but the papers were full of hatred, mistaking the source of the guilt.

The guilt was a shared one, Jackie thought, a handed-down one. Everyone's hands were dipped in blood; blood of intolerance. He'd thought about it so much, knew the kind of prevalent and often justified anger of Irish republicans. In Kerry they were eccentrics. One IRA man he knew grew the best marijuana in Kerry and decorated it with Christmas decorations come Christmas. Often Northern republicans fled to his house, men with trapped eyes. Reaching to them was like reaching to dynamite. They hit back easily.

So Jackie and Moira assumed responsibility for the deaths of the Earl of Mountbatten, the Dowager Lady Brabourne and the two children killed with them. They walked about London with the air of criminals. The newspapers had ordained this guilt. Jackie and Moira accepted it, not as slaves but with a certain grandeur. They were Irish and as such bore a kind of mass guilt, guilt for the republican few, for the order of the gun, the enslaved and frightened eyes, the winsome thoughts of Patrick Pearse. It was all part of their heritage; to deny it would be like denying the wet weather. But in accepting a certain responsibility both knew, Jackie more than Moira, of a more real tradition which never met English eyes, the tradition of the great families of Kerry, the goblets of wine, the harp, the Gregorian chant.

They'd left Kerry with their wolfhounds, going to Europe, but something was always ready to be disturbed of this tradition, a hedge-schoolmaster behind a white hawthorn tree reading Cicero; O'Connell, another Kerryman, in Clontarf telling the Irish proletariat that the freedom of Ireland is not worth the shedding of one drop of blood; Michael Davitt in Clare leading a silent pacifist march against English landlords.

Jackie knew, as all sensitive and knowledgeable Irish people knew, that the prevalent philosophy of Irish history was pacifism and he could therefore accept the rebukes of the English newspapers with glee, with a certain amount of wonder, knowing them to be founded and spread in ignorance.

But Moira wasn't so sure. He'd noticed her fluctuating somewhat. Although outwardly calm there was a new intensity in her dancing. She was going back, quicker than he could cope with, to the ballroom floors in Kerry, the point at which all is surrendered, the days of drudgery, the nights of squalid sex in the backs of cars. She was trying to be peaceful with a violent heritage.

In a dancehall one night there was a fight. Someone hit someone else on the head with a chair. A woman started singing 'God save Ireland said the Heroes' and in moments Jackie's dreams of pacifism were gone. A young man made a speech about H-Blocks on the counter and somewhere an auburn-haired woman described her lust for a Clare farmer.

Jackie took Moira home. She began crying, sitting on a chair. In moments it was gone, a summer of harmony. The tears came, scarlet, outraged blue. Afterwards it was the silence which was compelling. She was steadily recalling the corners of a mental hospital, the outreaches of pain. Her heart in a moment had turned to stone.

It was a curious stone too which her heart had become, exquisite and frail in its own way. She began going to dances by herself and one night she did not return. Jackie sat up, waiting until the small hours. When there was no sign of her he went out for a while, hugging himself into a donkey jacket. Autumn was coming.

People are like doctors. We live with one another for a while. We cure one another. Jackie saw himself as physician but too late. Moira no longer needed his physician's touch. She was sleeping around, compulsively giving herself, engineering all kinds of romances. And when she stopped talking to him much he too searched the night for strangers. At first unsuccessfully. But then they came, one by one, Argentinians, West Indians.

She perceived the domain of his life, said nothing.

'Pope visits war-torn country,' the papers warned. It was true, John Paul was coming, giving an ultimate benediction to the dance-halls, the showbands, the neon lights, the jukeboxes that shook jauntily with their burden of song.

He saw the look on Moira's face and knew she was destined to return. Nothing could hold her back. Dancing to an Irish showband singer's version of 'One Day at a Time' he realized her need for the hurt, the intimacy, the pain of ballroom Ireland. She wanted to be immolated by these things.

There was nothing he could say against it. It was his life against hers and she saw his life as a shambles. He couldn't tell her about the boys with diamond eyes, no more than she could tell him about the lads from Cork who jumped on her as though she was an old and unusable mattress. In mid-September she announced her decision.

A bunch of marigolds sat on the mantelpiece, a little throne of tranquillity.

'Will you come too?' she asked.

'No,' he said and half-naked he looked at her. He wanted to ask her why it was necessary always to return to the point where you were rejected, but such questions were useless. The Pope was coming, the music of ballroom Ireland was strong in her ears.

He took her to Euston and she asked him if he had any messages for their parents.

'Tell them I won't be home for Christmas,' he said.

She looked at him. Her eyes looked as though they were going to pop out and grapple him and take their mutual pain but they did no such thing.

Later that night Jackie wandered in Shepherd's Bush. He knew he'd deceived himself, going from body to body, holding out hope he'd meet someone who'd fulfil some childhood dream of purity.

All his life he'd been trying to reconstruct her, not so much Moira, as that virgin of Ireland, Our Lady of Knock, Our Lady of the Sorrows, that complacent maiden who edged into jukebox cafés, into small towns where apparitions had taken place in the last century and now neon strove into the rain.

He wouldn't go to Copenhagen. He'd go south. He'd pack up his things and leave, knowing there was a certain compulsion about the sun, the Mediterranean, the shine of the sun on southern beaches.

Before leaving London there was one thing he wanted to do, dress up like any other Irish boy, comb his hair, put on his green Chinese tie and dance until all was forgotten, the lights of Killarney, the whine of the jukebox, the look on Moira's face as she stared over a stone wall in Kerry, into a world which would consume their knowledge of the sea, their knowledge of stone, their reverence of one another.

# The Mourning Thief

Coming through the black night he wondered what lay before him, a father lying dying. Christmas, midnight ceremonies in a church stood up like a gravestone, floods about his home.

With him were his wife and his friend Gerard. They needn't have come by boat but something purgatorial demanded it of Liam, the gulls that shot over like stars, the roxy music in the jukebox, the occasional Irish ballad rising in cherished defiance of the sea.

The night was soft, breezes intruded, plucking hair, thread lying loose in many-coloured jerseys. Susan fell asleep once while Liam looked at Gerard. It was Gerard's first time in Ireland. Gerard's eyes were chestnut, his dark hair cropped like a monk's on a bottle of English brandy.

With his wife sleeping Liam could acknowledge the physical relationship that lay between them. It wasn't that Susan didn't know, but despite the truism of promiscuity in the school where they worked there still abided laws like the Old Testament God's, reserving carnality for smiles after dark.

A train to Galway, the Midlands frozen in.

Susan looked out like a Botticelli Venus, a little worried, often just vacuous. She was a music teacher, thus her mind was penetrated by the vibrations of Bach even if the place was a public lavatory or a Lyons café.

The red house at the end of the street; it looked cold, pushed away from the other houses. A river in flood lay behind. A woman, his mother, greeted him. He an only child, she soon to be a widow. But something disturbed Liam with excitement. Christmas candles still burned in this town.

His father lay in bed, still magically alive, white hair smeared on him like a dummy, that hard face that never forgave an enemy in the police force still on him. He was delighted to see Liam. At eighty-three he was a most ancient father, marrying late, begetting late, his wife fifteen years younger than him.

A train brushed the distance outside. Adolescence returned with a sudden start, the cold flurry of snow as the train in which he was travelling sped towards Dublin, the films about Russian winters.

Irish winters became Russian winters in turn and half of Liam's memories of adolescence were of the fantasized presence of Russia. Ikons, candles, streets agleam with snow.

'Still painting?'

'Still painting.' As though he could ever give it up. His father smiled as though he were about to grin. 'Well, we never made a policeman out of you.'

At ten, the day before he would have been inaugurated as a boy scout, Liam handed in his uniform. He always hated the colours of the Irish flag, mixing like the yolk in a bad egg.

It hadn't disappointed his father that he hadn't turned into a military man but his father preferred to hold on to a shred of prejudice against Liam's chosen profession, leaving momentarily aside one of his most cherished memories, visiting the National Gallery in Dublin once with his son, encountering the curator by accident and having the curator show them around, an old man who'd since died, leaving behind a batch of poems and a highly publicized relationship with an international writer.

But the sorest point, the point now neither would mention, was arguments about violence. At seventeen Liam walked the local hurling pitch with petitions against the war in Vietnam.

Liam's father's fame, apart from being a police inspector of note, was fighting in the GPO in 1916 and subsequently being arrested on the republican side in the Civil War. Liam was against violence, pure and simple. Nothing could convince him that 1916 was right. Nothing could convince him it was different from now, old women, young children, being blown to bits in Belfast.

Statues abounded in this house; in every nook and cranny was a statue, a statue of Mary, a statue of Joseph, an emblem perhaps of some saint Mrs Fogarthy had sweetly long forgotten.

This was the first thing Gerard noticed, and Susan who had seen this menagerie before was still surprised. 'It's like a holy statue farm.'

Gerard said it was like a holy statue museum. They were sitting by the fire, two days before Christmas. Mrs Fogarthy had gone to bed.

'It is a museum,' Liam said, 'all kinds of memories, curious sensations here, ghosts. The ghosts of Irish republicans, of policemen, military men, priests, the ghosts of Ireland.'

'Why ghosts?' Gerard asked.

'Because Ireland is dying,' Liam said.

Just then they heard his father cough.

Mr Fogarthy was slowly dying, cancer welling up in him. He was dying painfully and yet peacefully because he had a dedicated wife to look after him and a river in flood around, somehow calling Christ to mind, calling penance to mind, instilling a sense of winter in him that went back a long time, a river in flood around a limestone town.

Liam offered to cook the Christmas dinner but his mother scoffed him. He was a good cook, Susan vouched. Once Liam had cooked and his father had said he wouldn't give it to the dogs.

They walked, Liam, Susan, Gerard, in a town where women were hugged into coats like brown paper accidentally blown about them. They walked in the grounds of Liam's former school, once a Georgian estate, now beautiful, elegant still in the East Galway winter solstice.

There were Tinkers to be seen in the town, and English hippies behaving like Tinkers. Many turkeys were displayed, fatter than ever, festooned by holly.

Altogether one would notice prosperity everywhere, cars, shining clothes, modern fronts replacing the antique ones Liam recalled and pieced together from childhood.

But he would not forfeit England for his dull patch of Ireland,

Southern England where he'd lived since he was twenty-two, Sussex, the trees plump as ripe pears, the rolling verdure, the odd delight of an Elizabethan cottage. He taught with Susan, with Gerard, in a free school. He taught children to paint. Susan taught them to play musical instruments. Gerard looked after younger children though he himself played a musical instrument, a cello.

Once Liam and Susan had journeyed to London to hear him play at St Martin-in-the-Fields, entertaining ladies who wore poppies in their lapels, as his recital coincided with Remembrance Day and paper poppies generated an explosion of remembrance.

Susan went to bed early now, complaining of fatigue, and Gerard and Liam were left with one another.

Though both were obviously male they were lovers, lovers in a tentative kind of way, occasionally sleeping with one another. It was still an experiment but for Liam held a matrix of adolescent fantasy. Though he married at twenty-two, his sexual fantasy from adolescence was always homosexual.

Susan could not complain. In fact it rather charmed her. She'd had more lovers since they'd married than fingers could count; Liam would always accost her with questions about their physicality; were they more satisfying than him?

But he knew he could count on her; tenderness between them had lasted six years now.

She was English, very much English. Gerard was English. Liam was left with this odd quarrel of Irishness. Memories of adolescence at boarding school, waking from horrific dreams nightly when he went to the window to throw himself out but couldn't because window sills were jammed.

His father had placed him at boarding school, to toughen him like meat.

Liam had not been toughened, chastened, ran away twice. At eighteen he left altogether, went to England, worked on a building site, put himself through college. He ended up in Sussex, losing a major part of his Irishness but retaining this, a knowledge when the weather was going to change, a premonition of all kinds of disasters and ironically an acceptance of the worst disasters of all, death, estrangement.

Now that his father was near death, old teachers, soldiers,

policemen called, downing sherries, laughing rhetorically, sitting beside the bed covered by a quilt that looked like twenty inflated balloons.

Sometimes Liam, Susan, Gerard sat with these people, exchanging remarks about the weather, the fringe of politics or the world economic state generally.

Mrs Fogarthy swept up a lot. She dusted and danced around with a cloth as though she'd been doing this all her life, fretting and fiddling with the house.

Cars went by. Geese went by, clanking terribly. Rain came and church bells sounded from a disparate steeple.

Liam's father reminisced about 1916, recalling little incidents, fights with British soldiers, comrades dying in his arms, ladies fainting from hunger, escape to Mayo, later imprisonment in the Curragh during the Civil War. Liam said: 'Do you ever connect it with now, men, women, children being blown up, the La Mon Hotel bombing, Bessbrook killings, Birmingham, Bloody Friday? Do you ever think that the legends and the brilliance built from your revolution created this, death justified for death's sake, the stories in the classroom, the priests' stories, this language, this celebration of blood?'

Although Liam's father fought himself once, he belonged to those who deplored the present violence, seeing no connection. Liam saw the connection but disavowed both.

'Hooligans! Murderers!' Liam's father said.

Liam said, 'You were once a hooligan then.'

'We fought to set a majority free.'

'And created the spirit of violence in the new state. We were weaned on violence, me and others of my age. Not actual violence but always with a reference to violence. Violence was right, we were told in class. How can one blame those now who go out and plant bombs to kill old women when they were once told this was right?'

The dying man became angry. He didn't look at Liam, looked beyond him to the street.

'The men who fought in 1916 were heroes. Those who lay bombs in cafés are scum.'

Betrayed he was silent then, silent because his son accused him on his deathbed of unjustifiably resorting to bloodshed once. Now guns went off daily, in the far-off North. Where was the line between right and wrong? Who could say? An old man on his deathbed prayed that the guns he'd fired in 1916 had been for a right cause and in the words of his leader Patrick Pearse had not caused undue bloodshed.

On Christmas Eve the three young people and Mrs Fogarthy went to midnight mass in the local church. In fact it wasn't to the main church but a smaller one, situated on the outskirts of the town, protruding like a headstone.

A bald middle-aged priest greeted a packed congregation. The cemetery lay nearby, but one was unaware of it. Christmas candles and Christmas trees glowed in bungalows.

'O Come All Ye Faithful', a choir of matchstick boys sang. Their dress was scarlet, scarlet of joy.

Afterwards Mrs Fogarthy penetrated the crib with a whisper of prayer.

Christmas morning, clean, spare, Liam was aware of estrangement from his father, that his father was ruminating on his words about violence, wondering were he and his ilk, the teachers, police, clergy of Ireland responsible for what was happening now, in the first place by nurturing the cult of violence, contributing to the actuality of it as expressed by young men in Belfast and London.

Sitting up on Christmas morning Mr Fogarthy stared ahead. There was a curiosity about his forehead. Was he guilty? Were those in high places guilty like his son said?

Christmas dinner; Gerard joked, Susan smiled, Mrs Fogarthy had a sheaf of joy. Liam tidied and somehow sherry elicited a chuckle and a song from Mrs Fogarthy. 'I Have Seen the Lark Soar High at Morn'. The song rose to the bedroom where her husband who'd had dinner in bed heard it.

The street outside was bare.

Gerard fetched a guitar and brought all to completion, Christmas, birth, festive eating, by a rendition of Bach's 'Jesu, Joy of Man's Desiring'.

Liam brought tea to his father. His father looked at him. ''Twas lovely music,' his father said with a sudden brogue, 'there was a Miss Hanratty who lived here before you were born who studied music at Heidelberg and could play Schumann in such a way as to bring tears to the cat's eyes. Poor soul, she died young, a member of the ladies' confraternity. Schumann was her favourite and Mendelssohn came after that. She played at our wedding, your mother's and mine. She played Mozart and afterwards in the hotel sang a song, what was it, oh yes, "The Star of the County Down".

'Such a sweetness she had in her voice too.

'But she was a bit of a loner and a bit lost here. Never too well really. She died maybe when you were a young lad.'

Reminiscences, names from the past. Catholic names, Protestant names, the names of boys in the rugby club, in the golf club. Protestant girls he'd danced with, nights at the October fair.

They came easily now, a simple jargon. Sometimes though the old man visibly stopped to consider his child's rebuke.

Liam gauged the sadness, wished he hadn't said anything, wanted to simplify it but knew it possessed all the simplicity it could have, a man on his deathbed in dreadful doubt.

Christmas night they visited the convent crib, Liam, Susan, Gerard, Mrs Fogarthy, a place glowing with a red lamp.

Outside trees stood in silence, a mist thinking of enveloping them. The town lay in silence. At odd intervals one heard the gurgle of television but otherwise it could have been childhood, the fair green, space, emptiness, the rhythm, the dance of one's childhood dreams.

Liam spoke to his father that evening.

'Where I work we try to educate children differently from other places, teach them to develop and grow from within, try to direct them from the most natural point within them. There are many such schools now but ours, ours I think is special, run as a cooperative; we try to take children from all class backgrounds and begin at the beginning to redefine education.'

'And do you honestly think they'll be better educated children than you were, that the way we educated you was wrong?'

Liam paused.

'Well, it's an alternative.'

His father didn't respond, thinking of nationalistic, comradely Irish schoolteachers long ago. Nothing could convince him that the discipline of the old style of education wasn't better, grounding children in basic skills.

Silence somehow interrupted a conversation, darkness deep around them, the water of the floods shining, reflecting stars.

Liam said goodnight. Liam's father grunted. Susan already lay in bed. Liam got in beside her. They heard a bird let out a scream in the sky like a baby and they went asleep.

Gerard woke them in the morning, strumming a guitar.

St Stephen's Day, mummers stalked the street, children with blackened faces and a regalia of rags collecting for the wren. Music of a tin whistle came from a pub, the town coming to life. The river shone with sun.

Susan divined a child dressed like old King Cole, a crown on her head and her face blackened. Gerard was intrigued. They walked the town. Mrs Fogarthy had lunch ready. But Liam was worried, deeply worried. His father lay above, immersed in the past.

Liam had his past, too, always anxious in adolescence, running away to Dublin, eventually running away to England. The first times home had been odd; he noticed the solitariness of his parents. They'd needed him like they needed an ill-tended dog.

Susan and he had married in the local church. There'd been a contagion of aunts and uncles at the wedding. Mrs Fogarthy had prepared a meal. Salad and cake. The river had not been in flood then. In England he worked hard. Ireland could so easily be forgotten with the imprint of things creative, children's drawings, oak trees in blossom. Tudor cottages where young women in pinafores served tea and cakes home made and juiced with icing.

He'd had no children. But Gerard now was both a twin, a child, a lover to him. There were all kinds of possibility. Experiment was only beginning. Yet Ireland, Christmas, returned him to something, least of all the presence of death, more a proximity to the prom, empty laburnum pods and hawthorn trees naked and crouched with winter. Here he was at home with thoughts, thoughts of himself, of adolescence.

Here he made his own being like a doll on a miniature globe. He knew whence he came and if he wasn't sure where he was going, at least he wasn't distraught about it.

They walked with his mother that afternoon. Later an aunt came, preened for Christmas and the imminence of death. She enjoyed the tea, the knowledgeable silences, looked at Susan as though she was not from England but a far-off country, an Eastern country hidden in the mountains. Liam's father spoke to her not of 1916 but of policemen they'd known, irascible characters, forgetting that he had been the most irascible of all, a domineering man with a wizened face ordering his inferiors around.

He'd brought law. He'd brought order to the town. But he'd failed to bring trust. Maybe that's why his son had left.

Maybe that's why he was pondering the fate of the Irish revolution now, men with high foreheads who'd shaped the fate of the Irish Republic.

His thoughts brought him to killings now being done in the name of Ireland. There his thoughts floundered. From where arose this language of violence for the sake and convenience of violence?

Liam strode by the prom alone that evening, locked in a donkey jacket.

There were rings of light around distant electric poles.

He knew his father to be sitting up in bed; the policeman he'd been talking about earlier gone from his mind and his thoughts on 1916, on guns, and blazes, and rumination in prison cells long ago.

And long after that thoughts on the glorification of acts of violence, the minds of children caressed with the deeds of violence.

He'd be thinking of his son who fled and left the country.

His son now was thinking of the times he'd run away to Dublin, to the neon lights slitting the night, of the time he went to the river to throw himself in and didn't, of his final flight from Ireland.

He wanted to say something, urge a statement to birth that would unite father and son but couldn't think of anything to say. He stopped by a tree and looked to the river. An odd car went by towards Dublin.

Why this need to run? Even as he was thinking that, a saying of his father returned: 'Idleness is the thief of time.' That statement had been flayed upon him as a child but with time as he lived in England among fields of oak trees that statement had changed; time itself had become the culprit, the thief.

And the image of time as a thief was forever embroiled in a particular ikon of his father's, that of a pacifist who ran through Dublin

helping the wounded in 1916, was arrested, was shot dead with a deaf
and dumb youth. And that man, more than anybody, was Liam's
hero, an Irish pacifist, a pacifist born of his father's revolution, a
pacifist born of his father's state.

He returned home quickly, drew the door on his father. He sat
down.

'Remember, Daddy, the story you told me about the pacifist
shot dead in 1916 with a deaf and dumb youth, the man whose wife
was a feminist?'

'Yes.'

'Well, I was just thinking that he's the sort of man we need now,
one who comes from a revolution but understands it in a different
way, a creative way, who understands that change isn't born from violence but intense and self-sacrificing acts.'

His father understood what he was saying, that there was a remnant of 1916 that was relevant and urgent now, that there had been at
least one man among the men of 1916 who could speak to the present
generation and show them that guns were not diamonds, that blood
was precious, that birth most poignantly issues from restraint.

Liam went to bed. In the middle of the night he woke muttering to himself, 'May God have mercy on your soul,' although his
father was not yet dead, but he wasn't asking God to have mercy on
his father's soul but on the soul of Ireland, the many souls born out
of his father's statelet, the women never pregnant, the cruel and violent priests, the young exiles, the old exiles, those who would never
come back.

He got up, walked down the stairs, opened the door of his
father's room. Inside his father lay. He wanted to see this with his
own eyes, hope even in the persuasion of death.

He returned to bed.

His wife turned away from him but curiously that did not hurt
him because he was thinking of the water rising, the moon on the
water, and as he thought of these things the geese clanked over,
throwing their reflections into the water grazed with moon which
rimmed this town, the church towers, the slate roofs, those that slept
now, those who didn't remember.

# Portrait of a Dancer

His mother sat over the fire warming her palms. She stared, merely stared. Colours furiously froze and spat.

She sat in blue. Her hair now was tinged with grey but still held a marmalade colour; right now it was brightened and delighted with flame. She sat pondering her own beauty. He stood by the door, lingering, waiting for her to notice him but she didn't, she continued to stare, continued to ponder, continued to absorb.

'Mother.' She turned. 'Damian.' She was not surprised to see him. 'How are you?' 'Well.' He lay down his books. 'Tired?' 'No.' She moved towards the table. 'I have duckling. I hope you don't mind it being a bit burnt.'

He sat down, ate.

'Well, how's it going?'

'Well.'

Two months at art school he was already frittering his time.

Bored, he was drawing nudes without much conviction.

His career was chequered to say the least. His mother's need to move had caused his childhood to be a stream of cities, nucleus of colours, white of desert sands, neon of downtown New York. His mother had been an original New Yorker, a model in the 1940s until she met an Irish poet who fathered him. The poet had died early, of drink. His marriage had been unperturbed by the affair. A woman had mourned him, his wife. Damian's mother had nourished her own grief quietly, first in New York, then in a variety of places, passing among the rich and the famous.

He'd been sent to school first in Marrakesh, then in Scotland in a free school.

Out of school six months he'd begun at art school, his mother settled now, less than serene, in a London apartment. She hung a picture of herself over the fireplace, one in which the world could see her as pretty. It was a reproduction of a painting by an eminent modern artist housed in a New York art gallery. In the painting her neck swung towards her nape like a swan's neck. Her eyes rang with laughter. Her face was thin and pinched and her lips smote the vision like a paper rose.

'Damian, did you have a good day?' '

'Yes.' Then he said, 'No. No I didn't.'

He went to bed early reading Chekhov, sleeping with it on his chest.

, The first time he met her was in November. She was late coming to the school, an Irish art teacher. She was about thirty-two, had black hair, carved like a Cretan. 'She was pretty,' Damian thought to himself. New York expressions still in his head, American gentleness.

She taught him to paint. She hovered across his figure, staring downwards. He enjoyed her closeness and often wondered at her face, being Irish it should have spoken of violence.

Instead it was calm—like the Book of Kells, which Damian had once seen in Dublin, lying open in Trinity College.

She was from Connemara. The name sung in Damian's ears. His father had lived there, a father he'd never met, just heard about.

'Hi.' He spoke to her one day in the canteen. She approached, looking through him almost.

They spoke. They mentioned backgrounds. They parted.

That night Damian realized he was in love.

His mother sat by the fire as though in prayer.

She sat staring into the flame.

'How are you?'

'Well.'

He went to his room and packed his clothes. He was moving

out. His mother sat as usual by the fire when he returned from school on the following days.

He told her he was going and she hardly seemed perturbed.

'Where are you going?'

'To squat in West Harrow.'

His mother shrugged. 'Don't get cold whatever you do.' The squat consisted of high Edwardian buildings, fronted by rubbish dumps.

Damian got a room in one of them with the assistance of a friend. First he tacked a picture of Pablo Casals on the wall.

Then he arranged a matted quilt on the bed. The quilt was multicoloured. He would sleep beneath colours.

There was a fireplace in the room and he lit warm fires in the afternoons, sitting beside them with a warm rugged polo neck on.

He usually tracked down the Irish teacher on her way to the bus, dwelling a few minutes in conversation with her as leaves merely rested on dusty earth.

He was going to ask her out. He planned it for weeks.

The squat in which he lived housed runaway girls who wore long black coats and big Edwardian hats. Their maroon and pink colours dashed into afternoons of black sidling rain. 'I want to make love,' Damian told himself, 'I want to make love to this woman.'

He invited her to tea one day.

She was at first surprised by the invitation. Then she accepted. 'I'd love to,' she said.

He bought a cake iced in a Jewish bakery and they ate sweet things.

She left early. He watched her go and knew how deep was his attraction for her. An attraction to calm, simplicity, the hush her voice was.

His mother had joined a mystical group and was reading the words of Greek and Russian mysticists. Years previously she had known a man in California who had known the mentor of her group, Gurdjieff, and this single fragment had inspired enough confidence to move, search. She was going out again and very, very slowly talking about her travels and her affairs and her intimacies with artists, widely known and little heard of.

The teacher came to Damian one day, uninvited. She brought with her tomatoes.

She took off her gloves and her coat.

'I hope you don't mind me calling,' she said.

He smiled. 'I suppose I was feeling lonely today,' she said.

'Lonely?' He laughed. 'Do you miss Ireland?'

'I was hurt by Ireland,' she said. He didn't ask her any more but made tea and smiled at her and poised Tchaikovsky on the record player he'd recently bought. 'These days my mother talks of Central Park,' Damian said. 'It's like as though it's a womb.'

Madeleine—the teacher—looked at his ring. 'It's lovely,' she said. 'Silver?'

'Yes.' She stared at him. 'It's good to know someone I can come to see.' He took her hand.

He kissed it. She withdrew, shivered almost. He moved towards her. In moments they were lovers.

They made love from love. This was an experience never to be repeated. It was her world and his that merged, the colours, sombre, green, of Ireland, the mad dash of kaleidoscopic colours that had been Damian's travels.

They looked at one another afterwards, recognizing friendship, friendship never to be repeated.

She rose, put on her clothes, walked away. He stood with her outside a Seventh-Day Adventist church, attending a bus. Her brow was furrowed. He was willing to wait for a long time, he was willing to wait until an eternity. He wanted to tell her that together they'd discovered what his mother had never found in her travels—the experience of creativity. But before he could open his mouth a bus came and she was taken from him, chocolate papers brushed the pavement already wet with afternoon rain.

His mother was reading Isaiah when he called. 'And the leopard shall lie down with the kid,' she said snapping the book closed, almost accusing Damian. Damian quietly made tea while she talked about his father, the poet, times with him in retreat in the West of Ireland. 'A highly illicit affair,' she declared, almost shouting.

Damian ate sweet cakes that his mother fetched from a confectionery shop in Soho. Damian stared at the flames, penetratingly. He knew that moment that he, a person without a country, his mother, also a person without a country, were now crossing paths, realizing that one moment of love could exonerate one of a life of loneliness.

He saw her often. She came to his house and they slept in the big bed and they spoke about countries by firelight.

She whispered, 'Someone told me I was frigid in Ireland. They said I was frigid to hurt me. You have repaired me.' Damian was drinking cocoa. 'They told me I was frigid because I was rather spiritual, because I kept to myself and observed certain laws, laws of solitude, laws I hoped of love. The Irish are a people at war with themselves. England has given me an order.'

He turned to her, momentarily observed pain, pursed his lips and looked again at the stars, little silver stars sparkling and spitting in the flame.

At Christmas she returned to Ireland. He walked her to Euston and observed her board a train and felt very much the young lover with his genitals ringing as wheels clattered. He walked away, hoping the Guinness pubs would not defile her and when she returned she spoke of change, the rosettes of white houses in Connemara, new buildings, new blood.

She spoke of having seen a punk-rock band play in a hall that lay among fields where stones were gilded with moon and how she saw toothless couples dance to the mad murderous music. They made love, out of a hush, out of a calm left by conversation. They renewed physical contact and then Madeleine wept and she wished she could return to Ireland but defiled by it she was an exile at heart, an exile in abeyance to wounds.

Wood crackled in January as they sat on Saturday afternoons drinking coffee, talking, the photograph of Pablo Casals curling up in agony.

'I knew a girl at school,' Damian said, 'who had long hair and played a guitar and would run across fields like a fairy. Sometimes we'd just sit on the grass not saying anything, just holding hands.'

'School is the most creative experience of one's life,' Madeleine said. 'God speaks to us at secondary school, light through the doorway, a plant on the window, a picture of Joan Baez playing guitar in Birmingham, Alabama.'

'God?'

'Yes. Is that what's troubling all of us? Your mother, me, you; it is a terrible thing to believe, worse to doubt.'

'Aren't we all being driven by a force asking us for a simple gesture, a simple pain that is close to a real experience, an experience of life.'

His mother was happier now, thrilled almost.

Men and women were drifting into her apartment, supping coffee, discussing art, literature, religion. She was relinquishing her solitude and inviting the strands of her life, mislaid, to meet again. Her son came among these people, black knotted hair, a white shirt on him, his lips succulent. He was an added treat, youth, beauty remembered by all of them in circles in California where men spoke of Buddha or Indian philosophers emerging from the rainforests to speak of God to post-War dilettantes.

In February Damian told his mother he was having an affair. His mother took it philosophically until Damian mentioned his lover was Irish. Then his mother whispered, 'They're a cruel race, a cruel race.'

She was ill for a few days and when she returned to school Damian asked her if she'd accompany him to Greece.

'Greece!'

Early Easter holidays were approaching.

'We could get a bus.'

She'd been ill, she said over coffee, she'd stayed in bed.

'Why didn't you come to see me?'

Damian paused. He realized it had not occurred to him. He'd been in Madeleine's bedsitter but once. It was her custom to come to him. He'd never expected otherwise.

'I'm sorry.'

'You're used to being looked after,' Madeleine said. 'Yes, I'll go with you.'

He painted through March and was influenced much by Chagall whom his mother met in Venice once when he shook her hand with his pale, pale Russian hand.

He brought Madeleine to little cinemas and he cycled to school on an old bicycle picked up in Portobello Road.

On a grey day in March they caught a bus from Argyll Road to Athens, crossing Europe through snow and rain and reaching an island by boat where blossoms were shaping like curls on a baby's head.

They lived in a whitewashed cottage for three weeks, the sea daily becoming bluer and Madeleine's hair falling on her shoulders now and her face a sort of cow-like serenity.

'You're too young for me, you know,' she said over retsina one evening. Damian looked at her. He knew she was going to say that and that she'd just been holding back, waiting for this moment, watching Greeks, watching donkeys, watching priests with beards blowing in March breezes.

Madeleine's head dipped. She took hold of her wine glass like a pistol.

'I have been reading Chekhov,' she said. 'I found this quotation.' She read, almost in a murmur, ' "I don't believe in our intelligentsia. I believe in individual people scattered here and there all over Russia—they have strength though they are few." '

'Meaning?'

'That lives cross briefly, that we are in danger of losing ourselves unless we make supreme acts, reach out, know where to stop.'

'Like my mother,' Damian said.

'Like your mother, coming, going between people. The trouble is she never knew where to stop. But she has searched.'

Madeleine quietened. 'She has searched.'

They walked by the strand where the light on the sea reminded Madeleine of Connemara and where they spoke of the Atlantic where Madeleine came from, and where Damian's mother holidayed with Damian's secret father.

'The sea wills a strange power on us,' Madeleine said, 'a power of believing.'

They held hands and strode along until Damian quietly announced it was Easter Sunday and that it was believed Christ had risen on this day.

Back in London they saw one another less. In May Madeleine lived with him for a week and they slept in the big bed under the multicoloured quilt, and made love, his body seeking hers as though she was an immense bear, shielding him.

Then one morning she left—discreetly—before he woke and he saw her only at school after that. She didn't go home with him. She acted older than him, determined on the course of her life, refusing solicitude.

He was shattered. He pursued her with his eyes. She never acknowledged him. She studied the work of her students and left his looks unrequited, and when he followed her she said, 'Damian, it's unwise to go ahead with certain things. Forget it. Forget it.'

'What are you doing for the summer?' he asked.

'Going back to Ireland. I think I can come to terms with it now. I think I can get to know it.'

'Might you stay there?'

'Perhaps. England is not my country. They tell us Irish we're bombers whereas it's a few British subjects from the North who are planting bombs. I think I'll go home, teach in a small school, marry a farmer.'

'Madeleine, please come home with me,' he begged her.

'Damian.' She turned. 'Find yourself some nice nineteen-year-old.'

He could have killed himself. Instead he went to his mother. She was drinking brandy and saying sweetly to herself, 'Life is beautiful. Life is a collection of moods, moods, fine, peaceable, attractive. Life is a coloured shadow. Life is a coloured shadow.'

Damian realized she was quoting the Irish poet who'd been her lover. He went to his room and asked of it what he'd done wrong, realized that this impermanence was just living and decided to go south again for the summer. He didn't go south. Instead he went to Ireland where he hitched about, taking in Cork and Limerick, finding no trace of her but discovering mountains wild and blue, and sheep, rinsed yellow ochre and white. He sat in cafés thinking of her as American tourists clambered after tweed and would have asked the skies to show her to him had he not realized that was rather over-romantic and that anyway she was in another part of Ireland, one as yet unknown to him. He didn't go to Connemara because heavy squally rain began and wouldn't stop and he found himself one August morning in London, drinking steaming coffee.

In September back at school he discovered she had not stayed in Ireland, that she was teaching at another school and when he heard she was playing in an amateur production of Yeats's *Herne's Egg* at the school he went to see her in it. He caught a bus from the squat, through streets swishing with rain where girls in long coats and Edwardian hats ran.

He sat in the auditorium as she danced the part of Attracta, priestess of love, sombrely, fatalistically.

'She was Irish,' he told himself, 'she had been driven out again by a word, a look, a gesture back to London.'

Afterwards he waited in the cafeteria for her, in his white-blue embroidered shirt, whispering under his breath, 'I love you. I love you. I love you,' and when she didn't come he went home, took up a knife to cut his wrists and suddenly, just suddenly found himself pardoned by the glowing of the fire, which caught the knife, telling him sonorously of travels, travels through lives, faces, bodies, travels that wrought images of Irish women with black Cretan hair and faces that always looked as though about to give way or of women of middle age sitting by the fire, telling themselves over and over again that life was beautiful as flame glinted and eyes spat and hair that was grey turned gold.

# Memories of
# Swinging London

Why he went there he did not know, an instinctive feel for a dull facade, an intuition borne out of time of a country unbeknownst to him now but ten years ago one of excessive rain, old stone damaged by time, and trees too green, too full.

He was drunk, of course, the night he stumbled in there at ten o'clock. It had been three weeks since Marion had left him, three weeks of drink, of moronic depression, three weeks of titillating jokes with the boys at work.

Besides it had been raining that night and he'd needed shelter.

She was tired after a night's drama class when he met her, a small nun making tea with a brown kettle.

Her garb was grey and short and she spoke with a distinctive Kerry accent but yet a polish at variance with her accent.

She'd obviously been to an elocution class or two, Liam thought cynically, until he perceived her face, weary, alone, a makeshift expression of pain on it.

She'd failed that evening with her lesson, she said. Nothing had happened, a half-dozen boys from Roscommon and Leitrim had left the hall uninspired.

Then she looked at Liam as though wondering who she was speaking to anyway, an Irish drunk, albeit a well-dressed one. In fact he was particularly well dressed that evening, wearing a neatly cut grey suit and a white shirt, spotless but for some dots of Guinness.

They talked with some reassurance when he was less drunk. He sat back as she poured tea.

She was from Kerry she said, West Kerry. She'd been a few months in Africa and a few months in the United States but this was her first real assignment, other than a while as domestic science teacher in a Kerry convent. Here she was all of nurse, domestic and teacher. She taught young men from Mayo and Roscommon how to move; she had become keen on drama while going to college in Dublin. She'd pursued this interest while teaching domestic science in Kerry, an occupation she was ill-qualified for, having studied English literature in Dublin.

'I'm a kind of social worker,' she said, 'I'm given these lads to work with. They come here looking for something. I give them drama.'

She'd directed Eugene O'Neill in West Kerry, she'd directed Arthur Miller in West Kerry. She'd moulded young men there but a different kind of young men, bank clerks. Here she was landed with labourers, drunks.

'How did you come by this job?' Liam asked.

She looked at him, puzzled by his directness.

'They were looking for a suitable spot to put an ardent Sister of Mercy,' she said.

There was a lemon iced cake in a corner of the room and she caught his eye spying it and she asked him if he'd like some, apologizing for not offering him some earlier. She made quite a ceremony of cutting it, dishing it up on a blue-rimmed plate.

He picked at it.

'And you,' she said, 'what part of Ireland do you come from?'

He had to think about it for a moment. It had been so long. How could he tell her about limestone streets and dank trees? How could he convince her he wasn't lying when he spun yarns about an adolescence long gone?

'I come from Galway,' he said, 'from Ballinasloe.'

'My father used to go to the horse fair there,' she said. And then she was off again about Kerry and farms, until suddenly she realized it should be him that should be speaking.

She looked at him but he said nothing.

'Ten years.'

He was unforthcoming with answers.

The aftermath of drink had left his body and he was sitting as he had not sat for weeks, consuming tea, peaceful. In fact, when he thought of it, he hadn't been like this for years, sitting quietly, untortured by memories of Ireland but easy with them, memories of green and limestone grey.

She invited him back and he didn't come back for days. But as always in the case of two people who meet and genuinely like one another they were destined to meet again.

He saw her in Camden Town one evening, knew that his proclivity for Keats and Byron at school was somehow justified. She was unrushed, carrying vegetables, asked him why he had not come. He told her he'd been intending to come, that he was going to come. She smiled. She had to go she said. She was firm.

Afterwards he drank, one pint of Guinness. He would go back, he told himself.

In fact it was as though he was led by some force of persuasion, easiness of language that existed between him and Sister Sarah, a lack of embarrassment at silence.

He took a bus from his part of Shepherd's Bush to Camden Town. Rain slashed, knifing the evening with black. The first instinct he had was to get a return bus but unnerved he went on.

Entering the centre the atmosphere was suddenly appropriated by music, Tchaikovsky, *Swan Lake.* He entered the hall to see a half-dozen young men in black jerseys, blue trousers, dying, quite genuinely like swans.

She saw him. He saw her. She didn't stop the procedure, merely acknowledged him and went on, her voice reverberating in the hall, to talk of movement, of the necessity to identify the real lines in one's body and flow with them.

Yes, he'd always recall that, 'the real lines in one's body'. When she had stopped talking she approached him. He stood there, aware that he was a stranger, not in a black jersey.

Then she wound up the night's procedure with more music, this time Beethoven, and the young men from Roscommon and Mayo behaved like constrained ballerinas as they simulated dusk.

Afterwards they spoke again. In the little kitchen.

'Dusk is a word for balance between night and day,' she said. 'I asked them to be relaxed, to be aware of time flowing through them.'

The little nun had an errand to make.

Alone, there, Liam smoked a cigarette. He thought of Marion, his wife gone north to Leeds, fatigued with him, with marriage, with the odd affair. She had worked as a receptionist in a theatre.

She'd given up her job, gone home to Mummy, left the big city for the northern smoke. In short her marriage had ended.

Looking at the litter bin Liam realized how much closer to accepting this fact he'd come. Somehow he'd once thought marriage to be for life but here it was, one marriage dissolved and nights to fill, a body to shelter, a life to lead.

A young man with curly blond hair entered. He was looking for Sister Sarah. He stopped when he saw Liam, taken aback. These boys were like a special battalion of guards in their black jerseys. He was an intruder, cool, English almost, his face, his features relaxed, not rough or ruddy. The young man said he was from Roscommon. That was near Liam's home.

He spoke of farms, of pigs, said he'd had to leave, come to the city, search for neon. Now he'd found it. He'd never go back to the country. He was happy here, big city, many people, a dirty river and a population of people that included all races.

'I miss the dances though,' the boy said, 'the dances of Sunday nights. There's nothing like them in London, the cars all pulled up and the ballroom jiving with music by Big Tom and the Mainliners. You miss them in London but there are other things that compensate.'

When asked by Liam what compensated most for the loss of fresh Sunday night dancehalls amid green fields the boy said, 'The freedom.'

Sister Sarah entered, smiled at the boy, sat down with Liam. The boy questioned her about a play they were intending to do and left, turning around to smile at Liam.

Sarah—her name came to him without the prefix now—spoke about the necessity of drama in schools, in education.

'It is a liberating force,' she said. 'It brings out—' she paused

'—the swallow in people.'

And they both laughed, amused and gratified at the absurdity of the description.

Afterwards he perceived her in a hallway alone, a nun in a short outfit, considering the after-effects of her words that evening, pausing before plunging the place into darkness.

He told her he would return and this time he did, sitting among boys from Roscommon and Tipperary, improvising situations. She called on him to be a soldier returning from war and this he did, embarrassedly, recalling that he too was a soldier once, a boy outside a barracks in Ireland, beside a bed of crocuses. People smiled at his shattered innocence, at this attempt at improvisation. Sister Sarah reserved a smile. In the middle of a simulated march he stopped.

'I can't. I can't,' he said.

People smiled, let him be.

He walked to the bus stop, alone. Rain was edging him in, winter was coming. It hurt with its severity tonight. He passed a sex shop, neon light dancing over the instruments in the window. The pornographic smile of a British comedian looked out from a newsagent's.

He got his bus.

Sleep took him in Shepherd's Bush. He dreamt of a school long ago in County Galway which he attended for a few years, urns standing about the remains of a Georgian past.

At work people noticed he was changing. They noticed a greater serenity. An easiness about the way he was holding a cup. They virtually chastised him for it.

Martha McPherson looked at him, said sarcastically, 'You look hopeful.'

He was thinking of Keats in the canteen when she spoke to him, of words long ago, phrases from mouldering books at school at the beginning of autumn.

His flat was tidier now; there was a space for books that had not hitherto been there. He began a letter home, stopped, couldn't envisage his mother, old woman by a sea of bog.

Sister Sarah announced plans for a play they would perform at Christmas. The play would be improvised, bit by bit, and she asked for suggestions about the content.

One boy from Leitrim said, 'Let's have a play about the Tinkers.'

Liam was cast for a part as Tinker king and bit by bit over the weeks he tried, tried to push off shyness, act out little scenes.

People laughed at him. He felt humiliated, twisted inside. Yet he went on.

His face was moulding, clearer than before, and in his eyes was a piercing darkness. He made speeches, trying to recall the way the Tinkers spoke at home, long lines of them on winter evenings, camps in country lanes, smoke rising as a sun set over distant steeples.

He spoke less to colleagues, more to himself, phrasing and rephrasing old questions, wondering why he had left Ireland in the first place, a boy, sixteen, lonely, very lonely on a boat making its way through a winter night.

'I suppose I left Ireland,' he told Sister Sarah one night, 'because I felt ineffectual, totally ineffectual. The priests at school despised my independence. My mother worked as a char. My father was dead. I was a mature youngster who liked women, had one friend at school, a boy who wrote poetry.

'I came to England seeking reasons for living. I stayed with my older brother who worked in a factory.

'My first week in England a Greek homosexual who lived upstairs asked me to sleep with him. That ended my innocence. I grew up somewhere around then, became adult very, very young.'

1966, the year he left Ireland.

Sonny and Cher sang 'I've Got You, Babe'.

London was readying itself for blossoming, the Swinging Sixties had attuned themselves to Carnaby Street, to discotheques, to parks. Ties looked like huge flowers, young hippies sat in parks. And in 1967, the year *Sergeant Pepper's Lonely Hearts Club Band* appeared, a generation of young men and horned-rimmed glasses looking like John Lennon. 'It was like a party,' Liam said, 'a continual party. I ate, drank at this feast.

'Then I met Marion. We married in 1969, the year Brian Jones died. I suppose we spent our honeymoon at his funeral. Or at least in Hyde Park where Mick Jagger read a poem in commemoration of him. "Weep no more, for Adonais is not dead."'

Sister Sarah smiled. She obviously liked romantic poetry too, she didn't say anything, just looked at him, with a long slow smile. 'I understand,' she said, though what she was referring to he didn't know.

Images came clearer now, Ireland, the forty steps at school, remnants of a Georgian past, early mistresses, most of all the poems of Keats and Shelley.

Apart from the priests, there had been things about school he'd enjoyed, the images in poems, the celebration of love and laughter by Keats and Shelley, the excitement at finding a new poem in a book.

She didn't say much to him these days, just looked at him. He was beginning to fall into place, to be whole in this environment of rough and ready young men.

Somehow she had seduced him.

He wore clean, cool, casual white shirts now, looked faaway at work, hair drifting over his forehead as in adolescence. Someone noticed his clear blue eyes and remarked on them, Irish eyes, and he knew this identification as Irish had not been so absolute for years.

' "They came like swallows and like swallows went,"' Sister Sarah quoted one evening. It was a fragment from a poem by Yeats, referring to Coole Park, a place not far from Liam's home, where the legendary Irish writers convened, Yeats, Synge, Lady Gregory, O'Casey, a host of others, leaving their mark in a place of growth, of bark, of spindly virgin trees. And in a way now Liam associated himself with this horde of shadowy and evasive figures; he was Irish. For that reason alone he had strength now. He came from a country vilified in England but one which, generation after generation, had produced genius, and observation of an extraordinary kind.

Sister Sarah made people do extraordinary things, dance, sing, boys dress as girls, grown men jump over one another like children. She had Liam festoon himself in old clothes, with paper flowers in his hat.

The story of the play ran like this:

Two Tinker families are warring. A boy from one falls in love with a girl from the other. They run away and are pursued by Liam who plays King of the Tinkers. He eventually finds them but they kill themselves rather than part and are buried with the King of the Tinkers making a speech about man's greed and folly.

No one questioned that it was too mournful a play for Christmas;

there were many funny scenes, wakes, fights, horse-stealing and the final speech, words of which flowed from Liam's mouth, had a beauty, an elegance which made young men from Roscommon who were accustomed to hefty Irish showband singers stop and be amazed at the beauty of language.

Towards the night the play was to run Sister Sarah became a little irritated, a little tired. She'd been working too hard, teaching during the day. She didn't talk to Liam much and he felt hurt and disorganized. He didn't turn up for rehearsal for two nights running. He rang and said he was ill.

He threw a party. All his former friends arrived and Marion's friends. The flat churned with people. Records smashed against the night. People danced. Liam wore an open-neck collarless white shirt. A silver cross was dangling, one picked up from a craft shop in Cornwall.

In the course of the party a girl became very, very drunk and began weeping about an abortion she'd had. She sat in the middle of the floor, crying uproariously, awaiting the arrival of someone.

Eventually, Liam moved towards her, took her in his arms, offered her a cup of tea. She quietened. 'Thank you,' she said simply.

The crowds went home. Bottles were left everywhere. Liam took his coat, walked to an all-night café and, as he didn't have to work, watched the dawn come.

She didn't chastise him. Things went on as normal. He played his part, dressed in ridiculous clothes. Sister Sarah was in a lighter mood. She drank a sherry with Liam one evening, one cold December evening. As it was coming near Christmas she spoke of festivity in Kerry. Crossroad dances in Dún Caoin, the mirth of Kerry that had never died. She told Liam how her father would take her by car to church on Easter Sunday, how they'd watch the waters being blessed and later dance at the crossroads, melodious playing and the Irish fiddle.

There had been nothing like that in Liam's youth. He'd come from the Midlands, dull green, statues of Mary outside factories. He'd been privileged to know defeat from an early age.

'You should go to Kerry some time,' Sister Sarah said.

'I'd like to,' Liam said, 'I'd like to. But it's too late now.'

Yet when the musicians came to rehearse the music Liam knew

it was not too late. He may have missed the West of Ireland in his youth, the simplicity of a Gaelic people but here now in London, melodious exploding, he was in an Ireland he'd never known, the extreme west, gullies, caves, peninsulas, roads winding into desecrated hills and clouds always coming in. Imagine, he thought, I've never even seen the sea.

He told her one night about the fiftieth anniversary of the 1916 revolution, which had occurred before he left, old priests at school fumbling with words about dead heroes, bedraggled tricolours flying over the school and young priests, beautiful in the extreme, reciting the poetry of Patrick Pearse.

'When the bombs came in England,' Liam said, 'and we were blamed, the ordinary Irish working people, I knew they were to blame, those priests, the people who lied about glorious deeds. Violence is never, ever glorious.'

He met her in a café for coffee one day and she laughed and said it was almost like having an affair. She said she'd once fancied a boy in Kerry, a boy she was directing in *All My Sons*. He had bushy blond hair, kept Renoir reproductions on his wall, was a bank clerk. 'But he went off with another girl,' she said, 'and broke my heart.'

He met her in Soho Square Gardens one day and they walked together. She spoke of Africa and the States, travelling, the mission of the modern church, the redemption of souls lost in a mire of nonchalance. On Tottenham Court Road she said goodbye to him.

'See you next rehearsal,' she said.

He stood there when she left and wanted to tell her she'd awakened in him a desire for a country long forgotten, an awareness of another side of that country, music, drama, levity but there was no saying these things.

When the night of the play finally arrived he acted his part well. But all the time, all the time he kept an eye out for her.

Afterwards there were celebrations, balloons dancing, Irish bankers getting drunk. He sat and waited for her to come to him and when she didn't rose and looked for her.

She was speaking to an elderly Irish labourer.

He stood there, patiently, for a moment. He wanted her to tell him about Christmas lights in Ireland long ago, about the music of

Ó Riada and the southern-going whales. But she persevered in speaking to this old man about Christmas in Kerry.

Eventually he danced with her. She held his arm softly. He knew now he was in love with her and didn't know how to put it to her. She left him and talked to some other people.

Later she danced again with him. It was as though she saw something in his eyes, something forbidding.

'I have to go now,' she said as the music still played. She touched his arm gently, moved away. His eyes searched for her afterwards but couldn't find her. Young men he'd acted with came up and started clapping him on the back. They joked and they laughed. Suddenly Liam found he was getting sick. He didn't make for the lavatory. He went instead to the street. There he vomited. It was raining. He got very wet going home.

At Christmas he went to midnight mass in Westminster Cathedral, a thing he had never done before. He stood with women in mink coats and Irish charwomen as the choir sang 'Come All Ye Faithful'. He had Christmas with an old aunt and at midday rang Marion. They didn't say much to one another that day but after Christmas she came to see him.

One evening they slept together. They made love as they had not for years, he entering her deeply, resonantly, thinking of Galway long ago, a river where they swam as children.

She stayed after Christmas. They were more subdued with one another. Marion was pregnant. She worked for a while and when her pregnancy became too obvious she ceased working.

She walked a lot. He wondered at a woman, his wife, how he hadn't noticed before how beautiful she looked. They were passing Camden Town one day when he recalled a nun he'd once known. He told Marion about her, asked her to enter with him, went in a door, asked for Sister Sarah.

Someone he didn't recognize told him she'd gone to Nigeria, that she'd chosen the African sun to boys in black jerseys. He wanted to follow her for one blind moment, to tell her that people like her were too rare to be lost but knew no words of his would convince her. He took his wife's hand and went about his life, quieter than he had been before.

# A Marriage in the Country

She burned down half her house early that summer and killed her husband. He'd been caught upstairs. It was something she'd often threatened to do, burn the house down, and when she did it she did it quietly, in a moment of silent, reflective despair. She had not known he'd been upstairs. She'd put a broom in the stove and then tarred the walls with the fire. The flames had quickly explored the narrow stairway. A man, twenty years older than her, had been burned alive, caught when snoozing. Magella at his funeral seemed charred herself, her black hair, her pale, almost sucrose skin. She'd stooped, in numbed penitence. There was a nebulous, almost incandesced way her black curls took form from her forehead as there was about all the Scully girls. They made an odd band of women there, all the Scully girls, most of them respectably married. Magella was the one who'd married a dozy publican whose passion in life had been genealogy and whose ambition seemed incapacitated by this passion. She'd had a daughter by him. Gráinne. That girl was taken from her that summer and sent to relatives in Belfast. Magella was not interned in a mental hospital. The house was renovated. The pub reopened. People supposed that the shock of what she'd done had cured her and in a genuinely solicitous way they thought that working in the pub, chattering to the customers, would be better for her than an internment in a mental hospital. Anyway there was something very final about internment in a mental hospital at that time in Ireland. They gave her a reprieve. At the end of that summer Boris came to the village.

Stacks of hay were piled up in the fields near the newly opened garage outside the village which he came to manage, little juggling acts of hay in merrily rolling and intently bound fields. All was smallness and precision here. This was Laois. An Ascendancy demesne. The garage was on the top of a hill where the one, real, village street ended, and located at a point where the fields seemed about to deluge the road. The one loss of sobriety in the landscape and heaviness and a very minor one. Boris began his career as garage manager by putting up flags outside the garage, and bunting, an American, an Italian, a French, a Spanish, a German and an Irish flag. He was half-Russian and he'd been raised in an orphanage in County Wexford in the south-eastern tip of Ireland.

Boris Cleary was thin, nervously thin, black-haired, a blackness smoothing the parts of his face which he'd shaved and the very first thing Magella noticed about him, on coming close, under the bunting, was that there was a smell from the back of his neck, as from wild flowers lost in the deep woods which lay in the immediate surroundings of the village. A rancid, asking smell. A smell which asked you to investigate its bearer. Magella, drawn by the rancid smell from the back of a nervous, thin neck, sought further details. She asked Boris about his Russianness which was already, after a few weeks, a rampant legend, over her counter. His father had been a Russian sailor, his mother a Wexford prostitute; he'd been dumped on the Sisters of Mercy. They had christened him and one particular nun had reared him, cackling all the time at this international irony, calling him 'little Stalin'. Boris had emerged, his being, his presence in the world, had emerged from an inchoate night on a ship in the port of Wexford Town.

How a September night, the last light like neon on the gold of the cornfields, led so rapidly to the woods partly surrounding the village they later lost track of; winter conversations in the pub, glasses of whiskey, eventually glasses of whiskey shared, both their mouths going to a glass, like a competition—a series of reciprocal challenges. Eventually, all the customers gone one night as they tended to be gone when Magella and Boris got involved in conversation, their lips met. An older woman, ascribed a demon by some, began having an affair with a young, slackly put-together man.

The woods in early summer were the culminative platform for their affair. These woods that were in fact a kind of garden for bygone estates. Always in the woods, oases, you'd find a garden house—a piece of concrete—a Presbyterian, a Methodist, a Church of Ireland chapel. Much prayer had been done on these estates. Laois had particularly been a county in bondage. Now rhododendrons fulminated and frothed all over the place. And there were berries to admire, right from the beginning of the summer. They found a particular summer house where they made love on the cold, hard, almost penitential floor and soon this was the only place where they made love, their refuge.

In September, just over a year after Boris had come to the village, they got a taxi and visited Magella's daughter in Belfast. She lived off the Falls Road, in a house beside a huge advertisement on a railway bridge for the *Irish Independent.* Gráinne dressed in an odious brown convent uniform. She had long black hair. She looked at Boris. From the look in her eyes Magella afterwards realized she'd fallen in love with Boris at that meeting.

What were they flaunting an affair for? At first they were flaunting it so openly no one believed it was happening. Such things didn't happen in Laois in the 1950s. People presumed that the young Russian had taken a priestly interest in the older possessed woman. And when they brought their affair to Belfast, Boris in a very natty dark suit and in a tie of shining dark blue, a gaggle of relatives thought that there was something comic going on, that Magella had got a clown to chaperone her and prevent her from acts of murderous madness. They brought glasses of orange onto the street for the pair—it was a very sunny day—and oddly enough there was a spark of bunting on the street, the ordination of a local priest recently celebrated. A bulbous-cheeked, Amazon-breasted woman spluttered out a comment: 'Sure he reminds me of the King of England.' She was referring to the King who'd resigned, the only member of royalty respected in nationalist Belfast.

But behind the screen of all the presumptions—and it was a kind of smokescreen—something very intense, very carnal, very complex was going on. Magella was discovering her flesh for the first time and Boris was in a way discovering a mother. She'd always been the licentious one in her family but flailing her flesh around cornfields at night when she'd been young brought her no real pleasure. In the carnality, in love-making now, she'd found lost worlds of youth and lost—yes, inchoate—worlds of Russia. She was able to travel to Boris's origins and locate a very particular house. It was a house in a wood away from the dangers of the time. In this house she put Boris's forebears. In this house, in her sexual fantasies, she made love to Boris, his forebears gone and only they, random lovers, left in it, away from the dangers and the onslaught of the time. There was a tumultuous excitement about being lovers in a house in a wood with many dangers outside the borders of that wood. There was a titillation, a daring, and even a brusqueness about it. But those dangers eventually slipped their moorings in the world outside the wood.

Early in the second summer of their affair someone saw them making love in the summer house. A little boy. Tremulous though he later was about the event he was matter of fact enough to wait for a good view of Magella's heavy white thighs. He was the butcher's son. A picture was soon contrived all over the village, Magella and Boris in an act of love that had a Bolshevik ferocity. Killing your husband was one thing but making love to a young Russian was another. Within the month Magella was in a mental hospital.

The funny thing was that she'd had a premonition that all this was going to happen some weeks before the little boy saw them. Fondling some budding elderberries in the woods she remarked to Boris, looking back at the visible passage they'd made through the woods, that they, she and him, reminded her of the legendary Irish lovers, Diarmaid and Gráinne, who'd fled a king into the woods, feeding on berries. They'd invested Irish berries with a sense of doomed carnality, the berries which had sustained them, right down to the last morsels of late autumn. Here in these woods many of the berries had been sown as parts of gardens and it was difficult to distinguish the wild berries from the descendants of a Protestant bush—

the loganberry, redcurrant, raspberry. These woods had been a testing ground for horticulture and parts of the woods had been cultivated at random, leaving a bed of mesmeric flowers, an apple tree among the wildness. Diarmaid and Gráinne would have had a ball here, Magella said. But for her and Boris the climate was already late autumn when the trees were withered of berries. Their days were up. She remembered the chill she'd felt at national school when the teacher had come to that part of the story of Diarmaid and Gráinne, reading it from a book which had an orange cover luminous as warm blood.

Boris tried to call on her in the mental hospital. He was wearing a suit. But there was a kind of consternation among nuns and nurses when they saw him—they weren't sure what to do—he stood, shouldering criminality, for a few minutes in the waiting room and then he turned on his heels and left. But there was a despatch from his childhood here. A statue of a frigid white Virgin as there'd been in the lounge of the orphanage. Magella had entered the house, all grey and fragmented with statues of Mary like falling crusts of snowflakes, of his childhood.

The years went by and the garage prospered. Gráinne came down from Belfast, having graduated from the convent. Her keen eye on Boris at their first meeting in Belfast led now, after all these years, to a romance. There'd been an unmitigated passion in between. Gráinne started walking out the roads with Boris, her hair cut short and the dresses of a middle-aged woman on her, dour, brown, her figure too becoming somewhat lumpy and, in a middle-aged way, becoming acquiescent. She was very soon linking Boris's arm. She and Boris went to see her mother who sat in a room in the mental hospital, a very quiet Rapunzel but without the long, golden hair of course. Boris, armed with Magella's daughter, was allowed in now. He approached Magella, who was seated, as if there'd been no carnality between them, as if he couldn't remember it, as though this woman was his mother and had been in a mother relationship with him. The affair with her, memory of it, had, in this Catholic village, evacuated his mind. Beside Gráinne he looked like a businessman, as someone who'd been operated on and had his aura of passion removed. He drooped, a lazily held puppet. There was a complete change in him, a complete reorganization of the state of his being, a change commensurate with collectivization in Stalinist Russia. Only very tiny shards of his former being remained, littered on the railway tracks of it, the thoroughfare of it. He didn't so much deny Magella as hurt her with an impotent perception of her. At the core of her love-making with him there'd been a child searching for his mother and now, the memory of passion gone, there was only the truth of his findings. A mother. The mother of a weedy son at that. The rancid smell at the back of his neck had turned to a sickly-sweet one. But Magella still ached for the person who would be revived as soon as she got her hands on Boris again. That person tremored somewhere inside Boris, at the terribleness of her ability.

The romance between Boris and Gráinne lapsed and Gráinne went off to work in a beauty parlour in Bradford where relatives of her father lived. A few months after her departure, Boris—there'd been tiffs between them—repented of his irascibility in the weeks before her decision to leave and he went looking for her. He ended up beside a slime heap in Bradford, a house beside a slime heap, exiled Irish people. The beauty parlour was a few streets away. People in Bradford called Boris Paddy which further confused his sense of identity and he went home without resolving things with Gráinne to find Magella out of the mental hospital and having reopened the pub which Gráinne had tentatively opened for a while. Everything was ripe for a confrontation between them but Magella kept a quietness, even a dormancy in that pub for months until one night she raged out to the garage, wielding a broom, a like instrument to that of her husband's death. He met her at the door of his little house alongside the garage that was closed for the night. 'You scut,' she said. 'You took two dogs from me once and never gave them back.' True, Boris had taken two ginger-coloured, chalk cocker spaniels for his mantelpiece on the condition he'd return them when he found something suitable for the mantelpiece himself. 'I want them back,' she said. He let her in. The dogs were there. She stood in front of him, not looking at the dogs. Where there had been black hair there was now mainly a smoke of grey. She stood in front of him, silently, broom inoffensively by her side, as if to show him the wreck of her being, a wreck caused by involvement with him. 'Come down for a drink some night,' she said and quietly went off.

He did go down for a drink in her pub. He fiddled with drinks on the counter. Then Gráinne came back and Magella burned the whole house down, everything, leaving only a charred wreck of a house. She was put back into the mental hospital. There'd been no money left in the bank. Everything was squandered now and everything had been amiss anyway before Magella had burned the house down. Maybe that's why she'd burned the house down. But this wreck, this cavity in the street was her statement. It was her statement before Boris and Gráinne announced plans for marriage.

What Gráinne did not know when she was earnestly proposed marriage to was that Boris and Magella had slipped away together for a honeymoon of their own in Bray, County Wicklow, the previous June. They stayed in a cascade of a hotel by the sea. The mountains, Bray Head, were frills on the sea. The days were very blue. Women walked dogs, desultory Russian émigrés in pinks, purples, with hats pushed down over their ears. You never saw their faces. Boris and Magella slept in the same room but in separate beds. There were rhododendrons on hills just over Bray and among the walks on those hills. Boris explained to Magella that she was the real woman in his life, at first a carnal one, then a purified, sublimated one. She'd been the one he'd been looking for. It was difficult for Magella to take this, that physical love was over in her life, but there was affirmation with the pain when she eventually burned down the house, on hearing of Boris's imminent marriage to Gráinne. She'd achieved something.

In Bray before they used to go to sleep Boris would light a candle in the room and sit up in bed thinking. 'What are you thinking of?' she asked. But he'd never answered. Nuns in Wexford, gulls streaming over an orphanage, poised to drop for crusts of bread on a grey playing area, sailors on the sea, migrations on foot by railroads in Russia, heavy sun on people in rags, a grandmother pulling a child by the hand, the only remaining member of her family.

'You've got to go through one thing to get to the other,' Boris said sagely as he sat up in bed one night, the lights still on, impeccable pyjamas of navy and white stripes on him which revealed a bush of the acrid black hair on his chest, he staring ahead, zombie-like.

In this statement he'd meant he'd gone through physical love with Magella to fish up a dolorous, muted ikon of a Virgin, of the untouchable but all-protecting woman. To get this holy protection from a woman you had to make her untouchable, sacred. For the rest of his life Magella would provide the source of sanity, of resolve, of belief in his life. She was the woman who'd rescued him from the inchoate Wexford night.

Magella was, of course, pleased to hear this but still restive. She did not sleep well that night. She longed, despite that statement, to have Boris, his nimble legs and arms, his pale well of a crotch, in her bed.

The marriage took place in July the following year. There was a crossroads dance the night before a mile or two outside the village. Rare enough in Ireland at that time, even in West Kerry and in Connemara, they still happened in this backwater of County Laois. People stepped out beside a few items of a funfair, a few coloured lights strung up. An epic, a tumultous smell of corn came from the fields. A melodion played the tune 'Slievenamon'. 'My love, o my love, will I ne'er see you again, in the valley of Slievenamon?' Lovers sauntered through the corn. Magella was packing her things in the mental hospital to attend the wedding the following day.

On their second last day in Bray, by the sea, he'd suddenly hugged her and she saw all the mirth again in his face and all the dark in his hair. An old man nearby, his eye on them, quickly wound up a machine to play some music. There was a picture of Sorrento on a funfair caravan, pale blue lines on the yellow ochre caravan, cartoon Italian mountains, cartoon-packed Italian houses, cartoon operatic waves. Magella had looked to the sea, beyond the straggled funfair, and seen the blue in the sea which was tangible, which was ecstatic.

Magella danced with Boris at the wedding reception. She was wearing a brown suit and a brown hat lent to her by her sister in Tihelly, County Offaly. She looked like an alcoholic beverage, an Irish cream liqueur. Or so a little boy who'd come to the wedding thought. She danced with him in a room where ten-pound notes, twenty-pound notes and, of course, many five-pound notes were pinned on the walls as was the custom at weddings in Ireland. The little boy had come a long way that morning. His granny, on the other side of his family, whom he called on on the way, in her little house, had given him a box of chocolates that looked like a navy limousine. He still had it now as he watched Boris and Magella dance, the couple, a serenity between them, an understanding. They'd been looking for different things from one another, their paths had crossed, they'd gone different ways but in this moment they created a total communion, a total marriage, an understanding that only a child could intuit and carry away with him, enlightened, the notes on the walls becoming Russian notes with pictures of Tsars and dictators and people who'd changed epochs on them, the walls burning in a terrible fire in the child's mind until only a note or two was left, a face or two, sole reminders of an enraptured moment in history.

At such moments the imagination begins and someone else, someone who did not live through the events, remembers and, later, counts the pain.

A little boy walked away from the wedding, box of chocolates still under his arm, not wanting to look back at the point where a woman was dragged away, screaming, at a certain hour, to a solitary room in a mental hospital.

Years later he returned, long after Magella's death in the mental hospital, to the woods, at the time of year when rhododendrons spread there. He bent and picked up a decapitated tiara of rhododendron. There was a poster for Paris in the village, a Chinese restaurant run by a South Korean, a late night fish-and-chip takeaway. The garage was still open at the top of the village. The only change was that Boris had put up a Russian flag among the others. It was his showpiece. He'd gotten it from the Legion of Mary in Kilkenny who'd put on a show about imprisoned cardinals behind the Iron Curtain. But it was his pride. It demonstrated, apart from his roots, the true internationalism of the garage. There were no boundaries here. A bald man, lots of children scampering around him for years, would come out to fill your car and his face would tell you these things, a brown, anaemic work coat on him, a prosperous but also somewhat cowed grin on his face.

At her funeral in 1959 Boris had carried lilies, and there, in the graveyard, thought of his visit to Bradford, the exiled Irish there, a cowed, depressed people, the legacy of history, and of the woman who'd tried to overthrow that legacy, for a while. He'd put the lilies on the grave, Magella's lover, no one denying that day the exact place of the grief in his heart.

Everybody walked away except the boy and Boris and then Boris walked away, but first looking at the boy, almost in annoyance, as if to say, you have no right to intrude on these things, flashing back his black hair and throwing a boyish, almost a rival's look from his black eyes that were scarred and vinegary and blazingly alive from tears. In those eyes was the wound, the secret, and the boy looked at it, unreproached by it.

Years later he returned to find that there was no museum to that wound, only a few brightly painted houses, a ramshackle cramming of modernity. He took his car and drove out by the garage and the bunting and the flags to the fields where you could smell the first, premature coming of the epic, all-consuming, wound-oblivionizing harvest.

Our mad aunts, the young man thought, our mad selves.

Lady of Laois, ikon from this incumbent, serf-less, but none the less, I expect, totally Russian storybook blinding harvest, pray for the night-sea, neon spin-drift, jukebox-beacon café wanderer.

# Ties

The Forty Steps led nowhere. They were grey and wide, shadowed at the sides by creeper and bush. In fact it was officially declared by Patsy Fogarthy that there were forty-four steps. These steps were erected by an English landlord in memorial to some doubtful subject. A greyhound, a wife? If you climbed them you had a view of the recesses of the woods and the places where Patsy Fogarthy practised with his trombone. Besides playing—in a navy uniform—in the brass band Patsy Fogarthy was my father's shop assistant. While the steps were dark grey the counter in my father's shop was dark and fathomless. We lived where the town men's Protestant society had once been and that was where our shop was too. And still is. Despite the fact my father is dead. My father bought the house, built the shop from nothing—after a row with a brother with whom he shared the traditional family grocery-cum-bar business. Patsy Fogarthy was my father's first shop assistant. They navigated waters together. They sold silk ties, demonstrating them carefully to country farmers.

Patsy Fogarthy was from the country, had a tremendous welter of tragedy in his family—which always was a point of distinction—deranged aunts, a paralysed mother. We knew that Patsy's house—cottage—was in the country. We never went there. It was just a picture.

And in the cottage in turn in my mind were many pictures—paintings, embroideries by a prolific local artist who took to embroidery when she was told she was destined to die from leukaemia. Even my mother had one of her works. A bowl of flowers on a firescreen. From his inception as part of our household it seems that Patsy had allied himself towards me. In fact he'd been my father's assistant from before I was born. But he dragged me on walks, he described linnets to me, he indicated ragwort, he seated me on wooden benches in the hall outside town opposite a line of sycamores as he puffed into his trombone, as his fat stomach heaved into it. Patsy had not always been fat. That was obvious. He'd been corpulent, not fat. 'Look,' he said one day on the avenue leading to the Forty Steps—I was seven—'a blackbird about to burst into song.'

Patsy had burst into song once. At a St Patrick's night concert. He sang 'Patsy Fagan'. Beside a calendar photograph of a woman at the back of our shop he did not sing for me but recited poetry. 'The Ballad of Athlone'. The taking of the bridge of Athlone by the Williamites in 1691 had dire consequences for this area. It implanted it forevermore with Williamites. It directly caused the Irish defeat at Aughrim. Patsy lived in the shadow of the hills of Aughrim. Poppies were the consequence of battle. There were balloons of defeat in the air. Patsy Fogarthy brought me a gift of mushrooms once from the fields of Aughrim.

Patsy had a bedding of blackberry curls about his cherubic face; he had cherubic lips and smiled often; there was a snowy sparkle in his deep-blue eyes. Once he'd have been exceedingly good-looking. When I was nine his buttocks slouched obesely. Once he'd have been as the man in the cigarette advertisements. When I was nine on top of the Forty Steps he pulled down his jaded trousers as if to pee, opened up his knickers and exposed his gargantuan balls. Delicately I turned away. The same year he tried to put the same penis in the backside of a drummer in the brass band, or so trembling, thin members of the Legion of Mary vouched. Without a murmur of a court case Patsy was expelled from town. The boy hadn't complained. He'd been caught in the act by a postman who was one of the church's most faithful members in town. Patsy Fogarthy crossed the Irish Sea, leaving a trail of mucus after him.

2

I left Ireland for good and all 11 October 1977. There'd been many explanations for Patsy's behaviour: an aunt who used to have fits, throwing her arms about like seven snakes; the fact he might really have been of implanted Williamite stock. One way or the other he'd never been quite forgotten, unmentioned for a while, yes, but meanwhile the ecumenical movement had revived thoughts of him.

My mother attended a Protestant service in St Matthias's church in 1976. As I left home she pressed a white, skeletal piece of paper into my hands. The address of a hospital where Patsy Fogarthy was now incarcerated. The message was this: 'Visit him. We are now Christian (we go to Protestant services) and if not forgiven he can have some alms.' It was now one could go back that made people accept him a little. He'd sung so well once. He smiled so cheerily. And sure wasn't there the time he gave purple Michaelmas daisies to the dying and octogenarian and well-nigh crippled Mrs Connaughton (she whose husband left her and went to America in 1927).

I did not bring Patsy Fogarthy purple Michaelmas daisies. In the house I was staying in in Battersea there were marigolds. Brought there regularly by myself. Patsy was nearby in a Catholic hospital in Wandsworth. Old clay was dug up. Had my mother recently been speaking to a relative of his? A casual conversation on the street with a country woman. Anyway this was the task I was given. There was an amber, welcoming light in Battersea. Young deer talked to children in Battersea Park. I crept around Soho like an escaped prisoner. I knew there was something connecting then and now, yes, a piece of paper, connecting the far-off, starched days of childhood to an adulthood which was confused, desperate but determined to make a niche away from family and all friends that had ensued from a middle-class Irish upbringing. I tiptoed up bare wooden stairs at night, scared of waking those who'd given me lodging. I tried to write to my mother and then I remembered the guilty conscience on her face.

Gas works burgeoned into the honey-coloured sky, oblivious of the landscape inside me, the dirty avenue cascading on the Forty Steps.

'Why do you think they built it?'

'To hide something.'

'Why did they want to hide something?'

'Because people don't want to know about some things.'

'What things?'

Patsy had shrugged, a fawn coat draped on his shoulders that day.

'Patsy, I'll never hide anything.'

There'd been many things I'd hidden. A girlfriend's abortion. An image of a little boy inside myself, a blue and white striped T-shirt on him. The mortal end of a relationship with a girl. Desire for my own sex. Loneliness. I'd tried to hide the loneliness, but Dublin, city of my youth, had exposed loneliness like neon at evening. I'd hidden a whole part of my childhood, the 1950s, but hitting London took them out of the bag. Irish pubs in London, their jukeboxes, united the 1950s with the 1970s with a kiss of a song. 'Patsy Fagan'. Murky waters wheezed under a mirror in a pub lavatory. A young man in an Italian-style duffle coat, standing erect, eddied into a little boy being tugged along by a small fat man.

'Patsy, what is beauty?'

'Beauty is in the eye of the beholder.'

'But what is it?'

He looked at me. 'Pretending we're father and son now.'

I brought Patsy Fogarthy white carnations. It was a sunny afternoon early in November. I'd followed instructions on a piece of paper. Walking into the demesne of the hospital I perceived light playing in a bush. He was not surprised to see me. He was a small, fat, bald man in pyjamas. His face and his baldness were a carnage of reds and purples. Little wriggles of grey hair stood out. He wore maroon and red striped pyjamas. He gorged me with a look. 'You're—' I did not want him to say my name. He took my hand. There was death in the intimacy. He was in a hospital for the mad. He made a fuss of being grateful for the flowers. 'How's Georgina?' He called my mother by her first name. 'And Bert?' My father was not yet dead. It was as if he was charging them with something. Patsy Fogarthy, our small-town Oscar Wilde, reclined in pyjamas on a chair against the shimmering citadels of Wandsworth. A white nun infrequently scurried in to see to some man in the corridor. 'You made a fine young man.' 'It was the band I missed most.' 'Them were the days.' In the middle of snippets of conversation—he sounded not unlike an Irish bank clerk, aged though and more graven-voiced—I imagined the tableau of love. Patsy with a young boy. 'It was a great old band. Sure you've been years out of the place now. What age are ye?' 'Twenty-six.' 'Do you have a girlfriend? The English girls will be out to grab you now!' A plane noisily slid over Wandsworth. We simultaneously looked at it. An old, swede-faced man bent over a bedside dresser. 'Do ya remember me? I used to bring you on walks.' Of course, I said. Of course. 'It's not true what they said about us. Not true. They're all mad. They're all lunatics. How's Bert?' Suddenly he started shouting at me. 'You never wrote back. You never wrote back to my letters. And all the ones I sent you.' More easy-voiced he was about to return the flowers until he suddenly avowed. 'They'll be all right for Our Lady. They'll be all right for Our Lady.' Our Lady was a white statue, over bananas and pears, by his bed.

3

It is hot summer in London. Tiger lilies have come to my door. I'd never known Patsy had written to me. I'd never received his letters of course. They'd curdled in my mother's hand. All through my adolescence. I imagined them filing in, never to be answered. I was Patsy's boy. More than the drummer lad. He had betrothed himself to me. The week after seeing him, after being virtually chased out of the ward by him, with money I'd saved up in Dublin, I took a week's holiday in Italy. The trattorias of Florence in November illumined the face of a young man who'd been Patsy Fogarthy before I'd been born. It's now six years on and that face still puzzles me, the face I saw in Florence, a young man with black hair, and it makes a story that solves a lot of mystery for me. There's a young man with black hair in a scarlet tie but it's not Patsy. It's a young man my father met in London in 1939, the year he came to study tailoring. Perhaps now it's the summer and the heat and the picture of my father on the wall—a red and yellow striped tie on him—and my illimitable estrangement from family but this city creates a series of ikons this summer. Patsy is one of them. But the sequence begins in the summer of 1939.

Bert ended up on the wide pavements of London in the early summer of 1939. He came from a town in the Western Midlands of Ireland whose wide river had scintillated at the back of town before he left and whose handsome facades radiated with sunshine. There were girls left behind that summer and cricket matches. Bert had decided on the tailoring course after a row with an older brother with whom he'd shared the family grocery-cum-bar business. The family house was one of the most sizeable on the street. Bert had his eyes on another house to buy now. He'd come to London to forge a little bit of independence from family for himself and in so doing he forwent some of the pleasures of the summer. Not only had he left the green cricket fields by the river but he had come to a city that exhaled news bulletins. He was not staying long.

He strolled into a cavern of death for behind the cheery faces of London that summer was death. Bert would do his course in Cheapside and not linger. Badges pressed against military lapels, old dishonours to Ireland. Once Bert had taken a Protestant girl out. They sailed in the bumpers at the October fair together. That was the height of his forgiveness for England. He did not consider playing cricket a leaning to England. Cricket was an Irish game, pure and simple, as could be seen from its popularity in his small, Protestant-built town.

Living was not easy for Bert in London; an Irish landlady—she was from Armagh, a mangy woman—had him. Otherwise the broth of his accent was rebuffed. He stooped a little under English disdain, but his hair was still orange and his face ruddy in fragments. By day Bert travailed; a dusty, dark cubicle. At evenings he walked. It was the midsummer that made him raise his head a little.

Twilight rushing over the tops of the trees at the edge of Hyde Park made him think of his dead parents, Galway people. He was suddenly both proud of and abstracted by his lineage. A hat was vaunted by his red hands on his waist. One evening, as perfumes and colours floated by, he thought of his mother, her tallness, her military posture, the black clothes she had always been stuffed into. In marrying her husband she declared she'd married a bucket. Her face looked a bit like a bucket itself.

Bert had recovered his poise. The width of his shoulders breathed again. His chest was out. It was that evening a young man wearing a scarlet tie stopped and talked to him under a particularly dusky tree by Hyde Park. 'You're Irish,' the young man had said. 'How do you know?' 'Those sparkling blue eyes.' The young man had worn a kind of perfume himself. 'You know,' he said—his accent was very posh—'there's going to be a war. You would be better off in Ireland.' Bert considered the information. 'I'm here on a course.' Between that remark and a London hotel there was an island of nothing. Masculine things for Bert had always been brothers pissing, the spray and the smell of their piss, smelly Protestants in the cricket changing rooms. That night Bert—how he became one he did not know—was a body. His youth was in the hands of an Englishman from Devon. The creaminess of his skin and the red curls of his hair had attained a new state for one night, that of an angel at the side of the Gothic steeple at home. There was beauty in Bert's chest. His penis was in the fist of another young man.

Marriage, children, a drapery business in Ireland virtually eliminated it all but they could not quite eliminate the choice colours of sin, red of handkerchiefs in men's pockets in a smoky hotel lounge, red of claret wine, red of blood on sheets where love-making was too violent. In the morning there was a single thread of a red hair on a pillow autographed in pink.

When my father opened his drapery business he ran it by himself for a while but on his marriage he felt the need for an assistant and Patsy was the first person who presented himself for the job. It was Patsy's black hair, his child's lips, his Roman sky-blue eyes that struck a resonance in my father. Patsy came on an autumn day. My father was reminded of a night in London. His partnership with Patsy was a marital one. When I came along it was me over my brothers Patsy chose. He was passing on a night in London. The young man in London? He'd worn a scarlet tie. My father specialized in ties. Patsy wore blue and emerald ones to town dos. He was photographed for the *Connaught Tribune* in a broad, blue, black-speckled one. His shy smile hung over the tie. Long years ago my mother knew there was something missing from her marriage to my father—all the earnest hot-water jars in the world could not obliterate this knowledge. She was snidely suspicious of Patsy—she too had black-berry hair—and when Patsy's denouement came along it was she who expelled him from the shop, afraid for the part of her husband he had taken, afraid for the parcel of her child's emotions he would abduct now that adolescence was near. But the damage, the violation had been done. Patsy had twined my neck in a scarlet tie one sunny autumn afternoon in the shop, tied it decorously and smudged a patient, fat, wet kiss on my lips.

# Players

For the week they were in town each year they changed the quality of life in the town; everybody submitted to them, shopkeepers, bankers, the keepers of the law. There was a certain light-headedness in puritans and moral flexibility in bigots. They were the players, the people who came to town, performers of the works of Shakespeare ever since the distant, Eamon de Valera mists of the 1930s.

The Mahaffy family gave their name to the players and Ultan Mahaffy commandeered the players. He looked much frailer than before in October 1958 when they came to town; one local woman, a businessman's wife in a perennial scarf, referred to him, in passing, in a conversation on the street as looking now 'like a sickly snowdrop'. Ultan Mahaffy should have been happy because 1958 was the first year his only son Cathal had played in the plays since he'd been assigned the roles of little princes, doomed to be smothered, when he was a child. Cathal had rebelled against the artistic aurora of his family and fled this emanation when he was seventeen to work as a mechanic in a factory in Birmingham. On his return you could see what a strange-looking lad he was: when he had been a child it had been suppressed in him, squashed down, but now he was an albino-like twenty-two-year-old, the whites of his eyes pink roses, the chicken bones of his pale chest often exposed by a loose shirt, his hair shooting up, a frenetic cowslip colour.

This mad-looking creature had been given the parts of Laertes in *Hamlet* and Hotspur in *Henry IV Part One* in 1958. The prodigal son had returned and conformed to the family notion of the inevitability of talent in all its members.

The week before they came the nuns had put on a show in the Town Hall; really a deaf and dumb show, schoolgirls in tights, berets on their heads, rifles by their sides—borrowed from the local army—standing immobile in front of a small cardboard prison that housed a cardinal (you could see the cardinal's meditative and lowered head through a window, a red bulb behind the cardinal's head).

There had been a bunting, made by a nun, of tiny hammer and sickle flags above the stage and this, more than anything, had excited gasps from the women in the audience and a round of applause. You weren't sure if it was the cardinal they were applauding for his endurance or the clever idea of the bunting. But with the coming of the Mahaffys there was one thing you could be sure of: that the bleeding church behind the Iron Curtain could be forgotten for a week. Only the Lenten missions united people in such common excitement. Immediately prior to the Lenten missions it was the excitement caused by the anticipation of so many sins due to be expunged. Immediately prior to a performance by the Mahaffys it was the excitement of knowing that you were going to be deliciously annihilated for a night by the duress of a play.

Mr and Mrs Mahaffy stayed by tradition in Miss Waldren's hotel at the top of O'Higgins Street. This hotel boasted a back garden inspired by the gardens of the local Ascendancy mansion, the garden full, for all its smallness, of walks and willow trees and little ponds drenched by willow trees.

This atmosphere was considered appropriate for the heads of the company but all other players stayed as usual with the two Miss Barretts in a more humble bed and breakfast house on Trophy Street. One of the Barrett sisters was about thirty, the other was near forty, the younger bright, exuberant, bristling with the thought of continual chores to be accomplished, the older usually seated, meditative, lank and arched of cheek.

The younger, Una, was small, pudgy, her head powdered with

anthracite black and celestial vague hair. The older, Sheona, was, by contrast, tall, demure, red-haired, the fluff of her red hair gripping her ears and her neck like forceps. They'd been parentless for a long time, running a bed and breakfast house since their parents died when Una had just entered her teens. They kept the circus people and the theatre people: many disreputables came to the house, of salesmen only licentious-looking ones, of lorry drivers only those continually drunk. Their family origins had become a mystery for many in town; it was as if they'd had no parents and stepped out of another planet very alien to this town because their manners and their decorum were different.

Of the two, Sheona was the most faraway. It was as if she'd spent a time in another country and was continually thinking of it as she sat by the natty peat fires that Una had prepared. She was queenly, erect, but was now nearing, without the sign of a man, the explosive age of forty.

Much satisfaction was expressed with this year's performances: Cathal Mahaffy, with his mad, upshooting blond hair, was particularly singled out; the redness in the whites of his eyes seemed to be the redness at the bottom of the sky in the evening after they'd gone, the sky over the fair green where the marquee had been. But Cathal hadn't really gone with the show. He came back again and again between performances of the plays elsewhere and it took some weeks before the people of town realized that he was having an affair with Sheona Barrett.

The realization came in a week of tender weather in November when he was seen again and again bringing Miss Barrett on the back of his motorbike on the backroads between wavering, stone-walled fields in the countryside outside town. The sky was very blue that week, the weather warm, and Miss Barrett, the near forty-year-old, often wore a summer dress under a cardigan and nothing other than the cardigan for warmth.

How did it happen? What had been going on among the crowd at the guesthouse? More and more women peeped through the curtains and saw the giant tableau on the sitting-room wall of Kylemore Abbey, Connemara, the tableau painted on to the wall by a destitute painter from Liverpool once, this work done in lieu of payment of rent. The painter had a red scarf around his neck and women in the town muttered that you'd have to be careful of his piglet fingers, where they went. Now they knew where Cathal Mahaffy's fingers went. They knew only too well. Sheona Barrett had shed forty-year-old skin and become a young woman.

It was Christmas that riled the women most though, Sheona Barrett going up to Dublin to attend a dinner dance with Cathal Mahaffy, at which the lord mayor of Dublin was present. She'd walked to the station, not got a taxi, and some people had caught sight of her on that frosty morning, of the erectness of her bearing and the pink box she carried in one hand. What had been in that pink box? And she still stood straight. People now, mainly women, wanted to knock her off balance. It was fine as long as the theatre came only once a year but now that it had been detained people were disconcerted. Superintendent Scannell, who always dressed in the same withered-looking, yellow ochre civilian coat, was seen chasing his civilian hat along O'Higgins Street one morning. A soldier's trousers suddenly fell down as the soldiers stood to alert in the square outside the church one Sunday morning. A teacher in the boys' national school suddenly started uttering a pornographic poem in the middle of a mathematics lesson. This man was swiftly taken to the mental hospital. A celibate, he'd obviously been threatened by a nervous breakdown for years.

But some other people were not so fortunate to get such an easy way out. The theatre had stayed in town and upset people, to the very pegs of their being, those pegs that held their being to the ground just as the players' tent was held to the verdant ground of the fair green by pegs.

Sheona Barrett did not seem even aware that she was upsetting people. That's maybe what upset them the most, that austere bearing of hers. It was a scandal but because it was a scandal that came from the theatre the scandal was questioned. This was the stuff of theatre after all, that people sat comfortably looking at. Now that it had been let loose on the streets you had to ask yourself: was the theatre not an intoxicating thing, like whiskey at a dinner dance? Did it not block out realities? In a way they envied Sheona Barrett for having taken something from a night of Shakespeare in a fair green and made it part of her life. They all dabbled with the thought of ensnaring some permanence from the theatre and when they realized it was impossible they decided, en masse, to destroy Sheona Barrett's relationship so they could have the theatre back for what it had been, a yearly festive balloon in their lives.

A Texan millionaire had come to live in a mansion outside town in 1957, a mansion in which the caretaker, who'd been there since the rich owners had departed to take up residence in Kensington, London, had murdered his half-wit brother. The millionaire was a divorcee and the parish priest had blocked the entrance to the mansion with his car one morning and stopped the millionaire's tomato-coloured American car from coming out. The priest had got out of his car and approached the millionaire whose head was cautiously inside the car under a wide cowboy hat and informed him that divorcees were not welcome here. The millionaire departed forthwith, leaving his Irish roots.

The same trick was got up with Miss Barrett but with less success because the parish priest was ill and his stand-in, Father Lysaght, a plump, berry-faced man with his black hair perpetually oiled back, was addicted to sherry, saying mass and giving sermons when drunk on sherry, mouthing out the usual particularities of Catholicism but given new accent on sherry. He was dispatched to pull back Sheona Barrett from her affair, arriving already drunk, was given more drink and spent the night on a sofa with Cathal Mahaffy, discussing the achievements of Cathal's father.

Eventually the priest began talking Greek because he thought that was appropriate, quoting poetry about carnal subjects from his seminary days, digging his snout-like nose into the air as he recited, and then he wavered and snortled his way home. The final agreement had been that only the theatre mattered, nothing else did, and the church and its sacraments palled in comparison to a good theatrical performance. The priest got to the presbytery gates, jolting out a refrain from *The Mikado* remembered from his days at boys' boarding school, boys in merry dress and many in ladies' wigs lined up to daunt the 1930s with colour and the smell of grease paint.

The relationship of Cathal Mahaffy and Sheona Barrett had been given a safe passage by the church. Sheona Barrett, by her

association with theatre people, had been elevated to the status of an
artistic person and as such was immune from the church's laws. You
had to titillate people through the arts with a sense of sin so as to
reaffirm all the church stood for. A thread united Sheona Barrett to
the artistic establishment of the country now and she knew this,
becoming so faraway looking she looked almost evanescent, as if she
was part of the clouds and the fields.

Cathal Mahaffy invoked her to many parts of the country and
she went swiftly. The townspeople knew now that the girls had been
left money they'd never spent much of before. That was evident
from the way Sheona Barrett could so readily draw on those funds
to get herself around the country. There'd never been any need of
that money very much before. Una Barrett groomed her sister, settling her hair. A taxi was often called to speed to some desolate town
in the Midlands, past derelict mill houses and past weirs and houses
that handed on an emblem for brandy on their fronts, to one another,
like a torch.

In August 1959 Sheona Barrett attended the Galway races with
Cathal Mahaffy. Her photograph was in the *Connaught Tribune.* She
looked like a new bride. In late September they spent a few days
together, again in Galway. They sauntered together by the peaceful
blue of the sea, holding one another's hands. Most of the holiday-
makers had gone and they had Salthill to themselves. The sea was
blue, it seemed, just for them. The blue rushed at their lovers' figures. There was a happiness for them in Galway that late September.
Sheona's hair was a deeper red and often there was red on both her
cheeks, 'like two flowerpots', one bitter woman remarked.

Cathal Mahaffy's body must have been lovely. He was so lithe
and pale. In bed with her he must have been like a series of twigs
that would seem almost about to break making love to this tall
woman. He looked like a boy still. He had this intensity. And he
challenged you with his pale appearance, his albino hair, his direct
smile. You always ended up for some reason looking to his crotch as
his shoulders sloped in his act of looking at you directly.

It was also clear that Cathal's parents approved of the relationship or at least didn't object to it. They were broad-minded
people. They were glad to have their son with them and he could

have been making love to a male pigmy for all they cared it seemed. They had seen many sexual preferences in their time and a lifetime in theatre qualified them to look beyond the land of sex, to see things that transcended sex: comradeship, love, devotion to art. Art had guided their lives and because of this they themselves transcended the land of Ireland and saw beyond it, to the centuries it sometimes seemed from the look on Mrs Mahaffy's face as she stood on a green in a village, the light from a gap in the tent falling on her face. But there was always some tragedy at the end of the route of tolerance in this country.

Shortly before the players arrived in Sheona's town in 1959 Sheona was set upon in a routine walk by the railway station, near a bridge over a weir, and raped. No one could say who raped her but it was known that it had been a gang. She had been physically brutalized apart from being raped and mentally damaged. When she was brought to hospital it was clear that some damage was irrevocable in her. There was a trail of stains like those of tea leaves all across her face when she sat up in bed and her eyes stared ahead, not seeing what she'd seen before. Una Barrett was there, holding a brown scapular she'd taken from its covert place around her neck.

The performances were cancelled that year. There was a mysterious silence around the players. The probable reason was that Cathal Mahaffy had opted out of the main parts in two Jacobean plays that weren't Shakespeare's. He'd made off on that motorbike of his after seeing Sheona in hospital, to mourn.

A rape, a job of teaching someone a lesson, had gone wrong. There had been an excess of brutality. The youths who'd run away from Sheona through the thickets by the river had probably been put up to it by nameless and sinister elders in town. That was the hazy verdict handed down. There'd been many accomplices and people, in a Ku Klux Klan way, kept silent about the event, kept their lips sealed as if it had been a figment of someone's imagination and there were often irritated howls years later when the event was referred to.

Sheona Barrett ended up in a home in Galway and she is still there; someone who saw her says her hair is still as red as it was then.

Cathal left the players permanently after the tragedy of October 1959, which months later still spread disbelief. He continued in the theatre in a ragged kind of way for a few years, his most celebrated role being as a black, scintillating cat in one of Dublin's main theatres at Christmas 1960 but after that his appearances became fewer and fewer, until eventually he was down to secondary roles in discontented American plays in the backstreet and basement theatres of the city of Dublin.

But his good looks flourished, that appearance of his became seraphim-like, and he was taken up by a rich American woman who'd moved into a top-floor flat in Baggot Street, Dublin, and he lived with her as her lover for a few years in this bohemian spell of hers, seen a lot with her in Gajs' Restaurant over its tables regulated by small bunches of red carnations or in narrow pubs packed with Americans and Swedes craning to hear uilleann pipes played by hairy North-side Dubliners in desultory red check shirts. He nearly always had a black leather jacket on as if he was ready to depart and move on and it was true that no relationship could really last in his life so haunted and fragmented was he by what had happened to Sheona Barrett; he felt irrefutably part of what had happened.

One day he did leave the American woman but she was already thinking of leaving Dublin so there was some confusion about his leaving her; no observer was sure which of the pair it was who sundered the relationship.

He spent a few months on people's floors, often on quite expensive antique carpets, around the Baggot Street, Fitzwilliam Square, Pembroke Road area of Dublin. The antique carpets were no coincidence in his life because he was actually working for an antique dealer now who had a shop on Upper Baggot Street and in Dun Laoghaire. The job was kind of a gift, kind of decoration for an aimless person and one Saturday when he wasn't working he did what he'd wanted to do for a long time, drove west on his motorbike to Sheona Barrett's town to try to find the answer to a question that had beleaguered his mind for so long: Why, why the evil, why the attack, what had been the motivation for this freak outrage, what had been the forces gathered behind it?

But in the town he discovered that there were other explanations for Sheona's state as if she'd been ill all the time. Una Barrett was a housewife, a guesthouse keeper, a mother, the wife of a man who had Guinness spilt all over his already brown jacket and waistcoat. The day was very blue: in the square there was an abundance of geraniums being sold; the sky seemed specially blue for his visit. All was happiness and change here. The past didn't exist. He was an exile, by way of lack of explanations, from the present.

But the more he stuck about, wandering among the market produce, the farmers made uncomfortable by the fact he wasn't purchasing anything, the more he knew. People did not like happiness. They distrusted happiness of the flesh more than anything. The coming together of bodies in happiness was an outrage against the sensibilities. It not only should not be allowed to exist but it had to be murdered if it wasn't going to unhinge them further. A swift killing could be covered up, it could be covered up forever; only the haunted imagination would keep it alive and that imagination would, by its nature, be driven out of society, so all could feel safe. There was no home for people like Cathal Mahaffy who knew and remembered.

With money he got from an unannounced source he purchased a house in a remote part of County Donegal in the late 1960s; the house up on a hill overlooking the swing of a narrow bay. There was much work to be done on it, a skeleton of a grey house peculiar and abandoned among the boulders that all the time seemed about to tumble into the sea.

On the back of his motorbike he ferried building materials from Donegal Town. These were the hippie days of the late 1960s and blue skies over the bay seemed arranged to greet visitors from Dublin. Often people got a bus to Donegal Town and then there was a liberated jaunt on the back of a motorbike around twists by the sea. There were benevolent fields to one side, the green early Irish monks would talk about, and stone walls dancing around the fields, finicky patterned stone walls.

These fields stretching to one side of him like a director's hand Cathal was killed on his motorbike one June day, a Lawrence of Arabia in County Donegal, all his motorbike gear on at the time, helmet, black leather jacket and old-fashioned goggles—a caprice? You felt he was being relieved of some agony he could no longer bear, that the day in June was the last he could have lived anyway, what with the pain in him people had noticed, a pain that scratched out phrases by the half-door of his house, into the Donegal air outside when he was under the influence of fashionable drugs transported from Dublin.

One of these last phrases, these last annotations had been—a woman about to play in a 1930s comedy revival in Dublin had sworn it, her lips already red for the part—'I don't know why they did it. Why? Why? Why? The innocent. The innocent.' This was mistaken as a premature eulogy for himself and because of it all the young rich degenerates in Dublin who saw themselves as being innocent and maliciously tortured by society gathered by his grave in County Wicklow for the funeral, making it a fashionable Dublin event, a young man later said to have epitomized the event, a young man who wasn't wearing a shirt and was advertising his pale, Pre-Raphaelite chest in the hot weather, a safe distance up from the grave, his chest gleaming, under a swipe of a motorcyclist's red scarf, with sweat and with a hedonist's poise.

Among the crowd from Dublin there were some strange rural mourners but no one identified them and anyway they were jostled and passed over in the crowd so awkward was their appearance, so nondescript was their floral contribution. But someone did, out of some quirky interest, get the name of the town they were going back to out of them. It was Sheona's town and the name was said almost indistinguishably so heavy and untutored was the accent.

Ultan Mahaffy did go back to the town a few times after 1959. The company was smaller but the spirit was still high despite losses of one kind or another. The players were greeted in the town with solicitude rather than with reverence. They were tatty compared to what they had been and the marquee in the fair green came to look almost leprous, unapproachable.

In October 1963 Ultan Mahaffy had a strange experience in the town, one which made him shudder, as if death had sat beside him. A man approached him in Miss Waldren's hotel, a tall man under a yellow ochre hat, in a weedy, voluminous, almost gold coat—the colour of the coat evoked stretches in the middle of bogs, slits of beach in faraway County Mayo; it was a kaleidoscopic bunch of national associations the coat brought but its smell was very definitely of decay, of moroseness.

'I beg your pardon, Mr Mahaffy,' a voice said. 'We respect you. You brought art to the town. You'll go down in history. You can't say anything to history. You can't say anything to history.' With that he turned his back and went off. What had he been saying? That Mr Mahaffy could not be impugned because he was part of history. Part of the history books like Patrick Pearse and Cúchulainn. But there had been others who were not quite so fortunate. Mr Mahaffy looked after the man and knew that he would not be coming back to this town again.

The following summer, before the new season, Mr Mahaffy had a heart attack in Blackrock Baths in Dublin while walking on the wall which separated the open air pool from the grey Irish Sea. He'd looked an exultant figure in his bathing togs before the heart attack, standing up there, stretching his body for all the children to see.

But anyway Mr Mahaffy's life's work had become irrelevant in Sheona Barrett's town. A few years before, on a New Year's Eve, when snow was falling, screens lit up all over the town with their own snow to mark the first transmission by Irish television.

# Elysium

It is nearly ten years now since I arrived in London. It is a long and involved story as to how I came here. I married at eighteen. I was, literally, a product of the bogs, but our bogs were close to, hugged Pontoon Ballroom in County Mayo. So from as early as fourteen years of age I was stealing over the bogs on a bicycle and creeping into the ballroom with older sisters. I presented myself, talcumed, usually in pale blue, a ribbon on; a piece of bog cotton, a flower from the meadows, a wrapt fluff of cloud. The men of Ireland looked me up and down. And I began to dance. My teenage years were ones of dancing and giving myself. I think it was my red ribbon that attracted attention to me first but the men always went for me. So there was a price on me. I got a lot of ice creams out of it in Castlebar. My body became worn very quickly because of it, my face became brazen, my tongue unsalacious as I licked ice-cream bowls. I was ostracized among my sisters; my success had swept them out of the scene. But there was Achill Island and bays I was brought to in the summer. In short to the men of Mayo I was a 'good thing'.

I slept uneasily on my sexual abandon. I had dreams of future catastrophes because of it. Nearby Our Lady of Knock appeared and she rummaged with my dreams. With St John and sometimes St Joseph she poked at me with a shepherd's stick and like a nun at school told me—in a broad Mayo accent—'to cop on'. As with nuns at school I refused her. I gave more of myself. My body turned from white to pink. I was eighteen and I met my man then. He owned a garage in the countryside near Castlebar. The Sheriff, he was called. He went around in American country and western apparel, big boots on him, a cowboy hat, valentine hearts embroidered into his shirt and his crotch always in evidence. I was 'his gal', he told me. He had lots of money, a garage in the countryside constantly attacked and mediated over by wild geese. We danced in Pontoon Ballroom for three months before marrying. My mother stood outside the cottage as he made off with me to our new home, a suburban house outside Castlebar. She had got rid of a handful but she had gained a prosperous son-in-law. I was a wealthy young woman now, all because of my body and my looks I told myself. I took trains to Dublin for hairdos. I wrote country and western songs in my spare time. Country and western songs became poems for me. That was the first sign of discussion. Little bits of poetry by loaves of brown bread in our suburban, blankly lighted kitchen, 'O Lord give me freedom. O Lord give me pain.' What I wanted pain for I was not sure but pain came when the children came, Tomás, Mícheál and Tibby—called after an American country and western singer— I had to fight to keep the pure lines in my body and with my physical beauty flawed by childbirth and the idea of lechery ruptured by marriage, my husband collected girls in the bogs and brought them off to Achill for weekends, making love to them under a crucifix situated high over the Atlantic.

All this is not telling much about me, my feelings at the time, the woman who walked about the house in country and western boots. I became very lonely. There was a big picture of mountains in our sitting room. I wanted to be buried like Queen Maeve on top of a mountain.

I realized too at that time that I was an exceptional kind of person. I was pretty, had blonde ringletted hair, did what most women in Castlebar could not do, wrote poetry. I recalled moments in childhood I'd heard voices in my dreams telling me to go to remote hills in the bog to receive messages from God. Maybe I'd missed what I should have been, a virgin, always a virgin, not a nun but a woman who drifts around the town declaring her virginity like a no-man's-land in war, a place of pain and thoughts and feelings too much to accommodate on any side.

I was curtailed, though, during these conjectures by memories of tender caresses from a young boy in a bog; Castlebar faced me, the mountains, the sea, years of suburban houses and masses of adulteries. The money was pouring in. My husband talked of holidays in Spain. It was summer and girls outside ice-cream parlours slouched, looking at me knowingly. A boy from Sweden passed the men's lavatory, a rucksack caked on his back. The girls were ones who travelled to remote corners with my husband. I was the wife, the mother. There were landslides within me; I walked as erect as possible, how a nun at school had ordained one should walk erect. Without the children— they had become bold, whingeing and brattish now—I found a rubbish dump on a beach by which I walked along, the sluice gates of sewers opening onto the beach and gulls diving down to question old, blackened contorted kettles. There was a face forming within me. It was a boy's face. I created a boy I wanted to get to know, not sexually, not anything like that. There was a photograph missing from inside me that should have been taken. I created, I invented an area; I wanted to conquer that area. I knew I would not find this boy in Castlebar but I was also sure he existed somewhere; there was the map of these finer things in me, the shape of a green squelching map of Ireland on the wall at school. I wanted a word to set me off wandering; I thought of fleeing with the Tinkers once or twice. Matt, the husband, smelled of semen. But the more I walked by a rubbish dump, the higher the ecstasy, the more suffocating the knowledge that I was trapped. There must have been thousands of Irish women in my position, I thought, millions of women. I did not intend to start the women's lib movement in Castlebar. Instead I wove wings of fancy. But they refused to fly very far. So I kept my eye on the shop in which I could buy tickets to England.

'Dear whoever you are, I went because—because I could not stand it any more. I could not stand being a lump of—I don't want to use a rude word. I went to try to salvage my most ancient dignity.' Words, notes were played with. I needed an excuse. By this time marriage, a husband, did not exist. He took a girl back home one day and made love to her on the couch. I smelt it, under the picture of Connemara mountains. This was just one of the incidents that slided into the sequence of going. I did not know what I was saying goodbye to when I purchased fresh emerald boat tickets to England in a shop in Castlebar in October for myself and my children. I'm sorry I cannot give you a dramatic incident that preceded my going; in fact between the first leaves of autumn and a boat journey to England there is only a blur, a blur on which is written a kind of Sanskrit. 'I am Mary Mullarney, twenty-four. I possess three yellow ochre cardigans and three children.' That month, in London, my life began, however dazed and erratic was its beginning.

London, refuge of sinners, of lost Irishwomen; its chief import is people from my part of Mayo. I often feel like addressing it; it is not England, it is not in the demesne of the Queen; it is an invented place. But a place that also dulls one, especially one who can hardly remember her former life.

'Piss off.' I had a sister in Harrow, 41 Bengeworth Road. I understood I could approach at her door. I was mistaken. She was married now to an Englishman who drove trucks to Aberdeen—she'd converted him to Catholicism—and the Harrow church hall was nearby. On this wall were photographs of herself among church committees. She was the one who when I was fourteen most hated me. I'd broken some rule of the dance-hall floor. I'd appeared in a blue taffetta-effect dress once. There were certain dresses you could wear and certain dresses you couldn't. She'd never forgiven me and one night—when her husband was probably plunging into beans at a motorway stop near Easingwold—she slammed a door on me and Tomás, Mícheál and Tibby in Harrow. Not before I'd noticed mathematical problems of lines and contortions on her face. She'd have to see Father-something-or-another in the morning to discuss the serving of coffee at the next meeting of the Mayo hurlers' association. The odd thing about families is that they're illusions. Far from being the closest to you they're very often the most diabolical of people. There were no ice-cream parlours open in Harrow and Mícheál, Tomás, Tibby and myself ended up in Westbourne Park late one night or early one morning. We had our bags, our rugs, I had my savings and we celebrated. It was a black perky girl who brought us to 'Elysium'.

'Elysium' was chalked in white on the right-hand column of a gate outside a generously decaying Edwardian house on a starlit night. Lenny, a scarlet ribbon in the laced strands of hair tied above her head, led us up the path. Tomás clashed against a dustbin and I bid him hush. I was entering a house in the fields of Mayo. The night was dark among the stone walls. I trod tentatively on the doorstep. The occupants were gone; to America, wherever. This house had a secret for me. It was after a dance. A door opened in a house in Mayo onto a house in London. There was a cooker, a fridge, heaters, bedding, everything we needed. The house was deserted, Lenny said, but for an Irish boy who never emerged from his room. Then she disappeared. After poking around a bit we lay down among Foxford blankets.

Great trouble had visited this house; the people were rich; the girls wore red tartan skirts. One of the girls became pregnant, tried to abort the baby among the streams that constantly cleansed the fluff of sheep, the red of her blood had run with the brook—a sign—and the whole family had left for America. But the boy. The father. I could see him against a half-door.

Raymond was from Belfast. I pulled back the door on him. He had a face, frail and white as Easter lilies against the Edwardian light of the window. Squatting on the floor, he was reading a poem by George Herbert out loud. 'Love bade me welcome; yet my soul drew me back. Guilty of dust and sin.' I was heading for the shutters that were not quite open. 'Isn't it time you were up having your breakfast. Hello there, I'm Mary. Yes, I know all about you. No need for introductions. We've moved in. We'll make a nice household. So you're from the Red Hand of Ulster. Sweet Jesus, you don't look like an Ulsterman. Come up and meet the children. The tea's made. How many sugars do you take?' I was now at the window, looking outside, my hands grabbing the worn-away cream of the shutters as the visions outside petrified me.

Already Cormac Fitzmaurice from Dublin was up, a large bottle of Guinness sprouting from his black maggoty coat picked up from a rubbish dump—among the florets of used Durexes and among the heroin syringes—shouting as he eddied to and fro about Synge Street Christian Brothers' School and one brother who used to ride a piebald pony, bareback, on Sandymount Strand at dawn. Behind him the graffiti on the pub opposite was choice. 'Come to Ballinacargy for pimples on your prick.'

Raymond struggled free from his Buddha position and quickly came to breakfast with me and the children. White shirt rolled up on his thin arms he charmed the children; Mícheál, Tomás and Tibby smiled gratefully at him. It was the first time really I realized I had children, not little piglets. I counted the freckles on Mícheál's nose that morning.

'I was born in a red brick part of a red brick city. There were hills and mountains around the city. My ma inherited a newsagent's from her dad. The *Irish Independent* was advertised outside. The front was whiney green. We were Taigs. My dad was jealous of my mother's shop and tried to burn it down one night. He worked at the station and shuffled along to work in the mornings under low mountains. At the local public baths Catholic and Protestant children swam. At the age of four I was nearly drowned by a Protestant boy of six who looked like a ferocious gorilla.'

I washed Raymond's shirts, often dots of darker white on them. 'Made in Italy' frequently boasted on the collar tag. Threads of blood disappeared into the water in the big, white, bath-like sink. I scrubbed inches of collar dirt on a washboard. The material was occasionally silk and pleasant to deal with. White shirts hung up in the kitchen like angels.

'Growing up in a city where blood has collected under the houses you have mischievous aunts and uncles. They canonize soldiers. There are wreaths around the pictures in their sitting rooms. Aunts and uncles sit like officers. They command imaginary armies. In another part of the city are other children whose aunts and uncles command different imaginary armies. One uncle of mine had a picture of Patrick Pearse in a frame and because there was no glass on it—they were too poor—Patrick Pearse's mouth was once stubbed away by a cigarette butt. He looked like Dracula then. Draculas sold Easter lilies outside the public baths. When I was fourteen Protestant children no longer swam at the public baths.'

In newly washed white shirts Raymond looked like a different person. I washed his hair one night over the kitchen sink and Tibby—

aged three—dried it. The kitchen smelt of lavender then. I realized that night my husband or the black-garbed nuns had not come looking for us. We were the Queen's property now. We had found another country.

'The first time you see death is the worst. I saw a child: its brains blown out. I thought of all the poems by Patrick Pearse blown to nothing. It was a Protestant bomb. You could always tell Protestant bombs because it was always children who seemed to be caught in them. Protestant Gods were different from Catholic Gods; they lived in houses of dark stone and punished children who carried rosary beads in their pockets.'

Raymond in a white silk shirt, rolled up, stripes of primrose and thrush hair on his shoulders, a cigarette in his fingers, he talking, his lips the colour of lips that have just been moistened by wine. That's one of the photographs taken in my mind at the kitchen table in November.

'Then came the real armies. In a city where the houses were armies, the eyes of houses in the hills, to encounter the real armies was to meet a ghost. Faces were painted out. It was all part of a logic; the grave too was part of a logic. Wreaths were wrapped in newspaper that would otherwise have held fish and chips and placed together with the news of local commandants in the paper, by wet grave slabs in Milltown cemetery. I remember one wreath of flowers, little pink and red flowers, miniature flowers, almost plastic flowers. It was a woman with a scarf on her head who laid this wreath for her son, a schoolfriend of mine. We were given berets and flags to compensate for the dead.'

Once or twice I pulled Raymond up, asking him what he meant by something or another and that stopped him really, so to fill in the gap, his white shirt catching the gleams of a candle we considered appropriate for the occasion, I mustered everything I had and took off where he stopped, in a mustard cardigan, arms folded, telling my life story as I concentrated on a pound of butter that had slipped into the shape of Croagh Patrick on the table.

'Where do I begin? Let's see. Let me rack my brains. Brown bogs. Creaking, spinning bicycles. Milk churns. Girls were solicitous about scapulars. Geese were coy. I shared a secret with the heavens.

I was to be sainted one day. Girls rummaged through bogs. Girls were friends until men came along. Girls stooped and lacquered their shoes with rival cream. There was a picture of Maria Goretti in our sitting room among millions of seashells and small pigeon feathers glued on the wall, and despite the fact that she was sainted for resisting the advances of a man, girls in newly laundered dresses and with new hairdos, before going to dances, fell on their knees in front of her and hands raised high in prayer begged her not to allow them to be shipwrecked in the jostle for a good man on the ballroom floor of their fledgling years.'

Funerals at first seemed to be the only point of contact between my discourses and Raymond's; hearses galloping through the brown marshes of Mayo, hearses, piled with their fill of flowers, languishing through Belfast. But the point of contact widened to an abstract and unstated notion which united us. This house was like the Irish flag. It brought a part of the green and a part of the gold together. It was the peaceable white between. I'd never before spoken at length with someone from the other part of my island. This city with its sleeping November dustbins afforded me the opportunity to do just that. This house was like a cavern of lost history lessons; nuns squawked with news of imminent invasions. In my dreams Raymond kept coming towards me. He came out of the white of the Irish flag. Reflections of water rippling on his face. Cowslips somewhere in the vicinity and the winnowing of the Irish flag sometimes wringing the sound of classical music. He came out of the tender things of my childhood. Like the fluttering of the flag he was caught in the act of motion; the expectation of his arrival was never met by his arrival. He was a part of me caught for years in the act of approaching and with all the attendant vagueness of line that entailed.

'A lad brought me out of a dance one moonlit night and confessed to me his ambition was to be a missionary priest in a Central American republic where the people would have to come to him for advice about revolution and sewers but first he had to do you-know-what with a young lady. So he asked me if I'd oblige him and lift my skirt. I said "No thanks, Father," slapped his face, pushed him into a moonlit brook and wished him luck with the holy revolutions in South America.'

London was the lifting of a weight; it was shuffling the Concise Oxford Dictionary at Maida Vale library; it was acquainting myself with the linear lonely hearts columns; it was paying a visit to a family-planning clinic and having something stuck in me. There I baulked. I returned to 'Elysium' and in the tradition of my mother baked a loaf of brown bread and kept repeating a phrase I concocted for Raymond a few nights previously: 'No white stale bread here as in Central America, Father. No white stale bread here as in Central America, Father.'

Gulls lolled over the grey Edwardian houses as if waiting for white bread. They got graffiti. Some of the graffiti was by my fellow countrymen. 'Life to those who understand and fuck the begrudgers.' My own language had become less auspicious. Black girls were trapped in red telephone kiosks. My children had improvised a see-saw among the syringes outside and I ordered them in once or twice. But there was more than just the grey outside to rescue them from. A creature halfway between the bygone hippie and the punk who was to come a few years later pulled himself along; the backs of Afghan coats had become lathery and polemical ex-public-school boys enlivened the world of Marx with candy-pink shoes. But confronting the grey outside one day I knew I could easily accommodate myself to it and all its ensuing threats; 'for better or for worse' as a green-toothed priest had spat at my white, backswept crown of a veil once—it was to be home.

*Dear Aunt Bethan,*

*I'm living in London now. It's a very grey city but there's also warmth here. You would not expect it at first arriving at Euston Station but it grows on you. It's like lifting a dustbin lid and finding salmon instead of chewed-away kippers. I live in a fine big house. In fact it's not unlike yours. I bought a brooch for you at Portobello market last Friday. I'll keep it to send later as I want to post this now and I'd have to wrap the brooch up. Tibby has taken all the tissue. The children are grand; Mícheál and Tomás are going to school. They learn about worms that enter your bloodstream if you bathe in African rivers which they never learnt at home. I hope you are well. Remember what you once said to me: 'One good lace blouse can be worth more than a marriage.'*

When I went to post that letter the mailbox refused to accept it. Aunt Bethan was a spinster aunt who lived alone in a big house by the river outside Ballina. She was the only one of my relatives I liked. As a child I'd been fascinated by the silver pointed pins in her pouch-like grey velvet hats.

'Why did I leave Belfast? You've got to leave, haven't you? It's one of the laps along the way. What am I going to do now? Don't know. Oh yes.' Raymond was going to say something but stopped. 'Red-brick cottages building into a palace. That's the dream. My father used always to want to eat cornflakes on Coney Island. It was a name that stuck in his head. Me?' Raymond shrugged. 'The funny thing about red-brick cottages under low mountains is that they kill me's.'

My children brought bread and honey to the genii in the lower room as offerings. We visited London Zoo; we visited big stores in which premature Santas had already made an appearance. But Raymond dominated. He never went out. He'd come with the house. He just sat surrounded by books and devouring their contents like a rat. Once or twice in the café of a big department store, a red tartan skirt on me, in sudden exultation I imagined, as in a Hollywood movie, Raymond, the other side of the table, clenching the white and tender part of my wrists mouthing some sublimity that made everyone in the café perk up and listen, his hair falling, a blond fluency—the colour of Raymond's hair fluctuated from dark to fair. But of course he never ventured out to make such a scene real. I'm sure he would have clenched my wrists like that had he come out. Not in any romantic way. We were friends now. Mates.

A gull spiralled into the air above our mansions, a festive eddying of a white uprising streamer. The gull climbed to a point where he could see all London. I had a part-time job now and Raymond when I went out looked after the children.

Raymond did go out. He came with us on our second visit to London Zoo. He wore a crocheted hat over his ears—one of mine—and he pointed to a polar bear on a grey November day and said that he'd always wanted a nose like a polar bear's, a nose that was so solemn and pacific.

I could not fully cope with our relationship on the level of the real so I created the fantastic; anyway our relationship always had buried in it an element of fantasy. I was the girl in the red tartan skirt in the house; he kept coming towards me. I was off to America. The smell of pristine new land, its riverside firs and its sluggish, congenial rivers already in my nostrils. But I was being separated from the boy I loved. For some reason there were always a dozen kegs of beer in the kitchen beside me so the smell of porter invaded the smells of the fir trees and unhurried waters. Raymond was always in white. That was his colour. And his hair was white. My arms were always waiting but he was entranced in a slow, continually revolving motion. I'd woken once or twice to find tears on my rich and ornate Foxford rug.

The winos up the road burned their house down. They came running out in the middle of the night, tails of their coats on fire but bottles of Guinness still outheld. Cormac Fitzmaurice was seen to be waltzing with a hot water jar on the opposite pavement, gurgling to his dancing partner that it was he who'd started the fire. As if to validate his Nero claims his cheeks were smudged in red lipstick and red lipstick daubed his lips. There were red smears on the hot-water jar. But Rome did not burn down that night. Just the house. As he danced Cormac had a litre bottle of whiskey sticking out of his pocket. The label had messages scribbled in red biro on it. A woman with a youngish face, her hair white as a bog cotton under a mauve chiffon scarf, her hands deep in the pockets of her plush whitish coat, then began screaming, affirmedly facing the house, that she was the culprit. A competition ensued between her and Cormac, who'd stopped dancing, the two of them looking at the burning house, Cormac revealing that he'd loved setting houses on fire since he was a child and he'd once incinerated alive an aunt and her two trimmed white poodles in her house in Blackrock, County Dublin. The children claimed they saw three burning rats perched on the roof of that house against the multiple stars and frenzied sparks that night.

A bomb went off in England. It tore through the entrails of the media. Many young people were killed. It ruptured the bowels of consciousness. We picked our way in a different planet for a few weeks. A Pakistani girl at school prodded Mícheál's bum with a compass and venomously informed him he was a murdering Paddy and should return to where he came from. I maintained queenly dignity at work—gracefully mopping floors—bald managers stooped towards me. Well it wasn't me who planted the bomb. What about the beam in your own eye? But the structure of my house was impaired. The landscape of England was transformed. Biting winds were said to have crept down motorways and isolated motorway cafés. A hideous orange light had overtaken everything. It glared in at night. Escaping it I descended to the cellars to try to discover the truth.

'The English invaded Ireland in the twelfth century and they've been a bloody nuisance ever since. They ruined the crops and ransacked convents.' An elderly, fragile nun at school contorted during history lessons. 'Mind you there were some decent Protestants. Theobald Wolfe Tone being one such. To him is the credit of the Irish flag, green, white and gold. Green for Catholic. Gold for Orangeman. White for a true and lasting peace between.' The only orange I saw was the orange of the light outside; it even changed the colour of Raymond's white dotted shirt as he crouched sacrosanctly on the floor. 'Let us all pray, girls, for a United Ireland.' Theobald Wolfe Tone slouched along Sutherland Avenue in an old manky coat, a newspaper cutting dripping from his pocket.

'My mother did not love my father but she married him. My father did not love my mother but he married her. My mother loved me but I was kidnapped by uncles with republican eyes. The annual Wolfe Tone commemoration was a great event. My uncles would get drunk in a nearby pub and start pissing on the other graves. That was the great festive point of the year. Pissing on graves in the cemetery Wolfe Tone was buried in. There was a little bridge over a brook nearby and in a short blue coat I'd run off there. I met a cow there once and we performed a pantomime together while the Wolfe Tone commemoration speeches were being made.'

The odd thing about Raymond was that since this bombing his load had lightened a bit; he'd begun telling foul jokes, he quoted poetry freely. The children loved his telling of stories. He'd got them from a grandmother who lived in a house in the Antrim mountains, he told them.

'My grandmother was Scottish really. She had boots in her voice, black boots. Children, we gathered. Her stories were of ghouls and headless men. She emphasized the blood around the rings of the headless men's necks. As a girl she'd been lifted to and fro on gentle waves by currachs. She was in a different land now and rewarded the natives with monstrosities.'

Where Raymond's granny came from there was a church; a Catholic church. The faith had been preserved there but the statues were unusually bloody. Christs with blood streaming from their wounds, Marys with blood congealed at their hearts and in their heavenward-gazing eyes. Always a story of moving from one place to another, the currachs on gentle waves eventually bringing them to waves of a more turbulent kind.

'There was a giant who lived in a castle on the edge of blackbog.' I became one of the children. I listlessly filed in for Raymond's story. Raymond's granny had made many shirts, embroidered them, so I bought a white shirt, and embroidered it blue for Raymond's birthday. A new shirt. A new human being. We dipped into wine and sang. December the tenth. It was drawing towards Christmas. I didn't send any Christmas cards to Ireland.

Raymond in an off-white embroidered shirt, serious creases in the shirt; his birthday. I had cut his hair, it had solemnized his head; candlelight caught and fiddled with gold locks. Raymond looked out—beyond the swooning candles what did he see? Mexico, Italy, Morocco. It was a time for currachs again but this time currachs would land in uncustomary blue waters.

My children looked as students put up barricades. The state was coming. Charred beams stuck out where the winos' house had been. The battering of hammers went on through the night. The local population of prostitutes, students, heroin merchants was threatened with eviction. The house I shared with Raymond was the only one without barricades. The state was welcome. We knew all about the state.

'Blood, blood in the gutters, blood on white-washed house fronts. Blood on an old lady's handbag. She looked at her bag with sudden disapproval as if the only appropriate thing was that it should fly away. The blood encircled her feet. It eddied under her. She started to scream and then I tried to scream and I couldn't and I woke and I found a rat peering out a hole with much curiosity at me.' Raymond was rambling. There was still an odd quiet hammer going. I'd brought him cocoa. I'd brought it right to his lips. A candle threw panoramic shadows in an Edwardian room. I'd had dreams like that as a girl in Mayo. I'd woken, gone to a window, tried to throw myself out. There seemed no returning from a state of madness. You had broken forever with the laws of logic. The laws that govern and make up everyday living. You had crossed some border into a hell. I suddenly looked into Raymond's pale blue eyes—they were the same colour as the walls in parts of this house—and saw he had broken forever with the logic that governs everyday living and sustains even the vaguest cohesion of a will for everyday survival.

Mícheál, hands behind his back, in a short blue coat, on a black and white day stood beside the charred beams of the winos' house; I went out to retrieve him from a photograph of Leningrad after the siege I'd seen in a book in Maida Vale library.

'Something's drumming in my head. Something's beating it in. I don't own it anymore. It's not mine. Once when I felt like this I used think of my granny as a girl in a red tartan skirt—she kept evil away—but it doesn't work any more. I'll have to think of something different. I can't. I'll think of you, Mary.'

Mary was preparing for Christmas; she was travelling to the perimeter of her mind, shores in West Mayo where mountains were hidden in the evening reflections. Mary in a yellow ochre cardigan began to say a kind of prayer, a prayer different from the ones she was taught. She said prayers for her children, for Raymond. She grappled again for words that were sacred as a child. London revived the glint of evening on mother-of-pearl beads. She found things she thought she had lost forever; it was Advent in London and mistletoe was brought for rides on the Circle line. A black man holding mistletoe opposite her as the tube was drawing towards Westbourne Park told her to cheer up, that Christmas was coming. She looked at him. She had not been doleful. She'd been thinking of anterooms of her existence darkened for years and now lighted by a strange and probing grey light.

Raymond became nervous, shivering. He carried trays about him with teapots on them. He began to act like a manservant, bringing tea to me as I lay in bed on Saturday mornings—the bed had been transported in from a skip by four friendly West Indians. 'Leave it there,' I'd ordered him. Then I'd search out his face. Every day I looked into it I saw something new crashing in it.

'I wanted to say something. I wanted to tell you something. But I couldn't find the words. Words are strange aren't they? They've declared a war on my words. They've tried to take my vocabulary from me.'

The state did not come. The state did not show much interest as yet in the decrepit houses. Students hitched home for Christmas. Prostitutes put their legs up and watched their little yelping TVs.

'I wanted to tell you something. I wanted to tell you something. I wanted to tell you something.' Raymond managed to scream one night but when I tried to put my arms about him he began shuddering; he did not want me to hold him.

Why wasn't he hitching home for Christmas? Why was I devoting so much time to him? I started becoming annoyed with the idea of him. There were some days I wanted to shake him but I was restrained by the presence of a dream: a boy in white and a girl in a red tartan skirt. This house was one I'd visited before. I was familiar with its rooms as I was familiar with its pain; I had come to relieve some of the pain from its big old walls.

Shortly before Christmas a new woman arrived on the street and she made speeches outside at night about the coming of doom; the judgment; the nuclear bomb. She was from Wexford. Somehow forebodings of the nuclear bomb got mixed up one night as she stood in the middle of the road with her autobiography. She was a Protestant. Her father was a vicar in Wexford. Someone had given her a large bottle of whiskey for Christmas and she raised it in the air and shouted, 'Does anyone have any holly? I'm itchy.'

I didn't see Raymond much before Christmas. I was working hard. London, its sea of Christmas, swept about me. Nigerian girls sang carols outside St Martin-in-the-Fields. I wanted to stop and thank them but the crowd was too thick and too onward rushing.

Two days before Christmas a boy in white who looked the image of Raymond passed. His face was tanned. He'd obviously been South. He was all in white except for an Afghan coat. He passed a bird who was snipping at a whole packet of white sliced bread thrown out into a dustbin.

'Hello. How are you?' I entered Raymond's room. He was just sitting there, saying nothing. 'Well Merry Christmas.' Christmas was a day off. Raymond did not want to talk and I closed the door, saying, 'We'll all be having turkey tomorrow night.'

I pushed around London that day; I floated on the crowd, I had no more shopping to do but I just wanted to be part of this intimacy. I belonged now, I was a member of this metropolis and I wanted to share with the crowd the day before Christmas.

Where do Cormac Fitzmaurices and drunk vicars' daughters go for Christmas? There was no one on the street that night. Just a youth passed. A pink chiffon scarf around his neck and his hands enveloped in his pockets and his head worriedly bent over.

I didn't go to midnight mass. With the children I stood at the window and looked in the direction of the church of Our Lady Queen of Heaven in Queensway. I knew I would not be going home again, except for their funerals, not for their marriages. 'Leave father, mother, sisters, brothers, and come follow me.' The half-remembered text of Christ in my mind. I had crossed a border now. There was no going back. My appearance had changed. My face had changed. I had no need of mother or father or sisters or brothers. Or husband. They'd tried to do me in. This city, this unkind sprawl, had given me back a modicum of self-respect and had pointed me on a road again. In the middle of the family-planning clinics and the abortion stopping points Christ was tucked into his crib in a church where winos snoozed and snortled now during midnight canticles.

I'd never been a very extravagant cook but I'd bought the *Times* cookbook and in its pages found the most elaborate Christmas dishes.

Sugar glazed gammon.

Slow roast turkey with chestnut stuffing.

Duchesse potatoes.

Purée of Brussels sprouts.

Apricots with brandy and cream.

Plum pudding with brandy butter.

And something called 'the bishop' on which we all got merry. Hot port with sugar, cloves, lemon and mixed spice.

Raymond in a three-piece dark suit I'd picked up for him hid and spluttered with laughter behind a bottle of Beaujolais nouveau. A fire blazed obligingly. I was wearing a white sleeveless blouse I'd presented to myself for Christmas. Daddy Christmas had abandoned ruminative toys under the Christmas tree. Wooden lorries from Norway. Dolls from Tibet. A reproduction of a Michelangelo print was now tacked uncertainly on the wall, Christ in the nude, rising. Mícheál bawled out a song in the Irish language. Tibby gave us a nursery rhyme in an English accent. Tomás yelled that he wanted more turkey after the final helping of the pudding. In our state of merriment we had party games and party games led to a play Raymond and I did together.

He took off his suit and played me, putting on a dress. I put on his suit. The children loved it. My whole life had been waiting for a play. There'd always been an imminent play. The mass. Ragged, scrawny pageants at school. To perform, to dramatize, the need to do these things, was always in my nature. This was an improvisation. There were no ready-made lines. But the script had been arranged.

Raymond: 'Well now, Mr. What's it you're after?'

Me: 'A nice young lady.'

Raymond: 'Haven't you found one yet?'

Me: 'I've been looking in all kinds of places. I fell in love with a nun but she up and slipped away when she was in my arms. She left a holy medal though.'

The children howled with laughter. But there was also another play taking place.

I have met you before in another time. This city brings other times, past lives together. I know your face. You're part of a shared guilt. We did it together.

I knew something that night I'd suspected for a long time. It slipped out. Beside Tibby Raymond in worn clothes suddenly began laughing and his laughter became drunken and hysterical and then it became crying and then it became screaming. He allowed me to hold him. He was shivering. He kept saying, 'It wasn't me. It wasn't me.'

Raymond: 'The city was orange. We arrived on an orange night. I'd been coming for years. My uncles had babbled on the journey about Gaelic football and heroes that had scored points in County Down years before. I'd heard all this before. I'd grown up with it.

There were many things I tried to do in my lifespan to be free of this babble. Read. Tried art school. Dabbled with self-portraits. But something always drew you into the smoky circle. The funereal voices, the faces contemplating the cards. It was as if there wasn't a you, couldn't be a you until you'd done something terrible to atone for an unknown past. Besides there were rungs on a ladder. Trying to be different wasn't easy. Trying to get out was impossible. We arrived and walked from the boat through the orange lights. My uncles had a slip of paper that was soiled with Guinness and tobacco. It was an address in this city. A woman answered. Her face was a skull in the orange light. I was the one who was going to place the device. In a Derry accent she to me, "Sure you have the face of a ewe."'

An outrage was done in this house once. A young woman separated from a young man. The female part of a person separated from the male. The childhood part of the person separated from the adult. The creative from the social. One part of a country was amputated from another.

Raymond was in my bed when they clambered in. It was six in the morning. I'd been lying awake; Raymond there, turned towards me. His face, his cold white body like a ewe's all right. We had not made love. Just slept together under a large multicoloured Tinker's shawl of a Foxford rug. One of the men from the anti-terrorist squad took up a position alongside us. He was squat and gruff. I'd been expecting them. 'Merry Christmas,' I said and one young fellow threw himself against the door, facing us with a revolver.

*Dear Aunt Bethan,*

*I'm nearly ten years in London and there's a lot I want to say to you. The reason I'm writing is because I passed the street the other day. There are brand-new council flats there, regimented ones. Raymond's been in jail now nearly ten years. It wasn't anything like a large bombing he'd been responsible for. A small and almost forgotten one. He writes poetry in prison now and some of his poems appear in republican papers. They mistake the images of doves as symbols of a struggle for a free Ireland. Needless to say I've polished my accent since. I did a secretarial course and am in quite luxurious employment as a secretary. The council long ago re-housed me and Mícheál and Tomás and Tibby. I'm a nice polite middle-class person now. Well almost. Mícheál is bigger than I am. He's grown to the ceiling. He teaches me things* about ancient Egypt and ancient Greece. Tibby wears tight pink satin jeans. I'm writing really to commemorate and celebrate coming to this city. I've kept my word. I never went back to Ireland. We wait here in our comfortable lodgings for the nuclear bomb, mushroom cloud, whatever, but in the meantime have a good time. There are lots of laughs, lots of celebrations but the laughter is innermost and most intense when I think of him in the corridors of his prison and I think of the cells of his poetry, now like Easter lilies they grow until they fill my mind and I want to appeal to the prime minister or the queen on his behalf, saying it wasn't his fault; it was other people. It was the pre-ordained. There'd been no one around to salvage his sanity at the time. But I know they would not listen to me so instead I try to teach my children what this city taught me: love. Yes, Aunt Bethan, love will bring us through the night of the nuclear bomb and the onset of middle age. It will bring us through the nights when the children and the people have gone. There was a night of accord once, a night of simplicity and that makes up for an awful lot, doesn't it?

# The Vicar's Wife

I

1959 was the year Joly won the local beauty competition and the year Colin came down from Trinity as a Teddy-boy vicar, a bouncing limousine of black hair in front of his forehead. 1959 was the year in which everything dangled precipitously on a scales, past and future, the end of things, the initiation of other things. There was something fearful about the things beginning. It was the year Joly and Colin met and became lovers.

There was such a mind-boggling difference in their backgrounds that their pairing didn't so much cause anger as a kind of earthquake; Barna Craugh's earthquake, 1959, the narrow roadway of Bin Lane opened and devoured a lady or two who had to walk up this disreputable lane because it connected the church with their part of town. Off Bin Lane Joly had been born. 'Born brown-haired!' people pronounced over and over again. Because now her award-winning curls were a cheeky peroxide blonde. It was her tits that had got her the prize, uncouth and bellicose farm labourers insisted. Her breasts were very large and she didn't try to sunder their largeness. It was those breasts the vicious and the jealous swore to themselves had attracted the attention of Vicar Colin Lysaght. Although much of the ultimate version was that he'd picked up a Catholic rose and transformed her into a black Protestant nettle. Joly Ward converted to Protestantism to marry the Teddyboy vicar.

The house was the most immeasurable leap for her; the house she moved into. It changed her automatically, from beauty queen to dark-haired, demure Protestant wife. That was the first word that came to her in the house. Fear filled her to a point at which she thought she was going to explode with it. But she kept silent. Shadows wrapped around her, twisted around her, shadows of dark banisters. Joly was in a house in the country, suffocated by gardens and by trees.

The wedding had been a pantomime, a joke, mainly lizard-like, old eccentric vicars at it, a flotsam of young ex-Trinity students. Ascendancy heirs rushed at champagne glasses, young men in snap-pily white shirts and in dark, casually askew jackets. There was a quick snow of champagne on a number of young, nearly-black moustaches. Joly was a proof of a Protestant sense of humour, a tes-timony to Irish eccentric Protestantism's ability to laugh at itself. She was in the line of a tradition of jokes; that day a dummy in white, an unwitting foible. Young Ascendancy men gauged her breasts in her wedding dress with their eyes. But her own family didn't look at her. They, to a man, did not come to the wedding. There was no Catholic there.

If she thought of it afterwards there were mainly men there and what women were there seemed to be stuffed into rag-doll textures of garments; their faces when you went close were blanks, their eyes didn't look at you. They looked through you. They were the faces of the dead.

Dead. There was death in this house. A subtle, omnipresent whine. She remembered the Catholic Church's teachings about pur-gatory but this house had more the reverberations of hell. No pos-sible escape within the mood of the house. Both Colin's parents were dead, Colin's father himself having been a vicar. She touched a ban-ister on her first arrival as Colin's wife—Colin hadn't let her see the house up to then—clinging to it for a moment, in a blue, matronly dress, for life. She knew that moment she had lost all worlds, the world of home, and the world of frivolous, combative youth.

Joly had gone against the grain from the time she was a little girl. Decked out in her holy communion costume, a veritable foun-tain of a veil, Joly had stampeded towards an obese member of the local town council, a very respectable man, his collar open, and plied him—successfully—for a russet money bill. She developed a relationship with this man, himself unmarried. At public functions, a St Patrick's Day parade, the crowning of the king of the fair, she always managed to get money out of him, a little prostrate flag of hair on the otherwise bald top of his head. It was unheard of, a relationship between a member of the town council and a child from Bin Lane. As a member of the town council you could be beneficiary for the sons and daughters of army colonels, of shopkeepers, of police superintendents. But not for a child from Bin Lane. Children from Bin Lane might as well have been squirrels with a contagious disease to the respectable people of town, and tawdry, unkempt squirrels at that. You could approach them, cautiously, at Christmas, with presents, in your annual symbol of generalized support for the Vincent de Paul.

A man on the local council and Joly; a photograph in the local press. Without a jacket, the man in a white shirt, his face round like a balloon, a meteor of a smile on his face, apple flushes on his cheeks. He looked quixotically retarded. It was this photograph which was the marked beginning of Joly's break with her own world and of her steep rise to stardom, notoriety and to the social grazing area of old, beak-nosed parsons. It had been a passport for her, her countenance in the photograph full of knowingness.

In 1959 she won the local beauty competition. The events that went into this success were manifold. Joly had won a scholarship to the convent secondary school, the first girl from Bin Lane to have done so. But the nuns at convent school immediately rejected her. She smelt, despite 'her brains' as they put it, raw. They had to admit the 'brains'. Joly seemed to be able to wriggle her way around any problem and she was able to come out with all sorts of information, adding even to the nuns' store of general knowledge. But she made them baulk. She was shameless in her gait. And it was this shamelessness combined with her nearly always manifest mental ability which made her such a special beauty queen for Barna Craugh. Her hair dyed blonde she'd turned down a secretarial job with a 'top-notch' firm of solicitors in Dublin to participate in the contest. It was both a joke and a gamble for her. A joke within the vocabulary of the effervescent way she looked at life—all rampant blonde curls and daring scarlet lips—and yet an ironic intellectual thumb in every joke. Was anything worth it really? The job in Dublin she turned down to parade herself in a beauty contest. It riled her family, her decision almost caused a revolution among them. They thought they had one member so near to success! And if it was a gamble for her it more than paid off. It seemed to bring her much further than any job with a solicitor in Dublin—after a brief secretarial course—could have done. It landed her in an altogether different stratum of society. She felt like Judy Garland when *The Wizard of Oz* turned from black and white into Technicolor. Her hair turned back to brown at the same moment and all her features, as well as her converted soul, seemed to become demure and tentative and Protestant. She merged perfectly with the landscape of the rural, grey, elongated house.

There was more to Joly's sudden fame in 1959 than the winning of the beauty contest. Winning the beauty contest would not, in fact, have been spectacular in itself. Given her unusual personality as well as her sharply striking looks she got a series of national offers after winning the contest. Her face was in a ladies' magazine, advertising the luscious red lipstick she liked so much. In another advertisement her blonde curls sported a hat which looked like a pink sandcastle. She was a bride in the most widely admired advertisement photograph. And that was appropriate enough. For Colin Lysaght saw the photograph and it was as if he picked the bride from the image as he would a bit of resplendent apple blossom. They were married in May 1960. Joly, though not in any way having been persuaded to, renounced Catholicism and became a Protestant to marry the delectable youth of a vicar and be an acceptable vicar's wife.

The morning she married, the nuns in her former school had the girls there send up shoals of prayers for her soul as if she had been their penultimately prize pupil, now having made a staggering fall.

Colin had been living in a town house beside the railway station since his father's death. After the wedding he brought Joly to the rural vicarage which had been industriously painted for weeks. It had been a secret. Now the secret unfolded. There was death and an ancient stagnation in the Teddyboy vicar.

What had she really known about him? Very little. She looked at gravestones in a nearby field the following autumn. Ignat Lysaght. An ancestor of Colin's. She was pregnant with a Protestant child. She was carrying the continuity of a contorted history inside her.

Autumn was the greatest wonder in this house; the greatest torrent of Technicolor in the house, apple on apple creeping across the lawn and gardens, all different in colour, some a hue of luminous gold, others more scarlet, more vermilion, apples very often a garish and unexpected clown's-cheek rouge. A gold too went into the green of the lawn, the gardens and the surrounding countryside, all of which had been a very dark and peculiar green throughout the summer. Tinkers' caravans in the backlanes had nestled in this green, taken a silent refuge among the green. Very few Tinkers seemed to emerge from the caravans and if they did they were archaic faces, very often male faces, that met you silently and seemed stranded on the roadway. All was atavistic here, skeletons were suggested very close to the surface in graveyards and frequently there were bones to be seen on graves, tussled among the clay. They would be strange sights for a child.

All summer long Joly had got to know her husband and herself better.

She'd looked in a mirror and had been amazed at the physical change in herself. She'd got plumper, more demure; her eyes seemed haunted by aspects of this house and of her husband's behaviour. She'd been made to seem meek in her demeanour by what she'd come to realize. Her husband, for all his Teddyboy looks, was one of the sequence of shapes of an ogre from the deepest past. He'd been contaminated and made violent by the past. That summer, before she became pregnant, he began to beat her up and the beatings continued after she discovered she was pregnant. She was in a prison. She could not go back. She had to stay where she was, with, for the moment, just one other cell mate.

Colin's face had changed once he'd got into the house; from a protruding frigate of an adolescent face it became debauched in appearance, mean, curdled. The lips, especially, looked dehydrated. With this life-despising change came the news of new life. News of new life came, it later seemed, with a solitary visit by Joly to a dark church with one, Technicolored, stained-glass window.

But, despite change in Colin, the church she'd been received into was still a statement for her; it was a statement of surrender of old values, the values of a totalitarian premiss on life, and the choosing of something new; something more liberated, something that gave her many choices; she was a Protestant by choice, a keeper of sentinel rows of geraniums, luminous in the mellifluous, vicarage, autumn sun.

She wore black a lot at Christmas. By then she'd accepted Colin's change of personality. The funny thing was that in the atmosphere of this house, in entry into this house, she was not surprised by the change in Colin. The source was a mystery to her, the emanation of this house. She was fighting with it. She served sherries to dried, old, outstretched, Protestant fingers that Christmas.

The baby was born in April. A boy. He came with medieval-Annunciation-painting trees of apple blossom, little celebratory bolls of apple blossom. She gave birth to the child in Barna Craugh's one hospital, a Catholic hospital, and a nun, in white, eyed her threateningly, her eyes saying that for this child's sake, if not for your own, pull back from the abyss. Audoen was baptized a Protestant child in a ceremony by a rural font. A wash of pale, hallucinatory May light came through the Technicolored window. Colin's face was alarmingly drained that day. He'd been ranting to himself in the nights previously. Another vicar, called into this parish especially, performed the ceremony.

Colin, in these days, had given himself over to Joly, asking for compassion, saying he was ill, that he had a disease, that his own father had treated his mother appallingly, that violence was rampant in male members of his family, that it was a rancid gene in the family. He was a boy in her arms now at night, the little boy who'd been cradled by other boys in a posh, Protestant school in Dublin, the little boy who'd dreamt of the Dublin Horse Show at night among evangelically laundered sheets.

In May 1966, when Audoen was five years old, he was run over on the road near the vicarage and killed. By then Joly had two more children. Colin was no longer a Teddyboy. There was a decrepit grey on the edges of his hair. For the funeral another vicar did not have to be brought in. It took place in Barna Craugh, which was part of another diocese, though close to the rural one where Colin presided. Audoen was buried in the Protestant part of Barna Craugh cemetery. Colin, face anaemic and blanched, bawled at the funeral. The faces of the women of Barna Craugh peered out from a dusk of their own in the cemetery. Justice had been done. God had punished this woman. But by then the teachings of the Ecumenical Council were creeping through and there wasn't as much gloating about the event as there might have been. Joly's marriage, bound together by children and a stoic compassion, was breaking up. The only thing that held it now was wonder on Joly's part at Colin's personality, wonder as to how such violence as she'd known and continued to experience could have insinuated itself so readily into a frame as aesthetically pleasing and as, almost shockingly, susceptible to the senses as Colin's had been. He'd had a pale adolescent face you could almost eat. But that face, the good looks, had been a mask.

The little rural hell was seven years old when she left Colin. On the day she got a taxi to the station from the centre of Barna Craugh she heard someone sing a refrain from 'O Lady of Spain I Adore You' on the main street. Her two children went with her. Colin had beaten her senseless with the leg of a chair a few nights previously, a leg from a chair which, before attacking her, he'd attacked, thus extracting the leg. She had bruises all over her on the main street the day she left. A woman looked closely at her, almost sympathetically. The bruises on Joly's face were like the marks of napalm. The bruises on her psyche from the vicar and from the town were worse and more enduring, as she was to find, than any television-screen napalm could suggest.

2

Comely Bank Grove, Edinburgh, was the address that she moved into with Midge, the Polish truck driver. She'd previously been living with a friend, from her school days, in Dundee. The friend had emigrated halfway through convent secondary education and the two girls had kept in touch. Joly's friend had not married, not wanted to marry. She nursed Joly, with a sense of vocation, for five years. There was a speechless communication between them, a distance, but sometimes in that distance bolts of desire from Joly's friend. But silent and ultimately stagnant bolts. The woman was so beholden to Joly for company, for purpose in life, that she even looked after Joly's children when Joly began going out with Midge. By then Barna Craugh was far away. Joly was a tart again, raspberry lipstick on her and her hair curled now, looking black rather than brown. Their most exotic occasions, hers and Midge's, were Chinese meals on Saturday nights in a Chinese restaurant among an industrial estate by the sea. Joly picked up bits of a Polish accent which she interspersed with her new Scottish accent.

Her children were Finn and Bríd. When eventually she moved in with Midge they might as well have been his children, judging by the ease of their appearance with him as they all sat around a table, joined in a meal. There was a conspiracy of pretences. But they all knew they were followed, by the sense of the children's father, by the inchoate hurt of Joly's friend. When she departed nothing in her mind had prepared her for Joly's departure. She even thought that by making it easy for Joly to see Midge she'd further strengthen her bond with Joly. But Joly went when Midge bought a house for a cheap price and there was a cocoon for her, her children, her relationship with Midge and her own confusion about herself and her past.

Not a day went by when she didn't try to unravel her relationship with Joly Ward, the multiple Joly Wards, the woman who had broken so many hearts and left so much patternless debris.

Ireland in Midge's mind was the country of grandiose scenery that they'd both seen in *Ryan's Daughter* in Dundee and Joly did not wish to disillusion him. For him she was haunted by the lofty tourist-brochure scenery that had something unexpectedly malevolent stuck in it. He did not realize and she never informed him that she came from flat land, nothing like the scenery of *Ryan's Daughter*. To have betrayed this would have been to betray a secret. You always had to keep secrets from lovers. However safe you felt with them you were also, always, on the run and you couldn't give too much away. In fact, even in love, you had to invent a pose rather than give your real self away. This was how Joly felt with Midge. Happy but incomplete. At worst an over-made-up character in a pantomime. A rather idiotic character, lots of lipstick on, her neck moving around in a kitchen, to the rhythm of a conversation, like a gander's neck, a half-wit's smile on her face.

The black, almost funereal doors of Edinburgh; mystery. Joly walked alone on winter nights when rain beat on these doors. She paused in front of these doors, staring at them in a nebulous gesture. What did they remind her of? Of the door of a vicarage, painted gleaming black. Of a brass knocker with a Cupid at its nub. Of a demure, dignified vicar's wife. Of the choice of hers to love a strange man. Colin. She was still under the spell of love for him. There was still a romantic yearning in her for a young cleric in black, with a Teddyboy flop of hair on front of his forehead; there was still a belief in her that the purity of this young man still existed. It only had to come to the surface, through complex effort and through earnest search. The past, the black bits of it, could be dispelled. The black bits in Colin came from a general blindspot in his ancestry. He only had to go through it, walk through it to the other side. Easier said than done. But everything was possible. She knew then he was searching for her. She wondered would he catch up on her. There were two persons in her now, the person who wanted him to find her and the tart who, partly out of laziness, wished to be without him. These parts of her were at war.

There was a war going on in Ireland. The rain here waged a war in sympathy to the mood of the war in Ireland. People rebuffed Joly for this war, mainly women. Irish. Irish had a dirty ring these days. Bodies. Mutilations. The bomb that surprised you from under your restaurant seat. Joly had to undergo the ritual of demoralization, because of the race she was from, again and again. Made to do so by people who understood nothing of Ireland or nothing of history. The incessancy of this eventually caused the straight beauty queen figure to look pinched, to have a hint of middle age in it.

The year Joly came to look middle aged she went south with Midge in his truck, on one of his journeys, through Yugoslavia to Greece and back.

The oxen in the fields, the peasant women, the rain of sun on the readiness of corn; renewal. Marigolds in a vase in a café in Belgrade, oh so lucid white wine in carafes on the shelf. Outside a man sweeping up a searing dash of yellow ochre leaves. The smell from those leaves; what did it remind her of? A vicarage. The first time she'd ever really experienced autumn.

She'd been a gauche girl before knowing autumn, but autumn, the smell of the leaves, of the opaque-gold apples, of the rain-haggard dwarf dahlias opened her to many other things; a view of life that transcended anything she'd known before. Autumn, a vicarage in the autumn, was history. It was a symbol of the subjugation of the land she came from. Remorse in some people who'd subjugated that land turned to terror, terror on wife, son, terror on self. Colin's father had committed suicide.

That floret of information was kept to the very end; squeezed tight in Colin's pale hands all those years. Colin's father had beaten him, tried to debilitate him in every way. The young man she'd encountered, who'd just come down from Trinity, was a temporarily escaped version of Colin, Colin after a few years of exuberance and oblivion. But there was the Colin tied to family. The demon Colin. History, family history, had not been worked through in Colin. And he took this inability to cope with what his father had tried to do with him out on Joly. In a kind of loyalty to his father he was crazed with his wife. There was a kind of metamorphosis that occurred late in the Lysaght night. Not only the suicide of Colin's father was lived over and over again in Colin but the vicious instincts which led to the suicide. Something was alive in Colin. A family ogre, a bogey man, untrammelled evil itself. Joly was to have been the cure for the evil, her peroxide curls were the bait, but she too became a victim to the evil. She left. But there was something she'd done. She'd set an erratic process of redemption in motion in Colin. She'd initiated a humility in his eyes. They were eyes she nearly saw telepathically in moments of intensity in a kitchen in Edinburgh when the music was uncharacteristically evocative on Radio 2.

3

Colin Lysaght had had a favourite toy when he was a child. A horse, white, with a scarlet drape on it. The horse had lain in a garden behind the house, inanimate there, striking against the verdure, always reassuring in its subliminal inanimateness.

This had been one of the few tokens of peace when he'd been a child. His father, Vicar Lysaght, outwardly a piece of genteel grey, his frame sometimes seeming to have been festooned in apple-tree lichen, had catatonic, totally transforming fits behind the doors and windows of the vicarage. He used to beat his wife, his son, lock his son in the nursery for hours with just a little, overfilled chamber pot for company, and a long-redundant playpen. Once Colin noticed apple blossom against a blue sky outside the nursery when he was locked in it and knew he'd escape some day.

Trinity College, Dublin; what fun. Colin was one of the brightest and the most popular of the students. Although following in his father's footsteps to be a vicar he headed some of the wildest of forays from Trinity, to the mountains, the sea, to dungeons of flats where bodies eventually twinned, in a sort of inveterate way. Colin was the rock and rolling would-be vicar, he led a dance once in a marquee, in his black clerical clothes, his oiled and extravagant hair as black. The idea of being a vicar seemed a clever extension of and a foil to being a rock and roll dancer. But still Colin passed all examinations with distinction and was ordained a vicar. He came down to Barna Craugh, just in time to meet Joly in her hour of success. The marriage was perfect, between the rock and roll vicar and the Bin Lane Marilyn Monroe. A few months before Colin was ordained a vicar though, his father had committed suicide and the impact of this event was still subsumed in rock and roll music as was the death of Colin's mother at the end of Colin's first year at Trinity. These events took their toll—after the wedding photographs.

## 4

Shortly after Joly left Colin gave up the trappings of being a vicar and went away himself, to Dublin, where he got a job teaching divinity and English literature in a boys' Protestant school. The black clerical clothes were exchanged for a characteristic chestnut sportscoat. The grey edges arbitrarily went from Colin's hair and it all became a subdued black, more curls in it, more divides. The vicarage had in fact belonged to the Lysaght family. So had a house in Barna Craugh. There was a complicated deal made whereby if they were sold most of the money went to the diocese where Colin and his father had functioned as vicars. Colin sold both houses. He got a small part of the price but what, for the needs of his life now, was a substantial amount of money. He banked most of that money for a secret, long-term plan. In Dublin he rented a second-floor flat in Terenure, near the school where he taught. He merged into his environment, becoming a leading member in the local branch of the Anti-Apartheid Movement, and of Amnesty International. He protested outside rugby pitches where South African teams played. He was photographed, looking distraught on these occasions, among the melée outside rugby pitches, by *The Irish Times*. He became a familiar protester on the front page of *The Irish Times*. Few people could have realized that this mellifluous-faced, rather autumnal-looking young man had been a wife-beater, in fact a wife-torturer. Colin shelved his secret on the neon-lit, late 1960s and early 1970s Dublin night. He bellowed protests at South Africans. He held a red flag against the sky outside the American embassy—the red was in fact part of a batik depicting Vietnamese blood, not the red of a communist flag. The October sun eddied through the batik in Ballsbridge. Flower children followed Colin, a line of Protestant, middle-class girls who had long, Pre-Raphaelite, blonde hair and who wore long, fussily floral dresses. Colin became a perfect child of his time and environment.

But he never stopped thinking of Joly and of his children: alone at night in a flat in Terenure, among the sheets soiled with haphazard, bachelor discharges, close to the socks that looked well during the day but smelt at night. In his bedroom the Dublin suburban night came in, the mountains—he kept the curtains always open—and excavated his mind. There were two Colin Lysaghts. The one he was running from. And the one he was now. But each time he imagined Joly both seemed to merge, in contrition. He knew he had to see her again. But he knew the risk of a journey to her. He had sanity in the covert-self he was now. Maybe he'd lose that sanity when he saw her. Anyway he didn't know where she was other than that she was in Scotland. He couldn't confront her family. So the years drifted until he had a letter from Joly. She wrote to say she needed to divorce him, to marry a Polish truck-driver.

5

Two people confronted in a kitchen in Edinburgh.
Colin said: 'Don't worry. I'm different.'
Joly said nothing.
Colin said: 'It's been hard. Being without you.'
Joly said nothing.
Colin said: 'The children?'
Joly said: 'They'll be in later.'
Colin said: 'Joly, I love you.'

Joly looked at him. She knew her face had become hard. She said nothing. She was the aged one. He was the younger one. There was almost a visible passage of bitterness, of sarcasm, through her face and then she knew that that wasn't worthy of this encounter and she softened. 'I'll make tea.'

She meandered almost drunkenly towards the stove. Scarlet print on a calendar told her it was August 1979.

The children came in later, Finn, Bríd, teenagers. Bríd was in emerald. Idiotically Colin thought she looked like an overgrown child in an Irish dance costume. There was no ambiguity about Finn's dress. He had metal earrings and his hair shot up in black, electric protest. Colin felt there should be a mediator, a talcum-haired priest from Ireland, a Reverend Mother from a local, prison-looking school, to negotiate them into some accord with one another; he made an erratic and abortive attempt to rise. But Finn saved the day. In heavy, working-class Scottish accent he said, 'Da, you've nearly axed yourself shaving.' Colin had badly cut his face shaving that morning.

Midge had gone. He'd left a month before. Having come to England in his early twenties he'd driven back to Poland. His mother was still in Warsaw and Warsaw, before his planned marriage in Edinburgh, got the better of him. He had to return there. He'd take it all, soldiers, police, everything for the sake of wholeness missing in his life for twenty-five years and for a kind of harvest-dream of Warsaw. He bade goodbye to Joly and the children and drove a company truck east to Warsaw, on an authorized errand, but this time he was going to stay. All that was left of Poland now were obsessive jars and jars of paprika and a picture of a Polish Christ. That picture made Colin think his wife and children were fervent Catholics now.

A working-class Edinburgh woman looked at a daintily dressed Dublin teacher. The social chasm was even wider and more perplexing than when they'd married. Colin looked like a harmless, over-trained chimpanzee now, all bones and angles. A woman, standing, looked at him, amazed at the scene that was happening. The children stared at him with convoluted stares as if they'd been expecting him all their lives and now that he'd arrived the epiphany was a curiosity more than a major event. Each time Colin opened his mouth now he shut it very quickly again, without saying anything. Joly suddenly remembered the seas of flagrant furze in the fields around the vicarage in spring.

6

It was her family she'd had to fight more than Colin then. They'd never imagined she'd made any really fundamental decision without consulting them, without involving them— they saw her as irritating them, driving them into furies. But when the moment came when Joly parted from them and became a Protestant they became petrified in their speech. It was unheard of, an Irish Catholic girl becoming a Protestant. An Irish Catholic girl acting on her own volition. An Irish person breaking from the rules, the taboos of their family. An Irish person going it alone, without their tribe. You could have tiffs, yes, but fleeing your family ... May God forgive her.

Joly had shaped a solitude inside herself in a society not made for solitude. She could hear their rancour in the vicarage gardens, their screams of bellicose outrage came to her ears. But she left these things some way outside her and resolved on going further on her own way, on plunging deeper into her perdition. Perdition took her to Scotland, to Edinburgh, to a kitchen where she'd tried to lock up all the pain of Ireland and throw it away. But she couldn't help arguing with them, taking them on in a mental wrestling match during an afternoon women's programme on radio, venting her opinions of them on them. They'd done everything in their power to destroy her, to strip her of her sensibility and make her one of them. This was what was left of the battle, this still outraged shell, this shell through which visible shivers of anger often went. They'd tried to divest her of everything that was her personality, besieging her in the vicarage. Yes she knew they were out there. And perhaps that sense of siege added unsteadiness to Colin's unhinged state. The vibrations going between Joly and her family, the smoke signals of livid argument. Something of what had happened in the vicarage was Joly's fault. There was a battle pressed inside her, a battle she couldn't share with him because he was one of the main reasons for the battle. She couldn't give them any success by having him drawn into the argument. They thought, ultimately, she was less than him. She couldn't let him know she feared that also. She couldn't let their stinking thoughts pollute her relationship with him. But in resisting them, in keeping them at bay, in the frozen stance she adopted any time she considered anything to do with them she offset something in Colin; whining choirs of his own hereditary demons. Their mutual demons met in the vicarage and created an abysmal furore, sometimes at the top of the stairs when, late at night, she and Colin looked in one another's eyes. The aspect of her blame, blame for what she'd brought to the vicarage, was one she'd always ignored. She too had an insanity caused by family. There had been a hole in her head, too. A transfixed void in her eyes. Two mad people couldn't have gone on living together and she left Colin, not without first having driven him to beat her, to flail his arms at her. She just hadn't been capable of response to his demons. So preoccupied and, in a way, in love had she been with her own. She'd failed the trusting Teddyboy. She'd gone away, carrying a further retinue of self-right-eous wounds, from Ireland, edified by her own sense of wounds. Now, the wounds had come full circle and encountered his wounds again. This time she knew she'd made the central wound in his life. She'd failed, totally, to drive away the dark in him. She'd been a bit of blonde mischief that had failed to understand the trust he was put-ting in her. He'd totally surrendered himself to her and all she'd done was look over his shoulder, arguing with the spectres of her family. The arms, legs, torso of a Teddyboy vicar, naked then, had counted for nothing, this show of tenderness, as against confrontation with a tribe, drawn up in battle ranks by a bedroom door. Privacy had been impossible between Colin and Joly. History and family had not allowed them privacy. But at least they'd stolen one or two pages from an epoch and danced together, before marriage, at an October fair, a couple, a marriage of opposites, beauty queen and vicar, an ikon—the ikon warmed by browns and golds, taking a bronze light from a marquee floor, shelving an image in a village mind, in a perpetuity of images. Together, ironically, Colin and Joly enhanced history. They were, that night, dancing to Buddy Holly, an atavistic reference point to which people would always return, in spite of themselves. They were a source of mystery, something of history and yet that broke with history. They were initiators. What came after didn't matter so much. They'd broken new ground together and as such would always have an odd craving for one another, be in default without one another. They were, in a strange way, one.

How he could have done those things to her he didn't know. They were all a strange dream in him now. In her arms, in bed, all the people he'd been since spiralled through him, the roles. The only reality was her face and body. He touched that face and body. His hands were no longer anointed hands. They had no special powers. They were no longer cursed. They retreated from her with a sense of redemption. He looked at them in amazement, as if he was seeing them for the first time. They, he and Joly, were starting right from the beginning. No demon in his past was telling him he had to be a vicar, was entrancing him into perpetuating this role in the family. He'd shed the need for this role. Joly was no longer the vicar's wife.

7

A new term in Dublin; a new direction in Colin's thoughts, a new countenance on him. He meditated more. He slumped into meditation at school, a chestnut-coloured jacket still on him. He'd journeyed from a Protestant, middle-class, Dublin experience to a house in Edinburgh where there was a woman he'd created in a way, a strange product of Ireland. There were so many lines on her face, so many. Lines further emphasized by a cloth she'd worn on her head a few times; amid the lines an always fresh swipe of strawberry lipstick. This had been his spouse. And his children? They were more like a brother and sister to the mellifluous-looking hulk of a man who'd crossed forty with an adolescent haze still around him. He had to deal with the new image of Joly, Joly with a penetratingly direct stare in her eyes. Joly as a very lonely woman, a sentinel of a woman in the middle of a kitchen.

Colin dragged his feet around Dublin; crimson autumn suns over the Ha'penny Bridge temporarily immobilized him. The way he dragged one of his feet that autumn he looked lame. And he also looked a bit hunch-backed. He was weighed down. Weighed down by what he'd done. By the rather awesome vision of Joly standing in the middle of a kitchen, something grandiose about her, something haunting, like the way a lighthouse on the west coast of Ireland, during early-winter twilight, haunted. Joly was total unto herself. She created a sense of scenery wherever she went. And it was this loneliness that made him love her again, made him want her, maybe out of guilt, made him want to protect the wounded frame of her, reach his arms about it. So correspondence began again and, from Dublin, supplications. They wrote to one another like teenage pen-pals, from two totally different backgrounds and aware of the different backgrounds. Except now the different backgrounds were Dublin middle class and Edinburgh downbeat working class. Joly agreed to visit Colin. She came at Christmas, a year and a half after he visited her, and stayed with him in the flat in Terenure, sleeping with him, a rather distant, very erect, somewhat pinched-looking middle-aged woman whom he met on a railway platform after she'd come from Belfast, lots of make-up on her and her hands on a handbag in front of a claret coat. She looked initially like some child's aunt from Barna Craugh; she was, ironically, a face from the main street of that town but with the days the reserve, the austerity, the fear even went and something trying to get out of Joly for years re-emerged, at first tokens, a Barna Craugh rasp in the accent, the desert-storm of freckles on the face becoming suddenly plainer—it was the beauty queen. With passion Joly became younger, vulnerable. She was going into marriage with Colin Lysaght again. In a state of vulnerability, of protective layers thrown away, she was stepping out of her world and going into Colin's again. She was leaving children and the intermediary years of exile, of flight behind. She was returning to a country that had changed, exposing herself to that country again.

She didn't know what she was doing with this man who had in a way ruined her life, walking down O'Connell Street with him, but there seemed to be an inevitability, an order about them being together; this time he was the protector, he was the guide of an innerly crippled person; he was bound to her by guilt. Such were the vicissitudes of life she thought, passing a go-go dancing model in Clery's window, that people should merge into a marriage again, brought about by guilt in one partner, now healed and whole, over the last marriage. Such was the ongoing nature of a lunatic marriage and maybe they had to find love in it to make it easier for both of them. The beauty queen and the vicar might not prove such a bad match after all.

But what immediately kept Joly going, down O'Connell Street, was fascination with the person beside her, the difference in him, the wholeness. A hurricane had gone through him and created a new person. There was ultimately, as in the first marriage, amazement and humility that this person should be interested in her. A recognition of her roots in Bin Lane and a renewed vision of them breaking from her in a flurry of distraught Easter doves, which made everything all right, pain, exile, solitude. Ultimately she was the little girl from Bin Lane who broke the rules and won, however it was done, however afflicted was the course in doing it, the heart of the obese and beaming town councillor. For the renewed hallucination of doves tearing away from an inchoate source, for the life-reinvigorating sensation of it—probably the same sensation young people in Edinburgh got from sniffing glue—she returned to Ireland. She groped her way back blindly. And the person who met her again was equally blind in guilt and in grief, looking over her shoulder at Amiens Street Station and seeing the person he knew she would obliterate forever this time, his father hanging from a roof beam. Or would she? Either way that image was subdued now, like an old war-flag in a Protestant church. He kissed her and asked her about the children she'd left in Scotland. It was spring. Three months since he'd last seen her. He took her baggage and carried it towards their new life together, an arc of light in the rainy sky you could see through the station bar window, like a strand of grey hair over the eye.

## 8

Colin gave up his job and purchased a gate-lodge in the countryside near the vicarage, with money left over from selling the vicarage and the Lysaght town house. He got a job, after some training, on a forestry near the gate-lodge. A new job for him, one that initially amazed the locals. Then they let him be. Joly went back to live near the town she grew up in, still very much a Protestant, growing nasturtiums, geraniums, chrysanthemums, goldenrod, marrows, braving the country that tried to destroy her. She didn't let it destroy her again. She didn't let it in on her. A new flush came to Colin's cheek. They seemed happy, an odd pair who didn't mix much, alone in a gate-lodge in a countryside of ghosts, ghosts of rural vicarages, of eccentric, set-back Ascendancy mansions that now looked out on thriving Free State forestry plantations, on the cars that sped on these backroads, bringing young couples to discos, on the nerve of change at last in this atavistic and laden green air.

When a statue of the Virgin Mary by a roadway was reckoned to have moved there was no hullabaloo, just smiles, and Joly was reminded of the time as a child she dressed up as Our Lady of Fatima for local children and played that part, in a shed, appearing on a stage of fragile boards. When this image returned to her she knew she'd changed once more; it was autumn, the nasturtiums ran through the garden in glittering rivers; a sort of miracle had happened; the Catholic and Protestant parts of her had merged as she remembered a very jocose Our Lady of Fatima, her veil slipping off, her hands joined in prayer and redcurrant, gleaming lipstick smeared on her lips that, try as they could, couldn't hold back a luscious, cherubic smile.

# Miles

'Miles from here.' A phrase caught Miles's ear as he took the red bus to the North Wall. Someone was shouting at someone else, one loud passenger at an apparently half-deaf passenger, the man raising himself a little to shout. The last of Dublin's bright lights swam by. What took their place was the bleak area of dockland. Miles took his small case from the bus. He had a lonely and unusual journey to make.

Miles was seventeen. His hair was manically spliced on his head, a brown tuft of it. He was tall, lean; Miles was a model. He wore his body comfortably. He moved ahead to the boat, carrying his case: foisting his case in an onward movement.

Miles had grown up in the Liberties in Dublin. His mother had deserted him when he was very young. She was a red-haired legend tonight, a legend with a head of champion chestnut hair.

She had gone from Ireland and insinuated herself into England, leaving her illegitimate son with her married sister. The only thing known of her was that she turned up at the pilgrimage to Walsingham, Norfolk, each year. Miles, now that he was a spare-featured seventeen-year-old, a seventeen-year-old with a rather lunar face, was going looking for her. That lunar face was even paler now under the glare of lights from the boat.

The life Miles lived now was one of bright lights, of outlandish clothes, of acrobatic models wearing those clothes under the glare of acrobatic lights; more than anything it was a life of nightclubs, the later in the night the better, seats at lurid feasts of mosaic ice cream and of cocktails. Dublin for Miles was a kind of Pompeii now: on an edge. He was doing well, he was living a good life in a city smouldering with poverty. Ironically he'd come from want. But his good looks had brought him to magazines and to the omnipotent television screen. He was taking leave of all that for a few days for a pilgrimage of his own. There were few signs of garishness on him. The clothes he slipped out of Ireland in were black and grey. Only the articulate outline of his face and the erupting lava tuft of his hair would let you know he worked in the world of modelling.

The night-boat pulled him towards England and the world of his mother.

2

She'd come to Walsingham each year, Ellie, and this year there was a difference about her coming. She was dying. She came with her daughter Áine and with her son Lally. She walked, propped between them, on the pilgrimage, the procession of foot from slipper chapel to town of Walsingham. Áine was a teacher. Lally was a pop star.

3

Miles was in fact late for the procession. He arrived in the town when the crowds were jumbled together. He looked around. He looked through the crowd for his mother.

4

Afterwards you could almost say that Lally recognized him, rather than he recognized Lally. Lally was discomfited by lack of recognition here. Miles recognized him immediately. 'How are you? You're Lally.' A primrose and white religious banner made one or two demonstrative movements behind Miles.

'Yeah. And who are you?'

Who am I? Who am I? The question coming from Lally's lips, funnelled mesmerically into Miles's mind on that street in Walsingham.

## 5

Miles was an orphan, always an orphan, always made to feel like an orphan. He was, through childhood and adolescence, rejected by his cousins with whom he lived, both male and female, rejected for his beauty. Nancy-Boy they called him. Sop. Sissy. Pansy. Queer, Gay-Boy, Bum-Boy. The ultimate name—Snowdrop. His enemy cousins took to that name most, considering it particularly salacious and inventive. Miles was none of these things. He looked unusually pretty for a boy. The names for him and the brand of ostracization gave him a clue as to his direction in life though. He found an easy entrance into the world of modelling. He was hoisted gracefully into that world you could say. At seventeen Miles had his face right bang on the front of magazine covers. He'd become an aura, a national consciousness arrangement in his own right. This success allowed him to have a flat of his own and, supreme revenge, wear suits the colour of the undersides of mushrooms down the Liberties. Miles sometimes had the blank air of a drifting, unpiloted boat in these suits in the Liberties. There must be more to life than bright suits his mind was saying; there must be more things beyond this city where boys in pink suits wandered under slender cathedral steeples. There must be more to life than a geography that got its kicks from mixing ancient grey buildings with doses of alarmingly dressed and vacant-eyed young people. His mother, the idea of her, was something beyond this city and Miles broke with everything he was familiar with, everything that bolstered him, to go looking for her, to stretch his life: to endanger himself. He knew his equilibrium was frail, that his defences were thin, that he might inflict a terrible wound on himself by going, that he might remember what he'd been trying to forget all his life, what it was like as a little child to have your mother leave you, to have a red-haired woman disappear out the door, throwing a solitary backward glance at you, in a house not far from the slender cathedral steeple, and never coming back again.

## 6

Who am I? Ellie Tierney had asked herself as she walked on the procession. Who am I, she wondered, now that she was on the verge of dying, having cancer of the bone marrow. An immigrant. A mother of two children. A widow. A grocery store owner. A dweller of West London. A Catholic.

She'd come young to this country; from County Clare. Just before the War. Lived the first year in Ilford. Had shoals of local children pursue her and her brothers and sisters with stones because they were Irish. She'd been a maid in a vast hotel. Met Peader Tierney, a bus driver for London Transport, had a proposal from him at a Galwaymen's ball in a West London hotel and married him. Had two children by him. Was independent of him in that she opened a grocery store of her own. He'd died in the early 1970s, long before he could see his son become famous.

## 7

Who am I? Lally had thought on the procession. The question boggled him now. He was very famous. Frequently on television. A spokesman for a new generation of the Irish in England. A wearer of nightgown-looking shirts. He felt odd, abashed here, among the nuns and priests, beside his mother. But he strangely belonged. He'd make a song from Walsingham.

## 8

Who am I? Áine had thought as she'd walked. A failure. A red-haired woman in a line of Clare women. Beside that young brother of hers nothing: a point of annihilation, no achievement.

## 9

It occurred to Lally that Miles had come here because he knew that he, Lally, would be here. Lally welcomed him as a particularly devoted fan.

'Where are you from?'

'Dublin.'

'Dublin?'

'Dublin.'

The hair over Miles's grin was askew. Miles waited a few minutes, grin fixed, for a further comment from Lally.

'We're driving to the sea. Will you come with us?'

10

The flat land of Norfolk: not unlike the sea. The onward Volkswagen giving it almost an inconsequential, disconnected feel; a feel that brought dreams and memories to those sitting, as if dumbstruck, silently in the car. Mrs Tierney in front, her face searching the sky with the abstracted look of a saint who had his hands joined in prayer. Walsingham was left behind. But the spirit of Walsingham bound all the car together, this strangeness in a landscape that was otherwise yawning, and to Irish people, alien, unremarkable—important only in that it occasionally yielded an odd-looking bird and that the glowering sweep of it promised the maximum benefit of the sea.

That they all considered it flat and boundless like the sea never occurred to them as being ironic; a sea of land was something almost to be feared. Only by the sea, in landscape, they felt safe.

Or in a small town like Walsingham which took full control over its surroundings and subjugated them.

The people of Britain had called the Milky Way the Walsingham Way once. They thought it had led to Walsingham. The Virgin Mary was reckoned to have made an appearance here in the Middle Ages. The young Henry VIII had walked on foot from the slipper chapel to her shrine to venerate her. Later he'd taken her image from the shrine and had it publicly burned in Chelsea to the jeers of a late-medieval crowd. Centuries had gone by and an English lady convert started the process of reconstruction, turning sheds back into chapels. To celebrate the reconsecration of the slipper chapel vast crowds had come from all over England on a Whit Monday in the 1930s. Ellie remembered the Whit Monday gathering here in 1946, the crowds on the procession, the prayers of thanksgiving to Mary, the nuns with head-dresses tall as German castles, pictures of Mary in windows in Walsingham and the flowers on doorsteps—a gaggle of nuns in black, but with palatial white headdresses, standing outside a cottage, nudging one another, waiting for the Virgin as if she was a military hero who'd won the war. The statue of Mary had come, bedecked with congratulatory pink roses. For Ellie the War had been a war with England, English children chasing her and brutally raining stones on her.

Her head slumped in the car a little now: she was tired. Her son, Lally, the driver, looked sidelong at her, anxiously, protectively. Her memories were his this moment: the stuff of songs, geese setting out like rebel soldiers in a jade-green farm in County Clare.

II

Lally was the artist, the pop star, the maker of words. Words came out of him now, these days, like meteors; superhuman ignitions of energy. He was totally in command: he stood straight on television. He was a star. He was something of Ireland for a new generation of an English pop audience. He wheedled his songs about Ireland into a microphone, the other members of his group standing behind him. His face was well known in teeny-bop magazines, the alacrity of it, the uprightness of it.

How all this came about was a mystery to his mother; from a shambles in a shed, a pop group practising, to massive concerts—a song in the charts was what did it. But a song with a difference. It was a song about Ireland. Suddenly Ireland had value in the media. Lally had capitalized on that. His sore-throat-sounding songs had homed in on that new preoccupation. Without people realizing it he had turned a frivolous interest into an obsession. He remembered— through his parents. His most famous song was about his father, how his father, who'd fled Galway in his teens, had returned, middle aged, to find only stones where his parents were buried, no names on the stones. It had never occurred to him that without him, the son of the family, there'd been no one to bury his parents. He had a mad sister somewhere in England who talked to chickens. Lally's father had

deserted the entire palette of Ireland for forty years, never once writing
to his parents when they were alive, trying to obliterate the memory of
them, doing so until he found his way home again in the late 1960s.

That song had been called 'Stones in a Flaxen Field'.

Words; Lally was loved for his words. They spun from him, all
colours. They were sexual and male and young, his words. They were
kaleidoscopic in colour. But they spoke, inversely, of things very
ancient, of oppression. A new generation of young English people
learnt from his songs.

And only ten years before, Ellie often thought, her grocery store
was stoned, one night, just after bombs went off in Birmingham, the
window all smashed.

Ah well; that was life. That was change. One day scum, the next
stars. Stars ... Ellie looked up from her dreams for the Milky Way
or the Walsingham Way but it was still very much May late-after-
noon light.


## 12

Her father told her how they used to play
hurling in the fields outside his village in County Galway in May
evening light, 'light you could cup in your hand it was so golden'.
There are holes in every legend. There were two versions of her
father. The man who ran away and who never went back until he was
in his fifties. And the man who'd proposed to her mother at a Galwaymen's ball. 'But sure he was only there as a spy that day,' Áine's
mother would always say. Even so it was contradictory. Áine
resented the lyricism of Lally's version of her father; she resented
the way he'd used family and put it into song, she resented this intru-
sion into the part of her psyche which was wrapped up in family.
More than anything she resented the way Lally got away with it. But
still she outwardly applauded him. But as he became more famous
she became older, more wrecked looking. Still her hair was very red.
That seemed to be her triumph—even at school. To have this almost
obscenely lavish red hair. She got on well at school. She had many
boyfriends. Too many. She was involved on women's committees. But
wasn't there something she'd lost?

She did not believe in all this: God, pilgrimage. Coming to Walsingham almost irked her. She'd come as a duty. But it did remind her of another pilgrimage, another journey, almost holy.

### 13

It had been when Lally was a teenager. She'd gone for an abortion in Brighton. A clinic near the sea. In winter. He'd accompanied her. Waiting for the appointment she'd heard the crash of the winter sea. Lally beside her. He'd held her hand. She'd thought of Clare, of deaths, of wakes. She'd gone in for her appointment. Afterwards, in a strange way, she realized he'd become an artist that day. By using him as a solace when he'd been too young she'd traumatized him into becoming an artist. She'd wanted him to become part of a conspiracy with her, a narrow conspiracy: but instead she'd sent him out on seas of philosophizing, of wondering. He'd been generous in his interpretation of her from out on those seas. His purity not only had been reinforced but immeasurably extended. While hers was lost.

There'd been a distance between them ever since. Lally was the one whose life worked, Lally was the one with the pop star's miraculous sweep of dark hair over his face, Lally was the one with concise blue eyes that carried the Clare coast in them.

Toady she saw it exactly. Lally was the one who believed.

### 14

Miles was so chuffed at being in this company that he said nothing; he just grinned. He hid his head, slightly idiotically, in his coat. The countryside rolled by outside. All the time he was aware of the journey separating him from his quest for his mother. But he didn't mind. When it came to the point it had seemed futile, the idea of finding her in that crowd. And romantic. When he looked out from a porch, near a pump, at the sea of faces, it had seemed insane, deranged, dangerous, the point of his quest. There'd been a moment when he thought his sanity was giving way. But the apparition of Lally had saved him. Now he was being swept along on another odyssey. But where was this odyssey leading? And as he was on it, the car journey, it was immediately bringing him to thoughts, memories. The landscape of adolescence, the stretched-out skyline of Dublin, a naked black river bearing isolated white lights at night as it meandered drunkenly to the no-man's-land, the unclaimed territory of the Irish Sea. This was the territory along with the terrain of the black river as it neared the sea which infil-trated Miles's night-dreams as an adolescent, restive night-dreams, his body shaking frequently in response to the image of the Irish Sea at night, possibly knowing it had to enter that image so it could feel whole, Miles knowing, even in sleep, that the missing mechanisms of his being were out there and recoiling, in a few spasmodic move-ments, from the journey he knew he'd have to make someday. He was on that journey now. But he'd already left the focus of it, Wals-ingham. What had come in place of Walsingham was flat land, an unending succession of flat land which seemed to induce a mutual, binding memory to the inmates of the car. A memory which hyp-notized everybody.

But the memory that was special to Miles was the memory of Dublin. This memory had a new intensity, a new aurora in the pres-ence of Lally; the past was changed in the presence of Lally and newly negotiated. Miles had found, close to Lally, new fundamen-tals in his past; the past seemed levitated, random, creative now. Miles knew now that all the pain in his life had been going towards this moment. This was the reward. It was as if Miles, the fourteen, fifteen-year-old, had smashed out of his body and, like Superman, stormed the sky over a city. The city was a specific one. Dublin. And remembering a particular corner near his aunt's home where there was always the sculpture of some drunkard's piddle on the wall Miles was less euphoric. The world was made up of mean things after all, mornings after the night before. That's what Miles's young life was made up of, mornings after the night before. Maybe that's what his mother's life had been like too. Now that he was moving further and further away from the possibility of actually finding her he could conjure an image of her he hadn't dared conjure before. He could conjure an encounter with her which, in the presence of an artist, Lally, was a hair's breadth away from being real.

## 15

Rose Keating had set out that morning from her room in Shepherd's Bush. She was a maid in a Kensington hotel where most of the staff were Irish. Her hair, which was almost the colour of golden nasturtiums, was tied in a ponytail at the back. Her pale face looked earnest. She made this journey every year. She made it in a kind of reparation. She always felt early on this journey that her womb had been taken out, that there was a missing segment of her, an essential ion in her consciousness was lost. She'd almost forgotten, living in loneliness and semi-destitution, who she was and why she was here. All she knew, instinctively, all the time was that she'd had to move on. There had been a child she'd had once and she'd abandoned him because she didn't want to drag him down her road too. She felt, when she'd left Dublin, totally corrupt, totally spoilt. She'd wanted to cleanse herself and just ended up a maid, a dormant being, a piece of social trash.

There was a time when it was as if any man would do her but the more good-looking the better: at night a chorus of silent young men gathered balletically under lampposts in the Liberties. Then there was a play, movements, interchange. Which would she choose? She looked as though she'd been guided like a robot towards some of them. All this under lamplight. Her face slightly thrown back and frequently expressionless. There was something wrong with her, people said, she had a disease, 'down there', and some matrons even pointed to the place. Rose loved the theatre of it. There was something *mardi gras* about picking up young men. My gondoliers, she called them mentally. Because sometimes she didn't in fact see young men from the Liberties under lampposts but Venetian gondoliers; the Liberties was often studded with Venetian gondoliers and jealous women, behind black masks, looked from windows. Rose had a mad appetite, its origins and its name inscrutable, for men. There was no point of reference for it so it became a language, fascinating in itself. Those with open minds wanted to study that language to see what new things they could learn from it. No one in Ireland was as sexually insatiable as Rose. This might have been fine if she'd been a prostitute but she didn't even get money for it very often; she just wanted to put coloured balloons all over a panoramic, decayed, Georgian ceiling that was in fact the imaginative ceiling of Irish society.

It was a phase. It hit her, like a moonbeam, in her late teens, and it lasted until her mid-twenties. She got a son out of it, Miles, and the son made her recondite, for a while, and then she went back to her old ways, the streets. But this time each man she had seemed tainted and diseased after her, a diseased, invisible mucus running off him and making him curl up with horror at the awareness of this effect. He had caught something incurable and he hated himself for it. He drifted away from her, trying to analyse what felt different and awful about him. Sex had turned sour, like the smell of Guinness sometimes in the Dublin air.

But Rose, even living with her sister, could not give it up; her whole body was continually infiltrated by sexual hunger and one day, feeling sick in herself, she left. The day she left Dublin she thought of a red-haired boy, the loveliest she had, who'd ended up spending a life sentence in Mountjoy, for a murder of a rural garda sergeant, having hit him over the head one night in the Liberties, with a mallet. He'd been half a Tinker and wore mousy freckles at the tip of his nose—like a tattoo.

London had ended all her sexual appetite: it took her dignity; it made her middle aged. But it never once made her want to return. She held her child in her head, a talisman, and she went to Walsingham once a year as a reparation, having sent a postcard from there once to her sister, saying: 'If you want to find me, find me in Walsingham.' That had been at a moment of piqued desperation. She'd written the postcard on a wall beside a damp telephone kiosk and the postcard itself became damp; people, happy people, sauntering, with chips, around her.

For a few years she found a companion for her trip to Walsingham, a Mr Coneelly, a bald man from the hotel, a hat on his head on the pilgrimage, a little earthenware leprechaun grin on his face under his hat. He had an amorous attachment to her. There was always a ten-pound note sticking from his pocket and a gold chain trailing to the watch in that pocket. But the romance ended when white rosary beads fell out of his trousers pocket as he was making

love to her once on a shabby, once lustrous gold sofa, she doing it to
be obliging, and he taking the falling rosary as a demonstration by his
dead mother against the romance. In fact he found a much younger
girl after that and he made sure no rosary fell from his pocket in the
middle of making love. He had been company, for a while.

Rose had geared herself for a life of loneliness. Today in Walsingham it rained a little and she stood to the side, on a porch and
watched.

## 16

Sometimes Áine's feelings towards her
brother came to hatred. She never pretended it. She was always cour-
teous, even decorous with him: the worst and the most false of her,
'schoolmistressy'. She resented his strident, bulbous shirts, the free
movements of those shirts, the colours of them. She resented what
he did with experience, turning it into an artifact. Artifacts weren't
life and yet, for him, they created a life of their own: those Botticelli
angels looking at him from an audience, full of adulation. Áine
wanted reports on life to be factual, plain; Lally, the Irish artist, threw
the facts into tumults of colour where they got distorted. Eventually
the words took on a frenzy, a life of their own. They were able to
change the miserable facts—rain over a desultory, praying horde at
Walsingham, crouched in between Chinese takeaways—and turn
themselves into something else, a miracle, a transcendence, an eleva-
tion and an obliviscence: wine turned into the blood of Christ at
mass. A mergence with all the Irish artists of the centuries. Of course
Lally was only a pop star and yet his words, she had to admit sometimes, were as truthful as any Irish writer's. His words exploded on
concert stages, on television, and told of broken Irish lives, red-haired
Irish women immigrants who worked in hotels in West London.

## 17

Miles had stood not very far away from his
mother that day and Lally had noticed Miles's mother, when there
was rain, as she stood talking to two men from Mayo. There was a
hullabaloo of Irish accents between Rose and the two men from

Mayo. Lally paused; a story. Then he went on. Miles didn't tell Lally in the car that he'd come in search of a red-haired woman. He said very little and was asked very little.

## 18

Rose, sheltering her body from the rain, got into a livid conversation with two men. They were bachelors and they were both looking for wives. They came to Walsingham, Norfolk, from Birmingham each Whit Monday looking for wives and they went to Lisdoonvarna, County Clare, in September looking for wives. So far they'd had no luck and their quest was telling on them: their hair and their teeth were falling out. One bandied a copy of the previous day's *Sunday Press* as if it was the portfolio of his life's work.

'And do you have a husband?' one of them asked.

'What do you think?'

'You've had your share of fellas,' the other one said grinning. 'A woman like you wouldn't have gone without a man for long.'

'What do you mean. A woman like me?'

'Well, you're not fat but you've loads of flesh on you. Like a Christmas goose. That's not derogatory. You look as firm as my grandmother's armchair.'

Rose screeched with laughter.

'And you both look as though the hinges are coming out of you.'

'Mentally or in the body?'

Rose laughed again.

'Whatever hope there is in Clare there's no hope here. Unless you want a Reverend Mother.'

'Oh, you'd be surprised.' A twinkle in the eye. 'Lots of randy women go on pilgrimages.'

## 19

Nearing the sea as though it was the Atlantic Ocean that blanketed the west coast of Ireland all kinds of words and images came into the head of Lally, the driver: sentences, half-heard at Irish venues—music festivals, Irish ballrooms—and elaborated on by him. So they could take their place in a narrative song. But more than words and images came now—an apotheosis came too. Lally was flying with the success and daring of his life. He was proud of himself. He'd turned something of the decrepitude and semi-stagnation of his parents' lives into art. More than that. Art for the young. He'd dolled his ancestry up in fancy dress.

## 20

How many days and months would she have to live? Ellie thought of Clare where she'd been born, the harvest fields there she'd walked before leaving Ireland, those blond, human fields, warm after days of summer sun. The imminence of death brought the friendliest images of her life.

## 21

The bastard, Áine thought, the bastard, he's taken everything that was of my creativity; he's used up my creativity. He's left me as nothing. There's no more to go around. He's a man, an exploiter, a rampant egotist. He doesn't see who he's trampled on to get where he's got, who he hurts. He doesn't see he's squashed my self-confidence out.

## 22

For Miles, as they neared the sea, it was a trip backwards: at least this journey, this expedition to Walsingham had allowed him to be solemn about his life, to see it: he sat back as though his life hitherto, as he could see it, was a state funeral.

There had been state funerals he'd seen in his life. De Valera's for instance, which he'd seen with his aunt, 'Ah, sure, look at his coffin.' All kinds of voices came back from Miles's life. Especially the voices of early adolescence. 'Ah, sure, look at the little eejit. The fool. Nitwit. Silly git.' All kinds of names were planted on Miles's always withdrawing figure with its gander legs in thin jeans. That figure was a continual epilogue, always disappearing around corners, always on the edge of getting out of the picture. But maybe that was because he knew there'd be an area where he could totally affirm himself, totally show himself—when the time came. Now there were ikons of Miles in fashion magazines, the young archangel in suave clothes. His tormentors in the Liberties would be bilious. But the young man in the picture was unmoved by this prospect. He seemed frigid of countenance. This loveliness was the product of pain. These secretive eyes in all the pictures looked back on tunnels of streets in the Liberties, streets where his mother had gathered men as if they'd been daisies.

As they neared Wells-next-the-Sea the sky, towards evening, had almost cleared and there were a few white clouds in it—like defeated daisies.

People in the car were mumbling, conversations were going on. Suddenly Miles wanted to go back to Walsingham.

'Mammy.'

### 23

Rose's shadow departed through the back door after her. Miles should have known there was something funny about her going that day. In fact he did know. Memory consolidated that fact. Rose's shadow writhed off a yellowy picture showing military-shouldered women in white, straw hats on their heads, holding bicycles, in some Edwardian wood of the Dublin mountains.

### 24

'And the queer thing is that Gabrielle knew Marty years before in Kiltimagh.'

Rose was in a Chinese restaurant in Walsingham with the two immigrants who were originally from Mayo. They'd discovered they had an acquaintance in common; a partisan in this tide of menial, immigrant Irish labour. Rose had encountered her in a hotel room once where the carpets had been rolled up after some VIP visitors had spent a lengthy stay. The room, grandiose in proportions, was being renovated. Rose did not know what to dwell on, the conversation with the two odd men or the drama of the encounter years before. Her concentration ultimately flitted between the figment of now and the thought of then. This caused an almost clownish agitation in her features.

'She had the devil of a temper.'

'Oh yes, she'd flare up at you like a snake.'

'There was cuddling in her though.'

'You dirty . . .'

Rose's mind had fled the banter between the two men. A woman in a hotel room in London years before, a blue workcoat on her, a conversation, commiseration, companionship then for a few months. But some family tragedy had brought the women back to Ireland and then Rose never saw her again; no more Friday evenings over a candle-lit, hard-as-a-horseshoe pizza in Hammersmith.

'Go on out of that. Don't be disparaging a woman's reputation. She's not around to defend herself.'

Rose's mind had drifted. She could see the sea, the grey sea such as it was piled up, a mute and undemonstrative statement, around Dublin and longed for it as though it had the confessional's power of absolution.

## 25

Miles stumbled by the sea. A few boats there, backs up. Now it was grey again, an overall grey. Walking done, the group went to a seaside café.

## 26

Words, they're my story, they're my life. Here by the sea, dusk, the jukebox going, Dusty Springfield, 'I just don't know what to do with myself', no song of mine on the jukebox. Chips, a boy, already tanned, looking from behind the counter, mystically, a Spaniard's or a Greek's black moustache on him. I'll make another song, another story. Stories will get me by, words, won't they, won't they? The stage, the lights, the mammoth audience. Is this a Nazi dream of power?

27

Today the religion they tried to kill. My religion. Remember when Peader and I went to the Church of the English Martyrs in Tyburn and we, privately, consecrated our marriage there on the site where the head of Oliver Plunkett, the Irish martyr, was chopped off, the nuns all singing, white on them. What will it be like to be dead?—back in that dream of a hymn sung in unison by nuns in white where Irish bishops in the long ago met their deaths.

28

Lally went obsessively, again and again, to the jukebox, standing over it, putting on more songs as though lighting candles in a bed of church candles. Midsummer dusk was out there, the strangeness of it. A woman soon to die looked at it. Lally's backside was very blue.

29

Loneliest of all was Miles, the stranger here, the one picked up and talked to as if being picked up was favour enough or as if he was supposed to sit in silent wonderment. He was an oddity from the sea of fans. He was an orphan among these people who, in a strange, unknowing way, patronized him.

30

The strangeness, the awkwardness became more evident as the number of coffees coming to the table multiplied, each set of coffees being ushered in more frenetically than the last. No one told their story aloud or was asked to.

31

Rose, though, was telling her story very loudly indeed not many miles away. Sweet and sour chicken, a plate of it, went by as she got to the part about leaving Ireland. Her immediate listeners were enthralled but their wonderment was more at how gauche exiles very often hid the most amazing secrets, how they hid horror, terror and great magnitudes of sin—incest, homo-sexuality, lesbianism, prostitution, now, rare enough, nymphomania. England dusted off the sins and made people just foolish—just foolish Irish folk.

'The child? The little lad?'

'Sure he's grown now. He wouldn't want to see me.'

## 32

O Mother of God, Star of the Sea, pray for us, pray that we find loved ones. Someone's limbs to get caught up with in a mildly comfortable bed.

Lally remembered, from childhood, a Sacred Heart picture over the bed of a dying, bald uncle, a gay uncle who had a festive chamber pot under his deathbed, a chamber pot with crocks of gold running around it. Before AIDS was invented, that uncle seemed to be dying of something like AIDS. Or maybe merely an overdose of failure, an over-dose of incohesion. His version of Ireland didn't merge with England.

The harvest fields of Clare didn't get him by here: England scoured him. England debilitated him. England killed his spirit and then killed him. But not before he carried on a kind of maudlin homosexuality. The white hands of a corpse Lally saw, a rosary entwined in them, had been lain on his genitalia when he was a child, a St Stephen's Day Christmas tree behind the merry lecher, other people gone to bed.

Ireland kicked up such stories like sand in your feet on a beach: Ireland was so full of sadness. Ireland fed itself into Lally's songs now. They came out, these stories, renewed, revitalized, pop songs for a generation who swayed and sometimes jived to them and couldn't be unnerved by them.

Star of the Sea, pray for the wanderer, pray for me. Lally's blue-shirted wrist wrestled with a bottle of Coke now. He was on to Coke. And he being the pop star, everyone watched the movement of his wrist, everybody's attention had gone to his wrist in alarm, people realizing that they'd been neglecting Lally for a while and that his wrist was telling them so.

And despite resenting him a little maybe they were glad for the coherence he gave to something of their lives. Even to death.

'Beach at Brighton, Baby-death.' Áine was looking at her brother in stillness now, not in anger or resentment.

### 33

As stars came out they walked on the beach. Lally tried to identify the stars in the sky. The Walsingham Way? Next week he'd be in California. By the Pacific. Watching the sky of stars over the Pacific. But he'd take something from here. Pointers to his mother's life and death. Ellie too saw her life and death in the stars tonight. A constellation of stars like a constellation of wheat fields in County Clare. 'A time to plant and a time to pluck up that which is planted.' Áine saw London classrooms in the sky, children of many races, rivers of children's faces. Miles, away from the group, dissociated from it, didn't look at the stars but poked the sea with a stick.

### 34

'Goodbye to yis all now.' Drunk, unpilgrim-like, Rose tottered out of a pub near the Chinese restaurant in Walsingham, looking behind at a constellation of lights in the window of that pub that might have distinguished it as a brothel if it had been in a city. The lovers stood at the door, goodbyes in their eyes. They were bent on returning, getting *stociously* drunk and staying the night in Walsingham. A bus would take Rose home. Her hair down on her shoulders she was a manifestation of Irishness in her dowdy coat. Her back stooped a little: she was an aged pilgrim. The successive pilgrimages were gradations, demarcations of age. But there was a wicked youthfulness about the way she stepped on the bus and turned around, shouting back to the men who hadn't yet gone back into the pub. 'Up Mayo.' Bandy knees afar twitched in response to her salutation: two Mayo bachelors looked suddenly spectral, looked like a vision in a wash of white light from a turning car. Then they were gone, gone into the album.

## 35

In the middle of summer in Wells-next-the-Sea there would be boys with faces pugnaciously browned by sun, boys whose crotches would be held in by aerial blue jeans, battalions of these boys unleashed on the place and their eyes, the explosive look in their eyes, turning the nights into a turmoil. Boats would be lined up on the beach. Lanes would meander down to the beach as they did now. The jukeboxes would be more active. England would come here to be loved, ladies from Birmingham, factory boys, boys with backsides tight and fecund as plums. This is where England would take a few weeks off, the boring country of England becoming carnal, becoming daring, becoming poetic. Caution and pairs of cheap nylon stockings would be thrown to the nervy summer breezes. The grey would go for a few weeks, making room for a blue that visited the place from the deep Mediterranean.

Ellie would be dead in July. Her funeral would be in West London on a very hot day. Áine would cry more than anybody. Lally would be silent, a pop star in black and white, no tie, white *fin de siècle* shirt spaciously open in the cemetery. There'd be a red rose in his black lapel. The sun would be gruesomely hot. Áine would be crying for a country she never really knew, a country for which her red hair was an emblem.

Miles would start losing his soul that summer, if soul you could call it; his sensitivity, vulnerability, belief in something. Walsingham and Wells-next-the-Sea would have been the last stops for his openness. After that, though still in media terms outrageously beautiful, he'd start becoming hard, calculating, eyes, those brown eyes of his, focused on attainment. All he'd want to do would be to be a star and oblivionize, kill anything else in him. There'd be no sign of Rose in this Italian suit dolled-up boy.

36

Rose let herself in the hall door. 14 Boling-
broke Road, Shepherd's Bush, London. Inside the light wasn't
working. The smell of urine came from the first-floor toilet. She was
a little drunk still. Her drunken form merged with the darkness. The
smell of urine was aquatic in the air the further she walked in. But
the darkness was benign to her. It shrouded her unhappiness, the
unhappiness which had suddenly come on her in the bus as she
remembered what she'd been trying to forget for years, what she'd
been successfully putting Walsingham between it and her for years.
Now pilgrimages, trips to Walsingham, the cabbalistic charades of
them and the inexact hope they gave off didn't work any more and
all she could see, right in front of her, was the greyness, the no-hope,
the lethargy land of *it*.


37

The lights of a motorway going back to
London and the lights rearing up at you, daisy trails of them. Four
silent people in the car, one sleeping, the strange boy, a phrase coming
to Lally's head as he drove, a phrase he wouldn't use in a song, an
unwelcome phrase even. It came from a prayer of his mother's he
remembered from childhood.
'And after this our exile.'

# Martyrs

Ella was an Italian woman whose one son had been maimed in a fight and was now permanently in a wheelchair, still sporting the char-black leather jacket he'd had on the night he'd been set upon. Ella's cream waitress outfit seemed to tremble with vindication when she spoke of her son's assailants. 'I'll get them. I'll get them. I'll shoot them through the brains.' The formica white walls listened. Chris's thoughts were set back that summer to Sister Honor.

The lake threw up an enduring desultory cloud that summer—it was particularly unbudging on Indiana Avenue—and Chris sidled quickly by the high-rise buildings which had attacked Mrs Pajalich's son. Sister Honor would have reproached Ella with admonitions of forgiveness but Chris saw—all too clearly—as she had in Sister Honor's lucid Kerry-coast-blue eyes the afternoon she informed her she was reneging on convent school for state high school that Sister Honor would never forgive her, the fêted pupil, for reneging on a Catholic education for the streams of state apostacy and capitalistic indifference. Chris had had to leave a Catholic environment before it plunged her into a lifetime of introspection. She, who was already in her strawberry and black check shirt, orientated to a delicate and literary kind of introspection. Sister Honor's last words to her, from behind that familiar desk, had been

'Your vocation in life is to be a martyr.'

The summer before university Chris worked hard—as a wait-ress—in a cream coat alongside Mrs Pajalich. Beyond the grey grave-stone citadels of the city were the gold and ochre cornfields. At the end of summer Chris would head through them—in a Greyhound bus—for the university city. But first she had to affirm to herself, 'I have escaped Sister Honor and her many mandates.'

Ella Pajalich would sometimes nudge her, requesting a bit of Christian theology, but inevitably reject it. Ella had learnt that Chris could come out with lines of Christian assuagement. However, the catastrophe had been too great. But that did not stop Ella, over a jam pie, red slithering along the meringue edges, from pressing Chris for an eloquent line of heaven-respecting philosophy.

Rubbing a dun plate that was supposed to be white Chris won-dered if heaven or any kind of Elysium could ever touch Ella's life; sure there were the cherry blossoms by the lake in a spring under which she pushed her son. But the idea of a miracle, of a renais-sance, no. Mrs Pajalich was determined to stick the café bread knife through someone. If only the police officer who allowed his poodle to excrete outside her street-level apartment. Ella had picked up the sense of a father of stature from Chris and that arranged her atti-tude towards Chris; Chris had a bit of the Catholic aristocrat about her, her father an Irish-American building contractor who held his ground in windy weather outside St Grellan's on Sunday mornings, his granite suit flapping, a scarlet breast-pocket handkerchief leaping up like a fish, his black shoes scintillating with his youngest son's efforts on them and his boulder-like fingers going for another volu-minous cigar. 'Chris, you have the face of fortune. You'll meet a nice man. You'll be another Grace Kelly. End up in a palace.' Chris saw Grace Kelly's face, the tight bun over it, the lipstick like an even scimitar. She saw the casinos. Yes she would end up living beside casinos in some mad, decadent country, but not Monaco, more likely some vestige of Central or South America.

'Chris, will you come and visit me at Hallowe'en?' The dreaming Chris's face was disturbed. 'Yes, yes, I will.'

Summer was over without any great reckoning when Sister Honor and Chris slid south, through the corn, to a city which rose over the corn, its small roofs, its terracotta museums by the clouded river, its white Capitol building, a centrepiece like a Renaissance city.

Sister Honor had imbibed Chris from the beginning as she would a piece of revealing literature; Chris had been established in class as a reference point for questions about literary complexities. Sister Honor would raise her hand and usher Chris's attention as if she was a traffic warden stopping the traffic. 'Chris, what did Spenser mean by this?' Honor should have known. She'd done much work in a university in Virginia on the poet Edmund Spenser; her passion for Spenser had brought her to County Cork. She'd done a course in Anglo–Irish literature for a term in Cork University. Red Irish buses had brought her into a countryside, rich and thick now, rich and thick in the Middle Ages, but one incandesced by the British around Spenser's time. The British had come to wonder and then destroy. Honor had come here as a child of five with her father, had nearly forgotten, but could not forget the moment when her father, holding her hand, cigar smoke blowing into a jackdaw's mouth, had wondered aloud how they had survived, how his ancestry had been chosen to escape, to take flight, to settle in a town in the Midwest and go on to creating dove-coloured twentieth-century skyscrapers.

Perhaps it had been the closeness of their backgrounds that had brought Chris and Honor together—their fathers had strad-dled on the same pavement outside St Grellan's Catholic Church, they'd blasted the aged and lingering Father Duane with smoke from the same brand of cigars. But it had been their ever-probing interest in literature which had bound them more strongly than the aesthetic of their backgrounds—though it may have been the aes-thetic of their backgrounds which drove them to words. 'Vocabu-laries were rich and flowing in our backgrounds,' Sister Honor had said. 'Rich and flowing.' And what did not flow in Sister Honor she made up for in words.

Many-shaped bottoms followed one another in shorts over the verdure around the white Capitol building. The atmosphere was one of heightened relaxation; smiles were 1950s-type smiles on girls in shorts. Chris found a place for herself in George's bar. She counted the lights in the constellation of lights in the jukebox and put on a song for Sister Honor. Buddy Holly. 'You Go Your Way and I'll Go

Mine'. A long-distance truck driver touched her from behind and she realized it was two in the morning.

She had imagined Sister Honor's childhood so closely that sometimes it seemed that Sister Honor's childhood had been her childhood and in the first few weeks at the university—the verdure, the sunlight on white shorts and white Capitol building, the fall, many-coloured evening rays of sun evoking a primal gust in her—it was of Sister Honor's childhood she thought and not her own. The suburban house, hoary in colour like rotten bark, the Maryland farm she visited in summer—the swing, the Stars and Stripes on the verdant slope, the first- or second-edition Nathaniel Hawthorne books open, revealing mustard, fluttering pages like an evangelical announcement. In the suburbs of this small city Chris saw a little girl in a blue crinoline frock, mushrooming outwards, running towards the expectant arms of a father. Red apples bounced on this image.

Why had she been thinking of Sister Honor so much in the last few months? Why had Sister Honor been entering her mind with such ease and with such unquestioning familiarity? What was the sudden cause of this tide in favour of the psyche of a person you had tried to dispose of two years beforehand? One afternoon on Larissa Street Chris decided it was time to put up barriers against Sister Honor. But a woman, no longer in a nun's veil, blonde-haired, hair the colour of dried honey, still tried to get in.

Chris was studying English literature in the university—in a purple-red, many-corridored building—and the inspection of works of eighteenth- and nineteenth-century literature again leisurely evoked the emotion of the roots of her interest in literature, her inclination to literature, and the way Sister Honor had seized on that interest and so thoughts of Sister Honor—in the context of her study of literature—began circulating again. Sister Honor, in her mind, had one of the acerbic faces of the Celtic saints on the front of St Grellan's, a question beginning on her lips, and her face lean, like a greyhound's, stopped in the act of barking.

'Hi, I'm Nick.'

'I'm Chris.'

A former chaperon of nuclear missiles on a naval ship, now studying Pascal, his broad shoulders cowering into a black leather jacket, accompanied Chris to George's bar one Saturday night. They collected others on the way, a girl just back from the People's Republic of China who said she'd been the first person from her country to do a thesis at Harvard—hers was on nineteenth-century feminist writers. George's bar enveloped the small group, its low red, funeral-parlour light—the lights in the window illuminating the bar name were both blue and red.

Autumn was optimistic and continuous, lots of sunshine; girls basked in shorts as though for summer; the physique of certain girls became sturdier and more ruddy and brown and sleek with sun. Chris found a tree to sit under and meditate on her background, Irish Catholic, its sins against her—big black aggressive limousines outside St Grellan's on Sunday mornings unsteadying her childhood devotions, the time they dressed her in emerald velvet, cut in triangles, and made her play a leprechaun, the time an Irish priest showed her his penis under his black soutane and she'd wondered if this was an initiation into a part of Catholicism—and her deliverance from it now. The autumn sun cupped the Victorian villas in this town in its hand, the wine-red, the blue, the dun villas, their gold coins of autumn petals.

Chris was reminded sometimes by baseball boys of her acne—boys eddying along the street on Saturday afternoons, in from the country for a baseball match—college boys generally gave her only one to two glances, the second glance always a curious one as she had her head down and did not seem interested in them. But here she was walking away from her family and sometimes even, on special occasions, she looked straight into someone's eyes.

What would Sister Honor have thought of her now? O God, what on earth was she thinking of Sister Honor for? That woman haunts me. Chris walked on, across the verdure, under the Capitol building beside which cowboys once tied their horses.

The Saturday-night George's bar group was deserted—Nick stood on Desmoines Street and cowered further into his black leather jacket, muttering in his incomprehensible Marlon Brando fashion of the duplicity of the American government and armed forces—Chris had fallen for a dance student who'd raised his right leg in leotards like a self-admiring pony in the dance studio. The plan to seduce him failed. The attempted seduction took place on a mattress on the floor of his room in an elephantine apartment block which housed a line of washing machines on the ground floor that insisted on shaking in unison in a lighted area late into the night, stopping sometimes as if to gauge the progress of Chris's and her friend's lovemaking. In the early stages of these efforts the boy remembered he was a homosexual and Chris remembered she was a virgin. They both turned from one another's bodies and looked at the ceiling. The boy said the roaches on the ceiling were cute. Chris made off about three in the morning in a drab anorak, blaming Catholicism and Sister Honor, the autumn river with its mild, off-shooting breeze leading her home. Yes, she was a sexual failure. Years at convent school had ensured a barrier between flowing sensuality and herself. Always the hesitation. The mortification. Dialogue. 'Do you believe we qualify, in Martin Buber's terms, for an I-thou relationship, our bodies I mean?' 'For fuck's sake, my prick has gone jellified.'

Chris knew there was a hunch on her shoulders as she hurried home; at one stage, on a bend of the river near the road, late, home-going baseball fans pulled down the window of a car to holler lewd-nesses at her. She's never been able to make love—'Our bodies have destinies in love,' Sister Honor rhetorically informed the class one day—and Chris had been saving her pennies for this destiny. But tonight she cursed Sister Honor, cursed her Catholicism, her Catholic-coated sense of literature and most of anything Sister Honor's virginity which seemed to have given rise to her cruelty. 'Chris, the acne on your face has intensified over Easter. It is like an ancient map of Ireland after a smattering of napalm.' 'Chris, your legs seem to dangle, not hold you.' 'Chris, walk straight, carry your-self straight. Bear in mind your great talent and your great intelli-gence. Be proud of it. Know yourself, Chris Gormley.' Chris knew herself tonight as a bombed, withered, defeated thing. But these Catholic-withered limbs still held out hope for sweetening by another person.

Yes, that was why she'd left convent school—because she per-ceived the sham in Sister Honor, that Sister Honor had really been fighting her own virginity and in a losing battle galled other people and clawed at other people's emotions. Chris had left to keep her much-attacked identity intact. But on leaving she'd abandoned Sister Honor to a class where she could not talk literature to another pupil.

Should I go back there sometime? Maybe? Find out what Honor is teaching. Who she is directing her attentions to. If anybody. See if she has a new love. Jealousy told Chris she had not. There could never have been a pair in that class to examine the Ecclesiastes like Honor and herself—'A time of war, and a time of peace.' Chris had a dream in which she saw Honor in a valley of vines, a biblical valley, and another night a dream in which they were both walking through Spenser's Cork, before destruction, by birches and alders, hand in hand, at home and at peace with Gaelic identity and Gaelic innocence or maybe, in another interpretation of the dream, with childhood bliss. Then Sister Honor faded—the nightmare and the mellifluous dream of her—the argument was over. Chris settled back, drank, had fun, prepared for autumn parties.

The Saturday-night George's bar group was resurrected—they dithered behind one another at the entrance to parties, one less sure than the other. Chablis was handed to them, poured out of cardboard boxes with taps. A woman in black, a shoal of black balloons over her head, their leash of twine in her hand, sat under a tree in the garden at a party one night. She was talking loudly about an Egyptian professor who had deserted her. A girl approached Chris and said she'd been to the same convent as Chris had been. Before the conversation could be pursued the room erupted into dancing— the girl was lost to the growing harvest moon. Chris walked into the garden and comforted the lady in black.

'Dear Sister Honor.' The encounter prompted Chris to begin a letter to Honor one evening. Outside, the San Francisco bus made its way up North Dubuque Street—San Francisco illuminated on the front—just about overtaking a fat negro lady shuffling by Victorian villas with their promise of flowers in avenues that dived off North Dubuque Street, heaving her unwieldy laundry. But the image of Sister Honor had faded too far and the letter was crumpled. But for some reason Chris saw Honor that night, a ghost in a veil behind a desk, telling a class of girls that Edmund Spenser would be important to their lives.

Juanito was a Venezuelan boy in a plum-red T-shirt, charcoal

hair falling over an almost Indian face which was possessed of lustrous eyes and lips that seemed about to moult. He shared his secret
with her at a party. He was possessed by demons. They emerged
from him at night and fluttered about the white ceiling of Potomac
apartments. At one party a young man, José from Puerto Rico, came
naked, crossed his hairy legs in a debonair fashion and sipped vodka.
So demented was he in the United States without a girlfriend that
he forgot to put on clothes. Juanito from Venezuela recurred again
and again. The demons were getting worse. They seemed to thrive on
the season of Hallowe'en. There was a volcanic rush of them out of
him now at night against the ceiling. But he still managed to play an
Ella Fitzgerald number, 'Let's Fall in Love', on a piano at a party.
José from Puerto Rico found an American girlfriend for one night
but she would not allow him to come inside her because she was
afraid of disease, she told him, from his part of the world.

Chris held a party at her apartment just before the mid-term
break. Juanito came and José. She'd been busy preparing for days. In
a supermarket two days previously she'd noticed as she'd carried a
paper sack of groceries at the bottom left-hand corner of the college newspaper, a report about the killing of some American nuns
in a Central American country. The overwhelming feature of the
page, however, had been a blown-up photograph of a bird who'd just
arrived in town to nest for the winter. Anyway the sack of groceries
had kept Chris from viewing the newspaper properly. The day had
been very fine and Chris, crossing the green of the campus, had
encountered the bird who'd come to town to nest for the winter or
a similar bird. There was goulash for forty people at Chris's party—
more soup than stew—and lots of pumpkin pie, apple pie and special little buns, speckled by chocolate, which Chris had learned to
make from her grandmother. The party was just underway when five
blond college boys in white T-shirts entered bearing candles in
carved pumpkin shells flame coming through eyes and fierce little
teeth. There were Japanese girls at Chris's party and a middle-aged
man frequently tortured in Uruguay but who planned to return to
that country after this term in the college. He was small, in a white
T-shirt, and he smiled a lot. He could not speak English too well
but he kept pointing at the college boys and saying 'nice'. At the end

of the party Chris made love in the bath not to one of these boys who'd made their entrance bearing candles in pumpkin shells but to a friend of theirs who'd arrived later.

In the morning she was faced by many bottles and later, a few hours later, a ribboning journey through flat, often unpeopled land. The Greyhound bus was like her home. She sat back, chewed gum, and watched the array of worn humanity on the bus. One of the last highlights of the party had been José emptying a bottle of red wine down the mouth of the little man from Uruguay.

When she arrived at the Greyhound bus station in her city she understood that there was something different about the bus station. Fewer drunks around. No one was playing the jukebox in the café. Chris wandered into the street. Crowds had gathered on the pavement. The dusk was issuing a brittle, blue spray of rain. Chris recognized a negro lady who usually frequented the bus station. The woman looked at Chris. People were waiting for a funeral. Lights from high-rise blocks blossomed. The negro woman was about to say something to Chris but refrained. Chris strolled down the street, wanting to ignore this anticipated funeral. But a little boy in a football T-shirt told her 'The nuns are dead.' On a front page of a local newspaper, the newspaper vendor forgetting to take the money from her, holding the newspaper from her, Chris saw the news. Five nuns from this city had been killed in a Central American country. Four were being buried today. One was Honor.

When Chris Gormley had left the school Sister Honor suddenly realized now that her favourite and most emotionally involving pupil—with what Sister Honor had taken to be her relaxed and high sense of destiny—had gone, that all her life she had not been confronting something in herself and that she often put something in front of her, prize pupils, to hide the essential fact of self-evasion. She knew as a child she'd had a destiny and so some months after Chris had gone Honor flew—literally in one sense but Honor saw herself as a white migrating bird—to Central America with some nuns from her convent. The position of a teaching nun in a Central American convent belonging to their order had become vacant suddenly when a nun began having catatonic nightmares before going, heaving in her frail bed. With other sisters she changed from black to white and was seen off with red carnations. The local newspaper had photographed them. But the photograph appeared in a newspaper in Detroit. A plane landed in an airport by the ocean, miles from a city which was known to be at war but revealed itself to them in champagne and palm trees. A priest at the American Embassy gave them champagne and they were photographed again.

There was a rainbow over the city that night. Already in that photograph when it was developed Honor looked younger. Blonde hair reached down from under her white veil, those Shirley Temple curls her father had been proud of and sometimes pruned to send snippets to relatives. In a convent twenty miles from the city Honor found a TV and a gigantic fridge. The Reverend Mother looked down into the fridge. She was fond of cold squid. A nearby town was not a ramshackle place but an American suburb. Palm trees, banks, benevolent-faced American men in panama hats. An American zinc company nearby. The girls who came to be taught were chocolate-faced but still the children of the rich—the occasional chocolate-faced girl among them a young American with a tan. Honor that autumn found herself teaching Spenser to girls who watched the same TV programmes as the girls in the city she left. An American flag fluttered nearby and assured everyone, even the patrolling monkey-bodied teenage soldiers, that everything was all right. Such a dramatic geographical change, such a physical leap brought Honor in mind of Chris Gormley.

Chris Gormley had captivated her from the beginning, her long, layered blonde hair, her studious but easy manner. Honor was not in a position to publicly admire so she sometimes found herself insulting Chris. Only because she herself was bound and she was baulking at her own shackles. She cherished Chris though—Chris evoked the stolidity and generosity of her own background; she succeeded in suggesting an aesthetic from it and for this Honor was grateful—and when Chris went Honor knew she'd failed here, that she'd no longer have someone to banter with, to play word games with, and so left, hoping Chris one day would make a genius or a lover—for her sake—or both. Honor had been more than grateful to her though for participating in a debate with her and making one thing lucid to her—that occasionally you have to move on. So moving on for Honor meant travel, upheaval, and finding herself now beside a big Reverend Mother who as autumn progressed kept peering into a refrigerator bigger than herself.

A few months after she arrived in the convent however things had shifted emphasis; Honor was a regular sight in the afternoons after school throwing a final piece of cargo into a jeep and shooting—exploding—off in a cantankerous and erratic jeep with other nuns to a village thirty miles away. She'd become part of a cathectics corps. Beyond the American suburb was an American slum. Skeletal women with ink hair and big ink eyes with skeletal children lined the way. Honor understood why she'd always been drawn to Elizabethan Irish history. Because history recurs. For a moment in her mind these people were the victims of a British invasion. At first she was shy with the children. Unused to children. More used to teenage girls. But little boys graciously reached their hands to her and she relaxed, feeling better able to cope. The war was mainly in the mountains; sometimes it came near. But the children did not seem to mind. There was one child she became particularly fond of—Harry after Harry Belafonte—and he of her and one person she became drawn to, Brother Mark, a monk from Montana. He had blond hair, the colour of honey, balding in furrows. She wanted to put her fingers though it. Together they'd sit on a bench—the village was on an incline—on late afternoons that still looked like autumn, vineyards around, facing the Pacific which they could not see but knew was there from the Pacific sun hitting the clay of the vineyards, talking retrospectively of America. Did she miss America? No. She felt an abyss of contentment here among the little boys in white vests, with little brown arms already bulging with muscles. Brother Mark dressed in a white gown and one evening, intuiting her feelings for him—the fingers that wanted to touch the scorched blue and red parts of his head—his hand reached from it to hers. To refrain from a relationship she volunteered for the mountains.

What she was there would always be in her face, in her eyes. Hornet-like helicopters swooped on dark rivers of people in mountain-side forests and an American from San Francisco, Joseph Dinani, his long white hair likes Moses' scrolls, hunched on the ground in an Indian poncho, reading the palms of refugees for money and food. He'd found his way through the forests of Central America in the early 1970s. There were bodies in a valley, many bodies, pregnant women, their stomachs rising out of the water like rhinoceroses bathing. Ever after that there'd be an alarm in her eyes and her right eyebrow was permanently estranged from her eye. She had to leave to tell someone but no one in authority for the moment wanted to know. The Americans were in charge and nothing too drastic could happen with the Americans around.

She threw herself into her work with the children. For some hours during the day she taught girls. The later hours, evening closing in in the hills, the mountains, she spent with the children. They became like her family. Little boys recognized the potential for comedy in her face and made her into a comedienne. In jeans and a blouse she jived with a boy as a fighter bomber went over. But the memory of what she'd seen in the mountains drove her on and made every movement swifter. With this memory was the realization, consolidating all she felt about herself before leaving the school in the Midwest, that all her life she'd been running away from something—boys clanking chains in a suburb of a night-time Midwest city, hosts of destroyers speeding through the beech shade of a fragment of Elizabethan Irish history—they now were catching up on her. They had recognized her challenge. They had singled her out. Her crime? To treat the poor like princes. She was just an ordinary person now with blonde curly hair, a pale pretty face, who happened to be American.

The Reverend Mother, a woman partly Venezuelan, partly Brazilian, partly American, took at last to the doctrine of liberation and a convent, always anarchistic, some nuns in white, some in black, some in jeans and blouses, became more anarchistic. She herself changed from black to white. She had the television removed and replaced by a rare plant from Peru. An American man in a white suit came to call on her and she asked him loudly what had made him join the CIA and offered him cooked octopus. Honor was producing a concert for harvest festivities in her village that autumn.

There was a deluge of rats and mice—no one seemed quite sure which—in the tobacco-coloured fields that autumn and an influx of soldiers, young rat-faced soldiers borne along, standing, on front of jeeps. Rat eyes imperceptibly took in Honor. They had caught up with her. A little girl in a blue dress crossed the fields, tejacote apples upheld in the bottom of her dress. A little boy ran to Honor. They were close at hand. At night when her fears were most intense, sweat amassing on her face, she thought of Chris Gormley, a girl at a school in the Midwest with whom she'd shared a respite in her life, and if she said unkindnesses to her she could say sorry now but that out of frustration comes the tree of one's life. Honor's tree blossomed that autumn. Sometimes rain poured. Sometimes the sky cheerily brightened. Pieces moved on a chess table in a bar, almost of their own accord. In her mind Honor heard a young soldier sing a song from an American musical: 'Out of My Dreams and Into Your Arms.'

The night of the concert squashes gleamed like moons in the fields around the hall. In tight jeans, red check shirt, her curls almost peroxide, Honor tightly sang a song into the microphone. Buddy Holly. 'You go your way and I'll go mine, now and forever till the end of time.' A soldier at the back shouted an obscenity at her. A little boy in front, in a grey T-shirt from Chicago, smiled his pleasure. In her mind was her father, his grey suit, the peace promised once when they were photographed together on a broad pavement of a city in the Midwest, that peace overturned now because it inevitably referred back to the turbulence that gave it, Irish—America, birth. And she saw the girl who in a way had brought her here. There was no panic in her, just an Elysium of broad, grey pavements and a liner trekking to Cobh, in County Cork. 'Yea, though I walk through the valley of the shadow of death, I will fear no evil: for thou art with me; thy rod and staff they comfort me.' In the morning they found her body with that of other nuns among ribbons of blood in a rubbish dump by a meeting of four roads. No one knew why they killed her because after the concert a young, almost Chinese-skinned soldier had danced with her under a yellow lantern that threw out scarlet patterns.

Afterwards Chris would wonder why her parents had not contacted her; perhaps the party with its barrage of phone calls had put up a barrier. But here, now, on the pavement, as the hearses passed, loaded with chrysanthemums and dahlias and carnations, she, this blonde, long-haired protégée of Sister Honor, could only be engulfed by the light of pumpkins which lit like candles in suburban gardens with dusk, by the lights of windows in high-rise blocks, apertures in catacombs in ancient Rome, by the flames which were emitted from factory chimneys and by the knowledge that a woman, once often harsh and forbidding, had been raised to the status of martyr and saint by a church that had continued since ancient Rome. An elderly lady in a blue mackintosh knelt on the pavement and pawed at a rosary. A negro lady beside Chris wept. But generally the crowd was silent, knowing that it had been their empire which had put these women to death and that now this city was receiving the bodies back among the flames of pumpkins, of windows, of rhythmically issuing factory fires, which scorched at the heart, turning it into a wilderness in horror and in awe.

# The Airedale

The door of their house and the side gate to the archway leading to their yard, their proliferation of sheds and subsequently to their garden were painted fresh bright green. Green was the colour of the door and the side gate of the last house on the street, the house just before the convent. The nuns were always eager to get hold of the house and they did eventually. If you pay a visit to the town now it is merely an eventual part of the convent premises.

The stone of the house was dark grey and if you peeped through the bony windows you'd see shining wooden floors and above them paintings of the maroon and purple mountains of the West. We lived in the Western Midlands. East Galway. Mrs Bannerton was from Poland. She had blonde sleeked hair. She had taken a bus from the War and arrived in Ireland. In Dublin she'd married a surgeon. They lived now in our town. Denny was the son. Their one child. He was my friend.

I came from a family of five brothers. There were certain obscenities within my family. I can now see that friendship was one of them. Denny should have been from a suitable class background for closeness with me but my mother detected something she did not approve of there. Looking out the window at Denny trailing along on the other side of the street, beside rugged curtains she spat, 'You're not to play with him. He's wild.'

Denny was wild; he had wild chestnut hair, wild confluences of freckles, wild and expansive short trousers. He kept a milling household of pets, lily-white, quivering-nosed rabbits, garden-trekking tortoises, cats of many colours, at one stage a dying jackdaw, but monarch among the pets was Sir Lesley the Airedale. Denny tended his menagerie carefully, kneeling to comb the fur of cats and rabbits with a horn comb he assured me had been part of his grandmother's heirloom in Lublin. Later discovering that Lublin had been the site of a concentration camp struck home memories of a childhood where imaginary storks cascaded over a town which often looked, in its loop of the river, that it had been constructed as a concentration camp. Denny in white sleeveless jersey and white trousers combed a cat's fur and muttered a prayer he insisted was Polish. It was in fact gibberish. Denny did not know a word of Polish because his mother refused even to speak a consonant of it. Some languages are best forgotten. The town had its language. My family had its language. But the Bannertons spoke a different language and I owe them something; I owe them what I am now, for better or for worse. Denny's gibberish addressed to one of his cats is a language I still hear. We move from one country to another; we move from one language to another. But certain remembrances bind us with sanity. Denny's addresses to his cats is one of them for me. Another is the red in Denny's hair. Denny's red. My own hair was dull brown and I always vied for red hair so when I first came to live in this city I had a craze and dumped a bottle of henna into my crew cut, stared into my eyes in a mirror then and saw myself as an inmate in a concentration camp.

Denny and I sat together at school and we heard the words of William Allingham together:

Adieu to Ballyshannon! where I was born and bred
Wherever I go, I'll think of you, as sure as night and morn.

That we were elevated at an early age by the romance of words was also a saving grace of this town. The speaker of these words, a grey-haired headmaster with a worn and lathery black leather strap, is now lying in his grave. After doing his purgatory for the mutilation of poor boys' hands—boys from the 'Terrace', the slum area of town—he will surely be transported to heaven on a stanza of

Thomas Moore. That was the duality we lived with. But Denny's home in the afternoons dominated at school. Toys on the wooden floor were trains winding through Central Europe. Snow toppling on the trains—litter from Denny's hands. We saw a midget woman alight from a carriage on the floor, look around her and wander through the bustling streets of an anonymous Central European city.

Mr Bannerton had a large penis. From Denny I first heard mention of the word 'penis'. He kept me in touch with his father's and mother's attributes. I presumed Mr Bannerton's large penis was to do with his medical profession.

Denny taught me history; the entire history of the world; he knew this from books; Denny read Dickens and Louisa M. Alcott. These authors owed their life in the town to Denny. He frequented their worlds. He borrowed their books from the library. Denny was a parent. At eleven he had a wide and middle-aged freckled face.

Everything was lovely about Denny, his father, his mother, his hair, his clothes, everything except his face. He had an ugly face. When I met him in later life he had kept that face like a chalking-up area for pain.

In Denny's home I first heard Mozart; I first spoke to a jackdaw; I first was kissed by a blonde woman; I first acquainted myself with the names of herbs. In Denny's home I first hated my mother and my father. I despised my brothers. There were no cats or dogs in our home. No Airedales. I swapped passports in their home and took out citizenship of a country situated between bare wooden walls.

I was ten when Denny left. God threw snow out of a spiteful heaven. He was borne away in the furniture van. On the main street I cried. They were going to a city in the very South. I was wearing a short blue coat. Tears stung in my eyes and if I stay awake long enough at night I can still feel them.

All their property had gone, everything, except the Airedale. He'd been too big to carry away and whether they donated him to a neighbour or not he strode majestically around town for weeks. In the mornings on my way to school I nodded to him though he did not acknowledge me. Then one day I passed his carcass beside a dustbin. They left his carcass there for weeks, below the dustbin, until fleas got into it. I supposed it was to demonstrate to everyone the folly of being lofty and having once been the pet of a gifted family. The Bannertons went on to be part of a big city. There was an opera house in this city and a river which divided into two. There were many hills in this city and many churches. Now that I had been left my brothers turned upon me, beat me up, locked me into rooms on grey afternoons. It was a grey February afternoon for a long time now. One grey February afternoon I left to be a priest in Maynooth.

What happened in the meantime had been a kind of breakdown. My parents, fearful of consequences, confiscated stamp albums, books. Stamps were slightly suspicious, books were dangerous for me. They knew no better, my parents. They were peasant people, their parents having graduated to businesses in towns. The only book my mother had ever read was the penny catechism, and my father, a more jovial sort, had his joviality truncated by my mother. My brothers were all going to be accountants. At fifteen I borrowed my father's razor blade and slashed my wrists. Blood ran from the wound of a white hamster. They did not bring me to the main hospital but to the mental hospital. On the way there, like Denny, I began muttering gibberish. Gibberish saved my life.

Maynooth was rusted pipes alongside the grey walls of premises which were alleged to be haunted by catatonic ghosts; Maynooth was young clerics in black soutanes, hands digging deep into their soutanes, staring collectively at gutters; Maynooth was razor blades the colour of congealed blood, deftly taken from private lockers. There were sonorous prayers and professors of medieval philosophy who went around spraying snippets of Simon and Garfunkel. But eventually a prayer became too nasal for me; a part of my brain leapt into self-awareness again; before being ordained, a hitherto placid clerical student boarded a plane from Dublin to London, first having attended a film in his favourite cinema on Eden Quay. The city I arrived in was experiencing its first buffeting of punk hairdos;

skies were bleached, dustbins overladen. Hands were generally shrouded in pockets. From a room in Plumstead I looked for work, got a job on a building site and a year later started attending a film school. Boats pushed past on the Thames outside my door. Plumstead marshes nearby conjured skeletal boats on the Thames. There was a ghost running through and through me as I sat, meditating, in my room in Plumstead. I could make little communication with fellow students. Something in me was impotent and my favourite occupation was sitting on a stool, meditating on my multiple impotences and creating a route out of them. One day I knew I'd walk out of inability. Charitable notes drifted through from Maynooth. There were short films made. There were eventually relationships made. Sex stirred like a ship on the Thames. But I touched one or two people. I made gestures to one or two people. I was released from the school with accolades. I made my first film outside school. A short film. On that ticket I returned to Ireland.

Adieu to Ballyshannon! where I was born and bred
Wherever I go, I'll think of you, as sure as night and morn.

A plane veered across lamb-like clouds. Below me was a southern Irish city. My film was being shown in the annual film festival. I was sitting next to the window. I'd never been to this country before. I was an outsider now. I'd prepared myself and preened myself for that role. But a wind on the airport tarmac ruffled my demeanour and cowed me back again to Good Fridays and Pentecost Sundays on a grey small-town Irish street.

Cocktails were barraged towards the glitter of the light. Young women in scanty dresses and with silken bodies flashed venomous eyes at me. I was invited to bed chambers that always seemed by implication to be above the bars of cinemas. I declined these invitations. The night my film was shown, afterwards, I met Denny Bannerton. Dr Denny Bannerton. We said hello, made polite comments to one another, and arranged to meet the next night. There was no award for my film. Silence. Unmuttered blame. It had been a trip to Ireland though and I was glad of it. In a gents' toilet full of mirrors

I congratulated myself on my black, polka-dotted tie, a narrow
stripe of a tie purchased on Portobello Road and subsequently
endearingly laundered and ironed. It was as if someone was affec-
tionately pulling my tie in the direction of London. But first I had
an appointment. A camera went off and took a photograph of me,
dark glasses on and a smile winter days living by London cemeteries
had given me.

A blank, broad freckled face with black glasses. A grey suit—a collar
and tie. Unusual accoutrement for a film reception. Denny's face was
still the same in a way. We met in a pub the night after. The night was
young, Denny explained when we met; there were many bars in this
city to travel through. I sat on a high stool and gazed into a purple
spotlight falling on a many-ringed male finger. We had ventured into
the gay scene of this city. We were about to step further.

Swans, very clean swans; little neon-emblazoned retreats; hills;
wave-like lanes. A spiralling journey. Conversation. I was the film-
maker. Denny Bannerton was an auspicious and regular part of the
newspapers and behaved as such. I was treated to propaganda. I listened to the water, the breeze and the swans. The tricolour flew for
some reason over a Roman pillared church. As Denny's conversation
battled with the breeze, as young men in white shirts behind coun-
ters, glasses being cleaned in their hands, enthusiastically saluted him
among purple light, I made a mental film of his life.

The most important discovery in Denny Bannerton's life had
been that of his homosexuality. He discovered it at thirteen. With a
white rabbit. In the back garden of a red suburban house. The tenderness of his impediment connected him with inmates in a concentration camp near Lublin. He was still in short trousers at the
time. Broad, blank-faced, at fifteen he had an actual beauty. He had
a brief affair with a corporeal monk who was directing a Gilbert and
Sullivan operetta. Afterwards, having been rejected by the monk,
Denny's face resigned itself to ugliness. At university he took girls
out. But such relationships quickly collapsed. As a young doctor he
toured the world, had posts in Iran, in Venezuela, in Bristol. He
returned to Ireland. Returning to his city in the south he announced

his homosexuality. Affairs with Moslem, short-socked boys in the oil deserts. An affair with a piano-playing prodigy in Caracas. Nights of promiscuity in Bristol. Back home he politicized his loneliness. A doctor, he travelled the city with an expansive rose on his lapel. He was in the newspapers. He wrote irate letters to editors. He was a mirage on television discussion programmes. He'd peculiarly found his way home.

The questions asked of me were for the most part very factual; I knew what he was driving at. What were my sexual proclivities? I refused to answer. I just allowed myself to be led and occasionally I indulged in reminiscence. But it seemed reminiscence brought me back further than a garden. It brought me to a concentration camp in the suburbs of a Polish city.

Some of the nights in the desert had been like a concentration camp for Denny; the hot air, the arid flesh. Petrol had burned like pillars of flame. They had returned him to a geography before birth. Shirts were purple and pink in the dimly lit bars we slipped through. I was introduced to many people. A blond, furry-haired boy revolved his hand in mine in the pretence of shaking it. There had been the question of where Mrs Bannerton had really been from but now I knew. She'd been a mutual mother. Denny yapped on in a flaxen brogue, regardless of the images in my mind, furnaces lighting the night on the perimeter of a concentration camp in Poland.

Whether in reality or in dream she had traversed that camp. The skeletons had piled up in the dark. She'd heard the screams from those freshly dying. But in the middle of the skeletons and the screams she'd had an intuition of a limestone street, of an oak tree over a simple and pastoral pea garden, of an Airedale.

'So you're the film-maker. Heard your film was lousy. What are you doing beyond there in England? Pandering to Britannia. You should be home and drawing the turf of our native art.' An academic's lips seared with effeminacy. A gold chain sheathed the brushing of black hairs on display in the V of his pastel-blue shirt, the chain sinking into a tan picked up in Mexico. 'You're one of the quislings who won't admit they're queer.' He was asking me to concede my ratio of queerness. I said nothing, looked to the photograph of a scarlet-sailed yacht in Kinsale. Denny muttered something about camera work. The one word reserved for special treatment by the academic was Britannia; I saw a spring shower dripping off a stone, slouching lion.

Back in the night Denny ran down the list of his endeavours to bring gay liberation to Ireland: planting flags on the top of low, buttercup-covered mountains, leading straddling tiny marches through the city, chaining himself to the pillars of the Town Hall. He'd been wearing a brown T-shirt the day he'd chained himself to the Town Hall. Not a grey suit as now. A breeze from the sea suddenly slapped me with a drop or two of rain on the face.

The edges of her hair had burned against the lights of the concentration camp; again and again she strode across my vision. She wanted to exorcise it. She'd come a long way. Suddenly she'd been in Ireland and she'd lain down.

'My ma discovered I was gay. She was informed by a neighbour I was gay. She wasn't sure what that meant but contacted the mother of a boy who was known to be gay. That woman declared "Mrs Finuacane, don't fret. There were always gay men and women in Blarney but they didn't have the word for it then." '

I was speaking to a youth in one of the bars, interviewing him really. His hand was on a pint of Guinness. These rests in pubs interspersed with Denny's intense and self-engrossed mouthings.

In the same pub as I spoke to the boy I enquired about Denny's mother. She had stepped from a red brick suburban house into a big red brick hilltop mental hospital. Denny's mother had begun to eat her own fur coats. She was totally mad, Denny said. Totally mad.

In the Airedale I had seen it all; a crossroads. Denny had gone his way. I had gone mine. But some creatures lie down and die. Living becomes too much for them. Memory becomes too much for them. What she remembered I did not know. Could only guess. But she and her household of deranged hamsters had given me a residence in my mind. A new home. I had gone from their house, their world, with a life I would not otherwise have had; Denny had departed to this world. There'd been a juncture. An Airedale had marked the crossing. But a woman had held its thrall.

What had really caused an eddy in my gait had been the way Denny
had referred to his mother. It was as if there was plain reason to be
dismissory about her. She had sunk for him. Legend and myth had
walked out of his life but I had cherished it. She had grown for me.
She had marched across nights for me. In fact the first film I made at
film school I had thought of her. The blonde, ice-maiden-faced
Polish lady. The lights had centred on her. When Denny had made
his farewells I headed on into the night. There was a lot of way to go.

'See you now. Good luck with the films. I might see you tomorrow.' The phrases rang in my ears. I shovelled my hands into my
jacket. Denny was an arabesque of remarks. But I had sauntered
away from the Airedale a long time ago in this predestined black
jacket. There were already films in my face and Denny had already
changed in slinking away. There were worlds and corrosive thoughts
to stride through tonight.

'Goodnight. See you.' There'd been a room in her mind. A
chamber of torture. It had not necessarily been a concentration
camp, the proximity to a concentration camp, but the experience and
anguish of war. The worst anguish of surviving it. Storks and
domed palaces had perished in this war. But she had survived.

The scintillating blonde-haired lady in the garden imperiously
called to her husband. 'Bring me some lemonade.' A white rabbit
stuck its ears up at her. I watched from behind an oak tree, my right
hand clinging to the hoary bark.

The lights focused in on a girl's face. She had the features of
Mrs Bannerton. Why do I remember this face? What had this face
to say for me?

The city at night wound on. I unravelled the streets. There had
been a point on which I had coincided with this lady. You go past
pain. You come to meaning. I jotted little sentences in my mind. The
city by the river, its slim outlying houses, was Italianate.

The first time I made love to a woman I thought of her. Her
buttocks had asserted themselves through summer dresses, the dis-
daining quiver at the side of her buttocks. That quiver had said a lot.
'I'm not happy here. I'm not happy here.'

In the first few years after they went I used jumble words on
blue squared paper at school: 'loss', 'severity'. Gulls had looked in on

me, perching by an inedible crumb. I wanted to write to them, to all of them, but letters seemed inadequate to contain my feelings and anyway envelopes too frail to contain such corrosive letters as they might be. So I allowed myself to suffer. The Airedale had died. John F. Kennedy had died. My mother bought me a white sleeveless jersey one Christmas. At that point the Bannertons' house had been turned into classrooms by the nuns.

I'd wanted to write to her as well as to Denny. A letter to her had composed itself over my adolescence. There was place of pain we shared with one another. Not having any brothers I got on with I invented brothers in others, in boys who filtered through school— off to England after a short spate of studying at the priest-run boys' secondary school. There was chestnut hair, there were certain chest muscles behind white jerseys I envied in other boys. Boys from the 'Terrace'. Dionne Warwick sang me into a night of suicide. I woke up in Poland.

'Dear Mrs Bannerton ...' Always there was a beginning of a letter to her. But after my exercise in suicide attempts whatever they did to me in the mental hospital part of my brain slumbered. They had cajoled me into their universe. Maynooth College, its black bricks, was a logical upshoot from that universe.

On a night vaguely ingrained with rain in a hilly city in the very south of Ireland I finally scrambled off that letter to Mrs Bannerton. She was in a mental hospital in the vicinity, a house I thought I detected, shining with a light or two on a hill.

The times I was on the verge of doing something truly disastrous—being ordained a priest—when there was the immediate imminence of some irreparable lunacy she stopped me. She took strides with me when I was in my black soutane. It was that room that carried me from Ireland to England. The room where her blonde hair had looked red. Where toy trains spun around. Where trains stopped in towns you crept out into and had cold eggs showered in paprika in small cafés, the autumn sunshine shining through white wine and a leaf sweeper singing like a minstrel outside.

As a child I'd run up that street and peer in. There had been many ways of approaching a sight of the inside of that home. In the grey convent yard, a proudly decked member of the convent band, in claret dickie bow (which alternated occasionally with a miniature scarlet tie), white shirt, white long trousers, clashing a triangle, tripping in my clashing of it, one blue eye on the Bannertons' garden. What were Mrs Bannerton's limbs up to? Through the oblong window that stretched itself with narrowness on the street level you saw the brown wooden room and the journeys that the trains encompassed. Your mind gyrated with Europe's railways. Sometimes she stood in the middle of that room returning over these journeys, trembling in a leafy tight summer dress in the room. There was a person or a budgie she spoke to often. If it was a budgie it was to be seen, a cheeky lemon and lime thing. If a human being he was invisible. There were also ways you spied into that house in your dreams, through the chimney, on that roof that sent slates flying down in March. One night I travelled in the sky over their house on a broomstick and in my magician's capacity observed her dreams, trains snuggling into stations packed with marigolds and girls. But even being inside the house was always just an attempt. There were barriers. I was not one of them. The Airedale disdained me with one eye.

'How are you?'

A middle-aged man in a Charlie Chaplin-type bowler hat cascaded into me in the night. 'You're the young man who makes the films.' As a celebrity in my own right I sat beside him on a high stool in a late night café on a hill, Elvis Presley in maroon and pink on the wall, looking as if he'd been blasted on to it, as we discussed my films and my intentions with new films. As a cappuccino lever was pulled down—the café was Italian—a voice in my head in a County Galway accent said, 'Now you are their world.'

A woman in a room crossed her own barrier to be again in the boulevards and the parks of childhood. The edges of her hair had been red in remembrance. They had stood out, flames. Mrs Bannerton had had red hair as a child. She'd coveted a wooden sleigh with emerald tattoos on it. I too had a barrier to cross to remember. In the night my relatives webbed in me, no longer the demons I'd always presented to myself, but innocent. My mother, her frail sisters beside her, on station platforms in June during their youths. Many of my mother's sisters had died. Of purple lilac. Of tuberculosis. Purple lilac had flagged on russet, peeling railway bridges. Further back there was a room in history. A concentration camp. A war. A famine. There had been an operating theatre where innocence and joy had been removed. I had to make my way through ancestral minds to the joy in myself. The task in a black jacket seemed easy.

'Dear Mrs Bannerton ...'

It was not to her I ended up giving most of my thoughts but to the young man I'd spent the evening with, her son. Whether we knew it or not those times we enacted pageants in the thick shrubbery outside the men's club—a black canvas-covered hut—we were seeking to return to a corner of history; Ireland before subjugation. In white bed sheets we had been the kings of an undefiled Munster and undefiled hobgoblin world. The garden had pointed the way to an innocence. That oak had shaded the wounds of history; the memory of war. It had covered a part of a human being quaking because the sores distributed on her body were not apparent.

There was a bus; there was a journey. I'm not sure anymore what I left behind. I just remember a little boy in white trousers holding the white handbag of a woman. He was holding it up for the world to see. As if to ask why he was holding it. Why wasn't it with its owner who was probably dead or mutilated?'

The film scripts were beginning again. I could not stop them. A woman's voice reached me from the twinkle of a mental hospital light.

In a church at dawn under a cinder-blackened Christ I prayed for her and for her son who had disappeared into his grey jacket, into his spectacles and into the manifold expostulations of his cause. I tried to restate a part of myself I'd tried to forget. Pain too, the crossed mangled legs were necessary. They were a connecting point with the dots of our ancestors on the atlas. The world inside me now was created from childhood; from the gruesome logic of art. An attempt at art. But attempts at art could only lead back. To a room. In an ornately lettered mirror in a bar the edges of my hair were ghostly henna.

'We try to build; we try to grow. But we always build backwards. May God help me both to forget and to remember.' There were swans on the river. Graffiti flung itself against a urinal. There were turkey feet of aeroplane tracks through the clear sky. A path led out of here now. I had a ticket to depart. To leave a place where Mrs

Bannerton was incarcerated, where Denny Bannerton fought among the profusion of media attention, where a garden had been cemented over and an oak tree slashed down. The blood from the oak tree landed on the pavement of this city. I wanted to say over again, 'Thanks. Thanks for giving me birth.' But a chill had entered the air. It fingered the exposed headlines of newspapers. This was no country. It was no place. It no longer existed for me. All I was aware of were the aeroplane tracks in the sky. But there was a country in me now. There was a demesne. Sometime in the middle of the night I had gone back and picked up a child who'd been waiting on a street in Poland for a long time. There was a country where my child could be born or failing that where I could give birth to the latent little boy in myself. The terms of reference had changed; the language had changed. The chill in the air here no longer tortured me. The fate of the Airedale no longer bothered me. Soon Mrs Bannerton and Denny Bannerton would be forgotten. But walking back to the hotel I heard what I had not permitted myself to hear for many years.

The sound of Polish.

# Lebanon Lodge

The house became the property of a member
of the ruling party in the Irish parliament in the mid-1970s. With its
name definitively written on one of the gateposts it was clear that
that name, thought of in innocence—'The trees of the Lord are full
of sap: the cedars of Lebanon which he hath planted'—had become
a kind of public chalking-up area, in the minds of those who lived
in the vicinty of Dun Laoghaire, County Dublin, for the emotional
reverberations of events in one of the world's worst trouble-spots;
that name placed on the gatepost was a parallel to a stretch of the
front page of a newspaper which seared even the minds of these
complacent suburban citizens. A lethargic middle-aged woman in a
summer dress, her shopping beside her, often paused vacuously
beside it. What did it make her think of? Miles away and years away
in London, Lucien often fancied he was mentally writing its story as
he would the story of a house in the Catholic primary school he
attended in Dun Laoghaire for a while—this was a favourite task
given by Christian Brothers to nubile, teetering boys, 'A House Tells
Its Story', the irony of these Christian Brothers telling Lucien what
to do being of course that he was Jewish. What did a house
remember in inchoate nights in Maida Vale, London? What secrets
did its night-time bougainvillaea and arbutus protect? In a sentence
the history of an Irish Jewish family and particularly the history of

a young man who had escaped from that family and from the country that family had adopted. 'Alas, poor Erin! thou are thyself an eternal badge of sufferance, the blood of my people rests not on thy head.' Lucien often awoke in the night and imagined he was the receptacle for a history that was greater than him and yet had defined his own personality. Words, sentences, phrases of folklore came back; it was all built on legend of course, this history, but as he grew older Lucien, insurance broker, decided that he needed legend more and more, not just to escape but to sort out the bits of himself that Ireland had mangled and thrown into confusion—right up to an outwardly successful middle age.

The country his family had come to had been a strange one for Jews; they had come and gone since the beginning of the sixteenth century; Jews had been good spies for Cromwell; Jews had been jesters, Travellers on the roads of Ireland—no one knew if they were spies for the English or the French around the time of the planned French invasions at the end of the eighteenth century—Jews had shifted in and out of Jewish identity, not just on the roads of Ireland. There was a time when a whole spate of people, who had presented themselves as pious Catholics when it was difficult and even dangerous to be a pious Catholic, declared themselves to be Jewish on their deaths and asked for interment in the Jewish cemetery in Ballybough. Ballybough, a place by the sea, before it was a Jewish cemetery had been a burial place for suicides. Earth from Israel was imported into Dublin in the eighteenth century for Jewish burials, a handful of it thrown in after the corpse. Wine made from raisins was drunk on feast days and searches were made for tombstones, always disappearing and ending up as hearthstones on sale in market places, albeit hearthstones with Hebrew lettering—this story a comedy among Dublin working-class raconteurs. To this country came the Hoagmans, but not until after the synagogue at Mary's Abbey had been opened and a small bit of stability attained for Irish Jews, a symbol of stability in the new synagogue.

Where the Hoagmans began from was a mystery but there was no doubt where parlour legend allocated their beginnings—a fiercely black-haired woman left Hungary in Napoleonic times and met a man called Hoagman in Southern Bohemia, who had to flee his community—adhesive for false teeth which failed to adhere the teeth to the gum, brightly striped marionettes whose legs and arms quickly fell off, little, charred black Christs that quickly fell off their crosses—a marriage ceremony taking place before she fled with him to London. There they had two children, two boys, and it was the Famine of the 1840s which sent them to Ireland, all those Aid for Ireland events where Mrs Hoagman often got jobs serving soup or mopping marquee floors or attending the lavatorial areas, events so lavish and inspiring that they made you want to go to the land of reputed Famine, so loved did it seem by queens—who came in their carriages; by opera singers—who sang in cherry-coloured dresses on small improvised stages; by marchionesses—who baked huge, escalating cakes which were always threatening to fall, snowy, discreet Alpine peaks on those cakes; and by painters—who slapped people's portraits on in a few minutes.

It was not just this of course which made them go to Ireland— the glamour suggested by Ireland by way of people's eagerness to show their concern for it—but the fact that an Irishman was Jewry's greatest champion, Daniel O'Connell, and that Ireland's great leaders had always seemed to put a word in for the Jews as well as the Catholic Irish. It was a pull to a land promised by Famine aid events and by benevolent, languorous speeches from Irish leaders.

The city they arrived in was reeling under the Famine but still time was taken off to elaborately describe ladies' dresses at Castle balls in the newspapers. That was Mrs Hoagman's first impression of Ireland. A description of a young woman's dress, the woman dying a week after the dress description appeared when her coach fell into the canal near Portobello Barracks. In the early 1850s, when the Hoagmans found their feet, marionettes representing people with Jewish features were sold by women at College Green, and Dublin was held in the thrall of the legend of Pencil Cohen, a Jewish millionaire who'd started a halfpenny pencil industry and yet who slept under newspaper pages, visited and marvelled at by the ladies of Jewish relief organizations, an abundantly rich man who insisted on being a Rathmines Job. Magiash Hoagman, who'd started a small spice-box industry, soon had his own legend among the children of Chancery Street:

Magpie, Magpie sitting on the sty
Who, oh who has the dirty, greedy eye?

Ireland's tolerance for the Jews was even more considerably in
doubt when a Passionist father ranted from his pulpit that the
Dublin Jews had the crimson mark of deicide on their foreheads.
One of Mr Hoagman's sons stayed in Dublin and one disappeared
into the country and was never heard of by him again.

At this point Lucien, in London, would pause. So many unanswered questions, so many bits that didn't hang together. But that
had been the legend. And Pencil Cohen had indeed lived. Another
Dublin Jewish industrialist with the name Cohen was called Fresser
Cohen to distinguish him from his counterpart but he couldn't live
down the connection after Pencil Cohen's death, people eager for the
continuance of the legend, and he eventually left Dublin. But Mr
Hoagman was thriving then and there was no question of the Hoagmans, those that remained in Dublin, leaving this city. They'd found
an unexpected base under low, mellifluous, rainy mountains.

Every event concerning themselves was a legend among the Jews
of Dublin when Lucien was growing up—the night the new synagogue on Adelaide Road was opened in 1892, 'a night of snow', the
night of the Day of Atonement, 1918, when the electricity failed and
the ceremony was held by candlelight, 'the guns of the War of Independence going off outside', the day the newly extended Adelaide
Road Synagogue was reconsecrated in June 1925 and a celebration
held in a marquee by the canal afterwards, 'all the dignitaries among
the Jews there, justices in the new Irish state, businessmen; famous
actresses and authoresses all in their finery on the gorgeous sunny
day'. Lucien was born an exile. In Dun Laoghaire. His family had
exiled themselves from the Jews around South Circular Road, the
focus of Jewish population in Dublin, where the family had lived
since the 1880s. There was a crockery factory under the Wicklow
mountains, not far from Dun Laoghaire, and the family moved
nearer to it. But there was also the wish to associate themselves with
the most middle-class and secular environment in Ireland. But links
were forcibly kept up and Lucien was eventually sent to the Zion
Schools near Kelly's Corner, a marathon bus journey to be under-
taken each morning and each afternoon. When he tired of that or

his family tired of the effort of pushing him on his journey each morning they settled for a local primary school for him. That was the beginning of a more irrevocable exile for him.

Lucien was born in December 1932. That something terrible was happening to the Jews in Germany he was made aware of in gossipy gatherings of boys in school costumes at street corners around the archetypal corner, Kelly's Corner, boys who were as equally concerned with removing navy chocolate wrappers as they were with the fate of the Jews in Germany. Dublin in those years was a city of solitarily squirting rain clouds and of navy chocolate papers. Then it became a city of girls in navy convent uniforms. These girls had been whipped up by demagogues of Reverend Mothers into applause for fascist leaders, the saviours of the church against the Bolsheviks. Such was the hatred of one of these leaders, for the Jews, that he sent a plane to destroy the Jews of Dublin in January 1941. On the night of 1 January 1941 Greenville Hall Synagogue, on the South Circular Road, was half destroyed by a German bomber and the house of the second reader of the Adelaide Road Synagogue, who lived opposite the Greenville Hall Synagogue, totally destroyed. But no Jews in Dublin were killed. Greenville Hall Synagogue was reopened in September 1941 and Lucien was present.

Nights in London, his daughter making love in the house to a boyfriend, Lucien reconstructed another part of his family legend. This was the most extraordinary part and it was relevant to those war years, Dublin Jews with their own private war against a mass outbreak of anti-Semitism in Irish society. 'They're jealous of us,' his father would always say, 'jealous of our positiveness, our love of life.' This part of the family history was verified by an excavating Hoagman. The son of Magiash Hoagman, who'd left Dublin shortly after the family arrival in Ireland in the middle of the nineteenth century, had relinquished his Jewishness and become a Hogan, descendants running a butchering business in County Westmeath and fervent Catholics too. Their Jewishness had been totally oblivionized way back. It was not uncommon in Ireland for people to forget their recent heritage seeing that so many of the Irish middle class were survivors of quite recent famine or people who'd managed to cope after evictions from land. Irish family memory in general could not afford to go back very far. So the Hogans in Westmeath were really Jews who'd come to Dublin in the late 1840s. The very blackness of the hair of the Hogan girls could have made you suspicious. They were members of the Blueshirts, the Irish fascist organization, in the 1930s, their throng dotting the shores of Lake Derravaragh—legendary home of the Children of Lir, royal Irish children haplessly turned into swans, for three hundred years—for picnics. In 1941 Mr Hogan at an open-air wedding table, his black-haired daughters also at the table, made a speech saying that Ireland should do as Germany did and drive the Jews, 'those who'd crucified Our Lord', out. The speech was just one extension of the crazed Catholic triumphalism which gripped Ireland in those times. An excavating Hoagman confronted his relatives, and then rushed back to his business as picture-house owner in Dublin, not having, as he said himself, 'let the cat out of the bag'. But the Dublin Hoagmans could afford to be sly. They were rich, erudite and worldly people now, scoffing at the mores of the country around them and wearing laconic middle-class Dublin brogues. They were loved, despite the prevailing anti-Semitism in Dublin, for their laughter, their smiles and the way their eyes always seemed cocked in a joke. Uncle Adolphe, the picture-house owner, was the most loved one of all and he took on management of a theatre in which there was a pantomime each year until his death.

It was the influence of that uncle that played such a large part in Lucien's plans.

After leaving St Columba's College, Rathfarnham, in 1951, a Protestant secondary school founded so that landowners could address their tenants in Gaelic, Lucien entered Trinity College. There he befriended Ethel Bannion, a Catholic girl from Limerick, and spent two or three years going to plays with her and discussing the mainstreams of philosophy of the time with her. She was an eager, lonely girl, freckles like oatflakes on her face, eyes that startled out as from a statue of the Virgin Mary, auburn, even coppery curls in her hair. She followed him wherever he went; she was wafted by him. When he took lead parts in college plays she stared at him idolatrously. But when Libby Lazurus came along he fell carnally in love with her and made love for the first time. Libby, a Cork Jewess, came to Trinity in

1954. Hair black as Clanbrassil Street black puddings, eyes that were biblical, exotically alive. He made love to this girl, three years his junior, all over Dublin, in Killiney, Dalkey, in the wastes between Rock Road and the sea, on the top of the Dublin mountains, one day in a field in the Dublin mountains for Sunday picnickers to see. She was sexually carnivorous. She was unashamed. She was the most resplendent girl in Dublin. Then abruptly she threw in Trinity and left Dublin in the autumn of 1955 to go to an acting school. That threw him back on Ethel Bannion. He did not know how to make love to a girl after Libby Lazurus.

Lucien began working as an actor in Dublin in 1956. The world of Uncle Adolphe had exerted its influence over him. But he still had the safety of a university degree. Ethel Bannion was working as a secretary in a law firm, having failed all her way through college since Lucien began having the affair with Libby Lazurus. But still she saw him now and attended the theatre with him and watched him in rehearsal for the plays in which he performed. But there was something more subdued about her. She'd left college without a degree, having given up on it. And occasionally beside Lucien in the theatre seats, during a rehearsal for a play he was in, she came out with a rancorous remark under her breath. But still he tolerated her. The days were greyer in Dublin. The time was greyer. And then one day, beside a travel poster showing Chartres Cathedral at the juncture of Westmoreland Street and D'Olier Street, he saw Libby Lazurus. She was back. He was now twenty-five. She was performing in a pantomime that Christmas in his uncle's theatre. And he began having an affair with her again, as passionately and as mindlessly as before.

It was 1958. He turned twenty-six that December. On the night of his birthday Libby allowed him to make love to her under a bush on the cold ground in St Stephen's Green, the two of them, like winos, having skirted the railings. But there was a backlog of experience Lucien had not coped with. He'd tried to make love to other girls since Libby went and failed. Somehow the armoury of his body didn't work with anyone else, such had been the intensity of what had happened between him and Libby. Word quickly gets around Dublin and it was this word that killed the revival of his relationship with Libby. Full of masculinity, at a New Year's party, 1959, he was sud-

denly confronted by Ethel Bannion. Immediately he caught sight of
her he knew there would be trouble. She approached him, an almost
tangible smell of disuse off her. 'You're incapable. Incapable of physical relations with anyone except Libby Lazarus.' He was wearing a
white jersey. He stopped dead. 'You're a Jewish lesbian. You can't get
it up. You're a sexual failure. A wimp. Come on, show us what a cir-
cumcised prick that doesn't work looks like.' Her face, drunk, was an
aurora borealis of bitterness. The skin of her face like heaps and
heaps of dead porridge. This was her moment. Her speech. Then she
withdrew. He couldn't believe it. This was the Third Reich, the Tsarist
oppressions manifesting themselves at a Dublin theatrical party where,
if the revellers were not actors, they were ex-Trinity students. There
was silence. Ethel had made her impact.

He could not make love to Libby after that. In Ethel Bannion's
words he could not 'get it up'. She had destroyed something in him.
Not just his sexuality, but his belief in the steadiness of human
nature. He lost his innocence the night Ethel had attacked him.
Shortly after that, his ignominy with Libby and her quick with-
drawal from him, he left Ireland.

Yes, he gave up his pretensions to the theatre about the same
time. Was it a coincidence? Anyway he'd married the daughter of a
failed, rural Tory parliamentary candidate a few years later. She'd
brought him back to sexual life; she'd conquered, by her quietness,
the deadness in him. He was working for an insurance company in
the city by then and extravagantly successful at what he was doing.
'The righteous shall flourish like the palm tree: he shall grow like a
cedar in Lebanon.'

In the late 1970s he had occasion to visit Beirut for business reasons. He stood on a street in this city with evening hitting a few
high-rise buildings with a sun which was a perfect orange and
thought: nothing in this city, for all its carnage, can be worse than
what Ireland tried to do to me; it tried systematically to take the
flesh from the bone; it tried to eliminate me. He stood, perilously
still, a professional briefcase in his right hand.

By then, of course, Ireland was just a memory. His father died
in 1967. The burial was nostalgically Jewish. Clay from a black desert
in the Wicklow mountains under his head, his head tentatively

turned to the east—the verge of the Hill of Howth on the opposite side of the bay. Lucien recited the Hebrew prayers at Dolphin's
Barn Jewish Cemetery among a gaggle of half-embarrassed men in
heavy, charcoal coats. His father had always lit two candles on Friday
evenings in Dun Laoghaire so that often the candles were reflected
on the image of the sea; his father had inserted the Scrolls of the
Law back into the Ark of the Covenant in Adelaide Road Synagogue; his father had led the Jews of Dublin out of the old year
often as the Bridegroom of the Torah and brought them back to
Lebanon Lodge for festivities.

Lucien watched the silver bells tinkle on the Scrolls of the Law
the following Saturday in Adelaide Road Synagogue as he would
have as a child. But more than years separated him from then. He
was not really his father's son. He was not an heir. He wanted to get
away quickly from brothers who were forcing familial obligations on
him. He didn't want any of these arabesques. When his mother died
the house was sold and the money portioned among the family.
There was no house in Ireland now for him to bring his children
back to. But still it haunted him, Lebanon Lodge, a house become
more ghostly with the years. It was the house of the dead. Ironic that
Ethel Bannion, now grown fat, had married a member of the ruling
party in the Irish parliament, another parliamentary representative of
the same party having purchased the house. But political parties
come and go, especially in Ireland. Irish politics as everyone knows
are quixotic. But the house in Lucien's mind had a steadiness, a
ghostly permanence. It lived in a world of night in Maida Vale. His
relationship with his brothers was, as it had always been, negligible.
They were Dublin businessmen, intent on keeping the idea of family
up. He had an English accent now. The Irish connections had come
to nothing. One of his brothers kept the factory going and another
hovered around it. They were forever making overtures to him, those
overtures having begun as soon as he had thrown in the theatre for
business. But he suspected them. He had done with them. Yet something nagged him. About Ireland. About his youth there. He entered
the front door of Lebanon Lodge in his dreams and the whole of a
history of a Jewish family revealed itself to him, a history since their
arrival in Ireland. They had married Jewish history with Irish history

and made a covenant out of which he'd been born. He'd been the Jewish boy who'd vacantly written an essay entitled 'A House Tells Its Story' in a Christian Brothers' school in Dun Laoghaire. He fidgeted with the pen again in his mind and put the last strokes on the essay. It was the 1980s and his children were grown. His daughter worked in the theatre. She brought theatrical friends to his party on Christmas night in Maida Vale each year. Girls with short dresses and striped woollen stockings. Striped marionettes in Southern Bohemia? By default they'd become a kind of aristocracy. The children of the rich came to the party. Fenella, the heiress, of the long legs in the brief dress and of the little mirthful fountain of a head. Even the daughter, herself Jewish, of a man who made long and boring speeches in the Houses of Parliament, a girl with salient, tangerine lips. But for some reason he had to admit that his children, for all their easy artistic pursuits, were somewhat boring to him. They were beyond a border of understanding. Try as hard as they could they'd never be able to go back on that border. They were somewhat soulless, like their friends. People complimented him at the party for being so young-looking, as young-looking as his sons, his dark hair still shining and his skin pristine, that skin that had been married to Libby Lazurus's radiating skin once in a moment of total forgetfulness. But his lingering youthfulness made him oddly alone-looking there, standing among the hubbub of a Christmas night party in Maida Vale as he had stood on a street in Lebanon when the sun was going down and the high-rise buildings were aflame with meteors of colour, the tokens of the tired sun on them, and his mind had been shot through with an awareness of how close to extinction he'd come, whether extinction in Dublin during the War when the Germans were thinking of invading or extinction at a theatrical party in Dublin, not far from Kelly's Corner, when a woman had breathed her own brand of genocide into his body.

# Barnacle Geese

He would come early winter every year in his caravan to Kerry from a town in Tipperary where there is now a nude swim in the swimming pool the third Saturday of every month and swim on the different beaches, parking his caravan alongside them. He came when the barnacle geese arrived and he would explain to the boys on the beaches how barnacle geese got their names, that it had been believed they were born from ship barnacles.

Features smooth as a sea-stone, hare-lip, glass-grey eyes, sienna brows, Prussian crew cut.

He'd always stop at the Stella Café in Limerick on his way where the waitress had a steeple-beehive. Villages of flamingo-dolloped cakes under the casing on the formica counter. Toffee banana ice cream advertised. The speciality being Al Capone scoops.

There was a photograph on the wall of Willie Bevill in bermuda-length gym shorts. He'd used chest weights and spring grips before anybody was using them and he'd jump off the bridge at Parteen to swim in winter and he'd break the ice at Corbally Baths to swim.

On this stop he'd always have a cup of coffee and a slice of angel two-tone cake.

He'd swim in carnation-red underpants rather than a swimming togs and he'd carry his towel in a carpet bag.

In one village, after kicking up a peacock's tail of spray against the sunset on a beach where there were greyhounds' footprints like a little girl's acorn earrings, he'd have pig's head in a pub called Grunter's.

In the same village there was a sixteen-stone German man, brown as a picking berry, he'd join in a swim. The German came after the races every autumn and swam through the winter. People would come from all over to look at him.

But his favourite beach was Chapeltown where the swans gather on the sea before making journeys and after making journeys, and he'd swim out on winter evenings among the swans.

In his caravan were two photographs of a woman, one in a half-cup bra top, jersey trousers, shoes with high wedge heels, the other in a swimming suit with a key opening.

A picture of Alan Ladd in a yellow check waistcoat.

And a reproduction of Rubens' *Prometheus Bound* torn out of a library book. An eagle tearing at Prometheus. He turned downwards. His pubic parts just covered. Despite the savagery of his situation the clothes on his left side luxuriant—silvery and a deep twilight blue. The eagle chiaroscuro—some of his features gilded. The sky a mourning one—mauve, yellowy white.

When visiting boys would ask 'Who painted that?' and he'd say 'Rubens', they'd ask 'Was he a queer?'

In Killarney mental hospital there's a jigsaw reproduction of a Veronese painting in the corridor—Christ philosophically blessing wine in a tapered Venetian glass at Emmaus, little girls with spun gold hair, in décolletage, salmon petals on their silver brocade, playing with dogs at His feet, a little boy with a patina of hair fondling his own dog, a blonde woman with strawberry cheeks holding an infant, inevitably the masonry of the Renaissance—and his story was like a jigsaw picture.

'I lived with a woman. Then she took a heart attack. And I came to live in this caravan.'

Before her there'd been a boy.

'Slept out among the hop poles in Kent. Slept in a football field in Stepney Green. Used swim out to the coots' nest on Highgate Ponds.

'I met Bador. He was a good boy. But he liked the drink. What's this sex? An old cuddle and tickle. Sometimes he wouldn't come to me. He'd be out drinking with other candidates. He was sick. A bit of mental illness.

'Then we stopped seeing one another. He bent his head when he saw me.'

Silence is a tall order, the abandonment of a certain desire. At a street window in a town in Tipperary, gold clouds over a church spire like a wedding canopy in a synagogue, he remembered a Turkish bath in the East End that had a black and white portrait of Edward VII and Queen Alexandra at the burnt umber entrance.

He went to Dublin for a while and broke stones in Kilmainham for a living, and he'd swim from a shelter in South Dublin that had been built by British soldiers so they could get away from the wars, the turmoil, before they left Ireland.

He told the boys who visited his caravan that there was a place in Dublin called the Boys' Bathing Place. A ship called the *Inverisk* was shipwrecked just out from there in 1915 and boys used to swim out to it. There were rats on it so they'd bring dogs to protect themselves.

Before the woman in the photograph there'd been a few years in the FCA Barracks in Clonmel. There was a humpbacked Protestant businessman in another town in Tipperary, whose premises was stoned during the War of Independence, who rode his Harley Davidson every year to a Twelfth of July parade in a town just this side of the border, a town of almost all platinum-haired Protestants, where, wearing a sash, he'd march with the Orangemen, and he'd sit in Hearn's Hotel in Clonmel in the evenings with young soldiers in boat-necked jerseys.

He'd stay in Fenit for a few weeks and swim with the sidling blue light of the lighthouse in the evenings and the burning blanch light of the lighthouse in the early mornings.

On one beach, just before dark, as if in answer to his swim, dolphins would approach the shore speaking in short barks an almost human language. They'd play a kind of Ring Around the Rosie, going around in a circle, surfacing and submerging in the combers. Then they'd head out to sea again. It was as if they'd been telling a story.

Sometimes he could be seen pulling a small boy, whose freckled face looked like a wren's egg, speckled white, over and over again by the feet, down a chute of sand alongside a beach, rainbows playing like cubs on the sea.

There was a man near Ballinskelligs Beach who wore a trench-coat, winter and summer, and farmed marijuana.

On Inch Strand cobalt, violet and cerulean mountains were painted on the wet sands when the tide was out.

In one town, where he'd found a dead calf whale on the beach, there was a pub, an advertisement for whiskey with the four provinces of Ireland on it in the window, whose proprietress had once had a play performed at the Abbey Theatre and there was a photograph of her on the wall on stage on her opening night in a trapeze-line cock-tail dress with a silk flower under her bust, sling-back, high-heel san-dals, drop earrings, her hair in a high curled fringe. People would meet here at night and tell stories. It was cited in this pub by a Pick-wickian-faced man how in Ancient Ireland it was the storyteller's task to tell a story for each night from the beginning of November— *Samhain*—to the beginning of May.

The exploits of the Emperor Tiberius were related here, who had little boys he called 'minnows' nibble at him when he was swimming.

Sometimes people would repair from the pub to a ship in the harbour and one New Year's Eve on a Russian ship he saw Russian soldiers writing wishes on scraps of paper, setting fire to their wishes with candle flame, mixing the ash with champagne and drinking it.

A garda sergeant, in a jersey with a jacquard chequerboard design, who'd been interned in the Curragh during the Second World War for his Bolshevik sympathies, where the World's Classics were passed between prisoners, remarked that the French writer Stendhal was not only one of the few survivors of the Napoleonic invasion of Russia, but was always impeccably groomed on the way back to France. Outside there were flecks of snow in the sea air.

The proprietress of the pub stood on the deck in the snow in a chintzy boa.

He always called on a boy with a face nimbused by acne, a face that had known Killarney mental hospital, who lived in a fuschine house on one of the peninsulas, with a palm tree that had suffered in shape outside it, and who managed a garage that had an adver-

tisement for Coca-Cola that had faded to salmon beside it. This boy
had been brought up in an orphanage in a big town in Kerry by the
Brothers, a picture of a Penal Days mass on the wall, and his penis
had always been beaten when he'd wet the bed.

He spent the summer days now, when he wasn't working, driving
up and down the west coast, hoping to have his body franked by
swimmers—Bundoran, Strandhill, the changing huts on Glin Pier in
West Limerick.

He'd stand beside lifeguards' perches.

He'd never been to the East of Ireland and he never wished to
go. That was the way he'd spend his life; endlessly wandering the
West of Ireland.

Only on the west coast would touching have any meaning for
him.

When frost came he'd urinate on the gas cylinder in the mornings to get the gas flowing.

He'd kick a football in the evenings with the boys in a Black-
burn Rovers jersey, barnacle geese with their white faces, black caps
and black markings running from bill through the eye, scampering
in play or after a foe along the beach.

In the town in Tipperary he coached soccer and frequently on
Sundays he travelled with the boys in a coach to Armagh when the
Troubles were just breaking out, where a boy with shorn hair
holding the hand of a little girl in a long tartan dress with an Eton
collar and button-up patent boots might look towards the bus. In
the Middle Ages it was Malachy the anchorite, who, as Bishop of
Armagh, brought repute again to the city that had the blood of
Peter and Paul, Stephen and Laurence.

On Kilkee Strand, he'd tell the boys in Kerry, the Connaught
Rangers used to doff their scarlet trousers piped in green and play
naked football.

Inside the caravan he would often obsessively mention a film to
the boys he'd seen once in Tipperary. 'It's about these fellas who race
cars on cliffs. And one of them goes over the cliff. And the fellow
he was racing is blamed for telling the police about the lot of them.'

He'd spend the evening telling them football stories; of the Old
Handsel Monday Football Match played in Scotland in the Middle

254 / Desmond Hogan

Ages; of how football took over from bull-baiting and badger-
baiting in England at the beginning of the nineteenth century; of
how pupils of Rugby School where rugby began and pupils of Eton
where soccer began used hurl abuse at one another; of how the first
soccer star, Lord Kinnaird, who had a fiery beard to his waist, used
to play in a quartered cap and long white trousers and would be
pulled in his coach by fans to the players' entrance; of how Don-
caster FC was formed as a team to play Yorkshire Institute for the
Deaf; of how Arsenal got its name from a munitions factory in
Woolwich; of how Moscow Dynamos was founded by Lancashire
textile-men in pre-revolutionary Russia; of the confusion in the Irish
soccer team, who were featured on a set of cigarette cards, when Partition took place; of Dixie Dean who captained Everton at the age
of eighteen; of the Manchester United Team killed in the Munich
air crash on a freezing February day.

'In Liverpool there's a lot of touching, but no homosexuality,' a
boy said to him in England, whom he slept alongside one night,
peach pubic hair, a small amount of it, a ruche of a backside,
pressing his body as a child in Ireland would press a missal with gilt-
edged leaves and a cover of pearl with a picture of St Patrick with a
grandee-beard inset in it.

But here no one was touched and no one touched.

In Fenit a marine worker from Achill had once told him how
the prophecy that the last train from Scotland to Achill would bring
the body of a dead young man had come true.

Other prophecies come true too: 'And the almond tree shall
flourish, and the grasshopper shall be a burden, and desire shall fail.'

The boys would go home, walking with the aid of a flashlight.

The last beach he'd visit, before returning to Tipperary when
the peacock-green fields were brimming with black lambs and the
barnacle geese were about to return to Greenland, was Beal, where
the sea cabled in towards Limerick and the river came out, the ribs
of a wrecked trawler here and there, a landscape like a cowled monk.

The garda sergeant in the pub with the playwright proprietress
had told him, as the North of Ireland Troubles had intensified, how
the Book of Kells, the Book of Ardagh, were written in centuries of
early Christian peace in Ireland. But then the Vikings came and

monasteries began to war with one another—there were abbot and monk soldiers—and the art form was stone crosses with embossments.

Before leaving, in his caravan, in a Mao jacket, he'd sing a song for the boys who were visiting him.

> I never will marry, I'll be no man's wife
> I intend to stay single, for the rest of my life.

When asked what happened to him someone might shake their head and say, like the barnacle geese that fly so high no one can see them, 'He vanished off the face of the firmament.'

# Chintz

I met him my first time in Leningrad, New Year's 1989, in the Metropole Restaurant. I was dining with two friends who were part of my tour party, slices of sturgeon, a dessert of clementines. The orchestra played 'Let's Go to the Hop', 'I Celebrate My Love for You', 'Wild, Wild Party'. A man in a pinstripe blue suit and a girl with coronets on her high heels danced on the floor.

There was the chintz of the chandeliers, the chintz of the snow outside, the chintz of Alush's eyes when he came to the table, eyes of scabious blue. His hair was flaxen, an Arctic purity about it. He wore a shabby duffle coat. He was with a friend.

He'd come with bottles of champagne for my friends, five pounds a bottle. They'd met him on Nevsky Prospect, outside the Aurora Cinema. He sold T-shirts at Piskaryovskoye Cemetery where the dead of the Siege were buried. If caught he'd be sent to a detention centre in the country.

'Irish,' he said to me. Sometimes the Irish tourists on Nevsky Prospect showed him Irish money. They were easier with money than the British tourists.

A few days before he'd met an Irish boxer who lived in California who said that when you're a boxer you come to realize your body has peaks and lows. So you learn to time your boxing with your peak times.

He's played a Victorian boxer in a movie, wearing knee-length boxing pants and duck gaiters. He snorkled and swam through the winter with his seven-year-old son. 'He's better than me,' he said.

'Don't you feel the cold?' Alush asked him. 'No. You just jump in there,' he'd replied.

Sometimes, maybe in a boutique, in a sports shop in Southern California he heard the voices of Irish people or what he imagined were Irish accents. But then he remembered swimming in swimming pools in Belfast, where he was the only swimmer, with an armed British soldier outside and he didn't approach, he hid in the Southern California sun splash, exile outlined in his body. 'I'm a guest of the Pacific,' he said.

Alush and his friend invited us back to a flat in Ploshchad Vosstaniya for a small party where we could drink the champagne he'd sold my friends and smoke hash.

We got the metro. The flat, almost at the top of the building, was being rented to a couple for some hours so they could make love. The girl, in a long black coat and astrakhan hat, was thrown out into the snow while her boyfriend stayed. Under a poster of a naked-buttocked, helmeted Mercury guiding a girl in a transparent peplum through the sky, they played Frankie Ifield, 'Sweet Lorraine'. There was a bath in the kitchen as there'd been a bath in the kitchen of the flat of a friend of mine who died as a child.

I looked into Alush's eyes. I'd really, really despaired the previous year, thought I'd end up sweeping the streets.

I met Alush by arrangement the following day in a café, a fish lit up on a plate, over a bedding of pimentos on the wall. On the street outside an old lady in black carried a plastic bag with a girl in a flamingo bikini under spider palm trees on it.

When I told him my two friends were lovers he said, 'Homosexuals!', that he should have charged them more for the bottles of Georgian attar he'd sold them. He and his family who were devout Russian Orthodox celebrated the feasts and he named a few for me, that of St Nadezhda, of Sergius of Radonez, of the Glorification of the Mountain of Tabor, of the Protecting Veil of the Mother of God, of Our Lady of the Snowstorm.

We walked in Kuznechny indoor market where women threaded

dill and parsley and where eggs on pedestals had illuminations under them.

A few days later in Yelokovsky Cathedral the Patriarch of Moscow blessed the throng of which I was part for the Russian Christmas Eve.

Earlier I'd swum in Kropotkanskaya near Tolstoy's house, changing in a bleak room, then swimming through a tunnel out into an open-air heated pool. Snow was falling on ladies in bathing caps with baubles on them or daisies or little roses or summer anemones.

Alush haunted me over the next few months. I got a commission to write a travel piece about Leningrad from a woman whose cookbook I had used to cook a turkey my first Christmas in London and which gave me lasting recipes for a sponge cake and Irish soda bread.

I met him again, after a phone call to his family home, at evening in the Seagull Bar on the Griboyedova Canal. He was with, as if chaperoned by, a big, muscular friend, with a Tony Curtis quiff, who wore a T-shirt with a narrative about a rabbit and a tortoise on it.

He'd been in Gatchina mental hospital in the meantime. On February the third, the Feast of St Anna, he'd slashed his wrists in order to avoid the army. It was 'a cigarette for a fuck there', he said.

I knew in Stalinist times many people had gone technically mad in Russia. I had gone somewhat mad in Britain. The voices of Irish tramps, of Irish desolation, were omnipresent in London.

'Do you remember Bridget the Midget?'

'Are you a squaddie? Watch it or they'll beat you up.'

'Stay close to me. Just to be warm. I don't like what I'm going through.'

I met him again the following evening by the Stalin Gothic Palace of Youth where steps led down to the Neva. He flagged down a van. There was a blue circus tent with auric stars on it by the Neva and a boy in half-boots, cutaway jacket, shirt of glamorous salmon, stood outside it and looked at us. We went to an off-licence that was a man sitting on a bench in a park with bottles of wine under it. Walking along the Neva I put my hand on Alush's backside. There was the taint of love in my life again.

We took a boat down the Neva. A sixteen-year-old boy, in a

beige shirt with pandas and turquoise palm trees on it, who had the blond to cotton hair of a Polish woman who'd lived in my town and would give children's parties with servings in Dresden cups, was snogging with a girl from Silver City, New Mexico, who had a scarf of Killarney green in Native American style around her head.

Outside the Hermitage later, with its Caravaggio's *Youth with a Lute*—a boy, with a rose amid new greenery beside him the colour of his half-opened doll's lips, playing a lute, in an oyster-white smock with a vent for his stork-white chest, a girl's fluted veil hanging from the back of his English chestnut hair, a script with notes of music open in front of him beside a pear with a lascivious ferrule on butterscotch marble—as we listened to songs and to guitars a boy briefly touched my penis.

Caravaggio fled Rome after killing a man, first to Naples, after being knighted in Malta escaped another fracas to Sicily, died on the coast of Italy after walking a hundred kilometres only to find the boat carrying his paintings—the boys with bull earrings; the palm-readers with fillets on their heads; patterns of clothes breaking through like the lines of a palm—had already left. He undoubtedly died of a broken heart.

In a courtyard we stood in a queue and purchased the first bread of the morning.

In the evening I went to dinner in a flat of a girlfriend of his who lived in a block of flats in Prospect Veteranov. I was wearing Scout Master shorts. Women sitting beside a bed of marigolds in the courtyard howled with laughter at me. A little boy played handball by himself.

The next day was a red-letter day on the calender on the wall I saw as the girl served dessert in a strapless corselette—Anna Akhmatova's centenary day. Alush and I resolved to go to Komorova where she was buried.

On the way down a road through pine trees to the cemetery a woman, in a dress with tiny folded umbrellas on it like the umbrellas you got in a lucky bag when I was a child, ran towards us. 'The Patriarch of Leningrad is there,' she cried. We just missed him. Women who'd come in umber buses had left Anna Akhmatova's grave and run amok around other graves, reciting poetry.

It turned out they were reciting Akhmatova's friend Marina Tsvetaeva's poetry.

In Paris in the 1930s Marina Tsvetaeva had to borrow a white dress for a reading because she had only one woollen dress she'd been wearing all winter.

'Why didn't she leave Russia?' Alush asked me about Anna Akhmatova.

'Some people can't leave their country no matter what.'

'Why commit suicide?'

After visiting the cemetery we swam in the Lake of Pines and Alush, a muff daisy chain on now, slats of light running over his face, talked about escaping to the United States.

When I returned to Leningrad solo and not as part of a tour, as I had to do previously, by train from Berlin in March 1991, Leningrad under snow, I rang Alush's home and was told he'd gone to Manhattan.

I returned again by train in June 1991 from Berlin, met the friend who'd been snogging with the American girl, in a Byron-shirt and hat like the young Walt Whitman, on Nevsky Prospect, and he told me that Alush and his friends gathered on a rooftop in Manhattan every Sunday morning, wearing tie-dye T-shirts, smoking hash and shelling sunflower seeds. They had parties in the evening in the hall of the religious group who'd sponsored many of them coming to the United States, where they drank Dr. Peppers and ate tea-cakes under an inscription from Dietrich Bonhoeffer: 'Brother, till night be past pray for me.'

In early April 1997 coming from Southern California to New York on my way back to Ireland, the sun cutting through the sky-scrapers to the cherry and pear trees, which were a fleece of blossom against the brownstone buildings of Manhattan, I met him, by chance, in Chelsea bagel shop. He was wearing tie-dye shorts with red kisses on them as many young men in New York wore shorts on mild days in winter and early spring. Manhattan skyscrapers were powder blue in the afternoon sunshine. A man in elephant trousers, with a Pekinese on a red ribbon, paused and looked at us.

He was married to a girl from Long Island now.

A Russian friend had recently returned to St Petersburg on a visit and, despite the fact he spoke Russian, in a music club they asked 'Who's the foreigner?' and tried to charge him exorbitantly as they would a foreigner.

In New York on his arrival he spent a lot of time with American Romany Gypsies who'd sit under charts showing family trees in their kitchens. With his girlfriend he attended a Romany wedding in Pennsylvania. On the train journey there he'd seen Amish people riding in buggies.

At the Romany wedding they gave out scarves to the women as they would at a Russian funeral and handkerchiefs to the men. A pig was roasted. The amounts of money people donated as presents were announced. Alush saw his reflection in house trailers that had laminated pictures of beaches, palm trees, curtseying blue waves on them.

In a house trailer with a laminated stallion outside it, beside an egg timer with faded skyscrapers on it and the word Chicago underneath, was a photograph of Gypsies from the Kiev region who were gassed in one of the concentration camps; skirt with diamond shapes, a girl's white dress with honeycombed front and collarette, stockings with ticker tape, mare's tail of hair, raven scarves, polka-dotted waistcoat, a Tyrolean hat with medallions, a Montmartre hat, a moustachio, a soldier in forage cap, an accordion with a keyboard, a cello, violins.

'First a Jew, then an American,' said a Jewish boy at the wedding. 'First a Romany, then an American,' said a Romany boy at the wedding. 'First a Russian, then an American,' said Alush now.

'Before it wasn't easy to survive. Now everything must go through corruption. And before it wasn't easy corruption. But it was a way of meeting people. Now it's vicious, dangerous, violent and still there's the KGB, the army, the navy. They have the money. They are the mafia.'

He went to Fire Island in the summer, wore shorts, fifties shirts purchased in thrift stores, had his body universally admired in the flint aquamarine. But his body was exiled in marriage now.

Sometimes he and his wife camped by a lake near a Buddhist monastery in upstate New York.

Before I'd left England I'd moved from South-East London for the last few months to Hampstead, 'a place of transition', someone said, where people walked harlequin Great Danes on the Heath by the violet- and yellow-leafed elderberry trees and the torch-henna chestnut trees, where Goldilocks-yellow Virginia creeper garbed houses that once held silver spoons whose legend, as the dying Keats saw, drew hordes of 'gypseys' to Hampstead.

I met three American Dhamnapala Buddhist monks in golden robes coming out of Keats House and one in white robes. They'd left America and moved now between monasteries in Northumberland, Devon, Herefordshire, Sussex and monasteries near Kanderstag near Thun in Switzerland and Santa Cittorama in Sezze Romano, Latina.

'Will you go back to America?' I asked them.

'No, we'll keep moving.'

'Will you go back to St Petersburg?" I asked Alush now.

'Sometime. It's changed, it's not Leningrad anymore.'

For some reason as I said goodbye to him I thought of the Jewish man I'd seen during my last few months in Britain, on the night boat from Dover to Ostend, as I crossed to Amsterdam, in a prayer shawl, tallow and black striped, quietly droning prayers.

In this city I'd once asked an English boy if I could sleep with him. He was small, muscular, possessed of good looks, cleft in his chin, sleeper in his ear. We slept platonically alongside one another, his penis unaroused, gathered in. There'd been a Dutch boy, his flat-mate, in the next room. The English boy had once worked in community centres for Catholic and Protestant children in Belfast. A year and a half later he visited me in South-East London, shortly after I'd moved there, with his New York Jewish fiancée and brought sugar pretzels. A woman from Ireland, red-gold-haired, exiled in London, had come there a few weeks before—the same night as there'd been a little Irish-Mauritian boy present who had hair the colour of the candy carrot aloft a carrot cake—in a hobble skirt and in a wide-brimmed hat with chick feathers on it and called the food I'd prepared 'beauteous'.

In this city I'd once walked through Central Park as a concert of Jewish laments was being held. From this city I'd once returned to Iowa and the flag with the wild rose of Iowa on it blowing over the pumpkins alongside the Stars and Stripes, against the cornfields at sunset. In this city I'd once purchased a woollen tie of solid yellow for myself.

The fox has an earth and the badger a set but back in the part of the West of Ireland where I'd lived I had to look for a new abode.

The Traveller boys in cast-off Harris tweed or herring-bone jackets swim the horses in the river, bits of slate blue or citron, unpatterned material at their necks.

Later the boys in extreme viridian and chrome-yellow football jerseys, some with piercers in their brows, as a last sulky goes by on the bridge, will fish on the pier for white trout.

A priest at school one autumn had read Ovid's words about how, even after years in exile, he still broke down crying when he remembered his last night in the city.

*Cum sabit illius tristissima noctis imago …*

During my last days living in Berlin I'd gone to an American movie at the Berlin Film Festival and afterwards the director stood on the stage in loafers and jeans alongside the German youth who was introducing him, beautifully groomed, who looked from side to side, glad to be there, wearing a jacket threaded with chintz, a last pattern breaking from the palm of a hand.

I returned to Berlin very briefly that fall, when the German Coxes and the Kaiser Crown pears were in the fruit stores, standing beside the Stalingrad Madonna on Martin Luther Day, 31 October, in Gedächtniskirche with its algal blue light from the stained glass.

At the close of October I swam in Grünewald Lake. You could just make out a last swimmer on the other side and I remembered Alush telling me by the Lake of Pines in Komorova about those who broke the ice in winter to swim at the Men's Bathing Place on the

Neva where boys did somersaults into the river in summer, samizdat scrawls on the wall of the bathing hut, illustrations that looked like Cyrillic letters. On New Year's Day people held feast-day candles as they swam and there were presentations of bunches of red carnations.

I'd seen a wedding party there on one of the White Nights— they were from Belorussia (a boy in a shirt with a contraband pattern—an imbroglio of apricot tuxedos, black bow ties, teddybears who promised music—mimed driving a tractor to show that)—the groom and the best man, chintzy maidenhair fern in their lapels, urged on by a mother of one of the bridal pair in a Sultana's turban hat, by a girl in a Veronese green dress with ostrich-egg baubles around her neck, stripping naked and somersaulting into the lacquered water.

When I swim in the river at night, having cycled by the light of Chipland, which perhaps may have illuminated a face or two—boys in bricolage (olive, umber) combat trousers as though an echo of the Serbo-Croatian War—or perhaps having cycled in from the Shannon estuary where people used to make boat pilgrimages to the holy wells on the islands—near the Buddhist monastery in Santa Cittorama, Sezze Romano, Latina, a Buddhist monk told me in London, the monks roast artichokes in the hills in the evenings and once an Irish boy came and stayed with them and his face was lit up in the evenings, an intensity of lips and a dust of henna freckles, like a face someone was looking for and, like a Russian, by the fire, he'd recite poetry or prose passages, often in the Irish language, as if the act of memorizing and continually repeating was the sole survival, the indemnity, of these words—I can see the light of Shannon Airport circling in the sky on the other side of the estuary and sometimes the tail lights of a plane taking off from Shannon Airport, heading to the Atlantic, are reflected in the river and the side growth, and further down the river a cob cries out for a companion.

# The Bon Bon

My father used frequently take the train to Athlone to buy sweets in the Bon Bon: army and navy sweets, rhubarb and custard sweets, banana sweets, chocolate macaroons, Winter Mixture, Dolly Mixture, cough lozenges, fudge and lemon bon bons. If I went with him I was content with yellow, twisted sticks called Peggy's Leg. On the glass shelf was a picture of a woman in a poke-bonnet advertising Variety All Sorts.

Afterwards we'd have a Coppa Vanilla Italia in the Genoa Café where there was a picture of Eva Marie Saint for years beside an illustration of a Knickerbocker Glory, before it was replaced by a picture of Monica Vitti.

Boys with elephant-trunk hairstyles, in shoes with winkle-picker toes, girls in circle skirts, with anklets, would be sitting around the tables.

Shortly before, Seán South and Fergal O'Hanlon had been killed during a raid on Brookborough Barracks in Northern Ireland. When *Rock Around the Clock* with Bill Haley and the Comets was shown in the Town Hall there was a queue, mainly of elderly and middle-aged women, halfway down Society Street. Their number increased when its hasty sequel, *Don't Knock the Rock*, was shown.

It was in the Genoa Café that my father told me the story of the French film star, whom people had seen in Swanwick's Cinema, where there were potted plants beside the penny seats, play a monk who was burned at the stake, who gave street performances in Eyre Square in Galway, near the Imperial Hotel, in the autumn of 1937, exhorting people to join in with him.

In a pelerine—a long cloak for men—with back-swept Phoenician hair, beaked features, he looked like a raven.

He waved a sword embedded with hooks and a shillelagh of the type sold to American tourists, which he called the cane of St Patrick.

Waving these two appendages high in the air, he was spotted on top of Gentian Hill.

People, who'd once gone to Galway to see Edward vii—Teddy—and Queen Alexandra, took the train to Galway to see him.

A monsignor who was renowned for reciting filthy limericks in Galway parlours conversed with him about Euripides.

They sent him to the mental hospital in our town where he was detained for a few nights.

He recited a speech from *Richard II* for a file of mental-hospital patients being brought for a walk:

> So Judas did to Christ: but he, in twelve,
> Found truth in all but one; I, in twelve thousand, none.
> God save the King! Will no man say amen?

He then went on to Dublin by train where his exploits made national headlines. A man whom he exhorted to join him in a street performance hit him on the head with a crowbar at the suggestion. He was locked up in Mountjoy Jail and from there sent back to France in a straitjacket.

Perhaps because of his visit they started doing street performances on the boardwalk in Salthill in Galway during the War, plays about St Patrick and his bald charioteer Totmael, as well as doing displays of the four-hand reel.

The mental hospital staff started sending away to P.J. Bourke's for costumes and presented a play each Christmas.

When my father visited Dublin in the summer he always met Mr MacGonagle, the head of a travelling player company who came to town every October after the fair, always wearing a canadienne—a sheepskin coat—for his stay, because of the time of year, and went for a swim at the Forty Foot with him.

Mr MacGonagle had labourer's shoulders, pale scrolled face, luminary's lips.

He'd known Maud Gonne MacBride. In old age she had turned from politics to the theatre and would sit in her drawing room, in a raven's wing dress, entertaining travelling players.

Once when the three of us, Mr MacGonagle, my father and I, were walking by the railings of St Stephen's Green, Mr MacGonagle waved to a red-haired woman, in Spanish maya black, outside Smyth's of the Green. She was an actress.

'She's from Galway,' he said: fox-coloured West-of-Ireland hair—brindles, spears of gold in it; face masked with freckles; an elegance of stance, of shoulders; rallying nose, chin.

Mr MacGonagle always wore a leghorn to the Forty Foot.

He could tell us how Sir Walter Scott once swam here in snug trousers and the other swimmers applauded him; how just after the War, a garda sergeant raided the Forty Foot, arrested two young men for sunbathing in the nude, led them away through the pell-mell of villas, had them brought to court, both in zoot suits, one in a tie with skyscrapers, the other in a tie with a ketchup sunset, they were defended by a theatrical personality who wore white gloves and maquillage and the case was thrown out.

On one of those first visits there I remember a naked young man with Titian-red pubic hair standing against the sea with Hesperides becalment.

In our classroom, which had a picture of Morough of the Battle Axes beside a painting of a Titan Pope Pius xii standing among a flock of sheep which I did myself, Mr McWeeney, our teacher, who had a Franz Liszt haircut, often played John McCormack records on a gramophone, as well as playing records by Delia Murphy, whom he called Mrs Kiernan, wife to the Irish Ambassador to the Holy See.

I'd seen a photograph of Delia Murphy in the Sunday paper, in an evening dress with leg-of-mutton sleeves, long cape fringed with sable, pearl ear studs, with a cardinal in a skull cap, beside a headline which said: 'Irish girl bitten by shark.'

John McCormack was from Athlone and often on our walk

back from the Bon Bon and the Genoa Café to the train station my
father and I stopped on the bridge over the Shannon, the subject of
a poem Mr McWeeney frequently recited with thespian variations:

> Break down the bridge—Six warriors rushed
> Through the storm of shot and the storm of shell!

As a very young man with a roach à la pompadour who wore
drape jackets with beaver-fur trim, he'd sung for Queen Alexandra
who told him she was hard of hearing and could hardly hear the
brass band in the Albert Hall but she'd heard every word he'd sung
perfectly. Despite international celebrity he'd failed to impress Puccini and he believed this was because he was Irish. Neither Puccini
nor Athlone liked him. John McCormack was born on the banks of
the Shannon.

There was a boy from our town who went to Dublin, sat in the
Mug of Four Café in Townsend Street in the mornings, waiting to be
picked up for labouring jobs, returned as a Teddyboy in a dandy suit
with a velvet collar, sang Lonnie Donnegan's 'Rock Island Line'
against a curtain that has crescent moons on it at the St Patrick's
Night concert, was drowned while swimming in the Suck, near a
ruined Elizabethan fortress where Sir Philip Sidney, who was painted
by Veronese in Venice and the portrait lost, was said to have stayed on
his way to Galway in a pair of Poulaines—French boots—to meet
the sea-captain Grace O'Malley, the Teddyboy's shoes with 1¾-inch
soles, Persian melon socks, shirt with a harlequin pattern, Hi-Waist
Y-fronts, drainpipes found on the bank among the cuckoo flowers.

My true love hath my heart, and I have his.

In the Town Hall was a Men's Club above the cinema in which
there was a picture of Doris Day in house pyjamas and the men had
bored a hole in the wall so they could take turns watching the films.

They were taking turns watching *The Singer not the Song* with
Mylene Demongeot the night the Teddyboy was drowned, when a
Teddyboy friend of his walked in in a black V-necked jersey, black
Slim Jim tie with horserings and scintilla white circles, Santa Claus
red ankle socks, and played a game of billiards.

In the Royal British Legion Men's Club, which was a hut among a grove of oak trees nearby for First World War veterans, there was a mosaic of pictures and photographs of British Royalty arranged by a man called Rusty Pistol, including one of Edward VII and Alexandra of Denmark at sea—Alexandra: Geisha-doll features, black boater, polka dot, mandarin neck with brooch, black wasp-waist coat with epaulettes and wide, pinstriped collar. Edward: pepper-and-salt beard, beefy features, sailor's cap and sailor's jacket, anchor tie-pin on the knot. 'God save the King! Will no man say amen?'

Jumble Breetches, one of the First World War veterans, sitting on the Market Place wall, was rewarded with the sight of Princess Margaret driving through town in a Rolls-Royce, in a veiled flower toque and Marie Antoinette peruke, to visit her in-laws in County Offaly.

In the Town Hall, the autumn before the Teddyboy was drowned, the conductress, who'd studied in Heidelberg, who had a bosom thrust forward like a coast pigeon, wore lamé sheath dresses during performances, had slapped the face of the Lady of a rural manor who'd acquiesced to play Margot Bonvalet in Sigmund Romberg's *The Desert Song*, during rehearsals, which fact had more significance in the town than the 1916 uprising.

But the Lady of the Manor was nonplussed, returning to the Town Hall in early spring to play the changeling in Mícheál Mac Liammóir's *Ill Met by Moonlight*, walking about the stage in a trance in a bow-necked white organza nightgown from her own wardrobe.

The Teddyboy's father put an In Memoriam photograph in the *Galway Advertiser* each year—mouth nimbused by a moustache, poplin shirt, bootlace tie—like a lost portrait by Veronese.

John McCormack's ambition, when he was a boy in Athlone brought up on Dion Boucicault productions, was to own a Franz Hals, which he eventually did, purchasing Franz Hals' *Portrait of a Man* from the Blue Palace, Warsaw.

There was a priest in Loughrea who wrote a book that caused a great outcry but before that happened he used to bring John McCormack, when he was still only a teenager with a puppyfat chin, in wing collars and elephant ties with eclipses of the moon on them, to sing in the new cathedral, on which he'd worked himself, under a Sarah Purser stained-glass window.

'Ties had beautiful colours that time,' said my father who himself was wearing a Windsor tie, as we paused on the bridge over the Shannon, on the way back from the Bon Bon and the Genoa Café, to the train station.

I was carrying home—from a shop where a woman was forever in the window, watched by small boys, rearranging cartoon postcards with double-entendre captions, one clipped onto the other—a copy of *Photoplay* which had a colour photograph of Sandra Dee in a poodle skirt with Capri-blue slashings and black and white ones of Georgia Moll, looking like a matreshka doll in *The Cossacks*, and an ensemble of Cossacks doing a Soviet dance.

Objects were metonymies for my father.

As he spoke he took out of his pocket a crouched figurine from the top of a slice of iced madeira fruit cake he'd got in the Genoa Café when the Christmas tree on the shelf was decorated with pine cones wrapped in tinsel and with bon bons.

'Every colour you could think of. And beautiful designs.'

Ties were scarce. Businessmen and people like that always had them. In the country on Sundays and holy days people had ties.

Men only got a new shirt if they were married. The poor lads didn't know how to make a knot on the ties. They had to learn. It was an art.

The first thing you looked at in a photograph was a tie.

The men had stiff fronts and the mother had to iron them Saturday nights. Men's shirts had beautiful buttons. Some of them were so wide they covered the whole breasts.

'Sometimes they were tiny.'

'God of Abraham, Jacob, Isaac, have compassion for my children,' was a prayer Mr Vigoda, a Jewish tailor, who wore a kippa with mirror-moon discs, my father worked for in London EC in the 1930s, would recite aloud, behind algal brocade—a part of the world where Puccini's 'O Soave Fanciulla' from *La Bohème* or Puccini's 'O Mio Babbino Caro' from *Gianni Schicchi* dovetailed into 'Daddy Wouldn't Buy Me a Bow-Wow' and 'I'll Send You Some Violets'.

At the train station on our arrival, boys in forage caps and maxie kilts, with mica-bronze freckles, in Athlone for a match, played, with drums and fifes, 'The Brian Boru' and 'Brian O'Lynn', watched by a woman in a high turban, in pumps the blue of sea holly, with net uppers, clapped voraciously by thirteen- and fourteen-year-old girls, their hair sock-style, with brooches and hair clasps won in the lottery of Lucky Bags, and a Traveller man with an Elvis Presley cockscomb, in a polo-neck jersey, and his son who was in a corduroy jacket, short corduroy trousers, wellingtons, sold the County Clare colours, glitter-blue and lemon-gold.

# Winter Swimmers

Winter swimmers, you brave the cold, you know you've got to go on, you make a statement. A Tinker's batty horse, brown and white, neighs in startlement at the winter swim. A man rides a horse on Gort Hill, disappearing onto the highway. Tinkers' limbs, limbs that have to know the cold to be cleansed.

'The Tinkers fight with one another and kill one another. If someone does something wrong they beat the tar out of them. But they don't fight with anyone else. You never see a Tinker letting his trousers down,' a woman whispered in Connemara, sitting on a wicker pheasant chair. The flowering currant was in blossom outside the window.

A Traveller boy in a combat jacket with lead-coloured leaves on it stood outside his Roma Special, among washing machines, wire, pots, kettles, cassettes, tin buckets.

Some day later there were lightening streaks of white splinters across the road where the Travellers had been.

In early summer the bog cotton blew like patriarchs' beards, above a hide, the stems slanted, and distantly there were scattered beds of bog cotton on the varyingly floored landscape under the apparition-blue of the mountains.

I was skipping on Clifden Head when a little boy came along. The thrift was in the rocks. 'Nice and fit.' He wanted to go swimming. But he had no trunks. 'Go in the nude,' I said. 'Ah, skinny-dipping. Are you going again?' I was drying. 'No, I'll go elsewhere and paddle.'

'I used pass him in the rain outside his caravan,' the woman in Connemara told a story before she went to mass, about a Tinker man who died young, standing in an accordion-pleated skirt, 'sitting by a fire against the wall. "Why don't you go inside?" I'd ask him. "Sure I have two jackets," he'd say. "I have another one inside. I can put on that one if this one gets wet."'

'Are you a buffer or a Traveller?' a Tinker boy asked me. On their journeys there are five-minute prayers at a place where you were born, where your grandmother died.

There was a Traveller's discarded jersey in a bush. Buffer— settled—Travellers stood in front of a cottage with the strawberry tree—the white bell flower—outside.

A Traveller in a suit of Mosque blue came to the door one day to try to buy unwanted furniture, carpets. 'He had a suit blue as the tablecloth,' went the story after him. Part of his face was reflected in the mirror. It was as if a face was being put together, bit by bit.

A Traveller youth in a cap and slip-on boots which had a triangle of slatted elastic material held his bicycle in a rubbish dump against a rainbow. The poppy colours of the montbretia spread through the countryside in the hot summer. There were sea mallows between the roads and the sands.

You felt you were nuzzling for recovery against landscape.

The sides of the sea road towards fall were thronged with hemp agrimony. The seaweed was bursting, a rich harvest full of iodine. As I was leaving Galway the last fuschia flowers were like red bows on twigs the way yellow ribbons were sometimes tied around trees in the Southern States.

'Now therefore, I pray thee, take heed to thyself until the morning, and abide in a secret place, and hide thyself.'

You felt like a broken city, the one sung about in a song played on jukeboxes throughout Ireland. 'What's lost is lost and gone forever.' In May 1972 you heard a lone British soldier on duty sing 'Scarlet Ribbons' on a deserted sun-drenched street in that city.

Old man's beard grew among the winter blackthorns in West Limerick. Tall rushes with feathery tops lined the road to Limerick. Traveller women used fashion flowers from these rush tops.

The bracket fungus in the woods behind my flat was gathered on logs like coins on a crown, stories.

On the street of this town the Teddyboy's face came back, brigand's moustache, funnel sidelocks, carmine shirts, the spit an emblem on the pavement. He had briar-rose white skin.

'They'd come in September and stay until Confirmation time,' a woman in a magenta blouse with puff sleeves whispered about the Travelling people. When I was a boy Travellers would draw in for the winter around our town.

A pool was created in the river behind the house in which I was staying and I swam there each morning, the river, just after a rocky waterfall, halted by a cement barrier. On this side of the town bridge the river is fresh water. On the other it is tidal. Swans often sat on the cement barrier when only a meagre current went over it.

On this side it is a spate river and the current, always strong at the side, after rain, is powerful, I did not gauge its power and one morning I was swept away by it, over the barrier, as if by a human force. I had no control. There was no use fighting. I was carried down the waterfall on the other side of the barrier to another tier of the river, drawn in a torrent. I saw pegwood in red berry on the bank. I got to the side, crawled out. In Ancient Ireland they used eat bowls of rowan berries in the autumn.

One morning I tried the tidal part of the river at the pier called Gort. In Irish *gort* means field, field of corn. It is very close to the word for hunger, famine—*gorta*. The flour ships from Newcastle and Liverpool used come here. People would carry hay, seaweed to the pier. A slate-blue warehouse shelters you from view.

When I was a boy they used hold a rope across the river at the Red Bridge, someone on either side, swimmers clutching it and then the swimmers would be pulled up and down.

I remembered a man drying the hair of a boy in the fall of 1967.

I had a friend who used swim naked when he found he had the place to himself. One day someone hid his clothes in the bushes and a group of girls came along. He hid behind a bush until they went.

He was writing what he called a pornographic novel for a while. As we passed some Travellers' caravans one autumn day he told me a story. A boy, a relation, a soldier in Germany, came from England, slept in the bed with him. At night they'd make love. The evenings during his visit were demure. They'd have cocoa as if nothing had happened. My friend had a modestly winged Beatle cut, wore vaguely American, plum or aubergine shirts with stripes of indigo blue or purple blue.

A Traveller in a stove-pipe hat called to the door one afternoon and offered five pounds for a copper tank that was lying behind the house, his hand ritualistically outstretched, the fiver in it. I said I couldn't give it to him. It was my landlady's. The copper tank disappeared in the middle of the night.

An English Gypsy boy with hair in smithereens on his face, his cheeks the sunset peach of a carousel horse's cheeks, in a frisbee, carnelian hearing aid in his left ear, on a bicycle, stopped me one day when I was cycling and asked me the way to Rathkeale. I was going there myself and pointed him on.

In Rathkeale rich Travellers have built an enclave of pueblo-type and hacienda-type houses. They were mostly shut up, the doors and the windows grilled, the inhabitants in Germany, the men tarmacadaming roads. A boy with a long scarf the lemon-yellow of the Vatican passed those houses on a piebald horse.

I moved down the river to swim in the mornings, nearer the house where I lived, and swam among the bushes, putting stones on the ground where there was broken glass. There'd been a factory opposite the pool.

When I was a boy it was an attitude, swim in rain, ice, snow, brave these things, topaz of sun often in the wet winter grass, topaz in the auburn hair of a boy swimmer.

A group of young people used swim through the winter. Even when the grass was covered with frost and the blades capped with pomegranate or topaz gold. They'd pose for photographs in hail or snow. I was not among them but later I had no problem swimming in winter, in suddenly, after some months of not swimming, taking off a Napoleon coat in winter and swimming in winter in the Forty Foot in Dublin or on a beach in Donegal.

There was something benign about these young people. Mostly boys. But sometimes a few girls.

One day in Dublin I met one of the boys just after his mother died. It was winter. We didn't say much. But we got on the 8 bus to the Forty Foot and had a swim together. He went to the United States shortly after that.

Some English Gypsies were camped outside town and one day a boy on a Shetland pony, with copper crenellated mid-sixties hair and ocean-ultramarine irises, asked me, 'Did you ever ride a muir?'

'Look at the horse's gou,' he said referring to a second Shetland pony a boy with skirmished hair was holding, 'Would you like to feak her?'

It's like a bandage being removed I thought, plaster taken off, layer and layer, from a terrible wound—a war wound.

Christmas 1974, just before going back to Ireland from London, I slept in a bed with an English boy under a bedspread with diamond patterns, some of them nasturtium coloured. He had liquid ebony hair, a fringe beard. He wore his bewhiskered Afghan coat, spears of hair out of it. In bed his body was lily-pale—he had cherry-coloured nipples. On our farewell he gave me a book and I put the Irish Christmas stamp with a Madonna and Child against a mackerel-blue sky in it.

All the journeys, hitch-hiking, train journeys overlap I thought, they are still going on, they are still intricating, a journey somewhere. It's a face you once saw and it brushes past the Mikado orange of Southern Switzerland in autumn, a face on a station platform. It is the face of a naked boy in an Edwardian mirror in a squat in London with reflections of mustard-coloured trees from the street.

When I returned to England in the autumn of 1977 I went on a daytrip to Oxford shortly before Christmas with some friends and we listened to a miserere in a church and afterwards sat behind a snob-screen in a pub where tomtits were back-painted on a mirror. It was another England. I was sexually haunted. By a girl I'd loved and who'd left me. By a boy I'd just slept with.

In Slussen in Central Stockholm I once met a boy with long blond centre-parted hair, in a blue denim suit, and he told me about the tree in Central Stockholm they were going to cut down and which they didn't, people protesting under it. I bought strawberries with him and he brought me in a slow, glamorous train to his home on the Archipelgo, a Second Empire-type home. There were Carl Larsson pictures on the wall. It was my first acquaintance with that artist. He sent me two Carl Larsson images later. Images of happiness.

Years later I met that boy in London. He was working in the Swedish army and leading soldiers on winter swims or winter dips.

At the Teddyboy's funeral there were little boys in almost identical white shirts and black cigarette trousers, like a uniform, girls with bouffant hairdos, shingles at ears, in near-party dresses, in A-line dresses, in platform shoes, in low high heels with T-straps, with double T-straps, carrying bunches of red carnations, carrying tulips. In Ancient Rome, after a victory, coming into Rome, the army would knock down part of the city. At the Teddyboy's funeral it was as if people were going to knock part of the town.

The Teddyboy wore a peach jacket in the weeks before he was drowned. He was laid out in a brown habit. My mother said it was that sight which made her forbid me swim at the Red Bridge with the other young people of town. In the summer when I was sixteen I tried to commit suicide by taking an overdose of sleeping pills at dawn one morning. I just slept on the kitchen floor for a while. At the end of the summer a guard drew up on the street opposite our house in a Volkswagen, the solemn orange of *Time* magazine on the front of the car. He'd come to bring me to swim at the Red Bridge. Years later, retired, he swam in the Atlantic of Portugal in the winter.

At the end of the summer of 1967, when I was sixteen, I started swimming on my own volition.

In early February the wild celery and the hemlock and the hart's-tongue fern and the lords and ladies fern and the buttercup leaves and the celandine leaves and the alexanders and the eyebright and fool's watercress came to the riverbank or the river. There was the amber of a robin among the bushes who watched me almost each morning.

Here you are surrounded by the smells of your childhood, I thought, cow dung, country evening air, the smell the grass gives off with the first inkling of spring, cottages with covert smells—the musk of solitary highly articulate objects—and a mandatory photograph on the piano. My grandmother lived in a house like the one I lived in now. She had a long honed face, cheekbones more bridges, large eyes, Roman nose. She was a tall woman and spoke with the mottled flatness of the Midlands.

Here's to the storytellers. They made some sense from these lonely and driven lives of ours.

When I was a child in hospital with jaundice there'd been a traditional musician who'd been in a car accident in the bed beside me. There were cavalcades of farts, an overwhelming odour as he painfully tried to excrete into a bedpan behind the curtains but the insistent impression was, in spite of the pain, of the music in his voice, in his many courtesies.

You heard the curlew again. 'The cuckoo brings a hard week,' they said in Connemara. One year was grafted onto another. 'March borrows three days from April to skin an old cow,' they'd said a month earlier, meaning that the old cow thinks he's escaped come April. Two swans flew over the Deel and the woods through which golden frogs made pilgrimages among the confectioner's white of the ramson—wild garlic—flower, soldering stories.

On a roadside in County Sligo once I sat and had soup from a pot with legs on it with a Traveller couple. Now I knew what the ingredients were—nettles, dandelion leaves.

With May sunshine I started to go to Gort to swim each day. Traveller youths swam their horses in the spring tide, up and down with ropes, urging them on with long pliable horse goads with plastic gallon drums on the end. One of the Traveller youths had primrose-flecked hair. Another a floss of butter-chestnut hair. Another hair in cavalier style. 'You've a decent old tube,' said the boy with the primrose-flecked hair.

During the day I noticed his hair had copper in it.

One evening during spring tide I saw him stand in a rose-coloured shirt, not far from cottages, by the river where it was bordered by yellow rocket float down.

The first poppy was a bandana against the denim of the bogs of West Limerick.

In the evenings of spring tide when the Travellers came along and swam their horses I was reminded of St Maries which I'd visited twenty years before, when the Gypsies would come and lead their horses to the water on the edge of the Mediterranean. To Saintes Maries had come Mary, mother of James the Less, Mary Salome, mother of James and John, and Sarah, the Gypsy servant, all on a sculling boat. There were bumpers by the sea and in little dark kiosks jukeboxes with effects on them like costume jewellery. Lone young Gypsy men wandered on the beach, great dunes on the land side of the beach. A little inland horsemen with bandanas around their noses rode horses through the Camargue.

Back briefly in the river pool one evening I found the Traveller youth with the cavalier hair shampooing himself after a swim. His underpants were sailor blue and white.

Later that week when I came to Gort the boy with the primrose-flecked hair was there alone with his horse, a Clydesdale, ruffs at his feet. A few days' growth on his face, he was naked waist up. There was the imprint outline of a tank top—the evidence of hot days, his nipples not pink—hazel, a quagmire of hair under his arms, freckles berried around his body. His body smelt of stout like the bodies of young men who gathered in my aunt's pub in a village in the Midlands when I was a child. A rallying, a summoning in the body to dignity.

I am in the West of Ireland, I thought. Illness prevents me from seeing, from looking. Like a soot on the mind. Sometimes I raise my head. Like Lazurus recover life—especially vision.

One Friday evening as I cycled home from Gort the youth with the primrose-flecked hair introduced himself. 'Cummian.' And he introduced the other two youths. 'Gawalan. Colín.'

'You need a relationship,' he said.

When the tide came in in the evening again his horse had a wounded leg and he tied it to the ship rung on the pier and it would stand in the water for hours. Cummian stayed with it and he'd watch me swim and between swims he'd tell stories.

'There was a man who fucked his mares. He tied them to trees.'

'Someone sold a horse to a man who lived on Cavon Island off Clare and the horse swam back across the Shannon estuary to West Limerick.'

Two Traveller brothers troubled over a horse at Gort, their voices becoming muffled. They seemed to wager the tide. The river had a mirror-like quality after rain. Late one evening Cummian was sitting in the bushes to one side with some men, one of whom was holding up a skinned rabbit. Boys would often fish on the pier with the triple hook—the strokeall—for mullet. On the far side young men would hunt for rabbits with young greyhounds. On summer nights Travellers would draw up on the pier in old cars—Ford Populars, Sunbeams. In Scots Gaelic there's a word, *duthus*—commonage. That's what Gort was, people coming, using the place in common. The winter, the dark days were a quarter I thought, now I have to face people, I have to communicate. There was often a bed of crabs on the river edge as I walked in.

'If I wasn't married, I'd get lonely,' said Cummian one evening.

Water rats swam through the water with evening quiet, paddling with their forepaws. The tracks of the water rat made a V-shape.

Sometimes in the early evening there'd be a harem of Traveller boys on the pier in the maple red of Liverpool or the strawberry and cream of Arsenal or the red white of Charlton FC or the grey white of Millwall FC.

'Where are you from?' asked a boy in a T-shirt with Goofy playing basketball on it.

'You don't speak like a Galwayman but you've got the teeth.'

Cummian would tell stories of his forebears, the Travelling people—beet picking in Scotland, 'We lie down with manikins.' That ancestor used write poems and publish them in *Moore's Almanac* for half a crown.

Sometimes he got four and six pence. 'Some of them were a mile long,' said Cummian.

'They used stuff saucepans with holes with the skins of old potatoes and they'd be clogged. They used milkcans especially. Take the bottoms out of milkcans. Put in new ones.'

With his talk of mending I thought, recovery is like a billycan in the hand, the frail, fragilely adjoined handle.

In the champagne spring tide of late July Cummian rode the horse in a bathing togs as it swam in the middle of the river.

One afternoon there was a group of small boys on the pier fishing. One had a Madonna-blue thread around his neck, his top naked, his hair the black of stamens of poppies.

'I'll swim with you,' he said, 'if you go naked.' I took off my togs. They had a good look and then they fled, one of them on a bicycle, in a formation like a runaway camel.

Sometimes, though rarely, Traveller girls would come with the boys to the pier, with apricot hair and strawberry lips, in sleeveless, picot-edged white blouses, in jeans, in dresses the white of white tulips. Cummian's wife came to the pier one evening in a white dress with the green leaves of the lily on it, carrying their child.

Cummian was a buffer, a settled Traveller and lived in one of the cottages near the river, incendiary houses—cherry, poppy or rosette coloured—with maple trees now like burning bushes outside them. There'd be horses outside the Travellers' cottages—a jeremiad for the days of travelling.

One night Travellers were having a row on the green by the river—there was a movement like the retreat of Napoleon from Moscow, hordes milling across the green. Cummian, holding his child, looked on pacifically. 'You're done,' someone shouted in the throng.

There was a rich crop of red hawthorn berries among the sea-weed in early fall, at high tide gold leaves on the river edge. Reeds, borne by the cork in them, created a demi-pontoon effect.

A woman in white court high heels came around the corner one day as I stood in my bathing togs. 'This place used be black with swimmers during high tide. Children used swim on the slope.'

A swan and five cygnets pecked at the bladderwort by the side of the pier and the cob came flying low up on the river, back from a journey.

In berry the pegwood, the berberis, the rowan tree were fairy lights in the landscape. The pegwood threw a burgundy shadow onto the water. With flood the reflection was the cinnabar red of a Russian ikon.

One day in early November Cummian was on the pier with his horse alongside a man with a horse who had a sedate car and horse trailer. The grass was a troubled winter green. The other man, apart from Cummian, was the last to swim his horse.

'He likes winter swimming,' Cummian said of his. 'Like you. He'd stay there for an hour. And he's only a year.'

With the tides coming in and going out there was a metallurgy in the landscape, with the tidal rivers a metallurgical feel, something extracted, called forth. A sadness was extracted from the landscape, a feeling that must have been like Culloden after battle. On Culloden Moor the Redcoats with tricornes had confronted the Highlanders.

'Why do you swim in winter?' asked Gawalan who was with Cummian one evening.

'It's a tradition,' I said, 'I used to do it when I was a boy,' which was not true. Other people did it. I did it later, on and off in Dublin.

Jakob Böhme said the tree was the origin of the language. The winter swim sustains language I thought, because it is connected with something in your adolescence—the hyacinthine winter sunlight through the trees on the other side of the river. It is connected with a tradition of your country, odd people—apart from the sea swimmers—here and there all over Ireland who'd bathe in winter in rivers and streams.

A rowing boat went down the river one afternoon in late November, a lamp on the front of it, reflection of lamp in the water.

Gawalan and Colín went to England. They'd go to see female stripteasers first in the city and then male stripteasers.

With November floods there were often piles of rubbish left on the riverbank. A man in a trenchcoat, with rimless-looking spectacles,

cycled up to the pier one evening. 'I hear them dumping it from the bridge at midnight. It kills the dolphins, the whales, the turtles. You see all kinds of things washed in further down, pallets, dressers.' He pointed. 'There used be a lane going down there for miles and people would play accordions on summer evenings. A boxer used swim here with wings on his feet. There was a butcher, Killgalon, who swam in winter before you. He swam everyday up to his late eighties.'

The river's been persecuted, vandalized I thought, but continues in dignity.

Early December the horse swam in the middle of the river, up and down, and I swam across it. The water rubbed a pink into the horse.

Hounds, at practice, having appeared among the bladderwort on the other side, crossed the river, in a mass, urged on by hunting horns.

A tallow boy's underpants was left on the pier. Maybe someone else went for a winter swim. Maybe someone made love here and forgot his underpants. Maybe it was left the way the Travellers leave a rag, an old cardigan in a place where they've camped—a sign to show other Travellers they've been there—spoor they call it.

Towards Christmas I met Cummian near his cottage and he invited me in. 'Will you buy some holly?' a Traveller boy asked me as I approached it. Cummian's eyes were sapphirene breaks above a western shirt, his hair centre parted, a cowlick on either side.

There was a white iron work hallstand; an overall effect from the hall and parlour carpets and wallpaper and from the parlour draperies of fuschine colours and colours of whipped autumn leaves. He sat under a photograph of a boxer with gleaming black hair, in cherry satin-looking shorts, white and blue striped socks. On a small round table was a statue of Our Lady of Fatima with gold leaves on her white gown, two rosaries hanging from her wrist, one white, one strawberry; on the wall near it a wedding photograph of Cummian with what seemed to be a pearl pin in his tie; a photograph of Cummian with a smock of hair, sideburns, Dom Bosco face, holding a baby with a patina of hair beside a young woman in an ankle-length plaid skirt outside a tent.

We had tea and lemon slices by Gateaux.

Christmas Eve at the river a moon rose sheer over the trees like a medallion.

Christmas Day frost suddenly came, the slope to the water half-covered in ice. In the afternoon sunshine the ice by the water was gold and flamingo coloured.

Sometimes on days of Christmas the winter sun seemed to have taken something from the breast, the emblem of a robin.

Cummian did not come those days with his Clydesdale. I was the only swimmer.

I was going to California after Christmas. I thought of Cummian's face and how it reminded me of that of a boy I knew at national school, with kindled saffron hair which travelled down, smote part of his neck, who wore tallow corded jackets. His hand used to reach to touch me sometimes. At Shallowhorseman's once I saw his poignant nudity, his back turned towards me. He went to England.

It also reminded me of a boy I knew later who smelled like a Roman urinal but whereas the smell of a Roman urinal would have been tinged with olive oil his was with acne ointment. One day after school I went with him to his little attic room and he sat without a shirt, his chest cupped. There was a sketch on the wall by a woman artist who'd died young. He used often walk with his sister who wore a white dress with a shirred front and a gala ribbon to an aboriginal Gothic cottage in the woods.

He went to England in mid-adolescence.

He was in the FCA and would sit in the olive-green uniform of the Irish Army, his chest already manly, framed, beside a bed of peach crocuses on the slope outside the army barracks which used to be the Railway Hotel, a Gothic building of red and white brick, a script on top, hieroglyphics, the emblems of birds.

It snowed after Christmas. The trees around the river were ashen with their weight of snow. There were platters of ice on the water.

As I cycled back from swimming Cummian was standing with two Traveller youths in the snow. There was a druidic ebony greyhound in historic stance beside them. Their faces looked moonstone pale.

I knew immediately I'd said something wrong on my visit to Cummian's house. It didn't matter what I'd said, it was often that way in Ireland, having been away, feeling damaged, things often came out the way they weren't meant. Hands in the pockets of a monkey jacket, hurt, Cummian's eyes were the blue that squared school exercise books when I was a child.

There was a Canadian redwing in the woods behind my flat who'd come because of the cold weather in North America. Never again I thought, as I was driven to Shannon, the attic room of beech or walnut, a boy half-naked, military smell—musk—off him, a montage on the wall. Choose your decade and change the postcards. Somebody or something dug into one here.

I have put bodies together again here I thought, put the blond or strawberry terracotta bricks together.

In San Diego next day I boarded a scarlet tram and a few days later I'd found a beach, the ice plant falling by the side, plovers flying over, where I swam and watched the Pacific go from gentian to aquamarine to lapis lazuli until one day, when the Santa Anas were blowing, a young man and a young woman came and swam naked way out in the combers, then came in, dried, and went away.


The Red Bridge, a railway bridge, always porous, became lethally porous, uncrossable by foot. Cut off was an epoch, gatherings for swims.

People would trek over clattery boards who knew it was safe because so many people went there.

In the fall of 1967 trains would go over in the evening, aureoles of light, against an Indian red sun. You'd hear the corncrake.

A little man who worked in the railway would stand in the sorrel and watch the boys undress.

Shortly before he died of cancer he approached me, in a gaberdine coat, when I was sitting in the hotel, back on a visit. He spoke in little stories.

Of Doctor Aveline who wore pinstriped suits, a handkerchief of French-flag red in his breast pocket, and always seemed tipsy, wobbling a little.

Of Carmelcita Aspell whose hair went white in her twenties, who wore tangerine lipstick and would stand in pub porches, waiting to be picked up by young men.

Of Miss Husaline, a Protestant lady who went out with my

father once, who didn't drink but loved chocolate liqueur sweets.

Of the bag of marzipan sweets my father always carried and scrummaged by the rugby pitch; squares of lime with lurid pink lines; yellow balls brushed with pink, dusted with sugar, with pink hearts; orbs of cocktail colours; sweets just flamingo.

And he spoke of the winter swim. 'It was an article of faith,' he said.

# Caravans

The September river was a forget-me-not blue and the bushes on the other side were gold brocade. The old man who stood beside me as I got out of the river had glasses tied by a black strap around his head. He lived in a cream ochre ledge-top Yorkshire wagon with green dado, near the river.

'I've been here fourteen years but I'm moving tomorrow to a field near Horan's Cross,' he said, 'The children torment me. I hit some sometimes and I was up with the guards over it. We were blackguards too. They used wash clothes on stones in streams. There was an old woman who used wash her clothes and we'd throw stones at her.'

Looking at the river he said: 'A young butcher and a young guard used swim to the other pier, practising for the swim across the estuary in the summer. I used swim the breast stroke, the crawler. But then I'd put on swimming togs and go out and stand in the rain. It was as good as a swim.'

There'd been another caravan parked beside the old man when I first came to live in a caravan nearby and an Englishwoman lived in it sometimes dressed as a near punk—in an argyle mini skirt with a chain girdle—and sometimes as a traditional Gypsy with a nasturtium yellow shawl with sanguine dapples and a nasturtium yellow dress with sanguine dabs on it which had attenae.

In my first few weeks living in a caravan by a field there was the blood translucence of blackberries, the mastery of intricate webs, the petrified crimson of ladybirds on nettles.

On one of my first mornings the guards arrived in plain clothes. A guard with jeans tight on his crotch banged on the door. 'Mrs Monson has objected to you,' he said referring to a woman who lived in a cottage nearby.

In my first few weeks in a caravan I realized that living in a caravan there was always the laceration, the scalding of a nettle on you, the tear of a briar, the insult of a settled person. But you noticed the

grafts in the weather, mild to cold in the night, fog to rain. You saw the pheasant rising from the grass. Close to the river you were close to the hunger of the heron, the twilight voyages of the swan, the traffic of water rats.

In the night there was a vulnerability, a caravan by a field near a main road, a few trees sheltering it from the road, the lights of cars flashing in the caravan, a sense of your caravan's frail walls protecting you.

Coming to live in a caravan by a field near a main road was part of a series of secessions.

A few weeks after I'd come to live in West Limerick I was gathering firewood in the wood behind my flat, yellow jelly algae on the logs, sycamore, maple, ash wings on the grass, when a little boy in a frisbee and a shirt with chickens wearing caps and flowers and suns on it, came up to me on a bicycle. His hair had the gold allotted to pictures of the Assumption of Mary in secretive places. The sky over the river was a brothel pink. 'Pleased to meet you.' When I raised my axe a little he dashed away.

Sometimes as I walked in the fields in the winter I'd see him, tatterdemalion against the trunk of a rainbow. Dogs were often digging for pigmy shrews in the fields.

One day he was in the fields with two greyhounds of a friend on leashes, one white with marigold mottles, the other fleecy cream and tar black with a quiff on the back.

In the spring he knocked on my door. 'I'm looking for haggard for my horse. I wonder can I put a horse behind your house?' He had a seed earring in his right ear now.

'If I be bereaved of my children, I am bereaved.' Sometimes on summer nights when I swam in the artificially created pool in the fresh water part of the river behind my house he'd be there. On one side of the town bridge the river was fresh water. On the other side it was tidal water. He'd be leaping from the high cement bank with other Traveller children. Ordinarily he looked boxer-like but in swimming togs I saw that his legs were twig-like—almost as if he was the victim of malnutrition.

'On your marks, ready, steady, go,' he'd command the other children. 'Did you ever tread the water?' he'd ask me. Meaning being almost still in near-standing position in the water.

In the early autumn when I'd go to swim on the pier in the tidal part of the river he'd often be there with his horse, shampooing his horse's tail. The horse was a brown horse with one foot bejewelled with white and with a buttermilk tail. The boy's features were hard as a beech nut or an apple corn now. He'd look at me with his blueberry and aqua-blue mix eyes. 'I can't swim her now. She's in foal.' The foal when it came was sanguine coloured. The boy left both of them in a meadow on the town side of the pier. The foal would sometimes go off on a little journey, a little adventure, and the mare, tied, would whinny until his return.

I went to the United States and after my return in the spring I found the flat I'd been living in had been given away. I moved into another flat in the same house. It was unsatisfactory. Cycling to the pier I'd watch and listen for the little boy. There was no sign of him. I wondered if his family had moved on, if he was in England. Then one day at the end of April he rode to the river on his horse. The time for swimming the horses had come again.

Up and down the Traveller men swam their horses. Steel greys—white horses with a hail of dark grey on them, Appaloosas—speckled Indian horses, skewbalds—batty horses, piebalds.

Handsome horses with sashes of hair on their foreheads. A man with round face, owl eyes, stout-coloured irises, hard-bargained-for features, in an opaque green check shirt, spat into the water as he swam his horse. On his forearm he had tattoos of a camel, a harp, a crown.

The boy when he brought his horse to the water had a new bridle on her, viridian and shell pink patterned. He told me of the things that happened while I was away. In February the otters had mated by the pier.

I found a cottage in the hills outside the town and the boy's father who had kettle-black eyebrows, piped locks, roach hairstyle, wore a Claddagh ring—two hands holding a gold crown—on his finger, drove me there.

I put a reproduction of Botticelli's *Our Lady of the Sea* over the fireplace, her jerkin studded with stars.

'Say a prayer to St Mary,' an English boy, the son of a painter, who cycled to a flat of mine in London in an apricot T-shirt, said to me.

The cottage was near a church but despite that fact I soon found that local people were knocking on the back windows at night, cars were driving up outside the house at night and hooting horns.

I'd cycle to the river everyday. There were roads like Roman roads off the road through the hills. 'Finbarr Slowey bought a house there and brought his wife and children,' a Traveller man with Indian-ink-black hair and Buddha-boy features who was at the river with his strawberry roan, told me, 'and they drove up outside his house at night and hooted horns. If they don't want someone to live in their village they hoot horns outside their houses at night.'

Many sumach trees grew in this area as in the Southern States and I kept thinking of the Southern States. The bunch of ante-bellum roses; the tartan dickie bow; the hanging tree beside a remote bungalow with a dogtrot. The brother of a friend of mine from a Civil Rights family was killed by the Ku Klux Klan on the Alabama–Georgia border. This area was very similar to the border country of Alabama and Georgia. Great sheaves of corn braided and left out for hurling victors; boys in green and white striped football jerseys dancing with girls at the Shannonside to the music of a plat-form band; the shadow of a man in a homburg hat at night.

'The IRA's up there,' said the Traveller boy, 'And vigilante groups. They tar and feather people.'

At night when I'd be trying to sleep people would stand behind the house and bang sticks. I didn't think there was any point going to the guards. A guard with black lambchop sidelocks and a small paste-looking moustache came by at about eleven o' clock one night and asked me if I was working.

I couldn't sleep at night. I didn't see the Traveller boy by the river so I sought him out. I always thought his family were settled Travellers but when I enquired in the cottages near the river they said: 'He lives in a caravan up by the waterpump.'

A long sleek caravan with gilt trimming, occasional vertical gilt lines, flamingo shadows in the cream. Behind it, on the other side of the road, was a flood-lit grotto. His mother was standing by the window—buttermilk blonde hair, mosaic face over a shirt with leg-of-mutton sleeves—above the layette, the celestial cleanliness of aluminium kettles and pots laid out for tasks. She wore a ring with a coin on it. There was a little blonde girl with yellow ducks on her dress and a little boy with cheeks the yellow and red of a cherry and eyes a turquoise that looked as if it had just escaped from a bottle. On the caravan wall was a framed colour photograph of a boxer with a gold girdle and on a cupboard a jar of Vaseline. I remembered an English girl whose father was a miner telling me that miners always put Vaseline in their hair before going down into the mines. The Traveller boy was wearing wellingtons the colour of sard.

'You've no choice,' said his father, 'but to buy a caravan and move into it.'

The boy's father got a little caravan for me and I moved into it.

The hazelnuts were on the trees by the river the day I moved into the caravan. In being moved from house to caravan I found out the boy's name, his father referring to him. Finnian. A hawk had brought St Finnian the hand of an enemy who had tried to slay him the previous day.

A middle-aged single woman who had connections with the Travelling people moved into the cottage in which I'd been living and they started banging on her window at night. She couldn't sleep. A room was found for her on Maiden Street in Newcastle West. I'd often see Traveller boys with piebald horses on Maiden Street in Newcastle West.

Shortly after I moved into the caravan a little boy with a Neopolitan black cowlick and onyx eyes knocked at the door. 'I heard you like books. I have murder stories. Will you buy some?'

'Do you want to buy a mint jacket?' asked Gobán, a Traveller boy with a sash of down growing on his lips who lived in a caravan near Finnian's. He was wearing a plenitudinous pair of army fatigue trousers. He went into his caravan and brought it out. It was malachite-cream, double-breasted, almost epaulette shouldered, with a wide lapel.

He and Finnian would often come to my caravan and I'd get them to read poems.

> The nineteenth autumn has come upon me
> Since I first made my count:
> I saw, before I had well finished,
> All suddenly mount ...

Both Finnian and Gobán were in identical Kelly-green fleece jerseys. 'Will I tell you a joke?' said Gobán as Finnian read. 'Stand up and be counted or lie down and be mounted.'

Finnian and Gobán and I would have tea, and half-moon cakes and coconut tarts I'd buy in Limerick.

Sometimes when Finnian would be out lamping for rabbits at night he'd knock at the caravan door and request Mikado biscuits.

The boys would come at night and tell stories; of the priest who used go on pilgrimage to Lough Derg and bring a bottle of Bushmills around with him on the days of pilgrimage; of the local woman who dressed in religious blue, spring gentian blue, and broke into the priest's house one night and put on his clothes; of the single Traveller man with the handlebar moustache who lived in a caravan and had a bottle of Fairy Liquid for ten years; of Traveller ancestors who met up with other Travellers they knew from Ireland on Ellis Island before entering the United States; of a relative of Finnian's who went to America, joined the American navy and was drowned while swimming in Lough Foyle during the Second World War when his fleet was stationed there.

'Long ago in West Limerick,' said Finnian's father, 'they had rambling houses—went from house to house telling stories.'

Every year settled Travellers in Ireland—buffers—make a long walk to commemorate the days of travelling. One year it was Dublin to Downpatrick, County Down. Despite the insults, the contumelies heaped against Travelling people, you keep on walking.

On December twenty-first, the winter solstice, Finnian and Gobán and Gobán's smaller brother Touser brought a candle each and put them in the menorah in my caravan and lit them against the winter emerald of West Limerick. Touser had a fresh honey blond turf cut, a pugilist's vow of a body.

A rowing boat with a red sail had gone down the river that day.

Patrick—Patricius—had once lit the paschal flame in this country.

When he couldn't sleep Caesar Augustus would call in the story-tellers and as we had tea and Christmas cake they told stories and jokes and in the middle of stories and jokes came out with lines from Traveller songs—'I married a woman in Ballinasloe', 'I have a lovely horse'—and, the lights of cars flashing in the caravan, it was as though all four of us were walking, were marching through the evening.

# The Match

'Tell us the story of Mary, Queen of Scots,' Kevin and Will, the two Traveller boys would often say in my caravan. I would tell them the story again, how when Mary Stuart came from France to claim her Scottish kingdom she sent a naked swimmer to shore from each of her two ships, how people tried to make a match for her with many kings and princes but how she fell in love with the young tall bisexual Lord Henry Darnley and married him, how he was strangled on the streets of Edinburgh wearing nothing but his nightgown, how on her flight from Scotland she survived on porridge, how when captive in the English Midlands she would give alms to the poor when she went to bathe in a holy well, how when she returned to the Midlands from another place of captivity she told the beggars she was as poor as they were now, how when the thistles grew in the early summer around the castle where she had been beheaded they were called Queen Mary's tears.

'You've lived here three years,' Will said one day, when the bottom of the sky was smoked white with dapples of cerulean in it like the pattern in the breast panel of a medieval costume, 'and you've never gone with a boy. We know a big fellow—he's about seventeen or eighteen—who sucks langers. We'll bring him here for you.'

Will had parted glinting copper hair. Kevin had shorn sides with the crest dyed sunflower-yellow. Will wore an open-work choker with a gold medal on it. He had a body with ambition. Kevin had a string of diamanté jewels around his neck. Outside the caravan they'd hitched a chocolate and ice-cream horse with gold threads in its mane.

Some evenings later they led a boy dressed entirely in black across the fields.

'This is Conal,' Kevin said, 'but he has another name too, Clement.'

Conal had Spanish ebony hair like a lot of people in this area of Ireland. A year after Mary Stuart's beheading Philip II of Sapin had sent the Spanish Armada to Ireland and the ships had foundered off the coast of Kerry, many of the survivors settling in Kerry or making their way here to West Limerick.

Conal had the physical fullness and the block features of many boys in this area. His shoulders crouched the way the shoulders of boys crouched in First Holy Communion photographs.

With two names he was like a country with two languages. On one of his fingers he wore a virgin signet ring.

'Say the poem by Tommy Hardy about the ruined maid,' ordered Kevin. Both Will and Kevin behaved like matchmakers. They had me stand and recite the poem, making the appropriate music-hall, effeminate gestures. 'You should be in a concert,' said Kevin.

Thomas Hardy's poems were the favourite recitations.

'Take off your shirt and show your muscles,' commanded Will.

'Tell the story of Mary, Queen of Scots,' Kevin requested.

After I'd done what had been demanded of me I asked if each person in the caravan would tell a story.

First it was Will's turn and he told how he had his grandfather's false teeth.

Then Kevin told of a boat on the river with three men in it and how a hole came and one of the men stuffed it with his coat.

Will had another. The rats got into their caravan called Freedom and had baby rats and the caravan had to be burned to the ground. 'A rat would climb a caravan,' he said, 'a rat would climb a hostel.'

'Our father was in the army,' Kevin recounted, 'and he was forced to join the IRA. They told him he'd be kneecapped if he didn't join. He got out after a year.'

'Our cousins in Rathkeale swim in their clothes,' said Will.

'My father ties a rope around me and drops me in,' told Kevin.

With the bad summer there'd been few people at the river and I'd seen no swimmers. Flocks of teal skimmed it. The curlew had lived there and a crane and a mallard and the long-tailed silver bird. There'd been the glamorous blue of the watch on the other side.

Sometimes instead of swimming here I'd cycled to a banished beach on the Shannon estuary. 'No public person goes there,' the old lady, with hair of cultured pearl, in the nearby store had informed me. She told how the people who'd owned it had taken the sand from it, not wanting it there, but the sand came back of its own accord. You would never meet anyone there. The sea tides came in as they did to the river.

The landscape reminded me of the monastery of Lindisfarne in Northumberland, the way it was suddenly surrounded by water— water suddenly impinged on castles in curvaceous ruin.

A few evenings before as I was swimming there wild geese had flown over crying against the shades of peacock's tail in the sky, heading across the estuary.

On my way back I stopped at the old lady's shop. Some boys were sitting on a bench, drinking soft drinks. But her two grandsons who had carrot and apricot complexions were away at school now.

The mullet were jumping in the river when I swam on another stop. A heron bade my presence by skimming the water.

Now it was Conal's turn to tell a story.

'Des, St Colmkille would sleep on a pillar as a pillow in Donegal. Then he went over to the Island of Iona in Scotland and a crane followed him. St Colmkille said to a monk, "Look out for a crane because he's going to be very tired when he gets here and look after him." The crane arrived and the monk fed him and looked after him for three days. Then he went back to Donegal satisfied. St Colmkille saw a poor old woman pick nettles in a churchyard for her dinner. And he said from this day on I'll eat only nettles. And from that day on St Colmkille ate only nettles. St Colmkille was dying on a Sunday because he said Sunday is a day of rest and the white horse that carried the milk from the dairy to the monastery came up and laid his head on his chest. St Colmkille looked towards Donegal and he blessed it. He blessed the corn. And then he died, aged eighty-seven. And the white horse cried like a human being.'

We walked a little in the night, Conal and I, by the hawthorn bushes and the apple and pear trees, which gave only berried fruit now, in the field where my caravan was. The berries of the hawthorn had been cardinal red in the day's sunshine. By the estuary now were the raven berries of the blackthorn and the bog bilberry and the red berries of the guelder rose. The estuary was the blue of a blue butterfly these days.

'Did anyone ever catch you swimming naked in the river?' he asked.

I told him I swam more in the estuary now where no one could see you. With no one to talk to out there, a glissade of landscape by the ruined castle, I recalled people I'd met in my life.

That afternoon I'd thought of Evert, the little boy with punctured upper lip who sat beside me on the night bus from Johannesburg to Capetown one September, the South African spring, how his cousin, a soldier, with argent gold hair, had been standing at one of the bus stops, how the Christ-thorn had been in blossom in the Ceres mountains as we neared Capetown. Afterwards I sent him a postcard with the amaranth-purple Algerian Coffee Stores in Soho on it.

Streets change. A car started honking at a film-maker on that street who was walking to his favourite café. 'Hurry up, slow coach.'

He turned. 'I'm dying, you know.'

In a bar in Dublin once an Irish writer, wearing a cravat like the quiddity of a rugby-playing boy in the 1940s, had recited Paul Verlaine's poem about Soho to me.

Meetings, moments magical ...

When I'd arrived to live in London from Ireland a boy in a café in Soho with eyes the grey-green of orchard lichen had looked into my eyes. No one had ever looked at me like that in Ireland.

In my mind by the Shannon estuary today I sent a postcard to Evert. He'd be about eighteen now, with columnar locks maybe, in a jersey of harebell blue, slacks of royal blue, like a Limerick schoolboy, sitting at a café table in a park in Capetown under the yesterday, today and tomorrow trees in blue, white and mauve blossom.

In the night Conal said to me: 'I have a Saudi Arabian girlfriend.' And he took a crumpled letter from his pocket as if in evidence of sexual orthodoxy.

Pearse and Jonathan, two boys nearer Conal's age, had arrived.

Pearse wore a Foreign Legion beret and a Gypsy sleeper. In his face was the face of a girl I'd known who had boscage blonde curls like the blossom in some lost Arthur Rackham poster.

The blue of his eyes was the wheeling blue of the Mediterranean near Pisa where I walked with that girl once and saw an imaginary little boy. It was the forlorn blue of the sea asters among the rocks by the beach on the Shannon estuary, the urgent blue of the last scabious in the Shannonside fields.

That little boy had never been born but maybe he'd been the people I'd met, bits of people, children who'd leaned their head towards you on a bus in the night.

Pearse was born in the year of the Falklands War. Someone had told me a story about an English soldier who'd gone to battle in the Falklands with Sandy Denny's songs on his headphones. He'd been killed.

I often thought of her song 'Traveller by Trade' here.

Pearse sometimes stood on the town bridge saying 'This is Elvis singing' and singing Elvis Presley songs or 'Dirty Old Town'.

Jonathan wore a bull's earring and combats—army fatigue trousers. He had a cub muscular body like that of a boy I'd known at school who smelt of walnuts and brine from acne ointment.

His hair was crinkled 1930s style and his eyes had a gaping expression like a walrus in a state of surprise.

Pearse asked for some of my aftershave in a phial. He was going to a wedding. 'I'm going to wear Clarks shoes and a poplin shirt. All the boys will be there with cuff jewels. My little sister is going to be the peach girl.'

I asked Pearse and Jonathan to tell a story. Pearse told how a bullock was lost for days and found up a tree. Jonathan's was about how he borrowed a friend's billy goat and the goat ran away to a remote Shannonside ruin and the only way he could catch it was by borrowing a she-goat so the billy goat went towards her.

Sometimes they went to an old hall and sat in old-fashioned style, boys on one side, girls on the other, but danced to music like 'Sex on the Beach' or 'I Was Up at the RDO Glay'. But there were some boys who desired other boys—boys with earrings like the rung on the pier by the river where I swam to which ships used be tied at full tide—and turned up their collars.

But there was sometimes the answer of violence to desire—boys went home with bruised faces. The bruises on the face were a code for days.

Desire was as unanswered as it had been for a boy I knew when I was growing up who dressed entirely in black, had hair of India ink—an ancestor, maybe a survivor from the Spanish Armada—who had killed himself with rat poison.

The blue of that boy's eyes was found again in the autumn Roman skies, in the Michaelmas daisies old ladies ferried along Roman streets, in the eyes of young pilgrims of desire in the squares at night who were so at peace with their company that there was no need for desire.

'Do you have any more cakes?' Jonathan suddenly demanded. The last bun had been thrown across the caravan. As I lit the stove to make more tea Jonathan began blowing out my matches one by one without making any movement of his lips.

'I'll have no matches to make coffee for my breakfast,' I said.

There was no personality in the whites of his eyes. The atmosphere had changed so suddenly there was no connection with what had gone before, Jonathan requesting me to recite Lord Byron's 'So we'll go no more A-Rowing' and listening to it with the mellifluous expression of a young laird.

'Please leave me some matches for my breakfast.'

In my mind I saw the frieze of Lord Henry Darnley's Elizabethan auburn pubic hair as he was strangled on the streets of Edinburgh, the tartan shawl of an old woman who heard him crying for
mercy in the name of a noble, young laminated Christ.

'Stop blowing out the man's matches,' Jonathan told Conal. But
he continued to do it. Then suddenly he pushed Conal on to my
writing desk, completely smashing it. Everyone left then.

By the river where I would swim was a disused warehouse. At the
beginning of the century the paraffin for all the lighthouses on the
Shannon estuary was stored in it. The Lights House it was called.
One morning I came along to swim and there was a crowd of men.
They were turning it into a factory. You could no longer swim there.
A video camera lit up and filmed you at night if you approached the
pier. I left for the Atlantic coast.

Will and Kevin's father, the Traveller man, drove me, my goods
in a little trailer behind his car. We stopped briefly by the warehouse.
Teasel grew at the bottom of the lane which led from the road to
the pier.

'When I was a boy there were rocks there and seaweed grew on
them and people would gather the seaweed and sell it. Then they took
the rocks away,' the storyteller said. The previous evening there'd been
an old man on the bench in the old lady's shop. 'In Cromwell's time
they were building a bank by the Shannon here. So they didn't drive
us to Connaught. They left us here to complete the job.'

When I was a child the workhouse which saved lives during the
Famine burned down. In the morning I saw Billy Burgoyne, the
barber, cycle by the British Legion hut, past the oak trees which had
not been cut down yet, to see the smoking ruin. I don't know why I
remembered that.

# Wedding at Gallog

'Then he up with the story and told me ...'
There was a boy from Eton College called Daniel who came to the area, cherry outbreaks in his cheeks, keg of blond curls on his forehead, worked as a farm hand and swam the horses at Gort Pier, in a denim jacket blue as a coast cornflower, and he told her the story of Daniel and Susanna, how Susanna was falsely accused by the two elders of making love under a tree to a young man while bathing in the garden with soap and olive oil, and was being stoned to death when Daniel appeared, separated the two elders and asked them under what tree she was making love. One said a clove tree. The other a yew tree. So they were found out in their lie and Susanna's life was saved ...

Oonagh Cade got married to Cian Colleran, who was in the FCA in Duncannon, and the reception was held in a hotel in Gallog on a day the gilia blue of medieval skies, when the Himalayan balsam was in blossom along the Shannon.

The waiters were Lithuanian boys. They went to Norway in July to pick strawberries, in September to sow strawberries. In late autumn they came to work in this hotel. One of them, with a chin tuft, talked about Lithuania. 'My grandfather who is ninety says things were best in days of Stalin.'

The women, many with Venetian red hair that would warrant a

fire brigade, field-rose white skin, wore boleros, Far West leather cowboy trousers, prune and plum harem trousers, sunray pleated skirts; toques with veils, turbans with brooches; hoop earrings; stilettos with rosettes, stilettos with low vamps.

The men, many with the fiery red hair of the fox in autumn or the red berries of the lords and ladies fern, wore Palm Beach suits, suits the pink of the magnolia, drainpipe trousers; shoes with winkle-picker toes; Christopher Marlowe earrings; had their hair slicked back, with half-column locks, Regency locks.

Some of the small boys were blond porcupines.

Phyllis Griffenhagen, an English Gypsy with kipper-coloured hair, who had three royal photographs in her caravan—the amorous Edward VII and Queen Alexandra, George VI and Elizabeth Bowes-Lyon, Edward VIII and Wallis Warfield Simpson—wore a cocktail hat trimmed with feathers, a black dress with chiffon yoke, high heels with diamanté-studded T-straps. A Traveller woman, thin as an eel—pewter-coloured hair in a brindle on either side of her head—face veined like the outer leaf of a cabbage, sharp-featured as an axe, wore a floral-printed glazed cotton skirt and bootees with elasti-cated sides. Manus Culligan, who had been converted by the Jehovah's Witnesses and baptized his children in Kildimo Lake where men walk greyhounds in tartan surcoats, wore a tiger shirt.

Cian, rose-auburn hair, foggy green eyes with persimmon blazes in them, wore alligator shoes and a bootlace tie. On his ring was a Canadian coin.

Oonagh, Grecian nose, dark crock of gold curls, wore an Ottoman wedding dress, and, like an Arcadian bride, a headdress with silk roses and lillies of the valley with a silk-tulle veil.

In Amsterdam, where he'd lived with some Traveller boys from Limerick on Daniel Stalpertstraat, Cian had drunk too much in an Irish pub with the sign of the dolphin over the door beside it.

Outside the pub one night, beside a scarlet pavement post with gold stars on it, because he looked so forlorn, some Dutch boys from the provinces approached him and urinated around him as a sign of disgust.

In the mirror he looked like a self-portrait of the Dutch artist Jan Mankes, who died young, which he saw on a postcard.

Tubercular eyes, poppy lips, cheekbones like Jewish peoth.

He sat by himself one June day in St Francis Xavier Church on Singel. A woman and a little boy lit a candle in front of a statue of a gold Virgin with rubric undersleeves and a child with a gold bracelet on his wrist and gold apple in his hand.

He took a train the colour of a peeled apricot to Zandfoort aan Zee. On a windowsill was a statuette of an old Chinese woman kissing the nude breast of a young Chinese woman. Inside a house he saw a table with a small bible at each place.

On the beach were shells, saffron and white. Suddenly, when there was no home and no country, as if out of nowhere, against the sunset, a man in a Zouave cap went by in a sulky, an Irish Traveller in Amsterdam maybe. For a moment he pulled up and declaimed to his horse; what was his language—Dutch or Gammon? He pulled off his cap, the sides of his head were shorn, the top a mouse's nest, his nose was large, a patriarch's nose. His lips were slashed peach, the upper lip razor sharp. Then he tugged at the reins and continued, vanishing into the dark of the beach. That night Cian decided to go home to Ireland.

He joined the FCA in the cliff-side barracks in Duncannon in County Wexford. As the sea was coming in closer in the South-East the soldiers had the job of building dams of rocks on the beaches in the summer to ward off the sea, so much of the sand beaches had disappeared.

Recently the father of one of the soldiers in Duncannon had died and they'd brought him to his island in Connemara to bury him, the soldiers in uniform carrying the coffin over the sand at low tide. They carried the coffin past the cottage from which there were twelve brothers who were a football team in New York, a cottage in which there'd been a man who, when his wife was successively pregnant, a woman would come carrying a sack of potatoes and make love to him.

Cian's friend had told him of the father—he was a widower—and son on this island who were lovers. They were both winter swimmers, cycling to a small beach, having a summary swim each evening.

Complaining they have *meas madra*—respect for a dog—for you in Connemara, the boy, who had duck-egg-blue eyes and a cuckoo's egg expression, dark hair with blond lightings in it, went to New York, where he'd pick up fellow exiles from Connemara at last mass in St Patrick's Cathedral on Sunday mornings. 'Get any Connemara boy drunk,' he'd enjoin, 'and you'll get his trousers down.'

Sometimes in winter in Duncannon the soldiers had to swim in the sea as part of a survival course. Before he decided to marry Cian went to Cyprus alone and swam for fourteen hours to the next resort.

'Did you know that a badger always makes its own bed, brings out its feathers and straw in the mornings to air?' Oonagh's father would say to them on Gort Pier, where the heron snatched up frogs from the riverbank, when they were children, 'Did you know how a fox gets rid of flies? Takes a stick in its mouth and the flies go on to it. Backs into the water, and drops the stick.'

But it was of birds their father, whom they called Gearoidh, knew most. The crested titmouse. The woodpecker. The dunlin. The sand martin. The screech owl. The Pied flycatcher. The stonechat. The twite. The mistle thrush. The laughing goose.

In their French four-wheeler with a stove and a generator, under a picture of John F. Kennedy in a baby-blue tie, on winter nights, he told them that the heron had a powder down on the sides of his breast which he uses as a cosmetic. That when one starling of a nesting pair perishes the survivor immediately secures a mate and this mate is often of the same sex. That curlews used settle on ships bringing immigrants home, four or five hundred miles out of New York, flying alongside the ship by day, resting on it at night, until the Irish coast was sighted. That the woodcock stamps on the ground to bring worms to the surface.

That the male tern or sea swallow offers an eel to the female tern he's courting. That the herring gull decorates the edge of its nest with hyacinths. That coots have boxing matches in water. That a coal-titmouse makes its nest in a squirrel's drey.

That a blackbird will spend hours looking at its own reflection in a window. That the corncrake, who survives around St Ciaran's Monastery of Clonmacnoise and on the Aran Islands, when trapped pretends to be dead and at first opportunity flies away.

That a white cygnet is known as a Polish swan.

When Oonagh was a child there was a Protestant woman who

lived in a manor in the countryside near a Methodist church, a countryside of castellated walls where coal-tits flitted among the montbretia in summer, who had fallen into destitution. From the settlement around that church Methodists had gone to America and introduced the Methodist faith. But despite destitution the woman always arrived at the Protestant church in town on Sundays in her Bentley Continental, valiantly dressed. The Traveller girls, in their dresses with Peter Pan collars, would watch her as she stepped out, very erect and gaunt like an old poodle, her face the quavering, beak-like face of the magpie who came with the seventeenth century to Ireland. The Protestant lady was sometimes chaperoned by a girl with a Dutch cut, in a feather-threaded beret, knee-length boots with high heels. She herself in pink herringbone suits, blue tweed suits, cerulean hopsack jackets with crêpe-de-chine blouses; tocques with bird of paradise feathers; stilettos with almond toes.

In the countryside near the Protestant woman's house were a few surviving Methodists who, having fled here originally from the wars of Louis XIV in the Palatine, would gather in the church when the berries were blood-diamond around it, to commemorate Philip Embury, Barbara Heck, Robert Strawbridge, who introduced Methodism from Ireland to the United States; women with roll fringes, clubbed hair, men with long grizzled beards.

When she was a child she used to go with her father to a horse fair on the first Thursday of every three months in a town with braided facades, a topless Maid of Erin on the hotel facade, and it was there on the first Thursday of a February, when otters were mating at O'Rahilly's Pier and herons doing ballets for their spouses, she met Cian, on leave from the army, in the mimosa and green of Kerry. He'd proposed to her at the gannet colony at Loop Head.

A boy with porter-cake brown hair and a chaff of freckles, in a Capri-blue shirt and trousers with slash pockets, chosen to play junior soccer for Farm Hill in Dublin, says: 'I went to the sea once and I got lost in the crowd and I just walked and walked and I wanted to be at Paddy's Hole on the Blackwater where there are just a few lads.'

'Did you ever see an eagle?' asks a boy with a unicorn quiff, in a batik T-shirt with moon explorers.

'Them were the days,' says Gearoidh, in black frock jacket and ascot tie, under the voice of Philomena Begley singing 'Blanket on the Ground', 'We used go up the country to the dances. Roseland Moate. Fairyland Roscommon. Dreamland Mullingar. Edgeworthstown. Pontoon. Tureen. There was Bunny Joyce's band and Michael Cummin's band.'

In his teens he used go with the boys in February to fish for mackerel off Barra where the grey goose lives year round and where

you hear the song of the Hebridean song thrush. Cross from Larne to Stranraer when there was still snow on the Highlands. But they'd journey to Uig in violet rain.

On Barra there was a sense of Conquistadorial Catholicism. Christs with ichor on them in churches and the boarding house they stayed in had flaming colours in the carpets, in the lampshades, as if in sympathy with the churches.

Then he worked in England for a few years.

'Worked on the buildings in Croydon and Walthamstow when I first came to England. Standing out there at three in the morning like meat waiting to be picked up. Couldn't work so much in winter. For a while worked with Norfolk McAlpines.'

He gave this up, returned to Ireland, and dealt in scrap, driving as far as Donegal, often taking one of his young sons with him, stopping to look at the rabbit-fur nest of a wheatear in a stone wall or the nest of a chaffinch in an old shoe, stopping to have a nosh of Tayto crisps in the shelter over Tulan Beach in Bundoran, and, maybe as some soldiers walked back to quarters after a training session in the sand dunes, telling his son the story of Charles Stuart he'd learnt on Barra; there was a woman in town who with a hammer would break off bits of pink candy curled around a string that hung from the ceiling of her shop, who had his statue advertising whiskey, beside a man in Dutch trousers advertising rum—royal lychee features, snowdrop white tie wig, the Stuart white cockade in his bonnet, the blue ribbon of the Star and Garter on his chest, kilt with gold lace trimming, pale blue pilgrim flask at his side; a party was being held as his mother, a Polish princess, gave birth in Rome; there was a Hellfire Club in their town in those days where wealthy young men from all over Ireland used come and have orgies, kissing like ravens; the tzar of Russia sent the gift of a garment to the newborn prince; his mother was mourned with thousands of candles when she died shortly afterwards; from France he sailed to the Hebrides; carrying a blue and gold oriflamme he lead the Highlanders across the River Isk, in torrent, in winter, into England, two thousand men holding one another's collars and no one was drowned; in flight he was dressed as Betty Burke, an Irish maidservant; he wanted to carry a pistol and when Flora MacDonald, who used carry him on her back to boats so his feet wouldn't get wet, said they might discover it there he said, if they searched, they might find something else there; he looked like a very big woman on Skye, adjusting his bonnets; he hid in caves and got back to France; he returned to England, dressed as a monk, his turf-auburn hair blackened, a patch on his eye and was converted to the Church of England; in France he used bawl outside older women's houses at night and he had to flee back to Italy; his young wife, whom he used savagely beat, took refuge in a convent but first had an affair with a playwright; in the end he had weeping sores on his legs from war wounds and he was received back into the Catholic Church.

And passing Classy Bawn on the way home in the dark, where the Queen's cousin was murdered, he might add a royal refrain to his story.

Charles Stuart's brother became very pious and was made a cardinal; as Cardinal York he collected rare books, held musical evenings and had a young male lover; he lost his fortune in the Napoleonic Wars and fled to Venice where George IV, who used come and look at Beau Brummell arrange his cravat, gave him a pension.

But the stories didn't end there, they continued—about how Traveller soldiers used cross the Arabian Sea to India and come home wearing cobra-skin boots; how foxhounds were sent out from

West Limerick to South Africa during the Boer War for jackal
hunting and Traveller soldiers had the task of building kennels for
them by the White Umfolozi River; how the Black and Tans used
force girls to have sex with them and then put pig rings on their
backsides; how Seán Ó Conaill from Cahirdaniel used come to weddings in their area and tell stories and afterwards they'd play the
squeezebox and the fiddle; about how in a bad summer when the
herons had left for the Ballyhoura Mountains a petrel from the
Eastern Atlantic was found in a flowering furze bush on Gort Pier;
about how an arsonist, in a part of Scotland where the black-
throated divers scream, set fire to a hut full of sleeping spalpeens
from Ireland, burning them all alive; about young fishermen in a
storm off Barra holding one another's collars, like the Highlanders
led by Bonnie Prince Charlie across the River Isk and thus being
saved, the royal face, the royal features distilled again for some faces,
like lost causes, don't go away—until they reached Limerick city—
where children call on the caravan sites like the hunger cry of the
young cuckoo and where sulkies drive on the pavements in the
monochrome estates—and were on the estuary road.

'I have the job of shaving the pubic hair of wrestlers from Limerick,' confides Bryan Gammell, an adult tow-headed man with an
almost rhomboid face in an azure Sunday cardigan with a Greek key
pattern, under the voice of Eileen Reid singing 'I Gave My Wedding
Dress Away', 'They fly from Shannon Airport to pose for pornographic magazines in London. They all have girlfriends though.'

In his caravan on The Long Pavement, near a rubbish site where
fires constantly blaze, is a photograph of himself with some of those
boys by the Shannon in Parteen, he in a sleeveless vest, shorts.

One nude man, with a candified face, crouches, a towel touching
his pubic hair, raising a beer can to his mouth as though giving a
reveille with a trumpet. One in a zephyr loincloth, his bald pate
gleaming like a skull at an Ancient's feast. One holding what looks
like a facecloth in front of his genitals. Another fellow covering his
genitals with the *Evening Herald*.

He moved out of his caravan for a while, staying in a bedsitter—
gas oven that flamed like Mount Vesuvius, liver spots of damp on
the ceiling—in Mulgar Street where there was a mortuary for the

dead people from the asylum which they closed down, but he quickly returned to it.

'Remember everyone gave Job an earring of gold at the feast in his house,' says Manus Culligan. In the summer the Traveller boys who swim in Kildimo Lake have rings on their nipples, rings on their navels they got in Kiel, tattoos of grids and tubes they got in Marburg. Limerick is just a furlough for them now. When October comes, like swallows that have had a fourth brood, they migrate.

A young man in a moss and lemon check jacket, danton collar, sang 'The Fields of Shanagolden'.

Before he sang it he said that Michael McCarthy wrote that song and that he was dead now.

Oonagh's brother Pecker, in a laced shirt, black down like cyphers over his lips, smelling of Old Spice aftershave, told the story of how Blaiman, the son of the High King of Ireland, was hunting when a hare was killed on the snow and he asked was there a woman in the world as beautiful as those colours, hare's blood on snow, and a witch said there was, the daughter of the King of the Kingdom of the White Strand, but before he could marry her he had to kill the Three Giants. The sun was blinding him in the fight that went on for weeks and a robin put leaves on his eyes. He was hungry and a hound ran after a red-crested duck and got an egg and an otter put the egg in his mouth. And he married the daughter of the King of the Kingdom of the White Strand and they all drank buttermilk at the wedding.

A girl with gorse gold in her blonde hair, in an argent First Holy Communion dress, with a bonnet of petals, recited the poem that Patrick Pearse wrote in Kilmainham Jail the night before he was executed:

> The beauty of the world hath made me sad,
> This beauty that will pass ...

# Rose of Lebanon

'Just because you live in a caravan doesn't mean you're a Traveller,' Scolog Cahan hits out, 'Do you think you're a Traveller because you live in a caravan? You mulligan.'

Boy with coin face, delft-blue eyes, desert-sunset henna hair, pennon neck, champagne shoulders, in an oyster-grey bomber jacket with Rampage Club written on it and a coal-heaver's cap, who swears pledges on his knees in front of the Padre Pio picture in his caravan and who will identify the cuckoo's spit—larvae of the golden-tailed moth and the tiger moth—for you.

He pauses over a postcard reproduction in my album of a monochrome *Male Nude* by Pietro Pedroni; a young man, his back turned, right knee resting on upholstery, he holds a rod slant-wise— a possible instrument of punishment—his hair wet, vinous, after some athletic feat or some sexual act; a lonely silver light on his whole body, everywhere is evidence of submission, to an athletic discipline, to the artist who is viewing him.

I held my father's hand one Sunday afternoon as we approached the rugby changing room, the walls mottled, a lone rugby player taking a cold shower, his back turned to us, the ivory sheen of winter on his buttocks with their shoelace split, my father's hand tightening on mine.

'I knew them all. Trixie Leech, the tailor. Poteen Fallon, the publican. Scourge Fallon, the baker,' catalogued my father in St Patrick's mental hospital in Dublin, a few years before he died, against a jigsaw reproduction of Rembrant's *The Return of the Prodigal Son*, which had been one of the loose reproductions which had gone with a set of art books he'd given me when I was a boy—son with little bald patch, kneeling in groove of his father's body, cranberry red cloak on father, an observer with a staff, amber in the carpet.

Scolog's father Eochaid, who has ribbons of maize and bronze hair and wears an open-work choker-chain with a gold medal on it of St Christopher, patron saint of travellers—has been one of a group of Travellers who served with the Irish Army in Beirut; the Irish soldiers, says Scolog, used go to a casino and watch 'women with bare diddies ride elephants'; Eochaid tells of how at siesta time men in striped pyjamas used flee the liquid phosphorus attacks, holding children; of the miles and miles of red-dust cemetery with photographs of the dead person over each stone-marked grave; of the cats who'd eat bodies and became so dangerous the Irish soldiers used shoot them; how Palestinians used bring their bedding beside the Irish soldiers at night and recall how when they abandoned Palestine in 1948 the markouk bread was left baking because they thought they'd be back shortly. Eochaid brought back a violet-grey velvet suit which he wears at Travellers' weddings. In their caravan is a wall hanging of *Our Lady of the Ark*, mitre on her head, above the *White Rose of Lebanon*; beside it a postcard reproduction of a heron by Jan Mankes I gave Scolog.

When I gave it to him he said that in school he'd won third prize for a drawing of a swan and the fellow who drew the duck got second prize.

Once Eochaid and Senanus, a soldier from the Maigue at Croom, a foxy fellow, went home with some falafel-stand boys to Corniche Mazra's with its street barbers and ate red mullet and drank arak from gilt-edged glasses on the floor with them, under a Damascus-silk wall-hanging which showed a stork on a minaret, and afterwards had their bodies oiled with sandalwood and massaged by them.

The Irish soldiers used swim off the rocks at Raouche, bombed fish restaurants nearby, with areca palms which have white flowers, juniper trees, jasmine bushes, leopard lilies, peacock flowers and nettles growing beside them.

In the nineteenth century there was a Church of Ireland Missions Training College in Ballinasloe and one of their tasks was to try to convert the Travellers who came to the fair and in the Cahan family for generations was a bible, given to them by the Training College, in which there was a picture of a cedar of Lebanon against a deep azure sky on the front.

'I love to see the larch tree and the oak tree grow,' says Eochaid in Limerick shoes with extra-thick welts and a shirt of hot red, 'It takes a hundred years to grow a tree. It's terrible to knock it.'

Scolog goes to Dublin for the first time, with his father, when the Huguenot graveyard there is a cornucopia of bluebells and, having got the incentive from my album, looks at Rembrandt's *Rest on the Flight into Egypt*; a campfire, reflected in the fen water, barely indicating the minature refugees. Eochaid tells him that the Gypsies were people who followed Mary and Joseph and Jesus out of Egypt.

'It's a grand town. By the sea,' Scolog says on his return.

I tell him that Rembrandt used to go up to strangers on the street and ask them to pose for him and he wonders if David and Jonathan were strangers; David, plume in his turban, bidding farewell to Jonathan, who has shoulder-length hair, a scimitar by his side, cross gartered leggings.

Eochaid grew up on a Travellers' site in Wimbledon. 'My mother listened to Jim Reeves all day. She bought a bicycle between my sister and me. Both the Romanies and the Travellers had sulkies there but the Romanies had horses and carts—Totters we called them. Some of them had a pony farm and a donkey sanctuary in Vauxhall. There were zebras there too. There were many Romanies in Reading and in Camberley which is on the A30, out past Heathrow, the road to Staines and Ashford. There were many Romanies in Chertsey in Surrey. The Robinsons were there. Fairground people. I went there once and one of them asked my business. "I've come to buy a Ruby Austin 1934," I said. We returned to West Limerick. There was money in kerbing and paving and tarmacking. My father went back for a visit to Bridge North in Shropshire where he was born. An airforce town. He asked a question and they passed him on the street.'

When the woodcocks are roding in the woods and boys with the creamed whiteness of undrunk milk left out for cats in farmhouses are swimming in the Leap a youth with hair *en brosse*, Manchurian-black disc moustache and beard, in a jumpsuit with a slashed neckline, tells me, on the greensward by Gort Pier after I've swum, that the central affair of his life had been with a boy he'd seduced when he'd been babysitting and who would wait for him after national school. Then after secondary school. They'd make love in the woods by the Round Weir. The boy has a girlfriend now but there is still love between them.

'It all started with the Greeks,' he says.

'Sometimes when there's a storm we've got to get out of the caravan and sleep in the car for the night, hugging one another,' says Eochaid.

When the Cahans first returned to Ireland they used go to Tramore for the summer with its accordion set of coloured lights by the sea, where young people pulled up on dirt motorbikes on the sand dunes, and stay until the last Sunday of summer when the amusements were half price.

Now when the wild garlic is blossoming in Glin they go out to the coast with their caravan for the summer, past Glin Pier where the sea ends and the estuary becomes tidal—rock beach on one side of Glin Pier, mud flats on the other; spending a few days on Carrig Island by Carrig Castle, to which there is a bridge; then moving on to the open Atlantic, when the hedges are cascades of comfrey, where they swim their horse every day.

My parents honeymooned here at the end of the War.

Seaweed baths; there were changing booths on the beach then; a sudden foray towards the water, away from the years of palingenesis: a caterpillar of lights on the Clare side of the estuary at night.

They honeymooned in early September when the Atlantic is ultramarine and then lapis lazuli with waves which have antennae, then a deep lonely blue.

Then they returned to the teal-blue shop.

Before my father had married my mother he had a Protestant girlfriend, Miss Husaline. She never married, wore flying-squirrel furs, black georgette dresses, lived in a house with a clover green door and offered visitors tea from Aynsley cups—magenta cups with gold rims. She walked her King Charles spaniel along the street alone.

'I don't want to die yet. I want to go to the Isle of Man. I want to swim.'

Miss Husaline came into the church with her King Charles spaniel on a leash, carrying a bunch of red carnations, and stood beside my father's coffin.

Scolog returns with stories of the sea; of the leader of a missionary group in American-college red who preached on the beach, small bibles in their hands, who said his whole life had been beaches, he'd proposed to his wife in Helen's Bay outside Belfast; of the parson who took a roll of film to the chemist to be developed after lying on the beach and found there were three photographs of naked women on it—three women had taken his camera and photographed one another naked when he was in swimming; of the thin boy in a baseball cap and the fat girl in hot pants who regularly climbed down to a cave to make love and afterwards wrote pornography in the sand; of children from Belfast who woke at night screaming in their caravans.

In Beirut, during night watch, often under the green, white, red and black Palestinian oriflamme, as young Arabs played flutes made from the arbutus which grew all around the Lebanon as it did in County Kerry, the Irish Traveller soldiers used tell stories of their ancestry; how they were rivet-makers in pre-Christian Ireland; whitesmiths in early Christian Ireland; how king after king legislated against Irish Tinkers in the Middle Ages but to no avail; how the first Gypsies in Scotland danced for James IV in Holyrood House in Edinburgh, who paid them, and they told him they were pilgrims; how William Shakespeare travelled with Tinkers and collected stories from them ... 'drink with any Tinker in his own language'; how when Charles II expressed his astonishment to a learned cleric that he associated with John Bunyan, a mender of kettles and pans, the cleric replied that he wished he had the Tinker's ability to reach the heart; how Poor Law legislation in the early nineteenth century drove them back to Ireland; how many Travellers crossed to the United States during the Famine and most of them drifted south with the mule trade during the Civil War but they kept the Gammon; how their parents had sold ballad sheets purchased from Bob Cuthbertson, a publisher in Listowel, County Kerry, and how the favourite ballad was 'The Croppy Boy', 'I alone am left my name and race'; how Travellers' caravans in scenic areas were wrecked by hired gangs.

In the Lebanon was a people, many of them fair-haired like Irish Travellers, called the Druses, who'd come from Arabia. Sometimes they read the bible. Sometimes the Koran. It was said of them that a father sometimes cohabited with his daughter or a father made love to son.

A horse shed is converted into a gym, a poster of Manchester United's Dave Beckham on the wall, and Scolog trains there, pulling up his gammy shirt to show muscles like an outcrop.

'Keep the shovels flipping. You won't feel the time is slipping,' he sings as he lifts weights.

'Adonis,' a girl called him in Sinbin nightclub in Limerick, which he got into on a counterfeit pass. In Phoenicia in early spring people mourned the death of Adonis, carrying naked effigies of him in procession and then threw them into the Mediterranean. Women wailed and tore their hair. Next day they rejoiced and said Adonis had come again.

Before he leaves to try to get into Icon, a Limerick nightclub, on another counterfeit pass, Scolog studies *Venus, Adonis and Cupid* by Annibale Carraci in my album; Adonis in wolf skin, a bit of gold brocade slung on his chest but leaving his nipples exposed, leggings that leave his feet bare, his arms rippled with muscles, his gold hair crimped like a girl's and his blue-blood lips pursed as he beholds a naked Venus, who has a checked fillet in her hair, fondling a naked Cupid, Etruscan red drapery beneath Venus by which two Chinese white pigeons peck.

In the *Samhain samhradh*, the second summer, Scolog, in a black shirt with white lotus flowers on it, dries my back after I've swum, yellow blades of the gorse flower on it. 'You look like an age horse, you look like an age pony, you look like a weasel.'

When I was a child still in feral short pants I went one night— it was a Saturday night, a holiday granted to me—to the flat—near a house in which Russian horse dealers of the days of Catherine the Great had bivouacked, which put a summer cover on its historical

door on hot days—of the boy, with a pencilled quiff, who worked in
our shop, was a winter swimmer—he used swim in the river by a
willow-bend with young guards and young priests, one of the priests
claiming to have become a winter swimmer through bringing invalids
to Lourdes and taking the cold baths with them—and who sometimes wore a black shirt purchased in the priests' shop near the Pro
Cathedral in Marlborough Street Dublin and I slept in the bed with
him—he was from a part of Clare where there were aboriginal
national schools and goblin palm trees outside penal-looking bungalows—and he took off his clothes to put on his pyjamas, his backside ruddy like a robin's breast in patches and, like that, just the top
of his pyjamas on, he turned to me and quoted the travelling players
who had just visited the town, a Cleopatra in a leopard-spot body
stocking, about an Antony, like the Roman soldiers in the Stations of
the Cross in the church, with laced up persimmon legs, in a kindled
saffron cloak: 'For his bounty, There was no winter in't; an autumn
'twas That grew the more by reaping: his delights Were dolphin like.'

With his friend Naois, who has a pellucid ginger turf cut with an
asterisk quiff, black moiré eyes, Scolog sometimes goes and drinks
Lucozade under a cedar of Lebanon by a ruined house where a poet
lived. There is a man in the town who wears a chesterfield coat with
velvet lining, who lives in a decrepit cottage the way a robin builds a
nest in an old kettle, knows everything about the history of the town
and will tell you about the poet with owl features who lived in the
house; how he used sit under the cedar of Lebanon with a boy with
cuneiform sideburns from Pallaskenry who wrote a book about a
murder that was committed in West Limerick when a young lord
drowned the girl of lowly birth he'd married in the Shannon and
asked to go to his execution in a carriage; how the book made a fortune in England and the young man sent it to his parents in America,
joined the Christian Brothers, taught poor boys in Cork and soon
died; how the people of the house used row at summer's apogee,
when dolphins probe far into the estuary, to the Nuns' Strand and
explore the caves by boat; how, during the Famine, the poet's brother
brought a group of people who used dance at the end of the Ash
Avenue on Sunday evenings to Québec on a ship where they replen-
ished themselves on St Lawrence eels, as they would eat the conger

eel from Gort Pier at home, before disappearing to the United States; how the poet was converted to the Catholic Church and an atheist came to his house and, under the cedar of Lebanon, tried to persuade him not to but the poet said: 'I have lived as a Christian and I intend to die one.'

Scolog's friends, who wear fallal track suits, are going to the College of High Technology in Pallaskenry now or studying life-saving in Cork, spending their spare hours in Game Boy parlours; an iron curtain builds between him and them and a glass wall between him and me. With a Mohawk haircut, a cable of hair on top of his otherwise naked head, in a Laois white football jersey, he struggles through a passage of Russian literature in my caravan, carefully pronouncing the words.

Afterwards he summarizes it.

'God loves writing stories about prisoners.'

Naois in a sanguine Harp Lager T-shirt, who recently sang Skid Row's 'I Remember You' at a concert in Ballysteen, looking on, presses a button on a tape of the Prague Opera singing Handel's *Zadok the Priest* and tells a joke over it.

'Did you hear the story of the boy whose mother sent him to look for a bucket and a cocker spaniel? He went to the hardware shop and asked for a fuck it. He went to the pet shop and said "My cock is itchy." At the bus stop he said to a lady "Hold my fuck it. My cock is itchy."'

Scolog brings Arab horses to a fair in a town where boys with spartan haircuts collect golf balls as gannets do. In Clare they say young married men bring farmers' sons to the beaches and pay them for sex and he and Naois have taken the ferry across the estuary to investigate this rumour.

Scolog has a tattoo in the shape of a heron on his neck. 'You can just walk in in Limerick and get a tattoo. In Tralee you get a tattoo by appointment.'

Sometimes he flags down a bingo bus to the nightclubs in Limerick. He sees a lot of a girl from Shannon town who has purple-henna hair tied at the back with a black fillet, liquorice eye-make-up, wears a roll-neck jersey with a midriff and hoop earrings.

Maybe he'll join the army in Edward Street in Limerick. Some of the soldiers get an extra ninety pounds a week playing soccer in Markets Field.

He recounts a story from the *Sunday World* of a man in his twenties who has been sent to jail in Belfast for having sex with a teenage boy, giving it new material, embellishing it with images from my album, making a jigsaw painting with bits of Damiano Mazza's *The Rape of Ganymede*, Gerrit van Honthorst's *Saint Sebastian*, Jacques-Louis David's *Leonidas at Thermopylae*, and the way one story becomes another he retells the Children of Lir in the version given to them by the historian, the eagle which emerges from a naked boy's body in Damiano Mazza's *The Rape of Ganymede*, becoming a swan.

Lir, the King of Clare, bet in the election for High King of Ireland by Dearg, the son of Daghda the Druid, was summoned by Dearg to Lough Derg and told in compensation he could marry Dearg's foster daughter. Lir had his children sleep in a bed beside him and in the morning he'd get up and lie with them. As swans they returned from Inis Glóra off Belmullet in Mayo to Clare and found Lir's castle overgrown with nettles. Kemoc linked the children of Lir with a whitesmith's chain and their feathers fell off and they became old people and died.

When he finished Scolog picks up a letter which has an address in Donnybrook.

'Who's Danny Burke?' he asks in a betrayed voice.


'But when Herod's birthday was kept, the daughter of Herodias danced before them, and pleased Herod.'

In the Lebanon Scolog's father had seen the ruins of Chalcis where Salome was queen who'd danced before Herod Antipas and asked for John the Baptist's head as a reward. In my album Scolog looks at Salome from *The Feast of Herod* by Fra Filippo Lippi, the friar-artist who seduced an Augustinian nun Lucrezia Buti and had a son by her. Salome with crimped auburn hair, auric brows, pout lips, like a Traveller girl, in a cloth of gold dress with bat, fluted oversleeves, lace yoke, stares insolently at us as though she is looking at a camera. 'You need a bit of talent every now and then,' Scolog declares.

In the West Limerick countryside there is a small Methodist church. From the community around that church Methodists went to America and introduced the Methodist faith.

In Venice Paolo Veronese spent fifteen years painting a small church and in this travail 'grew wise'.

Before I leave to live on the coast when the barnacle geese are there and the estuary is pilgrimage-blue Scolog looks at Veronese postcard reproductions in my album; boys with the chestnut, bronze and carrot hair of Irish Traveller boys, auburn underchin growth, curls and twists of hair, Roman noses, orb chins; a patriarch with a vermilion hat forked out in two directions leaning over the Christ child in the temple; an alabaster Christ being laid out in the tomb by a ferociously strong young man in an emerald vest with lopped edge sleeves like an Ancient Irish hero, his copper hair swept back like flying horses's tails; a harlequin dwarf in apricot tussling with a black boy who has white, gold slashed sleeves; the cherry lips of male puberty, a dog nosing a pattern of pink pansies on Prussian blue; pomegranate stockings.

# Patterns

It was a day when the river was a smuggled indigo and the great, farthingale willow-herb was jutting out of the pier and the wintergreen was blossoming in the grass and three Traveller boys, two of them with their shirts off, were swimming a mare.

Connla, who had tangerine-henna hair, tadpole-brown eyes, a choker chain and a smaller chain with a starfish on it.

Felim who had turtle and hazel hair.

Small Taedy who had a platinum crest, dark sides, face and neck stabbed with hair.

'Get on her back. Get on her back,' Felim shouted at me when I was in the water.

I got on her back and she immediately threw me, giving me a good kick.

Connla thought I was drowning and jumped in after me. Three months later, a few weeks after I left to live on the coast, in a T-shirt with the words Live Intrusions on it he'd purchased on his American journey earlier that year, Connla was killed in an accident with his van on the way into Limerick.

Connla was brought up in an aluminium caravan on a Travellers' site off the Holloway Road in London.

In their caravan, beside a picture of Blessed Margaret Clitheroe, was a photograph of his grandparents taken in a Weymouth photographer's studio against a clock which had the face of Elizabeth I on it; his grandmother in a blouse with a sweetheart neckline, another blouse under that, Tara brooch on her bosom, with cuff ribbons, fur-rimmed ankle boots, her pigtails with bushends; his grandfather, who had seen the bonfires burn for the Silver Jubilee of George V on the Dorset Downs, in a suit with a long jacket with padded chest, black Mussolini shirt, aviator-hairstyle having used St John's wort for hairdressing, hands clasping his chest.

Connla's grandfather used drive to Ireland to buy holy statues in bulk in Monster House, Kilkenny and sell them to English Catholics. In Connla's caravan was one of his statues—St Rita of Cascia with a red spot on her forehead.

Uncle Derry, with eyes the blue of the blue in a willow-pattern plate, who had a brindle greyhound in West Limerick and would wear shamrock in September in West Limerick, would sometimes stay on the site in his caravan. He told Connla and his brothers what George I, who had Punchinello daubs on his cheeks, used do with his Turkish servants Mohamed and Mustapha.

Uncle Derry had served with Major-General Sean McKeown's troops in the Congo, had been involved in the siege of Jadotville, used ride a grey Syrian stallion by the River Congo with its water hyacinths. Members of the army Cumann Luasclas used fend off bats in their sleeping quarters with hurleys. Beside the pale blue Congolese flag with a yellow star in his caravan was a photograph of a great grandfather who'd served with the Young Jocks in the Boer War; in a Sam Browne belt with a frog, leggings, centre-parted pompadour, frisé moustache. He'd come back from the Boer War and found his wife was having an affair with another man, shot him dead with a blunderbuss from which emerged the leg of an ancient pot and was not charged as he'd claimed he'd found the man raping his wife.

Connla made his First Holy Communion in the Church of Our Lady of Assumption and St Gregory, in a dove-grey suit with black velveteen cuffs, white shirt, white tie, hair cut in a glib—a fringe.

Each year after they saw the Gerry Cottle Circus on Crown Meadow in Bromley Connla's family, the Dorans, used make a pilgrimage to Croagh Patrick in County Mayo for July 27. Patterns they called pilgrimages.

On the way they stopped at the graves of three Traveller children killed in Walsall when squad cars forcibly evicted Travellers from a site, towing caravans away, and who had been buried in Bilston.

Afterwards they'd have bacon and bubble in Wendy's Café in Walsall. They'd cross Ireland, stopping in Westport, where Connla's mother said they always had good cakes, to buy French Fancies, iced cups, pink apple slices, walnut slices, cream slices, custard slices.

Then they'd go out past Rockfleet Castle in Clew Bay where Grace O'Malley had lived, who'd captained her own ship on her journey to meet Elizabeth I to entreat for her imprisoned son, past Land's End and the Isles of Scilly, through the straits of Dover, into the Thames estuary where boys used swim then, borne up by pigs' udders; she was received in Greenwich Castle from which Elizabeth had expelled the friars, with its view of the Isle of Dogs, by Elizabeth—who wore cabochon earrings and a poisoned diamond ring—in a cloak of myrtle green, a crimson mantle on her head, in bare

feet; Elizabeth held her hand high but Grace was the taller of the women and the Queen had to reach up; a cambric and lace handkerchief was handed to Grace and she flung it in the fire after use and when upbraided for this declared they had higher standards of cleanliness in the West of Ireland; when Elizabeth offered to make Grace a countess, Grace said that was impossible because she was already a queen.

Connla's mother, who had flaxen and nasturtium hair, always wore a scarf with a pattern of kingfishers for the pilgrimage and cast-off kid pumps.

From Croagh Patrick they'd drive to visit a cousin from the

Sperrin Mountains in the Northlands who was in the Magilligan Prison for republican involvement and afterwards the boys would have a swim on Benowen beach beside the prison.

After Connla's mother had to start getting treatment in St Luke's, Woodside Avenue, Muswell Hill, the Dorans came to live in West Limerick.

Early in the year he was killed Connla made an American pattern.

In the Famine days a group of Travellers from West Limerick were brought in a ship by a doctor to Québec from where those who survived dispersed to the United States. They used to make a pattern of thanksgiving—a pilgrimage—every year in the United States or Canada. The last pattern was to the Passion Play in Hollywood Bowl in 1949.

Over the decades people with names like Cash, Cade, Colleran, used make pilgrimages to places like the St Katharine Drexel Shrine, who founded the Sisters of the Blessed Sacrament, in Bensalem, Pennsylvania; the Motherhouse Mission bell used to ring out to say goodbye to sisters leaving in carriages to cross the United States to serve black Americans and Native Americans and sisters would gather near the mission bell and wave snowflake-white handkerchiefs.

The Jesuit Martyrs' Shrine of Sainte Marie of the Hurons in Midland Ontario. The Jesuits were tortured to death in the 1640s after, having had to burn down their own mission station, their trek, with Huron Indians they'd converted, to Christian Island in Georgian Bay.

The Shrine of St Thérèse, Queen and Patroness of Alaska, a log church, overlooking Lynn Canal, on Crow Island—where a causeway was cut four hundred feet through wild tides from the coast where the great black-beaked gull feeds on dead calf whales. In Alaska Eskimo sleighs were decorated with the figure of St Thérèse of Lisieux.

The Shrine of Our Lady of Peace at Niagra Falls. In 1678 the Franciscan Father Louis Hennepin was the first European to sketch the Falls at Niagra. In gratitude for the beauty of this place Father Hennepin nailed a cross to a tree overlooking the Falls and offered mass to a congregation of Seneca Indians. The site was terminal for the railroad which aided the escape of slaves from the Southern

States. During the American Civil War, when General Grant issued an order expelling all Jews from Tennessee, Pope Pius IX dedicated Father Hennepin's site to Our Lady of Peace. It was consecrated during the Civil War by Archbishop Lynch who travelled by steamer from Toronto.

In New York Connla saw photographs of the pilgrims; women in Breton hats, astrakhan hats, dresses with pagoda shoulders, standing beside priests in priests' homburg hats and black Ford Model T cars at St Philomena's Shrine at Cherokee Village Arkansas, Shrine of the Sacré Coeur in Montreal, Shrine of St John Neumann in Philadelphia, Shrine of Our Lady of Fatima in Milwaukee Wisconsin, Dickeyville Grotto Wisconsin, Shrine of St Jude Thaddeus in Chicago, Church of the Seven Dolors in Minnesota.

Connla had driven south from New York in a Barracuda, stopping at Basilica of the National Shrine of the Immaculate Conception in Washington, down through Georgia with its flag with the Cherokee Rose blowing, through Alabama with its flag with goldenrod, stopping at truck stops where he heard Erskine Hawkins sing 'The Yellow Rose of Texas' and Bob Willis and his Texas Cowboys, across to California where he visited the San Carlos Borromeo Mission in Carmel Valley. In Southern California he saw the blue heron and in Northern California the black albatross. Then he drove to St George Byzantine Church on the Northwest Pacific coast.

Before I left for the coast he gave me a postcard of an ikon of Our Lady of Tenderness he'd bought there and he told me a story about how his great grandfather had travelled from Weymouth once to see Joseph O'Mara, who'd been educated in The Crescent, Limerick, and had sung in St Michael's Church Choir, in *Lohengrin* by Wagner—in a Prussian helmet with a spike and a demon-red cloak—sitting in the gods.

# Victoria

Kerrin Sanger was a little English Gypsy boy with a Romeo quiff, wheel-azure eyes, who used ride around, usually at a jogtrot, on a Shetland pony, in a Western shirt with enlarge check or a shirt with Hawaiian girls with camellias in their hair, jeans with turn-ups, black socks with planets on them, mauve-carmine shoes. He had a fracture of very small brothers with cream-blond hair who'd suddenly jump up from behind a gorse bush as I was passing on my bicycle.

Kerrin would get me to babysit the Shetland pony occasionally as it fed on a grassy bank and then he'd cycle to Rathkeale to visit friends who lived in a Spanish Colonial Revival house, leaving me there for hours.

The Cafferkey boys, Goll and Taoscán who had spider-silk hair crops, called him 'an English bastard', often from within balaclavas.

The Sangers lived in a Vickers trailer with chrome beading outside in a roadside meadow near Gort Pier. The interior walls were formica. In the Sangers' caravan was red stoneware Liverpool crockery with twisted dragons and contorted phoenixes, purchased on Scotland Road in Liverpool; lustre jugs; a tea-kettle; a delft Queen Victoria in a polka—an outing jacket; a framed photograph of the young Princess Margaret with a baluster hairstyle; an accordion set of postcards of Corby, Northamptonshire, which was given a

326 / Desmond Hogan

charter by Elizabeth I to hold a fair in gratitude for her rescue in a fog in the Royal Deer Forest of Rockingham by Corby people; a snapshot of a Gypsy boy with a cockscomb, wing collars seated in a pub which had barley-sugar pillars in Weymouth; a snapshot of a Christmas celebration in the Vale of Evesham, streamers with paper bells interlinking trailers. Outside was a nanny goat purchased in Mulhuddart near Dublin.

The Sangers wintered in Wilstead in Bedfordshire near where John Bunyan was born. The Bunyans had been menders of kettles and pans for generations in that area.

In May the Sangers attended the fair in Stow-on-the-Wold, which was the highest town in the Cotswolds, where the last battle of the Civil War was fought.

In early June the Epsom Derby.

From there they went north to the Appleby Fair in Westmoreland where Gypsy boys, in nothing but mid-thigh Union Jack shorts, swam their horses in the River Eden.

On the way they laid wreathes of red carnations, sometimes in the shape of bow-top wagons, at grandparents' graves in Fenny Drayton in Leicestershire.

From Appleby they went to Wisbech in Cambridgeshire for the last of the strawberry picking. Since he was three Kerrin was given a basket to pick strawberries at Wisbech.

Then beginning the first Monday in September the fair in Chipping Barnet, Hertfordshire, 'chipping' being the Anglo-Saxon word for bargain.

At these Gypsy men with greased quiffs still wore Teddyboy clothes; drape jackets with velveteen collars and floral cuffs; brocade waistcoats, suede Gibson shoes with thick crêpe soles or Eton Clubman chukka boots, shrimp-pink or canary ankle socks.

After the Barnet fair the Sangers crossed to Ireland and spent the rest of September and the month of October near Gort Pier.

Kerrin's grandfather Abiezer had spent the Second World War years in the meadow near Gort Pier to avoid conscription. He and his wife Iris lived in a ledge caravan which had no windows. On the wall was a newspaper photograph of the English soccer team saluting the Führer in 1936.

Just before the War the police had arrived in Bedford Twenty-Five-Seater buses at Epsom to prevent Gypsies gathering for the Derby.

The Travellers said of the Sangers that they were like the wren that builds its nest over other birds' nests—the mud saucer of a swallow, the spotted flycatcher's domed house.

Giraldus Cambrensis wrote that the woods of Ireland were full of wild peacocks and it was into the woods by the Round Weir Abiezer Sanger would go with a catapult seeking pheasants, woodcocks, grouse, finches.

Abiezer Sanger mended old china and umbrellas.

He mended a Quaker Pegg Derby set, with patterns of tulip trees, passion flowers, cranesbill, lady thistles, for the Taskers in Limerick who had been officers in the Royal Munster Fusiliers and Cyclist Company.

There was an aerodrome in Foynes then, on the Limerick side of the estuary, and refugees were borne there from Europe.

Abiezer mended the rayon umbrella with Japanese laquered handle of a woman who arrived, still in cosmopolite outfit—porkpie hat, silver fox windcheater, glacé kid pumps—before a turf boat took her across the estuary to Kilrush.

Whereas the Traveller women wore box-accordion pleated skirts or navy skirts with patterns of flora, Iris Sanger wore dresses such as a coral white dress with beetroot roses at the hem, a dress with a pattern of peacock's eye which had a shawl collar, a black dress with breast cups.

When she had sold paper flowers she'd made herself at people's doorways she'd take an eighteenth-century bow, like a drake in courtship.

Iris also went to the Nenagh Fair or the Races at Limerick Junction to sell her flowers.

At the St Patrick's Night concert in 1945, when the American armies crossed the Rhine at Remagen, in a dress with pale coffee-coloured roses, magpie pumps—white and black—she sang two songs: 'Three Little Fishes and the Mother Fishey Too' and a song with vocables like—'Maesy Doats and Doesy Doats and Little Lambsy Ivy'.

Goll and Taoscán's grandfather Conán joined the British Army during the Baedecker Air Raids on Plymouth, Coventry, Exeter in 1942, when lights crisscrossed in the sky in England at night.

The Cafferkeys used camp at Brews Bridge on the Clare side of the estuary and the Connaught Rangers, in forage caps, would come there from Renmore Barracks to recruit. Some of them had bulldogs on leashes. There was a bear ward with a pet bear who used sometimes do a dance.

In the snow near Robrovo in Serbia, Christmas 1915, the Clare Traveller soldiers met a Bulgarian who wanted to join the Connaught Rangers and fight against the Bulgarians because he hated his countrymen so much,

In December 1921, just two weeks before the Treaty was ratified by the Dáil, a Traveller boy from Ardrahan in County Galway enlisted in the Connaught Rangers.

Conán was allowed to travel to Ireland during the War because he was in the Army. He'd change into a suit at Holyhead, douse himself with lavender cologne, then travel on an unlighted boat, a lifebuoy around him.

He returned from the War in a jacket that had a supernumerary button and crab-coloured, gardenia-patterned lining, which he'd worn, before leaving London, to the London Hippodrome.

At the end of that summer a Christian Brother in Kilkee told him of Beau Brummell whom George IV used watch don his cambric and muslin cravat before they fell out. Beau Brummell ending up in France with only one trousers, having to stay in bed while it was sent out for repair.

The Christian Brothers used come from Tipperary, Galway, Ennis and line up in the nude on the rocks in Kilkee.

Farmers would go there and hire them for work in the fields because they were great workers.

Sometimes, shortly before he returned to England, when I came to swim at Gort Pier in the evenings, I'd find Kerrin there, on his Shetland pony, observing the flight of a smew or a red-backed shrike over the water.

It occurred to me that the reason the Sangers returned to Ireland every autumn was because there was an unresolved question about the Sangers' sojourn here during the War.

There was an unresolved question about the country, about provenance.

It was as if both Kerrin and I were soldering a broken pattern.

The Sangers attended the Ballinasloe Horse Fair in October 1944, to which Catherine the Great used send representitives, when the Warsaw Rising was finally suppressed.

A few nights before he returned to England Kerrin drew up at my caravan, tethering his pony outside, when I was telling Goll and Taoscán about Catherine the Great; how Sophia-Augusta, a fifteen-year-old German princess from the House of Anhalt-Zerbst, was invited to Russia by the childless Empress Elizabeth, daughter of Peter the Great; on her conversion to the Russian Orthodox faith she was given the name Catherine and became engaged to her second cousin who was chosen by Elizabeth as her successor, the future Peter III; in 1762, backed by guards, Catherine brought an end to the six months' reign of her husband and acceded to the throne herself.

Kerrin looked around my caravan as if it were a foreign country.

I offered him coconut snowballs I'd just put on a plate but he declined.

He took down my postcard album which was open on a nude Hélène Fourment—the girl Rubens married late in life after his first wife died—on her tiered, golden-syrup body, whom Goll and Taoscán admired for her 'powerhouse', and leafed through it, stopping at Gerrit van Honthorst's *Childhood of Christ*; Christ as a pubescent boy, in a wine robe, holding a candle as St Joseph works with a chisel, his lips suggesting he might be an early smoker, St Joseph with a fountain of a beard, the lines of his forehead illuminated, two girl Angels behind exchanging comments on the scene.

Then Kerrin asked: 'Do you have a story about Queen Victoria?'

And I told him how when Prince Albert died she said: 'Now there's no one left to call me Victoria.'

# Pictures

My father and I were looking at Veronese's *Saints Philip and James the Less* in the National Gallery in Dublin one summer's day when the curator approached us in a gameplumage tweed jacket and started explaining it to us.

The curator was from a part of the Shannon estuary where learned-looking goats ran wild and where bogland printed itself on sand. He'd been an officer in the Royal Field Artillary during the First World War, had twice been wounded at the Battle of the Somme in which men who gathered by the Lazy Wall in the Square in our town had fought.

The curator was renowned for his clothes.

Women would go to a church in Dublin to see him walking to Holy Communion in glen tweed suits, houndstooth cheviot jackets, rosewood flannel trousers, enlarge check trousers, Edelweiss jerseys, Boivin, batiste, taffeta shirts, black and tan shoes, button Oxford shoes.

A seated St Philip in a pearl-grey robe, sandals with diamond open-work, clutched a book as if he was afraid the contents might vanish, another book at his feet. St James the Less in a prawn pink robe, a melon cloak tucked into his belt, had a pepper-and-salt beard, carried a cross, and was talking to an angel with spun gold hair descending upon them both, perhaps asking the angel to help them save the contents of the books.

My father told the curator how I'd won first prize in a national art competition that spring.

I'd won it for a painting inspired by an episode of 'Lives of the Caesars' on radio that showed Julius Caesar, during a night battle off Alexandria, fireballs in the air, having jumped off a rowboat, swimming to the Caesarean ship, documents in his raised left hand, burgundy cloak clenched in his teeth to keep this trophy from the Egyptians.

I'd been presented the prize in a Dublin hotel by a minister's wife with a pitchfork beehive, a tawny fur on her shoulders that looked like bob-cat fur.

The hotel, I later learned, was one where young rugby players from the country spent weekends because the chambermaids had a loose reputation and they had hopes of sleeping with them.

My mother, usually silent, on the train back west, in a wisteria-blue turban hat with two flared wings at the back she'd had on for the day, spoke of the weeks after my birth when it snowed heavily and she used to walk me, past the gaunt workhouse, to the Ash Tree. A beloved sister died and the Christmas cakes were wrapped up and not eaten until the Galway Races at the end of July when they were found to have retained their freshness.

After we left the gallery my father and I took the bus, past swan-neck lamp posts, to the sea.

In a little shop my father bought American hardgums for himself and jelly crocodiles for me.

We walked past houses covered in Australian vine, with pineapple broom hedges, to the sea at the Forty Foot.

In winter, when I was off school, sometimes I accompanied my father on his half day to Galway. We'd have tea and fancies in Lydon's Tea House with its lozenge floor mosaic at the door and afterwards go to Salthill where we'd watch a whole convent of nuns who swam in winter in black togs and black caps.

I was spending a few days now in Dublin with my father. The previous summer I'd gone by myself to stay with an aunt and uncle in County Limerick for my holidays.

I arrived at Limerick bus station, a stand beside it of *Ireland's*

*Own*, where I read of the Limerick tenor Joseph O'Mara and of the stigmatic Marie Julie Jaheny, and of Russian cakes—almond essence, sugar syrup, chocolate.

In my aunt and uncle's village there was a Pompeian red cinema called the Melody. Outside it a picture of Steve Reeves in his bathing togs, standing in hubris, his chest mushrooming from his waist. In the film, which I saw while there, a prostrate Sylva Koscina, with a frizzed top, a racoon top, a racoon tail of hair by her face, clutches Steve Reeve's foot, who, as Hercules, is about to leave on an inexorable journey. The audience stamped its feet while reels were being changed. Boys, some of whom were reputed to have been in Cork Jail, on the steps outside during the day, spoke with Montana accents like Steve Reeves.

My uncle was a garda sergeant and wore a hat big as a canopy. In the kitchen at night, a bunch of nettles behind a picture of St Brigid of Sweden to keep off flies, he'd tell ghost stories. Of boys who were drowned in the river and who came back. 'The river always takes someone,' he said.

On 'Céilidhe House' on radio one night we heard a girl sing:

> And when King James was on the run
> I packed my bags and took to sea
> And around the world I'll beg my bread
> *Go dtiocfaidh mavourneen slán.*

My uncle told us of the Wild Geese who sailed to Europe after the Treaty of Limerick in autumn 1691 on the nearby estuary, and of how at the beginning of that century Red Hugh O'Donnell had ended O'Donnell's overlordship of Donegal by casting O'Donnell pearls into a lake on Arranmore Island.

On one of my first days there I was driven to a lake by a castle where about a dozen people with easels were painting pictures of the castle.

At the end of my holiday I was taken to a seaside resort on the mouth of the Shannon.

My uncle wore sports shoes and sports socks for the occasion. My aunt a cameo brooch that showed a poodle jumping into an Edwardian lady's arms. My two older girl cousins, who'd covered the walls of my room with Beryl the Peril pictures, saddle shoes—black with white on top and then a little black again at the tip. My youngest cousin, who'd recently made her First Holy Communion, wore her Communion dress so she was a flood of Limerick lace. My aunt recalled being taken by car with my mother to the Eucharistic Congress in Dublin when Cardinal Lauri granted a partial indulgence to all who attended the big mass.

On the way we stopped at a house where a poet had lived, a mighty cedar of Lebanon on the sloping hill beside it. I'd had to learn by heart one of his poems at school, 'The Year of Sorrow—1849'.

> Take back, O Earth, into thy breast,
> The children whom thou wilt not feed.

The poem was taught by a teacher who'd told us about the boy who ferried the Eucharist in his mouth in Ancient Rome and, John McCormack's 'My Rosary' frequently played to us on a gramophone, how when Count John McCormack returned to give a concert by the Shannon in his native Athlone no one had turned up.

On arrival in the resort, in a soda fountain bar on the main street, we had coffee milkshakes and banana boats.

On the wall was a photograph, cut out of *Movie Story* or *Film Pictorial*, of the Olympic swimming champion Johnny Weismuller in his Tarzan costume.

Johnny Cash sang 'Forty Shades of Green' on a public loudspeaker in the town.

'It's a lovely song, "The Forty Shades of Green"', my uncle said, 'Johnny Cash wrote it. Went around Ireland in a helicopter. The song tells you about all the counties. He saw them from a helicopter.'

Near the beach, on a windowsill, was a swan with a shell on its back, an Armada ship with sails of shells.

Women with their toes painted tulip red sat on camp stools on the beach. Young men wore ruched bathing togs. Little boys like bantam hens marched on the sea and afterwards some of them stood in naked, even priapic defiance.

'I'm so hungry I could eat a nun's backside through a convent railing', my uncle said after a few hours so we left.

There was a bachelor festival in the town and ten bachelors from different counties were lined up on a podium. They wore black, box, knee-length jackets with velvet-lined pockets, Roman-short jackets, banner-striped shirts, cowboy Slim Jim ties, crêpe-soled betel-crusher shoes. Some had slicked-back Romeo hair, some Silver-Dollar crewcuts. We were told about one of the bachelors, that he'd been a barber in County Longford, his business motto being 'Very little waiting,' that he'd recently migrated to one of the north-eastern counties but he was missed in Longford. He had a flint quiff, flint cheekbones, an uncompromising chin like Steve Reeves. John Glenn sang 'Boys of County Armagh' on the loudspeaker.

A man with the marcel waves of another era, who had been studying the bachelors, declaimed:

'I worked hard all my life. Training greyhounds. Can't sleep at night thinking about how hard I worked. Met a girl once. She liked going to dances and all that kind of thing. I liked greyhounds and greyhound races. So we stopped seeing one another. But it was a wonderful thing making love.'

On the way back my aunt sang 'The Last Rose of Summer' as she used to as a girl at ginger-ale parties in a room in my grandparents' house with a picture of a Victorian girl with the word 'Solitaria' underneath it.

> Oh! Who would inhabit
> This bleak world alone?

The fields of County Limerick were covered with yellow agrimony which was said to cure skin rashes and external wounds and yarrow which was said to cure the innards it looked like. Traveller boys called at the door selling dulse that they'd picked on the coast and dried themselves, popular with young guards because it was good for the physique.

Before I left my aunt and uncle gave me a large biscuit which was a walnut on a biscuit base buried under marshmallow sealed with twisted and peaked chocolate, and I clutched the canary's leg in a cage.

At Limerick bus station, where I wore a sleeveless jersey with a Shetland homespun pattern and mid-calf socks, a woman in a Basque beret said to me:

'Margaret Mitchell was a very small woman but she wrote a very big book.'

The Irish Sea was Persian blue.

My father and I had a swim and afterwards a man with a malacca cane, in a linen Mark Twain suit and a Manila straw hat, who had been watching us, told us the history of the Forty Foot.

Two boys listened intently to the lesson, one with a sluttish Jean Harlow face, the other with a Neptune belly and ant legs.

The Forty Foot was called after the Forty Foot Regiment stationed in the Martello tower built during the Napoleonic Wars. Twenty Men. Forty Feet.

At the beginning of the century Oliver St John Gogarty used to frequently swim between the Forty Foot and Bullock Harbour in Dalkey where monks had lived in the Middle Ages.

Oliver St John Gogarty had fox-blond hair then with an impertinent crescendo wave, eyebrows askance, shoulders poised for riposte, Galwegian lips.

He was Arthur Griffith's white boy.

Arthur Griffith had founded the non-violent Sinn Féin movement in 1905 in order to set up an Irish republic. He had a brush moustache, wore wire glasses, a stand-up collar, neckcloth.

One day, in his tailored swimming costume, he decided to swim to Bullock Harbour with Oliver St John Gogarty. He expired a few yards out at sea.

A few years after that visit to the Forty Foot, when my father bought me a set of art books, there was a reproduction of Titian's *Flaying of Marsyas* in one of them in which Titian depicted the death of self.

The Flute Player Marsyas is flayed alive, upside down, to the accompaniment of violin music, watched by a little Maltese dog and by King Midas, with ass's ears, who is Titian himself who'd recently given the prize of gold chain to and publicly in Venice embraced Veronese, lavish with red lake like himself, as his successor. Titian—his arms still muscular in the painting, his honeyed and diamanté chest strung with a salmon-vermilion cloak—painted it with his fingers.

I thought of the story of Arthur Griffith when I got the books, that it must have been the death of some part of Arthur Griffith's self that day.

Gogarty, who'd rescued a suicide in the Liffey by knocking him out, brought the leader to shore.

In the evening my father and I stopped at a fish and chip shop near the Forty Foot. On a cyclamen, jay blue and lemon jukebox the Everley Brothers sang 'Lonely Street'. A boy, in a blue shirt with white, sovereign polka dots, stood eating chips. On his wrist was a tattoo; the name of a place—army barracks or jail—and a date.

In the fish and chip shop I thought of a story my uncle told me as he brought me to Limerick bus station the previous year.

'They get baked jam roll and baked custard in Cork Jail. Better than they get from their mothers. One fellow was given a month and said to the judge, "That's great. I get baked jam roll and baked custard there that I don't get from my mother." "All right," said the judge, "I'll give you three."'

Later, in a room in a house in North Dublin where there was a false pigment art deco light shade with tassels, a picture of St Dymphna, patron saint of people with nervous disorders, my father spoke, as he was laying out a handkerchief of robin's-egg blue and rose squares as he might have laid out a Chicago tie once after a date with a Protestant girl in a tango-orange dress from whose house Joseph Schmidt could often be heard on the street singing in Italian, about cycling with other young men, some with aviator hairstyles, when General O'Duffy was president of the National Athletic and Cycling Association, to swim in the Suck at Ballygar.

# Larks' Eggs

There was a hotel on Tay Lane at the back of the town between river and canal, run by Pancake Ward, a little man in a spec cap with a Connemara weave who wore hobnail boots, where young, middle-class men hid out when their families were in dudgeon with them and my father had to stay there for a few days because of his relationship with a Protestant with bangs, Miss Husaline.

His hair still smelling from Amami shampoo after a trip to Dublin with Miss Husaline, in a tie with cedar-green and asparagus-green bars, flannel trousers, navy socks with jay-blue stripes; there was a chamber pot with purple peonies, pink anemones, fern under his bed, and by night a young English travelling player, with hair crescendo-curled to one side, who was staying there, would wander around in a Jaeger dressing gown, studying his part aloud:

> For valour, is not Love a Hercules,
> Still climbing trees in the Hesperides?
> Subtle as sphinx, as sweet and musical
> As bright Apollo's lute, strung with his hair;
> And, when Love speaks, the voice of all the gods
> Make heaven drowsy with the harmony.

In the mornings there was a view of the river, of Teampollín, an ancient church with surround houses where illegitimate and still-born children were buried. The monks who'd lived there wore iron chastity belts. Now there was an erotic air about the grass, the ruins.

In the summer women would wander on a monk's pass—a path leading from one monastery to another—by the Suck, collecting bur-marigolds for smallpox, measles, or to rub nipples during breast feeding, wild thyme for menstrual disorders, chest infections and sore throats, plantain—waybread—for dry coughs, haemorrhoids, beestings.

It was the year 1934. The calves had been slaughtered in Ireland in February of that year because of surplus and the Land Annuities dispute with England, and in August the Tailteann Games, re-enacting funeral games in honour of Queen Tailte of Ireland, had been held in Dublin. In January of the previous year Hitler had become Führer and in June of that year General von Schleicher, his wife and others were dragged from their beds and slaughtered. The carillon of children's voices could be heard from the Protestant national school, with its Gothic, diamond-pane windows, with a recitation:

Far as the tree does fall, so lyes it ever low.

A short while before my father stayed there an American in hobo dungarees had stayed in the hotel. He ran out of money and stood in the Square with the spalpeens—roaming men looking for a day's work. The Lazy Wall was on one side of the Square. The spalpeens gathered on the other. The American was carrying his banjo. When they asked him what he could do he said: 'All I can do is play the banjo.'

The English travelling players came to the town every October after the fair when the green in which they pitched their marquee was like a sea, the colours like that of a late autumn blackberry bush penetrated by late afternoon sunshine.

In the entr'acte of *Love's Labour's Lost* that he attended while staying in the hotel, Phoebe Rabbitte, a Protestant lady, in a hat with a cockatoo feather, offered my father a cigarette from a chased cigarette case. Phoebe Rabbitte's black Daimler could frequently be seen parked outside the chrome-green Medical Hall, from whose roof snipers used fire with Gatling machine guns during the War of Independence.

Pancake Ward, in a pearl-white waistcoat, held a party for the players. A man who sold football colours in crêpe paper at matches mimed to 'Champagne Charlie', 'Not for Joseph', 'I'll Send You Some Violets' on a horn gramophone and one of the players did a Highland dance on a table, lifting his royal tartan kilt to show his bare backside.

Bran Ahearne, a Jesse boy with a waxed moustache, could be heard telling an English player on a sofa with an antimacassar patterned with mice in friar robes: 'People on Tay Lane love taking opposite sides, during the Boer War some were Connaught Rangers and went into battle, only a couple coming back. Others were Boers and kissed the Tricolour by firelight on the Transvaal.'

On the canal side of Tay Lane lived a man with goat-whiskers who used his front garden as a lavatory and grabbed passing Rhode Island chicks as toilet paper.

Thomasine Solan and her mother, Tay Lane's courtesans, both in backless dresses, feathered boas and strings of bugle-beads, were present and were seated beside a flowering cactus in an Edward VII and Queen Alexandra coronation mug.

When she was a girl Thomasine's mother used accompany the Connaught Rangers to the station in the evenings with a cresset lantern.

When wings were falling from the sycamore, maple and ash trees outside the Protestant church, my father and Miss Husaline had gone to Dublin to see Douglas Fairbanks in *Mark of Zorro* at the O'Connell Street Picture House and afterwards they did the foxtrot at Mitchel's Tea Rooms before getting the train home.

In Miss Husaline's house was a soapstone elephant from India on which she put a mouse. Beside it, in an oxidized frame, a photograph of a Protestant orphan, Hyacinth Connmee, with a pudding-bowl haircut, against sea pools with submerged bunches of thrift. Hyacinth Connmee had been sent to a Protestant orphanage in North Connemara. A hotel owner there converted to the Church of Ireland and the Protestant orphans came back from England, from their houses with Margaret Hartness roses outside, and stayed in the hotel.

Beside the photograph was a postcard, 'The Lark's Song' by Margaret W. Tarrant, Hyacinth had sent from England.

My father and Miss Husaline had discovered larks' eggs on the

Hill of Down by the Suck, pointed oval, greenish-white, mottled with pale lavender, with markings of rufous.

Miss Husaline's father, who wore a cricket shirt winter and summer, had been at a wedding in The Park as a child when there'd been a pyrotechnic display—a golden fuschia tree in blossom, snow-drops in bloom, rose blossoms in violet stars, immense sheaves of wheat downfalling on the East Galway country.

Miss Husaline always served an aurora borealis of white-iced queen cakes or Boston sponge she made herself on a powder-blue Worcester plate that showed a Ho-Ho bird on a rock.

The bishop's palace used to be in the town but it moved to a town where a priest wrote a book which caused a great outcry, and the priest went to live in London where he was photographed in the English papers with women in flapper dresses who wore monocles. There was a doctor in town, who drove an Auto Carrier Aceca Six, who was a champion rugby player and one day, knocked out during a game on the mental hospital grounds, when some Campbeltown Malt Scotch whisky was poured down his throat, he leapt up, shouting: 'I am a teetotaller!'

There was rumoured to have been a homosexual orgy in the rugby changing rooms in the mental hospital grounds that winter, men whose genitals smelt of young mushrooms—the blame put on a few bottles of Canada brandy bought by a cross-border team with carp-rugby features who wore cloth caps during the game—and the orgy went down in town lore but all the participants married, except Éanna Geraghty who worked in the London brick-orange bank, rolled his own cigarettes with Wills' Capstan tobacco, and wore an Inverness cape.

He had a rendezvous with one of the Northern players, a youth with nougat-coloured hair, sheepdog-fringe, butcher-lie eyes, who wore an old Portoran tie, in Lyon's Corner House in London just before the War, having sallyslung and coffee with him.

In his flat opposite the house with an ivy-coloured door where Theobald Wolfe Tone had stayed, where the town makes a parabola and then a glissade towards Galway City, there was a print of Antonio Pollaiuolo's *Battle of Naked Men*. He attended dinner dances, however, at the Clonrickarde Arms Hotel with another bank employee, a woman with a bull fringe who on these occasions wore a lamp-black dress with a fishtail train or a rose-blue robe-de-style with a corsage of fritillaries.

The English players couldn't come to Ireland during the War so an amateur drama society was formed in the town and their first production was *Death's Jest-Book* by Thomas Lovell Beddoes, whose mother was from County Longford, about the Duke of Munster-berg in Silesia who was stabbed to death by his court fool. Éanna Geraghty played Isbrand the fool in Arabian slippers.

Phoebe Rabbitte cycled to performances in cavalry-cord trousers on a high nelly.

> Life's a single pilgrim
> Fighting, unarmed among a thousand soldiers.

For his holidays Éanna Geraghty would go to Bachelor's Walk in Dalkey. There was a swimming hole nearby where, before the War, he met a man from Plymouth whose only sport, because of spinal trouble, was swimming, who would swim out to Sorrento Point. When he was a boy Irish time and English time were different and when he got back to England from Irish visits, he told Éanna, he'd set his watch to Irish time because he loved swimming in the swimming hole in Dalkey so much.

In the evenings of his holidays, when v-2 rockets were falling on England, Éanna Geraghty would go to a hotel with mouldings of dolphins outside where a man in a grasshopper-green dickie bow, by a grand piano, incessantly played and crooned Jessie Matthews' 'Over My Shoulder Goes One Care, Over My Shoulder Goes Two Cares'.

At the end of the War he got a senior post in Aer Teoranta at Shannon Airport and when that closed in 1949 he went to Paris where he lived in an apartment block smelling of ammonia in the Faubourg outskirts and he'd attend rugby matches when the Irish team was playing and some of the Irish rugby players, young men with forelocks, came to his flat with a picture of Theobald Wolfe Tone's wife, Martha Witherington, in a sugarloaf cap on the wall and, on a bamboo-motif chair, by a Bauhaus lamp, he'd offer them Disque Bleu cigarettes and tell them how in Corfe Castle, Dorset, during the Middle Ages a football was accepted instead of a marriage shilling, by the local lord, from the most recently married young man, carried ceremoniously to him with a pound of pepper; how rugby was started at Rugby School in 1823 when a pupil, William Webb Ellis, picked up a ball and ran with it and in 1839 the Dowager Queen Adelaide, wife of William IV, visited the school to see the new game; how the Connaught Rangers marched through Alexandria at the beginning of the Dardanelles Campaign in July 1915 in khaki drill, playing 'Brian Boru', 'Killaloe' and 'Brian O'Lynn', led by the tallest of the company, an international rugby player who carried the Jingling Johnny with its red and black horse-hair plumes; of the scrummage in the winter of 1934 when there was yellow jelly algae on fallen logs in the mental hospital grounds, the ram's head push between other men's buttocks.

> Queenie, Queenie, who kicked the ball,
> Was he fat or was he small?

Queenie Waithmandle was a Protestant woman with Blanc de Madame de Courbet roses outside her house.

She always attended Sunday rugby games, in a trilby hat and a beaver-fur dickie front, or a jacket trimmed with monkey fur, or a pinstripe flannel jacket with boxy shoulders, stilettos with louis-type heels or monk-fronted shoes.

In the summer she'd go with relatives from Galway to North Connemara to catch up on the legations of ragged robin by the ocean and perhaps be awed by the dream of a nobby—a boat with a red sail.

When she was in her early fifties she became pregnant and went to England to live with relatives and have her baby. 'Mind yourself in this town as they say,' she bid me before getting the Dublin bus, as a man in a black shirt with puff sleeves in a marquee tent, in a performance of *The Duchess of Malfi* by the travelling players, which Queenie and I attended the same night, advised the audience to be 'mindful of thy safety'.

In Webster's day the Shoemaker's Guild in Chester would present the Draper's Guild with the handsel of a football on Shrove Tuesday. One year at a presentation a battle broke out between the two guilds which became known as the Battle of Chester.

My father was a draper.

In the eighteenth century in the East of Ireland football players wore white linen shirts.

A common prize for football winners was Holland linen caps with ribands.

Shortly after Queenie Waithmandle left, I held my father's hand at a Sunday rugby game.

The bulbous vein around the forehead, like a trajectory, the bald head, and yet still—the beauty.

One of the players that day was a young man with a roach like a duck's egg who'd been Queenie Waithmandle's lover.

When my father was a youth with cherry-auburn hair, field-green eyes, freckles big as birds' eggs, with a Shakespeare collar, a young British soldier was found shot dead by the River Suck where the otters run, with a picture of Marie Lloyd in his pocket, who once came out on the picket line on behalf of the most lowly of Music Hall workers.

The British soldiers used play rugby and hack one another—kick one another's shins—in the mental hospital grounds, in tiger-striped jerseys, the sforzandos from the field heard by the riverbank.

Fathers and sons, it's a smell from the genitals, a smell from the earth.

Sons come from sexuality—homosexual or heterosexual or a mixture. So your sexuality, homosexual or heterosexual, has to be protected. Sometimes there are people who would destroy it. So this means leaving one country for another. Or leaving that country and going back to the other.

On my return to Ireland, by the River Suck, in the place where the young British soldier was found shot dead, beside a clump of dandelion leaves—dandelion leaves cleansing for the liver and kidneys—I found some larks' eggs—olive-white, speckled with lavender grey, with markings of umber.

# Acknowledgments

The publisher gratefully acknowledges the following for permission to reproduce:

'Blow-Ball' and 'Foils' (*The Diamonds at the Bottom of the Sea* [Hamish Hamilton 1979])

'Teddyboys', 'The Last Time', 'Afternoon', 'The Man from Korea', 'Embassy', 'Jimmy', 'The Sojourner', 'The Mourning Thief', 'Portrait of a Dancer', 'Memories of Swinging London', 'A Marriage in the Country', 'Ties', 'Players', 'Elysium', 'The Vicar's Wife', 'Miles', 'Martyrs', 'The Airedale' and 'Lebanon Lodge' (*A Link with the River* [Farrar Straus 1989])

'The Hedgehog' (*The Honest Ulsterman*, ed. Frank Ormsby, 1972)

'Barnacle Geese' (*The London Magazine*, ed. Sebastian Barker, 2004; and *Southword: The Journal of the Munster Literature Centre*, ed. Philip McCann, 2004)

'Chintz' and 'The Match' (*Southword: The Journal of the Munster Literature Centre*, ed. Patrick Galvin, 2002)

'The Bon Bon' (*The Dubliner*, ed. Trevor White, 2005)

'Winter Swimmers' (*New Writing II*, eds Andrew O'Hagan and Colm Tóibín [Picador, The British Council 2002])

'Caravans' (*Southword: The Journal of the Munster Literature Centre*, ed. Patrick Cotter, 2003)

'Wedding at Gallog' (*Cyphers*, eds Leland Bardwell, Eiléan Ní Chuilleanáin, Pearse Hutchinson, MacDara Woods, 2004, in which some of the drawings also appeared)

'Rose of Lebanon' (*West47* online, Galway Arts Centre, 2003; and *American Short Fiction*, ed. Rebecca Bengal, 2006)

'Patterns' (*West47* online, Galway Arts Centre, 2004; and *Cúirt Annual*, ed. Mike McCormack, series ed. Maura Kennedy, 2005)

'Victoria' (*West47* online, Galway Arts Centre, 2003)

'Pictures' (*Element, 'writing the everyday'*, ed. Mari-Aymone Djeribi, Mermaid Turbulence, 2005; and *New Dubliners*, ed. Oona Frawley [New Island 2005])

'Larks' Eggs' (*The Irish Times*, ed. Caroline Walsh, 2005)